"The Promise of God unlocked areas of my imagination that I never had the courage to explore. From the outset, I was struck by the author's unflinching sense of purpose. An enth~~~~~~~~~~~~~~~~~~~~~~~~~~

\datto
: rabbi

"There are times when I've wonde~~~~~~~~~~~~~~~~~~~~~~~~~~~ out there in the universe that could persuade followers of the world's prominent religions to step back from their own rigid beliefs and take a fresh look at God from someone else's point of view. Of course, whenever most authors attempt to take us on such an excursion, the journey is generally derailed by the flurry of zealots who stop reading and start crying 'foul' as soon as their religious practices are questioned in any way.

"It is my hope that the highly entertaining story line Mr. Shapiro has utilized to deliver his message in *The Promise of God* will allow people of every faith to come along for the entire ride, and maybe, just maybe, come to the realization that we all answer to the same God. And if that's the case, we would all do well to show more respect and tolerance for the beliefs of everyone . . . not just the beliefs of those who attend our own particular church, mosque or temple."

—Reverend Dave Wollert
practicing minister and consultant to UCLA Writers Program

"We loved this book. It read quickly, with excitement, passion and energy. There is much teaching in this book—about Western religious ideas, messianic dreams, reconciliation, Judaism and Christianity. There is intrigue, mystery, danger, love—everything that is necessary for a great novel."

—Rabbi Jonathan Ginsburg
Temple of Aaron, St. Paul, Minnesota
adjunct faculty member of Metropolitan State University and
St. Catherine College
—Rabbi Julie Gordon
Temple of Aaron, St. Paul, Minnesota

"A magnificent tale of family love and commitment to truth and justice over many generations, *The Promise of God* speaks plainly of simple truths and the strength required to triumph over the past. With this insightful and remarkable account of the life and times of a remarkable leader, we become witnesses to a world struggling to overcome adversity and hardship in the wake of the darkest period in human history. This is a book for Jews, Christians and skeptics alike; for anyone who wishes to explore and understand humanity in a manner only a few dare to explore. *The Promise of God* is a tribute to author David Shapiro, for his great courage and foresight. He should be commended for this truly outstanding work and leap of faith."

—Rabbi Gabriel Elias
Congregation Mogen David

"*The Promise of God* is a spiritual journey; the awakening of something just on the edge of consciousness. Author David Shapiro has deftly woven a story that captures both the imagination and the spirit. Urgent, vivid and thoroughly original, the novel ponders profound questions with an ambitious plot that doesn't quit until its breathtaking conclusion—and even then, it lingers long after the last page is turned. It is a book of startling passion, of unexpected healing—a luminous search for the truth.

—Shari Cookson
award-winning documentary filmmaker

The Promise of God

A Novel

David Shapiro

SiMCHA PRESS
An Imprint of Health Communications, Inc.

Deerfield Beach, Florida
www.simchapress.com

Library of Congress Cataloging-in-Publication Data

Shapiro, David, date.
    The promise of God : a novel / David Shapiro.
      p. cm.
    ISBN 1-55874-744-3 (trade paper)
    1. Christianity and other religious—Judaism—Fiction. 2. Catholic Church—Clergy—Fiction. 3. Cardinals—Fiction. 4. Messiah—Fiction. 5. Jews—Fiction.
I. Title
PS3569.H34113 P76 2000
813'.54—dc21

                                        99-056095

©2000 by David Shapiro
ISBN 1-55874-744-3

Publisher: Simcha Press
              An Imprint of
              Health Communications, Inc.
              3201 S.W. 15th Street
              Deerfield Beach, FL 33442-8190

Cover design by Andrea Perrine Brower
Inside book design by Dawn Grove

In loving memory of my sister, Suzie,
whose tragic death at the age of forty-two
deprived me of my lifelong kindred spirit
and sent me spiraling through the odyssey
that culminated with this book.

And, most of all, to my wife, Cindy,
whose unswerving love since we were eighteen and
whose immeasurable personal virtue
are the greatest gifts God could have
bestowed on me.
May every man find such a partner.

Publisher's Note

The Promise of God is a work of fiction. The views expressed by the author are not necessarily shared by Simcha Press and Health Communications, Inc., and the story and characters represented herein are in no way meant by the author to denigrate the many righteous Gentiles throughout history, among whom are those who gave their lives and made other huge sacrifices in order to help Jews.

Book One

Everyone thought Grant Tyler was God. His employees, his golfing compatriots, every woman who ever saw him. Although he was treated in disparate ways by many different people, they all had one thing in common: an attitude of awestruck subjects to their king.

His employees were informed of the significance of their king's Christian name on the day they were hired. The personnel office would hand the new employee various forms to sign and one piece of paper designed to explain Grant Tyler's business philosophy. This paper, in stark terms, told of Tyler's father, James Tyler, naming his firstborn Grant for one simple reason. James Tyler, a student of military history, esteemed Ulysses S. Grant as the founder of modern warfare. Grant, he told anyone unlucky enough to be sharing a beer with him, was the first to understand total war, the first to understand that wrecking an army's economic base was as crucial as destroying the soldiers themselves. He wanted his son to know from birth, he said, that business was war and that all wars were the same: Give no quarter, ask no quarter, and always study and attack the opponent's means of support.

This attitude was inculcated in Grant Tyler from birth, and the vast news, sports and entertainment empire he had built from his father's radio station was dedicated to the same principle. The new employees used their intellect on the job and relegated any compassion to the department paper shredder.

Tyler's golfing associates were men from the same financial orbit. Unintimidated by his career because they were all super-millionaires, these men thought Tyler was God because, somehow, no one *disliked* Tyler. By contrast, nobody liked them because they were too rich, too successful. They distrusted everyone because they saw everyone as potential parasites, feeding off their success, their fame, their achievements. They saw how Tyler seemed at ease with everyone and everyone at ease with him. They marveled at his ability to be held as an object of reverence by people who should have been out of their minds with jealousy.

Women adored Tyler. He was fifty but looked forty, lean and handsome and distant. Many women tended to think of God as someone who was distant and intimidating—the strong, silent type. They wanted the strong, silent type because there was an air of mystery about that kind of man. Tyler had mystery in abundance. He usually replied tersely to questions, never had to have the last word and always seemed too busy to deal with trivial matters. No sultan could have matched Tyler's harem—had he wanted one.

The reason Tyler was so successful was that he was secure. Secure in the knowledge that he could succeed at whatever he chose, whether business or golf or marriage. His empire was the modern equivalent of any great ancient political empire; it spanned the globe, influenced millions and answered to virtually no one. He played golf the same way he did business: careful attention to each shot and not a moment's worry about a shot already taken. His marriage was twenty-eight years young, and he adored Becky, his college sweetheart, even more than when they had met.

If someone had asked Grant Tyler if he enjoyed being God, he would have shrugged off the question as irrelevant to the matter at hand (whatever the matter at hand was). There was always something to be done, and it was his destiny to make sure of it. Besides, to a man who shaped the world and its perspective, God was an unwelcome distraction. Tyler had never spent much time worrying or contemplating mystical issues, and he generally regarded them as a waste of time.

Until today.

Today was March 10. Tyler's news channel was humming with the news of another head of a corporation who had survived a heart attack. This was getting to be a chore for the reporters; this was the fifth corporation head who had survived a coronary in the past two weeks. The reporters had run out of ways to make the news audience interested in this phenomenon, and they resented their bosses for insisting on a fresh twist to the story. One young reporter joked that Tyler should be next; at least *that* would pique everyone's interest. The silence that followed his nihilistic attempt at humor sent him to the men's room to hide. The veteran reporters knew two salient points of which the young reporter was unaware or had forgotten: Tyler was God and gods don't die, and no one was less interested in dying than Grant Tyler.

The reporters were wrong on both counts. They would have been stunned to learn that Tyler was much more willing to die than they thought. Tyler also knew better than anyone that God didn't exist, and therefore that not only was he *not* God, but neither was anyone or anything else. And not only was the existence of God a lie, but even the life he had lived and was living was not real. Tyler knew this in a most profound sense by looking at the hospital bed in front of him.

Lying in that bed was the body of a person he had tightly clasped in his arms, the hands he had held through the years, the lips he had kissed with abandon, the eyes whose sparkle had captured his heart and soul at the age of eighteen and never let go. His memory flew back to the first time he had seen those eyes, filled with life and merriment and sending a shock wave through his young body that left emotional tremors still active thirty-two years later. The first time they had kissed he wanted to totally possess this girl, hold her so tightly that he would unite with her body and soul and they would become one living being, on fire with the life they would share and blazing a path that would brook no detours, a path that would defy any power in the universe to stand in its way. He remembered stroking her long, lustrous, thick hair. . . .

Her hair. *Try stroking that **now**,* he thought harshly. Try to imagine what kind of God would deprive the girl he had adored—the woman who had become that single soul with his own—of the hair that had been a hallmark of her womanhood, her femininity. She had no hair now, not even a strand of the hair that had been brushed and curled and dyed to be an integral part of how she had presented herself to the world, the only avenue the woman who shunned makeup had left herself to appear properly before others. She had never worn jewelry, never adorned herself with anything other than the radiance of her persona. That was enough, except for her hair, the one outlet for her need as a woman to show her care and attention for her appearance.

And that is what is being stolen from her, Tyler thought violently, *and no God has the right to humiliate her this way—and kill her, too.* The thought of Becky dead was so powerful that anxiety flooded his consciousness and left him no room for awareness of anything else. The realization that her soul was separate from his left him alone and acutely aware of his loneliness. He needed something—anything—to fill the emptiness.

Sound. He needed a sound to break the oppressive silence. Even the hospital room conspired against him—all white walls, white sheets, silver and gray drawers and cabinets and curtains. Even the colors of the room were silent. What he wanted was a room that had the multitude of colors that life offered, the visual splendor that enabled a man to assume that his own life had the same multiplicity of choices that he saw in the colors around him. Not in this room. This room was devoid of living, breathing colors that vibrated with life. Just white and gray and silver and silence. *Make a sound,* he told himself. *Say **something**. Breathe life into the room.*

"Becky." His voice was far back in his throat, almost a ghost of himself. "Becky, are you awake?"

A whisper of a sound. "Grant?"

"I'm sorry if I woke you. . . . I just wanted to make sure you were here." He had almost said *still* here, then caught himself as he realized the implications of that one word.

"Don't apologize . . . don't apologize . . . I drifted off . . . Grant?"

"Yes?"

"I had a bad dream . . . I dreamt that you couldn't get there. . . ."

"Where, Becky?"

"To the wall . . ." Tyler waited for her to continue, but she didn't. *What wall was she talking about?*

"What wall, Honey?"

"I dreamt that you couldn't get to the wall and I was behind it and . . . and we'd never find each other."

"*What* wall, Becky?"

"It was so tall . . . and old . . . ancient . . . I was so frightened. . . ."

"Of the wall?"

"No . . . no . . . that you wouldn't find me. . . ."

"Where was it, Honey?"

"I don't know . . . but just before I woke up a man told me to keep believ-ing . . . keep believing . . ."

"Who was he, Becky?"

"I don't know, but he had a beard and he had a black hat and black suit . . . Grant?"

Tyler, lost in thought, turned back to his wife. "Yes?"

"Keep looking for me . . . I'll be behind the wall . . . Promise me you'll find me . . . Promise. . . ."

* * *

Beverly Engler, Grant Tyler's assistant, was frustrated. The newsroom had called four times in the last twenty minutes for instructions regarding how to handle the rumors surrounding the eerily coincidental coronaries. Whispers of events bordering on the fantastic surrounded these heart attacks. Should the news report them? The newspeople wanted to be care-ful; some of the victims could be Tyler's friends. *Now what am I to do?* she asked herself.

Beverly had called the hospital, but Tyler had left strict orders not to be disturbed. The news was fifteen minutes from airing and an answer was imperative immediately. No news station wanted to miss a scoop, but no one wanted to look foolish later either. Beverly had worked for Tyler for seven years, and she reminded herself that Tyler's guiding principle was to ascer-tain who held the upper hand and act accordingly. What should he risk, the friendship of these men or the fastest news on the planet? Praying she was right, she picked up the phone.

* * *

"Good evening, I'm George Nelson. Tonight the Tyler News Network has learned of startling evidence in the continuing series of heart attacks strik-ing the heads of this country's major corporations. For a live report we go to Michael West in New York . . . Michael?"

"Good evening, George. Tonight Tyler News Network has learned that here at Mount Zion Hospital the chairman of the board of United States Motors, Perry Lindsay, was stricken by a massive heart attack today and died. . . . We have also learned that he was clinically dead for five minutes and then he was *revived*."

"That is unusual but certainly not unheard of, Michael."

"That's true, George. What makes this unique is that as soon as Lindsay regained consciousness, he immediately named the four other corporate chairmen that have been stricken in the past two weeks and insisted they must have a meeting with the utmost speed. He said it was of vital significance."

"How did he manage to be coherent so quickly?"

"No one knows. The doctors are still stunned at his recovery. And George, there's one more thing . . ."

"What's that?"

"Lindsay apparently asked for a pen so he could write something down before he forgot."

"Do we have any information on what he wrote?"

"Not yet. We're still trying to find out. We'll be here when further news breaks."

"Thank you, Michael. In other news . . ."

* * *

"Grant . . . Grant?"

Tyler suddenly realized that a hand was tapping his shoulder. He turned around in his chair to see Joel Alexander, the vice president of Tyler, Inc. Alexander's normally jovial countenance was not present; it had been replaced by a demeanor much more intimate, a look of utter, inexorable concern with the grief that he knew consumed Tyler. Alexander was not only Tyler's closest friend, he was also the one man Tyler trusted without reservation. They had worked together for twenty-seven years, from the time they had graduated from college to the present, and so Alexander knew Becky Tyler almost as well as he knew Grant. Alexander knew Tyler needed privacy now, but he also knew that Tyler would tear himself apart if he didn't get some relief from his proximity to Becky.

"Hi, Joel." The voice was a whisper.

"You asked me to remind you about the game tonight. . . . I would have waited longer but we only have half an hour before tip-off."

Tyler's hands, which had been gripping the arms of the chair, fell into his lap.

"Do you want to skip it? Would you rather stay here? You're exhausted."

"I think she's asleep. . . . Have any of the nurses heard her talking about some kind of wall?"

"Not that I know of, why?"

"Oh, nothing . . ." Tyler wearily rose to his feet. "I can't see much use in going to the game tonight." He waved off Alexander's attempt at speaking. "I know, I know it's a big one but even the owner is entitled to miss a game now and then."

"Why don't you ask Becky's doctor if he thinks you should go. You can zip right back here after the game; she'll probably still be asleep. Besides, they can always page you. Or Matt can sit here with her."

"Matt?" Tyler's voice suddenly sounded aggressive again.

"He's here, Grant. He drove in today."

"That was big of him."

"This is his *mother,* Grant. And you're still his father."

"Don't remind me."

"He's not evil, Grant. He's just mixed up."

"At his age, I was already running my own companies. I was married to Becky, too."

"You weren't measuring yourself against Olympus, though."

"What do you mean?"

Alexander walked over to the window. "All children have to find a flaw in their parents' armor, Grant. I used to say to Michelle that kids need to feel as if they are running against the incumbent. They have a need to find something they can do better than their parents did. My kids found enough cracks in my armor long ago. But you never left much to challenge. . . . Your life has been a perfect model. What was Matt supposed to do that would enable him to leave a mark of his own?"

"Was I supposed to purposely screw things up?"

"I'm not saying that. Just try to understand the shadow you cast."

"Every time I see that long hair and the earrings I want to send him to the marines."

"Someday he may surprise you and enlist."

"From your mouth to God's ears."

"I thought you were an atheist."

"If he enlists with the marines, I'll enlist with God."

In the corridor outside of his mother's room, Matthew Tyler stood silently. He gave no sign of having overheard the conversation inside except one. He took the ponytail holder out of his hair and let his hair fall to his shoulders.

Tyler and Alexander exited Becky's room, and Tyler strode directly to Matthew. Tyler was the same height and build as his son, but Matthew somehow seemed flimsy next to his father, in all likelihood because Tyler stood ramrod straight and Matthew stood slightly hunched over, almost as if he were awaiting the next strike life would deal him. Tyler set his hands on Matthew's shoulders and attempted to push them back, to straighten his son's posture.

Matthew pulled violently away and stared at his father.

"You two probably need some time alone," said Alexander unconvincingly. "I'll go ask the doctor about us leaving for a couple of hours, Grant, okay?" Tyler nodded. He watched Alexander's bulky form recede down the hall and then turned back to his son.

"Now that you've had your chance to embarrass me, can we discuss the possibility of you staying with your mother while I go out for a couple of hours with Joel?"

"Embarrass *you?* You're the one who embarrassed me! I don't need your help to stand up."

"Maybe not to stand up, but to stand straight you could use some help."

"I wasn't aware that my posture was of cosmic importance."

"It isn't. As a matter of fact, nothing of cosmic importance interests me, Matthew."

"That's a shock."

"Only issues that directly affect my life interest me."

"And just how does my posture affect your life?"

Tyler wanted to say, "Everything you do in your life affects me," but he then considered how Matthew would respond. "How?" Matthew would ask. "How does anything I do affect you? You've never altered the course of your life in any tangible way because of anything I've done. When I was caught dealing drugs in high school you hired the best attorneys to deal with the problem and went back to work. When I wanted the best guitar on the market you consulted the music experts and had the best guitar sent as a gift to me—and went back to work. When have you ever changed your life in any significant way for me?"

Matthew watched his father stand lost in thought and decided he couldn't wait forever. He opened the door to Becky's room, entered and quietly shut it behind him.

Tyler never noticed. He was still pursuing his train of thought. How did Matthew's posture affect him? He realized that he was contemplating issues that had never taken root before, issues that somehow weren't connected to anything tangible. *When people see my son stand like that does it bother me?* he asked himself. He acknowledged to himself that it did, but what if Joel hadn't been there, would he still have straightened Matthew up? Would the very fact of Matthew's apparent lack of regard for his appearance have gnawed at him? Why? *He's my son!* he thought fiercely. ***He's my son!***

Alexander returned from the nurse's station.

"The doctor said he thought it would be good for you to go out, Grant."

"It's not a question of what's good for me. It's what's good for Becky."

"Is it good for Becky when you haven't seen the sun for two days?"

"Pretty soon there won't be any sun for her, Joel. I think I can survive without the sun as long as I have to."

Alexander tried a different angle.

"Did you talk to Matt?"

"Not much."

Alexander gestured to the room. "Is he in there?"

"He had enough of my company."

Alexander heard the harshness in Tyler's voice. "Why don't you let him have a couple of hours alone with her? Maybe you two can talk more peaceably if he has a chance to be with Becky and you get some air. The nurses can page you if Becky wakes up."

Tyler relented. "Just tell the nurse to check in periodically and see if Becky is all right."

"I'll tell Matthew that we are going, too."

"You do that."

*   *   *

The night's basketball game was critical, at least if you were a sports fan. Tyler's Mules (named for the most popular metaphor used to describe U. S. Grant) were playing the Stallions in a battle for the supremacy of pro basketball. The two teams only played twice a year and the Mules had won the first meeting in January. They were led by Willie Daniels, the most incredible basketball player who had yet lived. Daniels had grown up in the ghettoes of South Los Angeles and was blessed with abilities that defied sportswriters to invent appropriate superlatives. He was only six feet, one inch tall, but he had high-jumped seven feet in high school, had incredible court vision and was the greatest pure shooter anyone had ever seen. This year he was second in the league in rebounding, first in scoring, first in assists and was getting more endorsements than any athlete in memory.

Willie Daniels was an anomaly in every way. His outstanding quality, which set him apart on the court as well as in his private life, was his ability to discern the "larger picture." Given the option between making a brilliant, flashy, behind-the-back pass to a teammate or a simple straightforward pass with the same result, Daniels invariably made the simple pass. He reasoned that a flashy pass had three drawbacks: It was more risky, it might infuriate the opposition, and his teammates might be distracted by the reaction of the crowd and momentarily lose their focus. It had always been the same outside of basketball, too.

Daniels had gotten his college degree in philosophy because he wanted to understand the deeper issues of life. He ignored the general manager who snorted that a degree in philosophy was hardly useful for basketball, and he refused to leave college early to turn professional. He had married his college sweetheart while still in college because he wanted to settle the most important issue of his life as early as he could so they could start building a sanctuary from which he could draw strength. Willie Daniels was not interested in trends, he was only interested in the eternal verities of life, and basketball was the gift he had been given to continue his search for them.

The game was halfway through the second quarter when Tyler and Alexander arrived. They walked wordlessly over to their seats ten rows up at midcourt and sat down. The fans around them were used to Tyler's presence and thought little of the fact that he did not extend his usual wave and grin to them; most assumed he was remote because he was late for the game and wanted to concentrate on the matter at hand. Alexander thought about waving but decided that what was really necessary was to focus on Tyler now.

"Look at that move." Alexander nudged Tyler. "Daniels is worth every penny you spent."

Daniels had leaped high above the Stallions' center to corral a rebound and, while still in the air, fired an outlet pass to a streaking teammate for a fast-break basket. The crowd was delirious, chanting "Wil . . . lie! . . . Wil . . . lie!"

"Grant? . . . Wasn't that spectacular?"

"Yeah . . ."

Alexander glanced sideways at his friend. Tyler normally sat forward in his seat, eagerly following the action, but now he sat slumped back against his seat, seemingly detached from his surroundings.

"Wil . . . lie! . . . Wil . . . lie!"

Daniels, facing his opponent at the top of the key, had executed a lightning-fast crossover dribble, left his opponent skidding in the wrong direction, and flashed through the lane toward the basket. In his way stood the opposing center, all seven feet, two inches of him, but Willie had soared *above* the leaping giant's flailing hands and thunderously rocketed the ball into the basket. The crowd was going berserk, pounding each other on the back, spilling their beers and thrilling the beer vendors, who started counting the number of refills they would now be able to sell.

Tyler remained motionless. Alexander turned back to the game to see Daniels steal a pass with one hand and simultaneously wave his teammates down the floor with the other, triggering another fast-break basket.

"This guy is unreal," murmured Alexander.

Tyler was alert but indifferent to everything around him. Still, the word *unreal* floated in the air around him until his mind reached out and seized it. That was the word for his world now. Unreal. All the commotion around him was just a distraction from the one essential fact of his existence: Becky was dying, and he was alone. Twenty thousand people surrounding him didn't change that fact.

"Mr. Tyler? . . . Mr. Tyler, sir?"

Tyler forced himself to turn and see who was speaking to him. He was startled by the beauty of the woman's face he saw because the only time he had ever seen that kind of perfection had been in his own wife. Although this woman was black and his wife white, the beauty they shared made them seem as if they had been cast from the same mold, even though this woman was in her early twenties and Becky's beauty was only a memory now.

"I'm Robin Daniels, Mr. Tyler . . . Willie's wife."

"We've never met, have we?"

"No . . . I like to keep a low profile." She hesitantly smiled and looked down self-consciously. Tyler hadn't taken his eyes off of her face, but he followed her gaze and realized she was in the late stages of pregnancy.

"I wanted to thank you for suggesting a good obstetrician to Willie. He's been thinking of nothing else, and I was worried that he would be distracted from his work. He's so focused, you know."

Tyler tried to remember speaking to Daniels about his wife's pregnancy, but nothing emerged from his memory.

"I'm glad I could help."

"He thinks so much of you, Mr. Tyler. He says that your life is a perfect model for him."

Tyler looked over at Alexander, who permitted himself a small grin at this echo of his own words only an hour before.

"I hope that I can live up to his vision of me, Mrs. Daniels."

"Mr. Tyler, I wanted to tell you one more thing."

"Yes?"

"I don't want to appear odd, but I saw on your news tonight that all these major executives have been having heart attacks and I thought of you. You mean a lot to Willie . . . and I just thought that . . . well . . . you should be careful and take care of yourself. . . . People seem to be dying all over the place. . . ."

Alexander winced and waited for Tyler's reaction. Tyler seemed to regard Robin Daniels from a distance before he spoke in return.

"Thank you for your concern, Mrs. Daniels. I can assure you that I think about my own death, or avoidance of it, quite a bit right now." He turned back to the game.

Alexander quickly said, "You just take care of that baby, Mrs. Daniels. We want Willie's children to see their father thrill them the way he thrills all of us." He glanced at Tyler again, who had resumed watching the game with detached indifference.

"Wil . . . lie! Wil . . . lie!"

Daniels had rebounded a missed opponent's shot, raced downcourt and leaped high in the air to score again. The crowd noise was deafening and Robin Daniels, smiling, held her hands to her ears as she started to return to her seat.

Suddenly, the crowd noise plummeted to a hush. Twenty thousand people sat frozen as they realized that Willie Daniels was lying on the court and not getting up. The players from both teams had circled Daniels's fallen body under the basket so tightly that he could not be seen. The crowd rose to its feet to see what was happening, but could only see both teams standing around Daniels while help was sought.

Alexander stood up to see and realized that Tyler was the only person in the building sitting down.

"Grant, Daniels is hurt and he's not getting up! You need to get down there!"

"I'm not a doctor."

"You're the owner, Grant. Come on, get up!"

"Don't push me, Joel."

"If you're not going, I will!"

"Suit yourself."

Alexander knew that Tyler was distraught over Becky, but he couldn't believe Tyler was this far gone. He ran down to the court to the Mules' bench and then onto the court, wedging his way between the players to stand next to Daniels. The Mules' trainer was taking Daniels's pulse and then doing CPR on Daniels until he saw Alexander. He looked up at Alexander, his face wet with perspiration.

"He's dead, Mr. Alexander."

"Call the hospital."

"It won't help. . . . He's gone."

"No! No! No!"

Robin Daniels was right behind Alexander. She burst through the players and threw herself down on Willie's chest.

"Come back, Willie. . . . Come back to me. . . . Please come back. . . ." She hugged her husband's face and kissed his forehead. "Don't leave me here. . . . Please come back." The trainer reached over to help her up, but Alexander held him back. Robin Daniels was sobbing quietly over her husband's body. The players hadn't moved from the tight circle they had formed around Daniels where he had fallen. Alexander started to turn away when he heard Robin gasp. He whirled around. . . .

Daniels's body moved. A tremor rippled across his face, and one eyelid fluttered. Then another. His eyes opened.

"Where am I?"

*   *   *

"Mr. Tyler, Mr. Tyler?"

Tyler couldn't see the person speaking to him. Everyone was still standing, craning their heads to get a better look at the court, and Tyler was still sitting down. He willed himself to stand and see the young usher who was speaking.

"Mr. Tyler, they told me to tell . . . ask you if you would come down to the locker room, sir."

"Why?"

"Willie Daniels asked for you, sir. He wouldn't even let them take him to a hospital. He said he *had* to speak to you."

"Why?"

"I don't know, sir."

"All right, I'm coming." Tyler slowly hooked one arm into his sports coat.

"Sir?"

"Yes?"

"He did say I should tell you something about a wall, sir."

2

Five thousand miles away in Brazil, a church was burning. The flames surrounding it devoured the building so rapidly that an observer would have sworn that the fire had a personal vengeance against the church. In fact, there were more than a thousand observers, and they knew that personal vengeance *was* involved, but not against the church, just one man. They had come to the church to hear this man speak, to hear the man revered by his people condemn evil in all its disguises. The people had never had the opportunity to see the cardinal face to face, and the prospect of seeing a man so devout and fearless had driven them to ignore the unusually intense hot weather and travel to a church too small to hold them. The speech was to have taken place at one o'clock on this blistering afternoon, but they had decided that the risk of heat stroke was worth it because the cardinal seldom traveled this far from Rio.

The cardinal had been widely quoted that he was making this speech away from his city because his vchement stand against the drug cartel had been largely ignored by the people of Rio, and the people of the country were not as cynical and street-smart as the city dwellers. He had made many speeches condemning the use of drugs and the drug cartel, and two attempts had been made on his life already.

The people of the country knew a threat when they saw it, and this church-burning was an obvious message to the cardinal from the cartel. As much as they respected the cardinal for his courage, they had a sneaking curiosity to see how he would react to this assault on his efforts. In all the pictures of the cardinal, his face looked as serene as Gandhi's. The rope that held the crowd back from the church grounds was unnecessary; they knew the cardinal would emerge from behind the church soon enough, for they had seen him run out of the church, his wiry frame followed by Father Juan, his aide, when the initial explosion had occurred. They waited patiently for him to return to them, for they still expected him to speak.

*　　*　　*

"Your Eminence, are you all right?"

The cardinal bemusedly looked up at the tall, distraught young priest beside him. "Why, yes, Juan, I must be in better shape than I thought. I haven't had to run since my soccer days." He studied Juan, who was still trembling from shock. "A more pertinent question would be if *you* are all right."

"Oh . . . I'm fine. Besides, if something happened to me it wouldn't be as bad as if something happened to you."

"Don't denigrate yourself. In your eyes I may seem more valuable, but in God's eyes your life is every bit as valuable as mine, Juan." The cardinal reached up and gently placed his hand on Juan's shoulder. "And my life's mission is to see the world as God's eyes see it, without my own vision clouding the view."

Father Juan shivered. "I didn't see you when the explosion happened. I was afraid that you had been hurt." He looked down at the cardinal, marveling that this man of relatively small stature could threaten an entire network of criminals. "Don't you think that you should have a bodyguard? This is the third time those maniacs have tried to murder you."

"I'm no martyr, Juan. I simply believe that if I'm to send the proper message to the public, they have to be able to see me as someone just like them."

"I don't think anyone sees you as ordinary, Your Eminence."

Juan thought of all the stories he had heard of the cardinal before he had met him. The story of the precocious boy who had astounded the nuns with his photographic memory. They had seen occasional prodigies before, but when they heard a five-year-old boy recite the entire Mass from memory—in *Latin*—the nuns had made young Isaac their personal project. That had been wonderful news for Isaac's mother, for she had wanted nothing more than for her son to devote his life to the Church since she regarded his birth as a miracle.

The cardinal's mother had tried unsuccessfully to have a child for twenty-five years and had, at the age of forty-four, given in to God's will and resigned herself to her fate. Her husband, an unusually spiritual man, had never given up hope that his prayers for a son would eventually be heard. When his wife became pregnant he told her that the boy (he never considered it would be a girl) would be named Isaac. His wife, a passionately religious woman, didn't have to ask why. She had studied her Bible thoroughly and knew that Isaac was given his name because his mother Sarah had laughed at the idea of conceiving a child at the age of ninety. When the cardinal was born, his mother started to dread the name Isaac. "You remember what happened to him in the Bible, Diego? He was offered as a sacrifice. I don't like it, Diego." Her husband had insisted, though, believing she was simply overwrought from achieving her dream of motherhood. "Remember, Gabriella, *that* Isaac in the Bible, he was all right in the end." This had assuaged her fears enough so that he had gotten his way, but for a price. To make certain that her son would be protected by God, Gabriella had insisted that his life be devoted to the Church. She had taught him the Mass at the age of four and saw the fulfillment of his destiny when the nuns made him their own.

When Isaac was in seventh grade, against the wishes of his teachers, he led his schoolmates into the slums of Rio de Janeiro to offer food and comfort to the poor. The nuns thought they understood what had motivated him, when in fact they didn't understand at all. They assumed that Isaac had wanted to feed the poor because he was gentle and affectionate, and was touched by the unfortunate slum dwellers. They assumed that he would deliver his food and be done with it. Isaac did deliver the food, but instead of turning around and leaving, he had gathered the recipients together and informed them that he would bring more food only if they attended church the next Sunday. When the nuns heard this they reprimanded him for speaking out of turn. Isaac responded that his proof would be counted on

Sunday. That Sunday, nineteen unfortunates from the slums had come to church, and Isaac's career as a future priest was born. His ferocious thirst for justice had led the cardinal, when still a young priest, to evict the wealthiest patron of his church from his cherished seat in the front pew because he had refused to give any money to charity. No threats to the church's coffers could sway him from his decision, and the patron had eventually succumbed and tithed 10 percent of his income and donated it to a charity of Father Isaac's choice.

The cardinal's brilliance had not gone unnoticed by his superiors in the Church. The entire hierarchy was aware of his photographic memory, his fluency in eleven languages, his encyclopedic knowledge of myriad subjects. He had risen at an astonishingly rapid rate to the rank of archbishop, and he had been made a cardinal soon after that. His courage in the face of the drug cartel was now legendary, and he was widely viewed as one of two or three candidates to succeed the present pope, who was eighty-five and in failing health.

What was the thread that ran through this man? Father Juan wondered. *What was the cardinal's outstanding feature?* After nearly fifty years of living, the cardinal still looked . . .

Passionate. That was the thread, passion. Passion for the Church, passion for justice, passion for knowledge of the truth, passion for the world to right itself from its unbalanced course. *Why would such a man risk his life unnecessarily?* Father Juan pondered.

"I don't see what having a bodyguard has to do with sending the right message to the public, Your Eminence."

"Juan, imagine yourself as a person confronted by a drug dealer. It's just the two of you, and you have only two choices: Do business with the dealer or risk incurring his wrath by your refusal. At that moment, your life may be in jeopardy and the only argument that would override the safety of your body is the safety of your soul. If I spoke out against the drug cartel while I was protected by bodyguards, my audience would have the right to dismiss me as a man who valued his body more than his soul. Could I expect them to pay heed to me?"

Father Juan smiled, against his will. *I love being defeated by this man,* he thought to himself. He looked to the front of the church grounds. "It looks as though the crowd is still waiting for you, Your Eminence."

"Then let's not keep them waiting."

*   *   *

As Cardinal Isaac Benda Cortes neared the crowd, the surge of energy was palpable. Of the thousand people waiting, almost no one had ever seen a cardinal in person. There was one exception: His name was Pablo de Cardoso, and he was the leading correspondent for Brazil's largest newspaper. He was a lapsed Catholic, and fierce in his opposition to the Church, which made covering the actions of the cardinal especially galling. *Every time I protest to the boss that there are bigger stories out there than the cardinal, something like this happens,* he thought to himself. *This guy gets natural publicity in a way that's beyond the normal.* He pushed and shoved to the front of the crowd just as Cardinal Benda Cortes climbed up on a makeshift podium in front of them and began to speak quietly.

"Good day to all of you. As you may know, I have come from my home to address you in yours." The cardinal gestured to the smoldering ruins behind him. "It is in the nature of those who practice evil to assume that they can control those around them by one force or another. This is not so. It is not so because of my will, or yours or anyone's. Evil cannot control the world because of our Lord." His voice suddenly thundered, "Because of our Lord!" The crowd was silent, rapt in their attention. He paused, then continued more softly, "Did he not say, 'If someone smites you on one cheek, turn the other cheek?' This is our strength, for our reward comes from heaven."

Pablo de Cardoso called out, "I thought you were here to present a path of resistance to the cartel, Your Eminence." The crowd looked around to see who would interrupt the cardinal. "This sounds like procrastination to me. Just words of consolation for a future life that doesn't exist!" The people around de Cardoso backed away from him, shocked.

Cardinal Benda Cortes looked straight at the journalist. "If you would care to let me continue, Mr. de Cardoso, I would be happy to grant your desire and present my thoughts on that very subject."

"Without referring to another world that doesn't exist?"

The people were thoroughly disgusted with de Cardoso and started muttering threats, which de Cardoso relished as his reward. *Someone has to awaken these believers from their slumber, even if the first step is to engender their hostility,* he told himself.

The cardinal noticed the movement of the crowd and held up his hand to quiet them. "As far as the references to heaven are concerned, Mr. de Cardoso, I give you permission to delete them from your report. . . . Just make sure that when the Lord greets you and you show him the article, he sees that the byline is yours, not mine." The crowd laughed and roared its approval.

A massive explosion shook the air. The cardinal whirled to his right toward the town and saw a fireball rising above the residential district. The crowd, panic-stricken, froze and then began to run toward the flames. De Cardoso remained motionless, staring at the cardinal, whose eyes followed the crowd and then looked up to the sky in silent wonder.

De Cardoso called to the cardinal, "I think you've lost your audience. The needs of the present outweigh the needs of the future right now, don't you think, Your Eminence?"

The cardinal looked at de Cardoso, pondered the question a moment, then started walking briskly toward his car, followed by Father Juan.

* * *

When the cardinal and Father Juan reached the site of the explosion, the remains of an enormous house were apparent, though the building had been decimated by the explosion. They found a huge crush of humanity that parted as soon as it was aware of the cardinal's presence. The area was eerily quiet, and the cardinal couldn't understand why an air of mystery hung over the scene until he realized that everyone was speaking in whispers. All that was heard was the crackle of the fire and thousands of whispering voices. As Father Juan walked toward the embers with the cardinal, he stopped and turned to an elderly bystander.

"Whose residence was this, sir?"

"It was the home of the Ganedos family, Father."

"Who are they?"

"They are very wealthy but good people, Father. They have lived here for hundreds of years. Their ancestors built our church. It is a terrible day for them, to lose their home and the church they built on the same day."

The cardinal had stopped with Father Juan to hear the elderly man's response. "Where is the family, sir?"

"I don't know, Your Eminence. They may have been inside."

A policeman walked quickly through the crowd to the cardinal. "Your Eminence, I am sorry to disturb you, but I think you should come see something right away." The cardinal excused himself from Father Juan and the bystander and followed the policeman to what was left of the front entrance of the house. He looked at the policeman inquiringly. The policeman pointed to the ground at the remains of the immense front door. Burned into the door were two images and one word written in huge letters: *SUINO* (meaning "swine"). Next to it was an image that looked like a triangle with a line drawn horizontally through the top of it. Some inches away from it, a cross was burned into the door.

"Do you have any idea what this is, Your Eminence?" the policeman asked worriedly.

"I don't have the faintest idea. Are the owners of the house anywhere to be found?"

"We have located three bodies. We think they are the mother and her two children."

"And the father?"

"He was badly burned. . . . I don't think he is going to live. He is with the priest at the rear of the house."

*　　*　　*

When the cardinal turned the corner at the rear of the house, he saw a priest on his knees next to a horribly burned man, giving him the last rites. It seemed as though the priest was listening to the man's confession, because he was leaning over the man, listening and nodding. The cardinal hurried to the side of the dying man just in time to hear him say ". . . there were three . . ." before the man's eyes closed forever. The priest anointed the body and then together the priest and the cardinal blessed the dead man.

The priest looked up to the cardinal and slowly rose to his feet. "Forgive me for not being aware of your presence, Your Eminence. I am Father Antonio. Ganedos was my benefactor . . . my friend. And he needed to speak while he could."

"What did he tell you? I heard him say there were three . . . three what?"

"Candles. He said that the fire happened because of last night, when his wife lit candles."

"That doesn't make sense. There was a huge explosion, we all heard it. Did he know of the marks on his front door?"

"He did, and he kept saying the fire was because of the candles."

"Did he say why?"

"No. He kept repeating that there were three of them."

"And that was all he said?"

The priest paused, then looked down at his feet. "He said that he knew why the word *suino* was on his door; it was because of his wife, because she lit the candles in the closet."

The cardinal was befuddled. Why would a dying man blame his wife for an explosion that killed her and their children, and then claim that the word swine applied to his wife all because she lit three candles? And why was she lighting candles in the closet?

Father Juan had made his way to the cardinal and quietly said, "Your Eminence?" The cardinal turned around. "Your Eminence, I was just told that the Holy See has heard of the bombings and telephoned to make sure of your safety. Shall we go to a telephone to inform them personally?"

"Yes, we will go." The cardinal spoke to Father Antonio. "I will stay here in the village tonight. Tomorrow morning I would like to meet to discuss this matter further. Can we meet then?"

"Certainly, Your Eminence."

*　　*　　*

Twelve hours later, at three in the morning, in the home volunteered by a wealthy member of the parish, Cardinal Benda Cortes sat in the downstairs living room, wide awake. Everyone in the house had gone to sleep hours before, and the cardinal was still trying to make sense of the day's events. Somehow, he sensed that the cross on the door was a reference to the bombing of the church, but what was the triangle with the line through the top for? And what was all this about the murdered wife being called *swine* for lighting candles?

A tap on the window caused him to jump up from his chair. He momentarily saw a man's face outside before it disappeared. The cardinal walked swiftly to the window and opened it.

"Please don't close the window." The voice came from outside.

"Who's out there?"

"I need to make confession. Please hear me, Your Eminence."

The cardinal stood by the window, suddenly more interested than afraid. "At this time of night?"

"You must promise not to try to see me, Your Eminence."

"I will remain where I am. What do you need to confess, my son?"

"I was among those who bombed the church today."

The cardinal moved toward the window involuntarily.

"I said not to look for me!"

The cardinal stood still, silent.

"The church was built by the Ganedos family. It could not be tolerated."

"Did you bomb their home also?"

Silence.

"I ask once again. Are you responsible for bombing their home?"

"They were swine."

"Why do you say that?"

"Check the mother."

"She is dead. You killed her, her husband and their children." The cardinal was enraged now. "By what right do you murder the innocent?!"

The voice outside became harsher, more venomous. "Check the mother." There was a rustle outside and the sound of running footsteps away from the house. The cardinal leaped to the front door and threw it open, but all he saw in the darkness were the leaves of the trees blowing spectrally in the wind.

3

W illie Daniels lay on his back on a table in the locker room, the only calm person amidst a sea of nervous, frenetic faces. It was halftime, and the room was filled with awestruck teammates, nervous coaches and story-smelling journalists. The journalists were unaware of the real story, though. All they knew was that Willie had lain on the floor for a minute and then gotten up. Normally they would have covered the story after the game, but the reaction of Willie's teammates and opponents when he had arisen made the journalists smell something out of the ordinary. Instead of simply returning to the game, the players had stood there frozen for two minutes, staring at Willie as he slowly made his way toward the locker room. When the referee approached and reminded them to return to the game, they moved, dreamlike, back to their respective benches. Now Willie's teammates crowded in a circle around him, firing questions at him so fast that the writers had to wait outside the circle, craning their heads to hear the whispered conversation.

"Willie, do you remember what happened?"

Daniels smiled. "I think so."

"What was it like, man?"

"Nothing much, I guess. Just peaceful."

One teammate pointed to the trainer, sitting in stupefied disbelief in the corner. "He said you were dead, dead the whole time."

Daniels looked over at the trainer. "Isn't Mel always right?" he quipped. "If he said I was dead, well, then, I must have been dead."

One teammate who had been on the bench when Daniels fell shouted out, "C'mon, Mel, you really think Willie was dead?"

At the word *dead* the writers whipped their heads around to face the veteran trainer. The trainer looked at Willie with quiet wonder. "He didn't have a pulse. Does that qualify?"

The writers, usually so quick to intrude, didn't move for a moment. Then one writer spoke. "Are you saying that Willie was dead out there? That he was *really* dead?" The other writers jumped in.

"If he was really dead how did he get up and walk away one minute later?"

"If he was dead why wasn't there any apparent damage? And why isn't he in the hospital?"

Mel's lips tightened. "Don't look at me. Willie's the one who refused to go to the hospital. I'm only the team's trainer, not the owner."

One reporter persisted. "Aw, c'mon, Mel, how could he have been dead?" He made a gesture toward Daniels, lying comfortably. "Nobody drops dead and is lying there joking ten minutes later."

The buzzer from the court sounded. The trainer stolidly looked at Daniels. "Believe what you want to believe, gentlemen. I have five minutes to get ready for the second half." He wearily rose to his feet and headed for the court.

The coach of the Mules, Al Knowles, came in from the adjoining room with his assistants. "Let's go, guys. We'll talk about all of this after the game." He turned to the writers. "If you want to talk to Willie, it'll have to wait until later. Mr. Tyler wants to talk with Willie alone right now, so everybody clear out."

The room quickly emptied, and Daniels was left alone on the table. Quietly the door at the far end of the room opened and Grant Tyler stepped in. He stood for a moment, letting his gaze travel around the room as though it were new to him, until his eyes settled on Daniels. Their eyes met and locked. Daniels thought that Tyler looked torn: eager to see him and yet afraid of what he might hear.

"I'm sorry about the game, Mr. Tyler. I feel fine, but the doc and the trainer won't let me go back out there." Tyler hadn't moved. "Have you seen Robin? She was here a couple of minutes ago, but I don't know where she went." Still no sign of a response. Daniels had been serene and detached until now, but Tyler's detachment was different; his detachment looked not serene but tormented. Daniels started to get nervous; sweat beaded on his forehead. "I told the ball boy to find you so I could—"

"What wall?"

"Sir?"

Tyler started to slowly walk toward Daniels. "Forget the rest. What did you want to tell me about a wall?"

Daniels suddenly realized that the vision he had experienced when he died and his compulsive need to tell Tyler were not a result of a lack of oxygen to the brain, which was what he had reduced them to in the minutes that had followed. Tyler stopped two feet from the table, his eyes boring into Daniels's, and Daniels could only wonder at the significance that the vision held for Tyler.

"I . . . I saw you at a wall, Mr. Tyler."

"Describe it."

"It was ancient, Mr. Tyler. Really old . . . made of huge blocks of stone."

"How tall was it?"

"It had to be fifty or sixty feet high. And it was light-colored rock, too."

"Was there an opening through the wall?"

"I don't know. . . ."

Tyler leaned over Daniels's face. "I have to know this, Willie. *Did you see a path through the wall to the other side?"*

Tyler's pager rang.

Daniels, with Tyler's face poised directly above his, closed his eyes and tried to recall the vision of the wall, hoping Tyler would answer the page and retreat from the table. The picture of Tyler and the wall was clear in Daniels's mind and he mentally searched it, but he couldn't see any gap in the wall anywhere. The pager rang again, and Daniels opened his eyes only to see that Tyler hadn't moved a muscle; he was still looking straight down at him.

"I didn't see any opening, Mr. Tyler. . . . Don't you want to answer that page?"

Tyler's face lost its fierceness. His hands came up to his face as if to ward off a blow, and he stood up and turned away from Daniels. He made no move to reach for his pager.

"I'm sorry, Mr. Tyler. I wish I *had* seen an opening." Daniels tried to find the words to comfort Tyler but he didn't even know what was tearing Tyler apart. Tyler started to walk away, head down, hands in his pockets.

"Mr. Tyler . . . I forgot to tell you . . . there was someone else with you at that wall."

Tyler stopped without turning around. His back was to Daniels, but Daniels felt the surge of energy radiate across the room as Tyler's head rose.

"He was an older man, and he had a beard. He was wearing a black hat and a black suit."

Tyler turned around and ran back to Daniels. "What else, Willie? Do you remember anything else? Did he say anything? Anything?"

The door where Tyler had entered flew open and crashed into the wall. Joel Alexander stood there, breathless and disheveled. "Grant, did you look at your pager? Beverly and the hospital have been paging you for five minutes! They finally called the press box. You need to get over there now!"

"Wait, Joel."

"Grant, Becky may be gone!"

"I have to talk to Willie for one more second!" He held Daniels's shoulders. "Willie, did the man say *anything?*"

"*He* didn't. But *you* said something."

"What?"

"You asked him if he could put your message *through* the wall instead of *in* it."

*　　*　　*

Five minutes later, Tyler and Alexander were in the back seat of a limousine speeding to the hospital. Alexander decided to jettison his cautious approach and invade Tyler's solitude.

"Grant, I'm sorry for barging in like that, but you told me to locate you if the hospital called."

For the first time that day, Tyler looked directly at Alexander. Alexander noticed that Tyler looked like himself again; the reverie was gone and his face had the decisive look that had graced a multitude of magazine covers.

"Skip it, Joel. How good are you at geography?"

"What do you mean?"

"Do you know of some ancient wall, fifty or sixty feet high, made of huge, light-colored stones, where someone could insert a message?"

Alexander stared at Tyler. "Does this have something to do with Becky?"

Tyler nodded. "It's crucial that I find this wall, Joel." He looked at Alexander and noticed to his surprise that Joel had become tense and silent.

"Listen, Joel, I have to find that wall. . . . I have to find it."

"Why, Grant?"

"Becky is behind it."

Alexander's eyes narrowed. "What are you talking about? We're going to see Becky right now at the hospital." Joel looked at Grant suspiciously. His voice grew harsh. "Is Daniels part of this, too? What the hell is going on here?"

Tyler was taken aback by the hostility of Alexander's response; he had never seen Joel so angry before. He waited a moment for Joel to regain his composure, then continued quietly but firmly.

"Why are you so upset, Joel? All I asked was if you knew of this wall."

Alexander pointed his finger at Tyler. "What kind of mystical crap is this? Just what did Becky say to you anyway? And what did Daniels tell you?"

"Look, Joel, if you don't tell me, I'll find out somewhere else. Are you going to help or not?"

Alexander turned to look out the window. "Grant, in all the years we've known each other, have I ever discussed religion with you?"

Tyler actually smiled. "That's when we became friends, remember? We were in that literature class in college and when the subject of religion came up, I walked out—and you were right behind me. We've never discussed religion since."

"Let's keep it that way, okay?"

Tyler's smile vanished. "No, it's not okay."

Alexander saw the determined look on Tyler's face, and astonishingly, he grasped that Tyler was obdurate, that Tyler would throw aside Alexander, his best friend, in his quest for an answer. Tyler turned toward the front of the limo. Without looking at Alexander, and with the air of utter finality, he spoke.

"You do know of this wall, don't you?"

Alexander spoke coldly. "You know, Grant, this had better not be some sort of twisted conspiracy some religious nut foisted on Becky and Daniels. Yes, I know the wall you're talking about. I ought to know, my ancestors built it thousands of years ago in Jerusalem."

*   *   *

Beverly Engler stood outside Becky's hospital room, waiting for her boss. Beverly was thirty-six, quite attractive, highly intelligent and never married. In her twenties, she had not accepted any marriage proposals (she received three) because she felt none of her suitors was her knight in shining armor. At the age of twenty-nine, she had fallen deeply in love with the man of her dreams. There was one problem, though, and it was not an uncommon one. The man was her boss, and he was happily married. Beverly was not the type of woman to break up a marriage, but she was also not the kind of person who could settle for less than the best, so rather than leave her boss to find someone else, she preferred to continue working for him just to be near him. She had consoled herself with the thought that she spent more hours with him than his wife did. Still, she resented his wife for finding him first, even though she knew that they had met when Beverly was four years old.

Beverly's attitude had changed one year ago when she finally met his wife. She had assumed that the reason she had never met her was that she was out spending her husband's money. She expected the wife of such a wealthy man to be pretentious and shallow; what she found instead was a woman so modest and at peace with herself that she had no need to make her presence known. This woman spent most of her days volunteering at the hospital cancer ward and quietly running several charitable foundations. The woman that Beverly had once privately disdained and scorned now became a role model for her, and Beverly often regretted that she had once wished this woman out of the way so that her husband would be free.

Those regrets were now intensified a thousandfold by her grief. The woman she had once despised and then grown to love was dying, and the dream Beverly had once cherished seemed as ugly now as it had seemed beautiful then.

The elevator doors at the end of the hall opened and Tyler and Alexander walked toward Beverly. She noticed tension between them. Normally they would talk to each other, but they both strode silently ahead to her. Strangely, Tyler looked expectant, but Alexander, who normally was warm and amicable, had antagonism written all over him. Beverly had expected Tyler to be withdrawn, the way he had been for the last two weeks, but Tyler's face was animated and charged with excitement. Beverly didn't understand what was happening, and she didn't know how to open the conversation. Tyler took charge immediately.

"What's the story with Becky? Why did the hospital page me?"

"Becky's asleep, Mr. Tyler. The hospital paged you because Matthew took off and left Becky without telling the nurses that he had gone. She had been left alone, and the nurses said you had left strict instructions that either you or your son had to be in the room with her."

"Where would he have gone?"

"I was thinking about that. . . . I think the Thrown Stones concert is tonight. He had telephoned me two weeks ago to ask if I could get two tickets."

"Thrown Stones? What the devil is that? Some music group?"

Alexander interrupted. "They're more than that, Grant. They're the biggest act in performance art today. All the kids swear by them."

"He left his mother to go to a concert!"

Beverly quickly said, "There was another reason you were paged, Mr. Tyler. It wasn't just about Matthew. There was a breaking story that I felt you should know about immediately."

"You mean that business about those dying executives? I heard about that at the game."

Alexander said, "You didn't hear all of the story, Grant. There's more to it than that."

Beverly put her hand on Alexander's arm to forestall him. "That's not the story I was referring to, Mr. Alexander. It's bigger than that."

Alexander raised his eyebrows. "Bigger than the most powerful executives in the world dropping dead and then jumping back to life?" Tyler shot him a surprised look. Alexander shrugged his shoulders and said sardonically, "It's getting to be routine. We just saw something like that at the game. No big deal. Crazy things happen all the time." Tyler shot him another look.

Beverly argued insistently, "This news may seem bigger than that, Mr. Tyler."

"I'm listening."

Alexander said pointedly, "We're all ears."

Beverly determinedly ignored him. "It's a breakthrough, Mr. Tyler. They've achieved cold fusion."

For a moment, Tyler forgot about Becky and the wall, and the reporter inside him took over. "Who has? Are you sure that this is true? Has it been confirmed?"

"They are confirming it as we speak."

Tyler turned to Alexander. "You know what this could mean, Joel."

"Sure, an unlimited source of energy . . . and political chaos all over the globe."

"I want you to cover this story yourself, no matter where it is. Take anybody you need with you; I don't care about the expense. I'll be here with Becky, and you call me when you have the details." Tyler looked at Beverly. "This is one trip I won't be making, I've got to be here with Becky. Where is Joel off to?"

"We got the call an hour ago from Jerusalem."

Tyler's head jerked as though he had been struck. Alexander, unbelieving, blurted out, *"Where?"*

Beverly glanced from one man to the other, startled at their reaction. "We got the call from Israel at eight o'clock our time." She looked at Tyler inquiringly. "Why? Is there something significant about Israel right now?"

Tyler looked shaken. He took three slow steps to a nearby chair and sat down. Beverly asked worriedly, "Are you okay, Mr. Tyler?"

Alexander crossed over to Tyler. "Grant, this has all got to be a coincidence. You know that, don't you?"

Tyler folded his hands together and stared at them for a moment. Then he stood upright and headed into Becky's room.

Just before he opened the door, he turned back to Alexander and Beverly. "Don't make any plans just yet. You both wait here until I come out."

*   *   *

Grant softly closed the door behind him and looked at his wife. Becky was exhaustedly trying to lift her head, and he swiftly crossed to her side to help her. Her eyes didn't appear to see him; they seemed to be staring out the window behind him. Grant followed her glance but all he could see from the fourth floor window was the night sky, thronged with stars.

The whisper of a voice. "Pencil."

Grant leaned over to hear his wife's voice. "What did you say, Becky?"

"Pencil."

Grant swiftly ran his eyes around the room. Not a pencil anywhere. He reached inside his suit for a pen, pulled the cap off and handed it to his wife. Becky took the pen and started to wave it wildly back and forth in the direction of the window. Grant couldn't figure out what she was doing but he saw her trying to mouth something. He could barely hear her.

"Daahh . . ."

What was she saying?

"Daahhh . . . Daahhhtt . . . Daahhhtttsss."

Grant looked at Becky's arm desperately attempting to write something. *What was it?*

"Daahhhtttsss . . . con . . . nec."

Grant stabbed the call button for the nurse. Seconds later the nurse, a white-haired woman in her sixties, hurried through the door. She took one look at Becky's behavior and Grant's distraught face and immediately sized up the situation.

Grant grabbed the nurse by the hands and pulled her to Becky's side. "What is she saying? I don't know what she's doing. Tell me what she's doing!"

The nurse studied Becky's waving hands for a moment and listened to the raspy whisper once more. "She is saying *dots*, Mr. Tyler. She's trying to connect the dots . . . the stars."

Grant didn't want to believe the nurse. He had been trying to prepare himself for everything, but no one had warned him that Becky would be delirious. He watched numbly as Becky continued to wave her arms wildly. "What can I do?" he asked thickly.

"There's nothing you can do, dear." Should she tell him? Did she have the right *not* to tell him? "This often happens . . . just before the end."

Grant's eyes began to fill with tears, the first time he had let himself cry. He covered his face with his hands.

The nurse found her own eyes growing wet. "Do you want to be alone, Mr. Tyler?"

"Yes . . . thank you . . . I'm sorry I called you away from your duties."

"Please don't be sorry. I'm here if you need me." She quietly left the room.

Grant watched Becky wave her arms more until he could stand it no longer. He reached over and gently pulled her arms down to her sides, then wrapped Becky in his arms and held her as tightly as he could. "I love you . . . I love you . . . I love you. . . ."

"You need . . . to go now."

Grant withdrew from his wife, startled.

"You . . . need . . . to go . . . now. . . ."

"You want me to *leave,* Becky?"

"Go now . . . I made dots . . . I go . . . the wall. . . ." She slumped onto her side.

"Becky? Becky? Becky! Becky!"

4

Cardinal Benda Cortes, with great effort, forced his eyes open. He had been having an intense dream, which was not unusual when he slept, but this dream had deeply disturbed him. He dreamt that he had returned to his mother's home, where he had spent his childhood, and searched through the house for something. He hadn't known what he was searching for, only that he had to find it because *the fate of the world depended on it.* What was disturbing about the dream was not that he was searching his mother's house, but that with the world at stake, he *hadn't* wanted to make the search; some outside force was compelling him to do so. In the dream, he had been opening drawers and cabinets with dread, a kind of dread he had never felt before, awake or asleep. Though he seemingly searched everywhere, he never found the object of his mission. Finally, after exploring every room but one, he found himself standing frozen in front of the huge double doors to the dining room, which were closed. He had wanted to run away, but something held him fast. Against his will, his right hand started to reach for the doorknob. Just as his hand touched the knob, he heard a knock from somewhere, and he awakened from the dream, forced his eyes open, and realized he was sitting in the chair in the living room where he had heard the mysterious confession of the previous night.

He glanced at the clock over the mantel: 6:30. He had slept for three hours. A knock came from the door to the living room, and the cardinal gladly forgave the visitor for awakening him.

"Come in."

Father Juan entered with Father Antonio, the priest who had administered the last rites to Ganedos, the dying man of the previous day. Father Antonio stood quietly by the door while Father Juan crossed over to the cardinal.

"Forgive me for bothering you so early, Your Eminence, but Father Antonio said he urgently needed to speak with you."

The cardinal looked quizzically at Father Antonio, who quietly awaited permission to speak. The cardinal beckoned him to sit on the chair across from him, and addressed him gently. "You look as though you haven't slept." Father Antonio nodded. "Have you eaten?" Father Antonio shook his head. The cardinal gestured to Father Juan. "Can a meal be prepared for Father Antonio, Juan? I would be most appreciative."

"And you, Your Eminence?"

"I will eat later, thank you." He cast a meaningful look at Father Juan, who started to leave for the kitchen, only to look back apprehensively at the two men as he exited. The cardinal turned back to face Father Antonio, who suddenly looked nervous.

"I owe you an apology, Your Eminence. I would have stayed after greeting you at the church yesterday, but after the explosion I was called . . . away to the village."

The cardinal studied the face of the priest across from him. He wanted to examine it closely before he responded. What he was trying to determine was the quality of the nervousness: Was it from guilt or exhaustion? Should he try to interrogate the man about the events of yesterday or let the information come on its own? He decided to forgo pursuing information aggressively and let events take their natural course.

"Was it for the sake of the apology that you came, Father Antonio?"

"No, Your Eminence. I need to make an urgent request."

"Yes?"

"I vitally need you to intercede with someone on my behalf."

"Who is it that you want me to confront?"

"Pablo de Cardoso, Your Eminence. The journalist . . ."

The cardinal was disappointed. He had hoped to hear some new information about the bombing, but Father Antonio obviously was headed in another direction. He stifled his discontent and acknowledged de Cardoso's name with a nod.

"You do know him, then."

The cardinal frowned. "Yes, he is my most potent adversary in the press. His cynicism makes him quite popular with much of the public."

Father Antonio agreed. "He doesn't have much of a following here; you seem to be more popular. We have a fine parish here. Our community may be uneducated and poor, but any violence here is in the fervor the people have for the Church. We are not like the big cities where they pray for salvation with one hand and bully and steal with the other."

"And yet it is here that a church is bombed and a family brutally murdered."

"You are Brazilian, Your Eminence. You know how the flame of a passion can eat at the heart and consume it."

"What does this have to do with Pablo de Cardoso?"

Father Antonio put his hands on the arms of the chair and pushed down hard to raise himself to stand. He walked over to the same window the cardinal had peered through the previous night. With his back to the cardinal, he continued.

"Your Eminence, somehow de Cardoso knows who was responsible for the Ganedos murder last night. I need you to tell de Cardoso to seal his lips, to suppress the story."

The cardinal rose to his feet and stared into Father Antonio's back. "Father Antonio, whom are you protecting?"

The priest didn't move or respond.

The cardinal repeated, "Whom are you protecting?!"

When he was unanswered, the cardinal moved to Father Antonio's side. To his amazement, he saw the priest was weeping, his hands covering his eyes, tears slowly creeping through his fingers.

"Your Eminence . . . Your Eminence . . . forgive me . . . I don't know what to do . . . I love him too much . . ."

"Who is it, my son?"

"I am all he has. . . ."

"Who?"

"My brother, Your Eminence . . ."

"Your brother!"

Father Antonio struggled to regain his composure. "He is my younger brother Dominic, Your Eminence. He always worshiped me, always tried to be more religious than I. He also wanted to be a priest . . . but he was refused."

"Why?"

"He was thought too fanatical, too unstable."

"It seems that judgment was justified."

Father Antonio wiped the falling tears with his sleeve. "He has only tried to be as good a Catholic as possible, even more than I. He knows the Bible from memory, and he continually quotes it to everyone. He is determined to purify the world."

"Have you told him that he must first cleanse himself of sin?"

"I have, but he is convinced of his own rectitude."

"Do you know why he would murder the Ganedos family?"

"The same reason that he bombed my church."

"What!"

"He has confessed both acts."

"To you?"

"No, to de Cardoso."

"He confessed to de Cardoso? Why not to you?"

"He said the Church had now been purified, but I was still tainted. He said he wanted to show the Church how to purify itself, that de Cardoso was an honest man and would tell Dominic's story to the world. He said that he had made one attempt to confess to a churchman, but he was rejected."

The cardinal grimaced, remembering his confrontation of the night before with the mysterious, fanatical voice from outside. He felt sure that the visitor must have been Dominic. What had he said that had alienated him? He closed his eyes and tried to re-create the conversation.

Check the mother. What had he said just before that?

They were swine. He remembered the other man's words more than his own.

By what right do you murder the innocent?! There it was: Those were the words that revealed his anger and drove the visitor away. Obviously the visitor had felt that the mother was not innocent, but guilty. But of what? All he had to help him was Father Antonio's testimony that Dominic was a fanatical Catholic. *A fanatic needs no rational reason to hate others enough to kill them,* he mused. *I will have to talk to de Cardoso to get the information.*

"How do I reach Pablo de Cardoso, Father Antonio?"

Father Antonio fell to his knees. "Oh, thank you, Your Eminence! Thank you for saving my brother from destroying himself and our name." He kissed the hem of the cardinal's robe. "I will take you to de Cardoso myself!"

There was a knock on the door and Father Juan entered with breakfast. The cardinal lent his hand to Father Antonio to help him to his feet, then pointed to the breakfast tray. "Can you eat while Father Juan drives?" he queried.

"The sooner we get there the better."

*   *   *

Pablo de Cardoso should have been delighted. This story was his exclusively, and he had only gotten it because the witness trusted him. Better still, the witness trusted him because of what he stood for, which was absolute honesty and integrity and devotion to his mission. Pablo had decided years ago that his mission was to awaken the world from its slumber and illuminate the truth. The truth was that religion was a scheme to redistribute money from the poor saps who believed what they couldn't see, to the institutions that encouraged the poor saps to go on believing. Every time he passed a new beautiful church he snorted out loud. The image of the Vatican on television almost drove him into a frenzy. All that money, and meanwhile people were starving in the streets of Rio de Janeiro. He knew that the Church had to be corrupt or tainted, and here was a fanatic from *inside* the Church who agreed with him. What better way to destroy an institution then to have it denounced by a devoted member?

He should have been delighted. Dominic had come directly to his room at the inn (how Dominic had found him so quickly was baffling) and asked to confess to him. When Pablo, amused, had asked him why he had not seen a priest, Dominic spat out viciously that priests were agents of the devil; even Cardinal Benda Cortes was Satan's agent. These words were gratifying to Pablo, who viewed the cardinal as his most formidable obstacle. He had hardly expected that Dominic was to confess any acts of significance, though, and his jaw dropped when Dominic admitted the bombing not only of the church, but of the Ganedos's home as well. When he asked Dominic's motive, and the response was that Dominic wanted to purify the Church of sin, Pablo congratulated himself on his good fortune. He had promised that he would help Dominic tell the story of the corruption of the Church to the world.

"I only need to know one thing, Dominic, and then you had better go home before I give the world the news. What was the sin of the Ganedos family and the church?"

"The Ganedos family were the builders of the church."

Pablo smiled. "Surely there is no sin in that. Many people build churches."

"The family was in the power of Satan."

"How do you know that?" He saw Dominic eye him suspiciously. "Not that I don't believe you, but my readers don't know you the way I do. They need something that they can understand. What was the sin of the family?"

"It was because of the mother. . . . I have watched her every week for months. . . ." And Dominic proceeded to tell Pablo of the act he had witnessed.

Pablo's hopes went up in smoke.

*   *   *

Now Pablo paced in his room, smoking feverishly, unsure of how to handle the story. Dominic had left immediately after stating the traitorous deeds he had seen, rejoicing in the belief that he had found an ally who would make him a national hero. Pablo had promised him that he would do whatever he could to help. In reality, Pablo needed time to clear his head. He had been pacing for two hours now, and he still didn't know what to do. Normally, he was so sure of himself. . . .

The knock on the door was crisp and imperious. Pablo knew immediately this was not an employee of the inn; this sound didn't beckon him, it summoned him. As he sauntered to open the door he felt a faint hope that someone else's certainty would help him escape from his own indecision.

"Who's there?"

The voice of Father Juan came through the door. "Cardinal Isaac Benda Cortes wishes to speak with you, Mr. de Cardoso."

Pablo swung the door open to see Father Juan flanked by Father Antonio. They stepped back to each side so that the cardinal stood directly in front of Pablo, who permitted himself a small smile of token welcome.

"Your Eminence. Come in, come in."

The cardinal and the two priests walked quickly past Pablo into the room and the cardinal motioned for the priests to be seated, while he remained standing in the center of the room, waiting for Pablo to follow. Pablo closed the door and unwillingly capitulated to the cardinal. He dawdled just enough to make Father Juan start to bristle, then walked to the cardinal and stood facing him.

"You need something of *me,* Your Eminence?"

"I understand that a man named Dominic came to see you early this morning."

Pablo was not surprised that the cardinal already knew about his meeting with Dominic. He firmly believed that one of the functions of the Church was to have an established network of spies who would keep the institution informed of the doings and whereabouts of its malcontents.

"That is correct, Your Eminence."

"I have been told that he confessed himself to you."

Pablo smirked. "I guess you don't have a monopoly on confession, Your Eminence. Somehow he felt more comfortable confessing to me. Is that a problem for you? Is that why you deign to visit me? Or is this visit to me your penance for something *you've* done?"

Father Juan leaped to his feet in anger, but the cardinal restrained him and gently led him back to his chair. Then he turned back to Pablo. "Mr. de Cardoso, if Dominic felt more comfortable confessing to you, I am delighted. First, my concern is with his soul, which cannot become whole if he is unaware of what he has done. Thus, his confession to you is a step in the right direction of awareness. Second, there is always the chance, however slim, that your exposure to spiritual matters may render your hostility obsolete." The cardinal took a step toward Pablo. "Now, may I ask you some questions regarding his confession?"

"You can ask."

"Did he confess responsibility for the bombings of the church and the Ganedos home?"

"Yes, he did."

"Did he maintain that they were related?"

"Yes, because the Ganedos family had built the church and they were agents of Satan."

"Agents of Satan!"

"That is correct. He stated that it was his responsibility to rid the Church of them so that the Church could be purified."

The cardinal thought to himself, *If Satan never existed we would have to invent him in order to justify the acts of the wicked.* "Did Dominic say why he considered the Ganedos family agents of Satan?"

Pablo was suddenly catapulted into his moment of decision. He had this moment to decide between two antithetical choices: One, to derive instant gratification from the utter shock that the three clerics would experience from the truth; or two, to withstand the urge to tell them now and let them see it later in the news. The drawback of the first was that if he divulged the information now, who knew how they would interfere with his plans for the story? The drawback of the second was that he wouldn't be present to see their reaction when the news hit.

Pablo wasn't aware of it, but the same factors that affected his decision in this matter also had been involved in his hostility to the Church. Pablo had always been a creature of the moment. The idea of a delayed return on any investment, material or spiritual, was anathema to him. From the time he was a child, he had been the despair of his parents. There had never been a time when he had not demanded instantaneous reward for good behavior. As an adult, he spent his money almost as fast as he earned it, with hardly a thought for the future. The teachings of the Church seemed the polar opposite of his obsession with living in the here and now, for they promised future gains that were unseen against the tangible benefits of the present.

Pablo was unconscious of his inner motives; he only knew that he wanted to see the churchmen squirm.

"You want to know why Dominic considered the Ganedos family agents of Satan?"

"Yes."

"Weren't you curious about the word *suino* that was written on their door?"

"I don't understand the connection between a pig and Satan. I also don't understand what the triangle on the door was supposed to represent."

"What triangle?"

The cardinal took a small piece of paper out of his pocket. He had drawn a replica of the triangle with the line across it that had been drawn on the Ganedoses' door. He handed it to Pablo.

Pablo perused the drawing, then looked delighted at the ignorance of the cardinal. "It all fits together so well. Tell me, do you have any other clues?"

Father Juan got up stiffly. "Must we stay and be insulted, Your Eminence?"

The cardinal was patient. "Mr. de Cardoso, I will tell you what little I know if it will enable you to help me. I know that Mr. Ganedos made reference to his wife lighting candles as the cause of the catastrophe—and that is the extent of my knowledge."

"How much do you know about the wife?"

The cardinal looked back at Father Antonio, who pulled himself to his feet and spoke. "We know that she was approximately fifty years of age and that she was devoted to her husband and children."

"Do you know her maiden name?"

Father Antonio scratched his head. "I think it was Gonzales."

"Correct." Pablo was enjoying himself immensely. "And her mother's maiden name?"

"Don't be ridiculous. I couldn't know that."

"Well, I *do* know that. It was Gonzales."

"So what? It is a common name."

"And the mother of the mother of the wife's maiden name?"

Father Juan, exasperated, exclaimed, "Gonzales! Is this of significance?"

Pablo smiled beatifically. "Would it be significant if I told you that the women in that family have kept the name Gonzales for five hundred years? Or, at least five hundred years that we know of? Or that the wife of Ganedos made a habit of lighting candles in a locked closet?"

The two priests, bewildered, looked at the cardinal. To their surprise, he was not paying any attention to them or Pablo. He was gazing out the window and looking far, far away.

The cardinal had thought he heard Dominic say "check the mother" the night before. Now he realized that the dream he had dreamt afterward had been triggered by those words. He had dreamt of his mother's house because he had somehow wanted to check *his* mother. That seemed logical enough, she was ninety and in failing health. That part of the dream made perfect sense. But now there was a more frightening connection.

He remembered now from his childhood that every Friday night as he headed up to his bedroom, his mother had gone in the dining room and locked the huge doors behind her. For many years he had assumed that she was cleaning the room after the evening meal. Then, one Friday night when he was ten years old, he had pretended to run upstairs and had instead hidden in the dining room. His mother had entered soon after that, locked the doors behind her and approached a cabinet at the other end of the room. When she reached it, she moved it to one side and opened a small door behind it. Then she furtively took two candles and two small candlesticks out of her pocket and, setting the candles in their holders, lit them, placed them in the small alcove behind the door, closed the door, replaced the cabinet and quietly started to leave the room. Isaac had watched his mother with a mixture of fear at being caught and curiosity, and when she had left, he climbed out a nearby window, shinnied up a tree that grew next to his window and crept into his bedroom. By the time his mother came upstairs, he was doing a marvelous impression of a sleeping child. It had seemed like a great game to him then, and as the years passed he had forgotten about it, for he adored his mother and hardly suspected her of doing something illicit.

Pablo grew impatient waiting for the cardinal to react. "Do you understand what the significance of all this is, Your Eminence? Maybe I should make things clear for all of you. Look here, gentlemen. Watch closely." The cardinal hadn't turned back from the window, so Pablo settled for the two priests. He took the paper with the triangle and the extra line across the top of it and drew two additional lines, one from each end of the single line down diagonally to meet under the bottom horizontal line of the triangle.

"Does this stimulate your imaginations?" he chortled. The priests stared.

It was a drawing of a Star of David.

5

The immense conference room was dominated by the enormous
cherry table that stood in the middle. It had been designed specifically for this room, for it was the longest cherry table anyone had
ever seen. It was important to the chairman that the table be cherry, not oak,
not anything less impressive, because he wanted to leave visitors with the
quiet impression of power. Normally the table could seat fifty, and it was
usually full. Today, however, there were only five men at the table, and the
necessity of using this particular room was not readily apparent. They certainly did not need a table of this size, and there was nothing to suggest they
needed a room of this magnitude either. This room was chosen for another
reason.

Doors. Massive double doors that provided the only entrance to the
room. Their size alone was of no significance. What distinguished them
from other doors was their weight; bank vaults had less substantial doors
than these. They were made this way for one reason: to prevent any sound
from escaping the room. The chairman wanted this conversation to be held
in absolute secrecy.

It wasn't that Perry Lindsay was paranoid, he was just careful. He had risen to the top of the United States Motor Company (USMC) by utilizing his two most dominant attributes: a high-caliber intellect and an ability to keep his mouth shut and listen. He never gossiped, he never indulged in disparaging others, and he never divulged a secret entrusted to him, which made him immensely popular with those who did, for they knew that they could confide in him with no fear of betrayal. In his twenties and thirties, he had been viewed as a son by the senior executives, then later as the brother they wished they had.

Now he was sixty-four, silver-haired, a grandfather of seven, earning 5 million dollars a year, and responsible for the single largest corporation in the world. He sat at the head of the table, flanked by four other men of similar stature. They were the executives who ran the four corporations that were next in size to the United States Motor Company.

Normally, these men would not have been sitting in the same room, let alone at the same table. Two of the men were direct competitors of USMC: Bill Eldridge, sixty-one, of Intercontinental Motors and Dan Bryant, sixty-nine, the head of Euro-Japan Motors. The other two were the chairmen of the two largest computer companies on the planet: Robert Hutchinson, fifty-two, of Worldwide Computer, and James Wolford, fifty-five, of Global Computer Systems. It wasn't that the men disliked each other—far from it—they each respected the others' achievements, but they were businessmen and under *normal* circumstances would consider this meeting a waste of time: no information to be gained, and no deals to be made.

These were *not* normal circumstances.

Perry Lindsay leaned forward in his seat at the head of the table. He locked his fingers together, placed his hands in front of him and looked from one man's face to the next. They all had the same expression on their faces, a worried, confused look that came from not knowing what to do—an unfamiliar place for them.

Lindsay spoke quietly. "I am so glad that you could come. This is not the kind of discussion I wanted to have over the telephone." The men nodded in agreement. "I wasn't sure that my internal experience was exactly the same as yours or if it was only the heart attacks themselves that we had in common. I'm only repeating what I saw in the papers, so I have to confirm it with you now. You all did have heart attacks, correct?" The men nodded again.

"And a few minutes passed before you regained consciousness?"

Bill Eldridge said uncomfortably, "I wouldn't call my experience a lack of consciousness, Perry. I'd call it more like . . ." He looked stupefied. "Hell, I don't know what to call it!"

Robert Hutchinson blurted, "I thought I was the only one who was going nuts. When you called me, Perry, I was hoping you might have a clue to what's been happening to all of us."

James Wolford added, "I figured one of us should know, that's why I came. You said on the phone that your attack triggered some kind of transcendental experience, and you needed to talk to me, Robert, Bill and Dan about it. I was left with the impression that you knew what was going on."

Lindsay winced. "I'm sorry about that. What I meant was for all of us to put our heads together and see if we could understand what has been happening."

Hutchinson grumbled, "Now you tell us." Eldridge nodded in agreement.

Dan Bryant, the senior member of the group, ran his hands through his thinning hair and glanced at Lindsay. "I don't think all of us would have come here if we hadn't shared some common experience, gentlemen. And I don't mean the heart attacks, either. I mean something beyond the normal. Why don't we put all the cards on the table. . . . I'm not afraid of saying I thought I was nuts, too. After all, it's not every day that I think I've seen the other side."

"The other side of what?" Hutchinson asked suspiciously.

"The other side of death. Why are you are so hostile, Robert? Did you see something that frightened you? Did you think that you were the only one here who was unprepared for dying?"

The droll tone of Bill Eldridge interrupted them. "You know, as a boy I used to dream of what I wanted heaven to be." He laughed. "Of course, I thought you got to play baseball all day long."

Hutchinson viciously slapped his hand down on the table. "I don't think that's funny. I don't like any of this. I want to know what happened to me!"

Lindsay waited for the fury of Hutchinson's outburst to pass, and then addressed the group. "Let's take this step by step. What was the first thing that you remember after the onset of the attack?"

Bryant said, "Everything went black, and then, almost immediately it seemed, I saw a light . . . the purest white I have ever seen."

Wolford and Eldridge nodded to each other, and Wolford spoke. "We did, too."

Lindsay said grimly, "I did, too. What about you, Robert?"

The men turned to Hutchinson. Abashed, he also nodded. Bryant took pity on the younger man. "You know, Robert, it's normal to be frightened by something you don't understand."

"It's not what I *saw* that frightened me, Dan! It's what I felt *afterward!*"

Lindsay broke in. "Wait a minute, wait a minute. One step at a time, remember? What happened to all of you after you saw the light?"

Eldridge said wonderingly, "That's the strangest part. I don't know how long that light lasted; I lost all track of time. Then the light disappeared, and I saw this word. At least I *think* it was a word. It was written in some ancient script that I didn't recognize. And I felt a profound need to know what it meant."

Wolford exclaimed, "You saw that word, too? I don't believe it!" His eyes moved to Bryant and Hutchinson. They dumbly nodded their heads.

Lindsay said excitedly, "Would all of you recognize this word if you saw it again?" An elation swept through the men. Lindsay pulled a piece of paper from his pocket and passed it around the table. The men's jubilant reaction left no room for doubt.

"Did you all feel the same urgency to know what this word meant?" Lindsay asked.

Bryant said seriously, "Yes, but I thought that if I admitted seeing that light, people would think I was crazy. Telling people I saw some word staring at me afterward would have bought me a free one-way ticket to the psychiatrist." The other men grinned, even Hutchinson.

Eldridge turned to Hutchinson. "But what was it that upset you, Robert? You said that you felt something that upset you."

Hutchinson waved off the question. "It's not important now, Bill." Eldridge looked at him worriedly.

Lindsay charged ahead. "Are we agreed that we need to discover what this word means as soon as possible?" The men nodded. Lindsay thought hard for a moment. "The best source of information is probably the library, but that could take days or weeks."

Hutchinson queried, "What about the newspapers? They have research people on their staffs."

Wolford shook his finger. "We need a specialist in ancient languages, perhaps a professor at a university."

Eldridge disagreed. "All those guys are *too* specialized. If it's not in their field of study, forget it."

Lindsay cautioned, "Not only that, Bill. We've got to keep this quiet. Somebody might talk. We need someone who can find this information and keep a lid on it."

Bryant hadn't responded. Lindsay respected him more than anyone, and he waited while Bryant pondered. Finally Bryant reflected, "Isn't Grant Tyler a good friend of yours, Perry?"

"Yes, we talk once a month or so."

"I've heard he runs a tight ship . . . a really tight, *silent* ship. Why don't you tell him to put his whole news apparatus on the job? They can go anywhere in a matter of moments, and they're used to finding anything on the planet."

Lindsay snapped his fingers and pointed at Bryant. "That's a great idea, Dan. I'll call him right away. Are we all agreed?"

The men didn't look confused now.

*   *   *

At the same time that Perry Lindsay was meeting with his fellow executives, someone who made more money than all five of those men combined was holding a meeting of his own. This meeting, unlike the one at the corporate building of USMC, was being held at a huge villa in Colombia. Another difference was the open, nonclandestine atmosphere of the discussion. Not only were there no doors to seal the room, there was no room, for this meeting was taking place outside at a large round table underneath a huge canopy.

Although the subject of discussion was as sensitive as the USMC meeting, there was no danger of the participants being overheard. The threat of a bullet to the head was more than sufficient to discourage anyone from eavesdropping. And the man conducting the meeting was more than willing to give such an order if it were necessary.

He was Cesar Carlos, the head of the cartel that supplied drugs to the rest of the world and terrorized anyone foolish enough to oppose them. This was his villa, and he had invited his lieutenants there to discuss a problem he had foreseen. Carlos was an extraordinarily intelligent man and had always had the gift of being more farsighted than his confederates in the drug trade. Other men in his line of work were just as ruthless, and there were others who were more cruel, but his vision surpassed them all.

He had been a wild, uncontrollable child. His parents had despaired of disciplining him, for when his father spanked him, Cesar would grin at him, daring him to punish him more harshly. His mother would talk softly to her son, trying to lure him back to what she thought was his better nature, but it was useless. The nuns at his school threatened him with their descriptions of hell, but he laughed and said that he would outlive them all and they could welcome him to hell when he arrived.

At thirteen, he had sought drug dealers who would sell to him. He had never used the drugs he bought; he was only interested in making contacts. He parceled the drugs into thirds and sold them to schoolmates for a neat profit. Once he had used his contacts to enable him to start smuggling drugs, he was in his element. His ascent in the cartel was about more than wielding power; the higher he rose, the more sophisticated were the government's attempts to catch him. He enjoyed the mounting challenge to his intellect posed by his adversaries. He had bided his time while the leaders of the cartel were pursued by the government. He was unremittingly loyal to his superiors and constantly urged them to let him (and others) smuggle more and more drugs. As with everything he did, he had an ulterior motive. Carlos figured that the higher the quantity grew, the more determined the governments of the West would be to capture the cartel's leaders, ensuring his rise to the top. His own capture he thought unlikely because he was not one of the leaders yet, and therefore he was out of the limelight. As it turned out, he was right. The collaboration of the U.S. and South American governments resulted in the capture or assassination of the leaders of the cartel, and Carlos ascended smoothly to the top.

Now he had been calculating the path of his nemesis, and he saw a good chance that his adversary could prove to be more powerful than ever. He studied the faces of his three most trusted associates with satisfaction. They were hard men, unyielding in their hatred of any opposition to their plans. He loved them as much as he could love anyone because they carried out his wishes and ensured the success of his ambitions. Carlos put his coffee cup down on the table.

"I see our favorite priest almost met his God yesterday, gentlemen. And we didn't even get a chance to participate . . . unless one of you knows something I don't." He eyed the other three men, who remained silent. He smiled. "I didn't think so. I am curious to know who would order such an attack without my knowledge; there aren't many people in the world who are like us, acting without a fear of eternal damnation."

Pedro Aguilar, his political advisor, spoke bluntly. "Cesar, that fear seems to be diminishing among the younger generation. They are distrustful of anything they cannot see with their own eyes. It is quite possible that some young man was looking for a chance to gain some notoriety by killing the spokesman who represents the lie that is the Church."

Ernesto Padillo, the man in charge of terrorist operations, disagreed. "I don't think that is plausible, Pedro. First of all, there were two explosions yesterday, which would require a certain amount of time to prepare, and the motive you are describing is usually manifested by a sudden killing. Second, the kind of explosion that destroyed the church seemed to be intended for the church itself, not the cardinal alone. No, there is something strange about all of this."

The third man, older than the other two, tapped his fingers on the table to gain the others' attention. "I am more interested in why you seem concerned, Cesar. What is the difference who kills this man as long as he is well and truly dead? Doesn't his death by any means satisfy our needs?"

Carlos let his mouth curve up into a tight smile. "You come to the point, Rodrigo. If the man were well and truly dead, I would be pleased and satisfied. But when someone attempts to kill him and fails, and his persona becomes more heroic and miraculous as a result, *then* we have a problem."

Rodrigo, who was Carlos's advisor in practical matters, asked the question that he was paid to ask. "You say we have a problem, Cesar. I am not sure how the public's view of this man can profoundly affect our plans."

Carlos's smile disappeared. "Do you think that the Church is unaware of its constituents, gentlemen?"

Padillo grumbled, "Who gives a damn about the Church?"

Rodrigo cautioned him. "Slowly, Ernesto, Cesar has a point to make. Although I am not understanding it just yet."

Aguilar massaged his temples with his fingers. "There is a political reason, Cesar? What are you hinting at?"

Carlos grunted, "Have any of you watched the news this morning?" He received two nods and one dissent from Padillo. "You saw the reverential treatment our Cardinal Benda Cortes is getting? The messages of encouragement from the many foreign governments? . . . Did you happen to note any other news of the Church?"

Rodrigo said slowly, "Of course . . . the news of the prostate cancer they discovered in the pope. Are you worried about the succession, Cesar? At the pope's age, the cancer could take years to be fatal. Besides, they have never had a Latin American pope before. Do you think they would elect Cortes?"

"Our friend in Sicily has informed me that Cardinal Benda Cortes is commanding more and more worldwide attention. He has also informed me that the cancer is more serious than the Vatican has divulged."

Aguilar shrugged. "So let us say that your fears become reality, Cesar, and this cardinal becomes the pope. Is that a cause for alarm?"

Carlos fumed. "Imagine the pope telling the entire Catholic Church that we are the enemy and that they are excommunicated and damned if they help us in any way. Even if many ignore him, many others will not. Should that concern us, or would you prefer we remain blind and stupid?" The three men looked down to avoid the wrath they heard in the voice of their chief. "This man is very close to a position where he could destroy us. I want to know who attempted to kill him, whether by accident or intentionally, and I want to find out as soon as possible. If these people have a hatred for this man, I intend to discover why and use them as best we can. Understood?"

*   *   *

Perry Lindsay was excited. It had been many years since he felt such a strong sense of adventure. To go on a quest, to search for something hidden, the whole undertaking brought him back the thrill of childhood, where anything was possible and the world was a giant game with him at the controls. He remembered playing hide-and-seek with his brothers and sisters, and the combination of being startled with fear and pleasurably surprised whenever he found someone hiding. He had the same sensation now. He hoped to be pleasurably surprised when he found the meaning of the word he was looking for, and he already felt a tinge of fear should he succeed, for who knew what might follow? Still, the thought of jettisoning the search never occurred to him. He had already faced death, and the experience of God's presence had been so real, so powerful, that he shrank from nothing. And the corroboration from his fellow executives had cemented his determination to pursue his mystical path.

The other four men had left immediately after the decision to call Grant Tyler had been made. They had all been as excited as Lindsay, each one saying that he wanted to be notified right away of any news. Lindsay asked them if they wanted to stay overnight so they could join him when he called Tyler the next morning, and he was touched by their response, which was that they trusted him to be in charge and get the expedition underway.

Now Lindsay waited for Tyler's office to answer his call. There had been three rings and still no one had responded, which was unusual; normally Tyler's people answered on the second ring at the latest. For a moment Lindsay felt an internal panic; this was the telephone call of his life and no one was there. He fought off the momentary anxiety and waited for the fourth ring.

"Mr. Lindsay? This is Beverly Engler. I'm so glad that you are well."

"Hello, Beverly. Nice job you folks did with that story about me."

"Why, thank you, Mr. Lindsay. We weren't sure whether you would approve of it."

"Actually, it was quite accurate, as far as it went. I'm only surprised that you didn't get more information than you did."

"I'll take that as a compliment. We try to give as many details to a story as we can without muddying the waters with trivial matters. Of course, anything connected with you would hardly be trivial."

"Oh, I have many mundane aspects, Beverly. Some I'm only beginning to discover. I would imagine that all of us find ourselves ordinary, sooner or later."

"For me the revelation came quite early."

"Ah, then you underestimate yourself. That kind of humility should only happen when you reach my age." Lindsay paused before he was ready to plunge ahead. "Is Grant in? I have an interesting problem for him. It's the kind of story I think he would like."

"Oh, I'm so sorry, Mr. Lindsay. Of course you didn't know, you were in the hospital. Mrs. Tyler died two days ago."

Shocked, Lindsay said, "Oh, my God, I didn't know Becky had deteriorated that fast . . . last month she was somewhat stable. I wish I had known. I could have offered Grant some support. Why did the cancer move so fast?"

"It hit her pancreas five weeks ago. Once that happened, it moved at lightning speed. The funeral was yesterday."

"No wonder I didn't know. I've been in and out of the country so much that my conversations with Grant only lasted five minutes. Is he at home? Maybe I could give him a call."

"Oh, he's not at home, Mr. Lindsay, and he'll be impossible to reach right away."

Lindsay felt that same attack of panic. "Impossible to reach? Why? Where is he?"

"He's on an airplane somewhere over the Atlantic."

"The Atlantic? Where is he going?"

"To Israel."

"To Israel? What for? Grant's not Jewish. He's not even religious!"

"All I can tell you is that his trip is about something that could change the world."

"When he calls in, you tell him that I want him to help me with something bigger than that. It can't wait. Tell him to call me day or night, okay?"

"Yes, sir. I'll tell him as soon as he calls."

"Good." Lindsay frowned slightly and thought, *Israel? Why Israel?*

6

Grant Tyler had flown countless times in his life, but there was one particular thrill that he had never lost. It wasn't the thrill that a first-time passenger gets from take-off, and it wasn't the thrill that those plagued by a fear of flying get from landing. It was the moment when the plane broke through the highest level of clouds and all that was visible was the blue sky and the sun. He always felt an incredible surge of optimism when he witnessed this and felt that he had the power and opportunity to achieve any of his dreams. Now, when he looked out the window to see the clouds fall away and the glory of the sky and the sun, he was aware of another feeling, one that he had never associated with this moment. Grant Tyler felt guilty: He was experiencing this moment and Becky could not. He was angry at even *allowing* himself to feel joy or optimism. He had no right to feel any of those things, no right to feel anything but grief. His mission to find Becky behind the wall seemed specious now, a vain longing for something he couldn't replace. His momentary fling with the mystical was now painful to him; he was a man used to dealing in the terms of reality, and whatever Becky had said about a wall, whatever Willie Daniels had said about a wall, the reality was that Becky was dead and she wasn't coming back.

He felt increasingly desperate now. His original response to the whirl-wind series of events since Becky mentioned the wall was a soaring hope that everything would be okay. That had lasted until . . . when? When had that feeling of desperation started? He mentally retraced his steps from Becky's hospital bed, with her lying dead in his arms, to the present moment. As he did, he tried to recapture that soaring feeling of hope. He remembered sitting next to Becky's body for what seemed like an eternity, but the hope was still there. He remembered Joel's arm around his shoulders leading him from the hospital room, and the hope was still there. He re-membered the funeral the next day. . . .

The services had been private. Grant had never been the type of man to make a public display of his feelings, and he wasn't going to start now. Eighty-five people attended, and all of them were either coworkers of Grant's or Becky's family members. In Grant's case, it was easy; his parents were already gone and he had no siblings. In Becky's case, her mother and sister survived her.

Becky's mother was eighty, and adored Grant. At the gravesite, she had tightly gripped Grant's arm with one hand and pulled his head down to whisper in his ear, "Wherever my daughter is, she knows that you were her destiny. I am so grateful to you for the life you gave her." Becky's sister Joanne, five years her junior, had quietly pulled Grant aside and said, "She couldn't have picked anyone as good as you, Grant. You were meant to find each other." Both remarks had further energized Grant to solve the riddle of finding Becky behind the wall, for her mother had mentioned destiny and her sister had referred to finding each other. He had nodded and smiled inwardly, for he knew that he would find his love again. There had been too many amazing coincidences already. He had even laughed at himself for ever doubting that there was such a thing as destiny, and he felt that his sepa-ration from Becky was only temporary and that once he found her again, everything would be all right.

His optimism was rudely shaken by the sight of his son Matthew stand-ing to one side of the crowd around the grave, wearing a sweatshirt and jeans, looking down at the casket. Matthew had been absent from the chapel where the services were held, and Grant had assumed that he was unaware of his mother's death, since both Grant and Beverly Engler had tried all night to reach him. Now he stood staring at Matthew angrily, ready to pounce on him, not caring if they had an argument. He walked aggressively to Matthew and stopped directly in front of him, between him and the grave.

"Where did you go last night? I came back from the game, and you had left your mother alone with the nurses. What the hell is wrong with you?"

Matthew continued to look down silently.

Grant tried to still the rage in his voice. "Where did you have to go that was so damn important?"

"Away."

"Away from what?"

Matthew raised his head to look his father in the face, and Grant saw tears streaming down his son's face. "Just away, Daddy."

Grant swallowed hard. He felt his anger drain out of him and found a surge of love for his son flowing through him. "Away from what?" he repeated.

Matthew wiped his eyes with the sleeve of his sweatshirt. "Away from the whole thing. I couldn't stand to see Mom suffer like that, so as soon as she fell asleep, I took off. She was talking about a wall, just crazy stuff. I couldn't stand it."

"She mentioned a wall? What did she say to you about it?"

"Something about how I could find her there. . . . I don't know. . . . It's not important."

"It might be *very* important, Matthew," Grant said eagerly. "Try to remember."

Matthew looked at his father, surprised and a little angry. "Since when does something like this interest you? You never cared about stuff like this."

Grant said evenly, "My views have changed. I don't scoff at things so quickly now."

Matthew's eyes narrowed. "You never felt this way when Mom was here. You used to say that anything that *sounded* crazy *was* crazy. And when I told you that one person's fantasy is another person's reality, you said that I'd better leave fantasy behind if I was to succeed in this world." He took a step away from his father and said resentfully, "Who's talking about fantasy now, Dad?"

"Look, Matthew, I was wrong, okay? I get it now. Just tell me what your mother said."

Intensity was etched across Matthew's face, "I'm going to give you your own advice, Dad. When someone tells you a cock-and-bull story, remember that the emphasis is on *bull*. *That's* what I think of what Mom said. She was mentally gone, Dad; she was finished. That story about the wall was as big a fish story as Jonah and the whale. I think you're just looking for an excuse to forget where she really is." He pointed at the grave. "*That's* where she is, Dad. She's dead . . . she's gone . . . and nothing you can do is going to bring her back."

Grant slapped his son's face.

Matthew's head snapped back from the impact. When he turned back to look at his father, Grant saw hatred burning in his son's face. Matthew's hands were clenched, ready to strike. The force of the blow had sounded like a pistol shot, and the people immediately turned to see what had happened. Matthew noticed the crowd watching him and his father, and turned abruptly to walk away from the grave toward the exit of the cemetery.

Beverly Engler was one of those watching, and she left Becky's mother's side and ran to her boss. Without thinking, she blurted out, "Are you all right, Grant?"

Grant, who had been rooted to the spot where he stood, spun his head around.

Beverly threw her hand up to cover her mouth, mortified that she had called him by his first name. "I'm sorry, Mr. Tyler. I'm really sorry. I forgot myself for a second." She temporarily lost her train of thought. "I just wanted to make sure you were all right. . . . It's a stupid question."

Grant looked at her bleakly. "No, it's not. I'm not all right, am I?"

"How could you be at this moment? You're allowed to be human, to make a mistake . . ."

"Not *that* kind of mistake."

Beverly had regained her composure. "*Especially* that kind of mistake." She said softly, "No one can enrage us like family can."

Grant gazed at her. She was shocked to see tears slowly wending their way down his face. He made no effort to wipe them away. She reached into her purse and fumbled through it for a handkerchief, finally grabbed it and started to offer it to him. He didn't move, and she realized that he was not going to take it from her. She hesitated, then saw the tears drop down on his shirt and raised her hand to his face and wiped the tears away.

Grant drew back from her.

Beverly understood and had the strength to remain silent without being hurt. She waited for Grant to say something. He closed his eyes, and she waited patiently; she could see him gather his strength before he spoke again. He placed his fingertips on his forehead and rubbed them back and forth. "I must get to Jerusalem right away and check out that cold-fusion report."

"I'll call the Nuclear Science Institute and set up an appointment for you. When are you leaving?"

"Get the jet ready as soon as possible. But don't set up an appointment on my first day there. I have one other stop I have to make." Grant tightened his lips. "One other thing. While I'm gone, I want you to follow Matthew. Not secretly, but openly. Wherever he goes, whatever he does, I want to make sure that he doesn't do something crazy. He's always been fond of you, so maybe he'll talk to you if he sees you. Tell Joel to find someone to cover for you, okay? I should be gone no more than five days."

"Are you sure that you'll be all right?"

He didn't answer.

*　　*　　*

She's dead . . . she's gone . . . and nothing you can do is going to bring her back.

Grant awoke groggily with Matthew's words ringing and reverberating in his brain. He didn't know how long he had been asleep. He hadn't slept for two nights, but now he looked through his window and saw the sun rising on the horizon so he figured he must have been asleep for a substantial time. Beverly had set Grant's jet to leave at noon the day after the funeral, calculating that the flight to Israel would take eleven hours and the time difference would add seven hours to that, so he would arrive at six in the morning. She knew that he was exhausted and would probably sleep on the plane, and, as usual, she was right. He tried to rouse himself; he had only one day free to get to the wall before his appointment at the Nuclear Science Institute the next day.

He felt the desperation rush through him to get to the wall in Jerusalem before something happened that he dreaded. He didn't know what he dreaded, just that it was vital that he get to the wall as soon as possible. Now, after reviewing the past forty-eight hours, he understood when his optimism had faded and the desperation had started. It was Matthew's remark. Before it, he had felt that all the incredible events he had experienced were a clear sign of a path being shown to him, a path that would somehow lead him to Becky again. But after Matthew had sounded a reminder of the power of reality, Grant's hope had been crushed by the force of his own realism. What Grant was holding onto now was a single thread of hope. He realized that it was because he had only a single strand left that he was feeling desperate. The enormous urgency to hurry was a result of his fear that the thread would break.

"Mr. Tyler, you need to fasten your seat belt. We are starting our descent to Tel Aviv."

Grant looked through the window to see the Mediterranean Sea below him. Although the sight of the sea sent a brief wave of tranquillity through him, he returned to the same feeling of desperation to hurry to the wall . . . and he thought that nothing else in the history of his life mattered at all.

*   *   *

Two hours and one taxi ride later he was standing in front of the wall Joel Alexander's ancestors had built two thousand years before. He was astonished by its massive scope; he only associated this kind of size with modern skyscrapers. He realized that it wasn't the wall's height that made it seem so tall, but all the people crowded around it at its base. All around him were men in black suits with beards, hundreds of them. They were all wearing prayer shawls over their shoulders, and each had some sort of small black box on top of his head that was held there by two straps that encircled the head and then dangled on either side of the neck down the front of the torso. Each had a similar box attached to his biceps by a strap that seemed to be woven around the left arm a number of times. It was obvious to Grant that they were praying because every so often they bowed low in the direction of the wall, the Western Wall of the temple destroyed by the Romans in 70 C.E. Grant was worldly enough to know that somehow this wall was the focus of Jews all around the world, although he didn't understand its full significance or even care. He was only interested in the wall because Becky and Willie Daniels had alluded to it.

What frustrated Grant was the impossibility of his situation. All Becky had said was that a man with a beard and a black suit and hat had told her to keep believing. She, not the man, had said she would be behind the wall. And Willie Daniels hadn't said anything about the mysterious man either. All Willie had said was that Grant wanted to put his message *through* the wall instead of *in* the wall. None of this was any good now. How was he supposed to find this man, anyway? Countless men around the wall fit Becky's description.

He noticed that some men were putting small pieces of paper into the spaces between the stones of the wall, and he remembered what Joel had told him; religious Jews believed that the divine spirit resided in a special room called the Holy of Holies in the temple, and the wall was the closest that they could come to approaching God with a request. *What's behind the wall?* he wondered.

He noticed one group of young men gathered around an old man with a white beard, listening intently. They were not wearing the black boxes or prayer shawls, and they stood as motionless as a squad of marines at attention, rapt in what the old man was saying. Grant was struck by the incongruity of the group; the men were certainly between the ages of eighteen and thirty, and the old man had to be at least in his eighties. What also made the situation unusual was that unlike the armed services in the United States, where a group of young men would pay attention to their superiors with the most deadly seriousness, this group of young men were just as respectful, but everyone was smiling. Grant couldn't ever remember witnessing a scene like this before, and somehow, he felt drawn to the old man. Intrigued, he walked toward him. As he approached, the old man suddenly looked up with the most lively eyes Grant had ever seen and stared straight at him. The young men followed their teacher's glance and stared at Grant, then some of them began excitedly talking to the old man. Grant came to a stop, ready to walk away, but the old man gave an answer to one youth, then turned back to Grant and beckoned him closer with his hands. Grant uncertainly continued walking to the group. The old man's eyes crinkled.

"You are Grant Tyler, the newsman?"

For some reason Grant winced. "You know who I am?"

The old man's eyes laughed. "My students informed me; I am not so knowledgeable myself. They say that you are a very important man."

Grant shrugged his shoulders. "Not so important."

"That's not what they tell me. They say that you are one of the most famous men in the world. And also one of the most powerful."

"I'm finding that power is a relative term."

"That is very true. We could be talking about governmental power, the power of an idea, or . . ." his eyes were suddenly piercing, ". . . the power of a new form of energy."

Grant looked at the old man, startled. "Who are you, may I ask? Are you a rabbi?"

All the young men smiled at Grant's question. One young man, unable to restrain himself, didn't wait for his teacher to answer. "Our Rosh Yeshivah is the greatest Torah scholar in the world!"

"Rosh Yeshivah?"

"Rosh is the Hebrew for head, Mr. Tyler. And a yeshivah is a school where our Torah, our sacred books, are studied. I'm very sorry, I should have introduced myself. I am Rabbi Eliyahu Hanviowitz of the Yeshivah Tahorah. What brings you to Israel? A story of a discovery, perhaps?"

Grant noticed the rabbi watching him closely. He said carefully, "Perhaps."

"It is a wonderful thing, to discover something. That is what we do, too."

"You mean when you study together?"

"We call it by a different name. We don't say 'We're going to do some studying,' we say, 'We're going to do some learning.' There is a profound difference between the two. When you study something, you are creating a division between the observer and the observed. You are *here*, the object you are studying is *there*. The object being studied may be fascinating, possibly even compelling, but it remains something apart."

Grant asked, "And learning?"

Rabbi Hanviowitz stroked his beard. "Learning implies a connection between the one learning and what he learns. When someone learns something, he is a changed person. Maybe his behavior is unaffected, but still, the knowledge gained by his learning makes him a different person than he was before, even if the change is a small change in the patterns of his brain. Therefore, we refer to our time with the Torah as learning, not studying, because we expect everything we learn to be connected to our lives and change them, most ideally to change our behavior, to come closer to what God wants from us. True learning does not take place in a vacuum."

"That's certainly an admirable goal, but most people are just trying to make a living. They don't have the time for all of that."

"And you, Mr. Tyler? Do you spend all your time at your job because you need the money?"

Grant was silent. The rabbi looked searchingly at Grant for a moment, then said something in Hebrew to his students. They all nodded and slowly moved away from the two men in groups of two and three.

Rabbi Hanviowitz turned back to Grant. He said quietly, "I'm sorry if I offended you, Mr. Tyler."

Grant shook his head. "You didn't offend me, Rabbi. It's just that you reminded me of someone else when you said that."

"May I ask who?"

"My wife."

The rabbi looked pleased. "If I gave similar advice to your wife's, that is very good. A man's wife is the fulcrum on which his sense of balance rests." He gestured toward the women's side of the crowd. "Is she here with you? I would be delighted to meet her."

"My wife died three days ago."

The rabbi was stunned. There was a moment while he considered, and then he looked piercingly at Grant once again. "And now you are here, in Israel? Why?"

Grant tried to decide whether to answer the old man.

The rabbi spoke calmly. "You're not here because of the cold-fusion project, are you?"

Now it was Grant's turn to look stunned. He managed, "How do you know about that?"

Rabbi Hanviowitz said, "With so many Jews working on the project, the chances of at least one of them being religious are pretty good, don't you think? Two of the scientists were once my students. We encourage our students to study science and nature. The more they learn about the way the world works, the more they will realize what a miracle the world is—which leads them right back to God."

Grant smiled grimly. "I hope you'll let me get the story first. It may be the biggest story of my lifetime."

"But is it so big that you would come here three days after your wife's death? You could have sent your best reporter." The rabbi studied Grant's face. "No, that is not the reason you are here. This must have to do with your wife."

Grant wanted to tell the rabbi everything, but something held him back.

"Was she Jewish?"

Grant shook his head.

"Then why are you here at the wall?"

Grant found himself waiting for a mystical sign of some kind before he would speak.

"Mr. Tyler, the reason I dismissed my students was because *I* wanted to speak with *you*. Three nights ago I had a dream that I would talk to a stranger at the wall. *I need to know why you are here.*"

Grant's eyes widened. "You saw me in a dream?"

"Not you, but a faceless man who needed to speak with me. Could you tell me why you came here?"

Grant told him everything, from the moment that Becky had spoken of the wall, to the encounter with Willie Daniels, to the news he had received of the success of the cold-fusion project. Rabbi Hanviowitz listened carefully, stroking his beard.

"Your wife said you could find her behind the Kotel?" He used the Hebrew word for the Western Wall.

"That's what she said."

"And your friend . . ."

"Joel."

"He knew it was the Kotel because the basketball player mentioned people putting messages in the wall?"

"That's right."

"And you thought you might find your wife if you came here?"

Grant looked embarrassed. "That must sound ridiculous. I've never done something like this before in my life. I've never had much use for religion or God."

"Did you ever consider that God might have some use for *you?*"

"I don't understand."

"We don't believe in coincidence, Mr. Tyler. We don't believe, as deists do, that God created the world and then left it to run by itself. We believe that God is active, involved in the affairs of men." He looked intently at Grant. "I don't think you are being ridiculous by coming here. In fact, I think it is part of the divine plan somehow. I don't think it is an accident that you have been directed here by a spiritual matter at the same time that the world is about to undergo a major change on the physical level."

Grant felt an enormous relief wash over him. This was an obviously rational, well-respected man telling him that his path was not a misguided attempt, not a venture into the absurd, but simply an endeavor whose purpose was still unrevealed to him and therefore confusing. Still, he didn't believe that God existed, and he felt guilty accepting consolation from this man.

The rabbi watched Grant's face. "It looks to me as if you would like to believe me but your skepticism prevents you from doing so." Grant nodded. "Maybe I should tell you what is on the other side of the Kotel?"

Grant felt his adrenaline race through his blood. "Is it something important?"

Rabbi Hanviowitz's eyes had a timeless look about them. "There is an empty space between two mosques, the Dome of the Rock and the El Aktzah Mosque."

"But Becky specifically referred to the wall. Why would she not tell me anything about the empty space behind it?"

"I would imagine that you need to go back fifteen hundred years before the mosques were built to answer that question. You see, when the temple was built, what lay behind the wall was the *Kodesh HaKodoshim,* the Holy of Holies."

"Which was where the divine spirit resided."

"Exactly, and many other things. It was the place from where we believe God started his creation of the world, the place from where all prophecy emanated, and the place where the Ark of the Covenant was located. And inside that ark were the two most sacred objects of our faith—the two tablets inscribed with the Ten Commandments and the Torah scroll that God dictated to Moses."

Grant said half-jokingly, "Are you telling me that Becky sent me here to be converted?"

The rabbi said seriously, "No. It is against Jewish law to attempt to convert someone. We are instructed to act only as examples for the world. For example, we have 613 laws to follow, while the rest of the world is enjoined only to follow the seven laws of Noah."

"And what are those?"

"They prohibit idolatry, murder, theft, blasphemy, adultery and incest, eating the flesh of a living animal, and one positive commandment: to establish courts of justice."

"That sounds simple enough."

"They all are predicated on one assumption, though. The belief in a single God who rules the world."

"That's a lot to assume."

"If he's not there, then what are you doing here?"

Grant realized that this was the question that had lain barely under the edge of his consciousness for the past three days. He looked up at the sky. All of his efforts to follow the path to Jerusalem were indeed based on the premise that someone was showing him the way. But why?

He heard the sound of running feet approaching. He turned back to the rabbi in time to see one of the young men who had been part of the rabbi's group reach the old man and unleash a torrent of Hebrew. Rabbi Hanviowitz's face, already aged, suddenly grew paler.

Grant didn't know what they were saying back and forth, but he was aware that it must be something profoundly important to the rabbi, for he was asking questions at a rapid-fire rate. The young man took off like a rocket, leaving the rabbi shaking his head, looking slightly unsure of himself. Then he seemed to be struck by a sudden thought, for he looked at Grant with a brightness in his eyes that was almost blinding in its intensity.

"I think I know why you are here, Mr. Tyler."

*　　*　　*

It was electric. What Rabbi Hanviowitz told Grant hit him like a thunderbolt and now, two hours later, he was on a plane heading back to the United States. He hadn't even seen the cold-fusion project, just given instructions to the Jerusalem reporter of the Tyler News Network to cover the story right away. What the hell was he doing?

Rabbi Hanviowitz had told him the news that the young yeshiva student had brought. Rabbi Hanviowitz's brother, Micah, terminally ill and in the hospital, had committed suicide. Grant felt bad for the old man, but said he had heard similar stories before.

"No, this is different."

"Why is that?"

The rabbi had rolled up the sleeve of his long black coat to display numbers tattooed on his arm. "We were both survivors of Auschwitz, along with my other brother, Daniel. Micah would never have killed himself, never!"

"Because he believed in God?"

"Because he *didn't* believe in God. He hated the idea of God. I am even forbidden to mourn him because he publicly disowned his Jewishness and declared the nonexistence of God. He held onto his life as tightly as a drowning man clutching a life jacket."

"So what does that have to do with me?"

"He had briefly come out of a coma, and before he took his own life he wrote down one word in some strange script that no one can understand."

"Yes . . . and?"

"I think that is why you were sent here, so that you would eventually be sent to him to decipher that word."

"Why me? Why not someone else?"

"Do you know who my brother was, Mr. Tyler?"

Grant shook his head.

"His name was Micah, but you probably knew him as Mike Hanvill. The financier?"

Grant almost shouted, "Your brother was Mike Hanvill?"

"The most powerful financier in the world."

"I knew him. He was the hardest man I ever met."

"Precisely. Don't you feel something else at work here? Is it possible that *this* is the story you were meant to pursue, that this ties in with everything that you have been experiencing, *that this will lead you to your wife somehow?*"

Two hours later Grant was flying over the Mediterranean.

7

Cardinal Benda Cortes was heading back toward his home, but it was not his home in the magnificent old church in Rio. It was the home of his childhood, where his mother, ninety years old and cared for by a nurse, insisted on living out the remaining years of her life. He had not seen his mother for three weeks, and normally he would have visited her just to see her and check her condition. Now he had another motivation for visiting her, one that possessed him and drove his thoughts in a radically different direction.

After the series of events starting with the bombing of the church, his lifelong certainty of his own identity as a Catholic had been shattered. The revelation that Ganedos's wife and children were descendants of Jews had been a surprise, but his sudden recollection that his own mother had also secretly lit Friday-night candles had shaken his world down to its roots. His resultant confusion had left him hurt and grieving for the presence of God, his lifelong companion, who was as much a part of his identity as his own name.

He had decided to return to his mother's house to learn the truth about his origins. Insisting on driving back alone to Rio de Janeiro to avoid arousing Father Juan's suspicions, he had suggested that Father Juan help Father

Antonio find his brother Dominic before the bombings became public and Dominic became the object of a massive manhunt.

"But what about Pablo de Cardoso, Your Eminence?" Father Antonio had asked anxiously.

"We have no control over what he does, Father Antonio. We must take aggressive action whether he prints his story or not. We must do two things: Find your brother before he can do further damage, and make it clear to the public that Dominic's point of view is not representative of the Church. The former is for you and Father Juan to accomplish; the latter is in my sphere of influence. That is why I am leaving for Rio immediately." He watched them closely. Did they suspect that he was concealing something?

Father Antonio could not restrain himself. He cried, "Then you are not going to prevent de Cardoso from printing the story?"

"I think that this man cannot be convinced of the importance of your brother's anonymity. De Cardoso's history suggests that his agenda is to destroy the Church, and whatever means he must use, he will use them. Therefore I believe we cannot prevent him from printing the whole story. My role, ultimately, is to protect the Church."

"And you are willing to sacrifice my brother in order to do so? What kind of Church do you propose to protect? Who is going to make up your Church?" He spat. "Dominic is a devout Catholic. You are supposed to protect *your* flock!"

"I thought that the Ganedos family were your friends."

"He is my brother. They are gone, and he is here. They are *gone.*" He said stubbornly, "I did not know they were Jews."

"Does that make a difference? They were human beings, and your brother murdered them."

Father Antonio said wrathfully, "Did not our Lord say, 'Take my enemies, who would not have me rule over them, bring them here, and kill them before me'? Did not our Lord say to the Jews, 'You snakes, you generation of vipers, how can you escape the damnation of Hell'?"

The cardinal was silent.

Father Antonio pointed at the cardinal. He said harshly, "Before I see my brother sacrificed like our Lord, I would see all my Lord's enemies destroyed first." His face was distorted with fury. "They're Jews, after all." He turned from the cardinal and walked away.

Father Juan, who had been shocked and silent throughout the entire exchange, looked at the cardinal, whose face had gone white. He asked quickly, "Should I go after him, Your Eminence?"

"Yes . . . until he finds his brother. Then see if you can talk to them. . . . I must return to Rio immediately."

"You are not angry with him, Your Eminence?" Father Juan was relieved. "I don't know why he has such violent hatred. He wasn't really angry with *you,* though. He doesn't really hate *you.*" He shook his head in confusion. "But such hatred of Jews . . ."

Like me? the cardinal thought painfully. "That is his prerogative," he said tightly.

Father Juan was bewildered. He had worked for the cardinal for six years, but he had never heard that tone in the cardinal's voice before. It was as close to bitterness as he could imagine, a sentiment that he would never associate with this man. Had he said something wrong?

"Did I say something to offend you, Your Eminence?"

The cardinal responded curtly, "Just follow Father Antonio and call me in Rio when you find Dominic." He abruptly walked away toward the car, leaving Father Juan confused and hurt. The cardinal never looked back.

$$*\quad*\quad*$$

They're Jews, after all.

Jews? What if he, Cardinal Isaac Benda Cortes, was a descendant of Jews, or more disturbing, if he were actually a Jew himself? He thought savagely about how all his life he had buried the memory of his mother lighting candles. He tried to forgive himself his self-deception, saying that as a boy he didn't know the significance of what he had seen, but no mercy was forthcoming. He had known about the Marrano Jews since young adulthood, when he had consumed hundreds of books on the history of the Church. He ransacked his memory for what he had learned. . . .

As far back as the sixth century C.E., the Jews in Spain had been subjected to proselytizing. King Recarred converted ninety thousand Jews to Catholicism in that period, but the successful Islamic invasion in the eighth century had temporarily halted the efforts at conversion. When Spain was reconquered by the Christians in the thirteenth century, though, Jews were again targeted for conversion. Very often it was done by force, and many laws made life for a Spanish Jew difficult, if not impossible, thereby easing the way for many Jews to seek an escape from their predicament by converting to Catholicism. They still practiced their Judaism in secret, lighting candles on Friday night to initiate the Sabbath, or eating flat crackers during Passover to obey the injunction to eat only unleavened bread. These Jews were often called *Marranos*—"Swine."

The Marranos became a major problem for the government because they were so successful. Laws were available to keep the Jews in their place, but a hidden Jew, a Marrano, could ascend to power and not be checked. Some even became bishops and archbishops of the Church. The public responded by riots against the Jews in 1378 and 1391. Soon after that, the Dominican friar Vicente Ferrer (later made a saint by the Church) suggested that the rooting out of heretics was the business of the state and the Church, not the people. By 1480, the Spanish Inquisition had been formally established. In the next twelve years, thousands of Marranos were condemned, and many were burned to death. Many of the Marranos fled Spain for Portugal, but in 1496 Portugal forcibly expelled her Jews and Marranos, too. A small percentage of the Jews left Portugal, went to Holland and later sailed to Brazil, where the tolerant Dutch who ruled there let them live in peace. That peace only lasted until 1600, when the Portuguese ousted the Dutch in Brazil and again persecuted the Jews. Some fled to America, but some merely hid their Jewish ancestry and remained in Brazil.

The wife of Ganedos had apparently been one of their descendants. Why all her maternal ancestors had kept their maiden names along with their married names was an enigma to the cardinal, but he abruptly remembered that his father's father's last name had been only Cortes. He had always assumed that his own middle name Benda was a family tradition, but strangely enough he had never asked about its origin. Now he wondered if somehow it came from his mother, and whether it was another clue to the burgeoning riddle of his existence.

The car phone buzzed. The cardinal had not wanted one, concerned that it was not truly a necessity, but Father Juan had insisted that there be a phone in the car so that the cardinal could be reached in case of an emergency. The cardinal, annoyed at the intrusion, frowned but answered the call anyway.

"Hello, this is Cardinal Benda Cortes."

The basso profundo voice of Father Mario, his long-time secretary, rumbled through to him. "Oh, Your Eminence, you surprised me. I thought Father Juan would answer."

"No . . . he is still in the village. I am coming to Rio by myself."

"I have Cardinal Scoglio on the line for you from the Holy See. Should I give him your car phone number and have him call you directly?"

Cardinal Scoglio, the cardinal thought. *What a time for him to call.* "Please ask him to wait one minute to give the line a chance to clear."

"Yes, Your Eminence."

Cardinal Benda Cortes winced. Cardinal Scoglio was the elderly pope's right-hand man, the man who was considered the leading candidate to succeed the ailing pontiff. He was sixty-eight, from Italy, and had always been aloof with Benda Cortes. The cardinal suspected that his own meteoric rise in the Church's hierarchy had engendered this response, for Cardinal Scoglio had slowly and carefully risen from a small church in Sicily to his present position and had been made a cardinal at the age of sixty-one, while Benda Cortes was made a cardinal at forty. Not only that, but Cardinal Scoglio thought of himself as a scholar, and word of Benda Cortes's incredible memory, range of knowledge and fluency in eleven languages had spread through the Church so powerfully that Scoglio had felt his own stature as the leading scholar jeopardized. Why, one of the languages in which Benda Cortes was fluent was Aramaic, the language that Jesus himself had spoken. Scoglio felt that knowing Aramaic was simply exhibitionistic, a tool that Benda Cortes used to show off. Once, at a conclave of the cardinals, he had even said so to Benda Cortes.

"There's no practical use for it, my young friend. What is really important is Greek." Cardinal Benda Cortes had simply nodded and kept his mouth shut, suppressing the fact that he had been fluent in ancient Greek from the age of seventeen.

Of late, Cardinal Scoglio had been openly critical of Benda Cortes's outspoken efforts to combat the drug cartel. He had stated that the drug issue was a temporal matter, not a spiritual one, and therefore should be dealt with by local governments. When Benda Cortes attempted to confront Cardinal Scoglio over the phone, he invariably found Scoglio was not to be found.

What does he want now? he wondered. The car phone buzzed again.

"Hello, this is Cardinal Benda Cortes."

"You were not hurt in the bombing, Benda Cortes?"

The cardinal couldn't tell whether Scoglio was disappointed or genuinely solicitous. "No, by the grace of God, I am unhurt."

"I think it is time that you were more circumspect in your activities, don't you?"

Cardinal Benda Cortes chose his words carefully. "Is that the judgment of the Holy See?"

There was a pause, then Scoglio's voice came crackling through the receiver. "The Holy Father has been too ill to attend to normal affairs. In his absence, I am handling crises that may erupt."

"Is it your view that my situation is critical?"

"You know my position in this matter. Your role is not to interfere in issues that should be the concern of the local government."

"Am I free to disagree?"

"I cannot speak for the Holy Father. His view may not be my own."

"Well, then, I shall pray for the Holy Father's health every day."

"I would hope that you are already doing that."

"Now I shall pray with *extra* fervor."

The line went dead. The cardinal felt better, much better than he had before the phone call. He had regained some of his natural fighting spirit. *I may have doubts about who I am and where I came from,* he thought, *but to quietly retreat from confrontation is not in my blood.* He pressed harder on the accelerator.

* * *

Cardinal Scoglio looked testily out the window of his office in Rome. He grunted, then picked up the telephone and made a call. He drummed the fingers of his left hand on his desk while he waited for his call to be answered.

"Yes?"

"This is Scoglio. Is don Sanguino there?"

"Wait a moment."

Cardinal Scoglio swung his chair around to avoid facing the crucifix on his wall.

"Scoglio, is that you?"

"It is I, don Sanguino. I regret that I have not called you these past few weeks."

"No matter, no matter. How is the pontiff?"

"The cancer is in the lymph nodes. At his age they are unsure whether chemotherapy is advisable."

"Do they have any projections of his future?"

"Not as yet." Cardinal Scoglio tried to suppress his anticipation. "I may be in this position for a bit longer."

"Would the chemotherapy hasten the pontiff's decline?"

"Quite possibly."

The silence that followed this statement was palpable in its implications. Finally don Sanguino spoke again. "You have influence with him?"

"Usually my word is listened to attentively. But lately there has been a curious change. The Holy Father has been ill, certainly, but even when we speak he seems to be distracted somehow."

"Perhaps it is the illness?"

"Possibly, but there has been another issue which has put us in confrontation. The cardinal from Brazil has been continuing his campaign against the drug cartel. When I spoke of my personal disapproval with the Holy Father, he dismissed my concerns as ill-founded and unnecessary. He even asked me to refrain from commenting at all."

Don Sanguino's voice became cold. "I thought that we discussed how to handle this man from Brazil. You were supposed to obtain the Holy Father's approval for a public reprimand."

"What more can I say to him without revealing too much? He must not know about our relationship. I was going to attempt to speak to him again, but when I heard about the bombing of the church I assumed you had taken matters into your own hands again. Have you spoken to Colombia as to why they failed this time?"

"I did, and they said they had nothing to do with the bombing."

"What!"

"They are trying to discover who was responsible."

Scoglio turned back to face the crucifix on the wall. "Someone else attempted to murder Benda Cortes?"

"That seems to be the case. The cartel is looking into it."

"That is essential. If we can find another to do our work for us, so much the better. I would prefer not to be involved."

Don Sanguino said brutally, "You have been involved since I built you that church forty years ago and made you successful. Never forget that, my friend. . . . You will keep me informed, I hope?"

Cardinal Scoglio started to answer before he realized that he was speaking to himself. He swung the chair around to turn away from the crucifix once more.

* * *

Cardinal Benda Cortes pulled into the driveway of his childhood home and came to a stop. He peered through the window to see the tree that he had climbed up as a child. It was still there, and his eyes followed the ascent of the branches until he saw the window of his bedroom. He felt a sudden nervousness and anxiety as he remembered why he had returned. He climbed out of the car, walked to the front door, and rang the bell. A moment later, Carlotta, the nurse he had hired to care for his mother, answered the door. She was in her mid-fifties, efficient and reasonably friendly. She smiled at seeing him.

"Your Eminence! This will be a welcome surprise for your mother. She was saying this morning how much she missed you. She just started eating in the kitchen. Should I wheel her in?"

"No, no, let her finish. I'll wait in the dining room for her."

"Yes, Your Eminence." The nurse retreated to the kitchen.

The cardinal stared at the huge doors to the dining room. Was there an answer for him behind those doors? Maybe that memory from his childhood had been a mistake? He hesitantly opened the doors and entered the dark, silent room. The curtains were drawn, and the only sliver of light came from a narrow break where the curtains met. He found that he was trembling a little as he approached the cabinet where his mother had lit the candles. He moved the cabinet aside, as quietly as he could and saw the door his mother had opened so many years ago. He reached for it. . . .

"Isaac . . ."

He whirled around at the ghostly, raspy voice. His mother stood silhouetted at the doorway to the dining room, leaning on her cane. He was so used to seeing her in a wheelchair, and she so rarely attempted to walk, that for a moment the cardinal lost all sense of where he was. A sudden flash of memory illuminated his mind. He remembered seeing his mother stand exactly in the same place, forty years ago, holding a tray of freshly baked cookies for him and his father. She had paused at the doorway so that the delicious aroma could waft across the room to them and smiled lovingly at his eagerness to partake of her gift. He had wanted to leap across the room toward the tray, but his father's stern glance made him wait in his chair, feet dancing above the floor, ready to fly. His mother had noticed the struggle within Isaac, and pleaded with her eyes to his father.

His father acted this way because to his chagrin Isaac had never eaten fish or meat of any kind. Isaac had assumed that it was because his mother abhorred killing anything. His father, on the other hand, relished eating meat, and it had been a constant struggle for his mother to make one meal for her husband and another for herself and her son. His father often retaliated by forbidding Isaac to eat dessert.

This particular time, his father had relented at the look in his wife's eyes, and Isaac found himself flying across the long dining room to his mother, grabbing a cookie, muttering a hasty prayer and burying himself in his mother's long skirt all in the same moment. The cardinal found himself blinking back tears as he saw this same woman, now frail and gaunt, valiantly try to stand erect for her son, to remain in every way the mother he had always worshiped.

"Isaac . . ."

He hurried across the room to her and, reaching her, glanced outside the room and saw the wheelchair hidden behind the stairs to the second floor. *Why does she want to disguise her infirmity now?* he thought. *I've seen her in that wheelchair for years.* He started to take her arm, and then he saw the fear written on her face. He gently took her arm and led her to the Spanish Renaissance armchair that had reputedly been in their family for five hundred years. He helped her lower herself slowly into the chair, and then brought a dining-room chair over to her side and sat down next to her.

"What's wrong, Mother? Why were you standing? I've seen the wheelchair before."

The yellowed eyes looked out of the aged face, frightened.

"Mother, it's Isaac."

The eyes blinked back at him. Once, twice, three times. The cardinal started to speak but then he saw a tear fall out of one eye, and he saw his mother look over his shoulder toward the cabinet and the hidden door. He followed her glance and then snapped his eyes back to her face. She was crying more freely now, and he felt helpless. He was not carrying anything to dry her tears, and he started to rise to get her something to wipe her face.

A grip like a steel vise held his arm.

"Don't go."

"Mother, you are all right?"

"I want . . . to talk to you."

"All right, I am here."

His mother released his arm. The cardinal rubbed it with his hand to restore the circulation. His mother bit her lips.

"I . . . I . . ."

"Can you tell me, Mother?"

She began to rock her body back and forth in the chair. "I promised her . . . I promised my mother. . . ."

He knelt on the floor in front of her.

"Is it true, Mother? Were we Jews? Am I . . . a Jew?"

"You are a Benda. . . ."

The cardinal did not understand. "What do you mean?"

"We have been Bendas for two thousand years. Ever since we left Spain we have kept the name . . . I have kept my promise. . . ."

"What promise?"

His mother drew a long, raspy breath. "When we fled Spain in 1492, the women were sworn to give all their daughters the name Benda as part of their name."

"But why?"

"I was never told."

"But I was your son. Why did you give the name to me?"

"My mother told me that you were the last child born in that line of daughters, and I had to give you the name."

"But what does it all mean? *Am I a Jew or not?*"

His mother turned her head away from him. He leaned forward in his chair and turned her face back to him. "I *must* know, Mother. I must know."

"You are a Catholic. I was there for your baptism, and you were destined to be the leader of your people." She started breathing rapidly. "You *are* going to be the leader of your people." She started to rise to her feet. "You will . . . you . . ." Her head jerked forward as she coughed violently. The cardinal instinctively jumped as a thin spittle of blood spattered across his lap. Blood formed around the edge of her mouth as she started to fall. He sprang to her and clutched her emaciated body in his arms.

"Carlotta! Carlotta! Come quickly! Quickly!" His mother's head lolled back on his shoulder.

He looked up in anguish, holding his mother's sagging weight. "Where are You? Why are You hiding from me? My God, My God . . . don't leave me here alone!"

8

Beverly Engler grimaced as she looked at the cars jammed in front of her. It had been ten years since she had gone to a rock concert, and she had forgotten what it was like to be part of a screaming mob. Most of the cars' windows were rolled down, and the pulsations of the raucous music could be felt by Beverly even though her windows were closed. *This could take forever,* she thought with exasperation. She consoled herself by twisting her head around and scanning the endless line of cars behind her. She permitted herself a grim chuckle, thinking, *They've got even longer to wait than I do. If I didn't love Grant, there's no way that I would suffer through this just to look for his son.*

She peered ahead toward the huge welcoming sign of the amphitheater. *Thrown Stones—March 10–13* flashed on its screen. The driver of the car behind her leaned on his horn, deafening her further. Why Matthew would go through this mess four nights in a row was beyond her.

She had tried to follow him yesterday after the funeral, but then she remembered that she had to make Grant's travel plans first. She had known Matthew was going to the concert all four nights; after all, she had arranged for the tickets. She had reasoned that she would have time after making

Grant's reservations to find Matthew at the concert. But by the time she was ready to leave the office, a huge downpour had started, and traffic was snarled throughout the city. She had lain awake most of the night, worried that she had let Grant down. This morning she had called Matthew at his apartment, and he had groggily answered "Hello, go away . . ." and then hung up immediately. She knew he would attend the concert in the evening and figured that he had gotten home at some ungodly hour and was trying to sleep, so she decided to try to attend the concert herself and find out how he was doing. Luckily, she kept records of everything, and she knew where he would be sitting. She made one phone call to a local ticket scalper and obtained a seat for the performance that cost three times its box office price.

Other cars started blasting their horns. *This show better be loud,* she thought, *I may lose my hearing before I even enter the theater.*

* * *

It was loud, all right. Beverly could feel the inside of her ears throbbing, violated by the assault of the roaring music. On stage, a long-haired, well-muscled guitarist had his back turned to the audience, urging the band members to crank it up. The band obeyed him, making a crescendo of gigantic proportions from what had been virtually deafening to what was absolutely stupefying. The music surged wildly to a peak until the band hit the last chord, and the frenzied fans went berserk. The band played one booming note and then paused. The crowd started to quiet down, sensing something imminent. The band played another note. The crowd was much quieter now, almost silent. The band played a third note, and the crowd was silent, waiting.

From the wings, a figure slowly started to cross the stage, one ponderous step at a time. The crowd saw him and started to clap, one clap for every step he took. The eerie pauses between each step and each accompanying thunderous clap from the audience sent chills down Beverly's spine. She had remembered to bring her binoculars to find Matthew in the crowd, and she trained them on the figure on the stage. She gasped at what she saw. A man in a long white robe and long beard was carrying a huge cross on his back across the stage, making his way toward a glass wall on the other side. At the wall waited a member of the band, holding what looked like a suit of armor. The crowd was silent except for the claps, and as the forlorn figure carrying the cross reached the wall, the crowd suddenly went silent. The bearded man was bent over from the weight of the cross, and another band member crossed over to him and started to help him don the suit of armor, all without letting go of the cross. The band played the single earsplitting note again, then another, and the mob began to clap with each note again. At the same time, three men came from the wings, each carrying what looked like another glass wall over to the first one. As the bearded man with the cross finished putting on his suit of armor, he was led to stand in front of the first glass wall. Quickly, the three other glass walls were attached to the first one, enclosing the bearded man and the cross within a square glass cage.

The stage suddenly went dark and silent. Then two spotlights shot out to encircle the glass cage with the bearded man at one end of the stage, and the long-haired guitarist-leader with his back to the audience at the other end. The leader pivoted to face the audience, and Beverly saw that he had a book in his hands. He cried through the microphone attached to him, "Who here knows what sin is?" Some in the crowd yelled back their encouragement. The leader roared this time.

"I *said,* who here knows what sin is? Say *I* do!"

"I do!"

"Who does?"

"I do!"

The leader yelled, "Is it a sin to lie?"

"Yes!"

"Is it a sin to lie?"

"Yes!"

"Then hear me, people!" He whispered now. "The man over *there* is a liar and a sinner!" He shouted, "A liar and a sinner! And I'm the man to show you why!" He paused. "Who here wants to know the truth?"

"We do!"

"Who *needs* the truth?"

"We do!"

"Then listen to me and I will bring you the truth! And the truth will set you free!" He started to dramatically flip through the pages of the book.

Beverly felt sick to her stomach. She had heard about groups that savagely attacked religion in this way but she had never seen it in person. She hurriedly fished through her pocket to find the piece of paper with

Matthew's seat number written on it, found it and shifted the binoculars to find the section he was in. There he was, sitting in the sixth row, dead center. He looked as eager with anticipation as everyone else.

The leader had found the page he was looking for. He pointed at the bearded man inside the glass.

"Did he not say, 'Love your enemies, bless those who curse you, and do good to those who hate you'?"

"Yes!"

"Then why did he also say, 'Take my enemies, who would not have me rule over them, bring them here, and kill them here before me.' Was he a liar?"

"Yes!"

"I said, was he a liar?"

"Yes!"

"Did he not say, 'Anyone who nurses anger at his brother must be brought to judgment'?"

"Yes!"

"Then why did he also say, 'Think not that I have come to send peace to the world. I come not to send peace, but the sword.' I ask you, was he a liar?"

"Yes!"

"I said, was he a liar?"

"Yes!"

"And haven't we all been taught that he will return to the world? It is two thousand years later, and he is not here. Another lie!" His voice sank to a whisper again. "And heavy is the soul that lies. As heavy to throw as . . ." He paused expectantly, waiting for the response the crowd was waiting to give.

"A stone!"

The leader powerfully ripped the book in half, dropped it to the stage, stood with one foot on each half, and swung his arms around to point with both hands at the bearded one.

"And people in glass houses shouldn't . . ."

The crowd roared, *"Throw stones!"*

Lights suddenly flooded the stage as the band played the single, deafening note again. The leader stood frozen in his position with his arms pointing at the glass cage. Two men strode across the stage toward the leader carrying two large metal buckets, left them on either side of him and retreated from the stage. The leader slowly turned his upper torso, bent from the waist, reached into one bucket to retrieve something, then repeated the action on the other side. Then he straightened up to stand erect, and Beverly felt faint as she saw what was in his hands.

Two large stones, as big as bricks.

The band started to slowly repeat the single thunderous note. The crowd not only clapped with each beat but stood up in unison and started to stamp their feet. Beverly could feel the floor pulsating under her feet, and when she looked up she saw the ceiling of the theater vibrating from the deafening roar.

"Do I lie to you?" the leader shouted.

"No!"

"Do I bring you the truth to set you free?"

"Yes!"

"I bring you the truth, and I do not lie. I AM SINLESS! . . . AND WHAT DID HE SAY? . . . He that is without sin among you, let him cast the first . . ."

"STONE!"

The glass cage began to rotate. As the speed of the rotation increased, the band accelerated the rhythm of the single note, and the mob kept pace with their hands and feet. Beverly felt her heart pounding in her chest and wildly looked around for an escape, but she was hemmed in and could not move. The crowd started to shout.

"Throw stones! Throw stones! Throw stones!"

The leader cocked his right arm and hurled the huge stone at the glass, shattering one wall of the whirling cage. The mob went berserk. The leader transferred the stone in his left hand to his right, and again hurled a stone at the cage, shattering a second wall. The noise level actually increased. The leader reached into the buckets for two more stones and hurled the third stone. Because two walls had been destroyed, two sides of the square cage were empty, and this stone hurtled through an open side and struck the bearded, armored figure, who stumbled back against one of the remaining glass walls and reached out with the cross to shield himself. The leader raised his right arm triumphantly. The crowd started to chant and raise their right arms along with him.

"Thrown Stones! Thrown Stones! Thrown Stones!"

Beverly scanned the crowd for Matthew and saw him with his arm upraised and chanting. He appeared as frenzied as everyone else. She shifted back to the stage, where the leader stood with the remaining stone in his left hand. He transferred the stone to his right hand, cocked his arm toward the spinning cage, then unexpectedly paused. He replaced the stone in his left hand and turned to face the audience. The cage slowed to a stop and the band, surprised, stopped playing. He dramatically lowered his voice.

"Are you sick of being powerless?"

"Yes!"

"I said, ARE YOU SICK OF BEING POWERLESS?"

"YES!"

"Do you hate all the rules they make for you?"

"YES!"

"Do you want me to empower you?"

"YES!"

"I SAID, DO YOU WANT ME TO EMPOWER YOU?"

"YES!"

The leader turned and indicated for the band to resume playing their single note. The thunderous clapping and stamping of feet began anew. The leader pointed to the armored, bearded figure.

"We must destroy the old to prepare for the new. Say it with me!"

"WE MUST DESTROY THE OLD TO PREPARE FOR THE NEW!"

"AGAIN!"

"WE MUST DESTROY THE OLD TO PREPARE FOR THE NEW!"

"AGAIN!"

"WE MUST DESTROY THE OLD TO PREPARE FOR THE NEW!"

The leader pointed to the audience. "I said WE." He turned to the band and cut them off. Pivoting to face the crowd again, he shouted, "We try something new right now." There was a deadly pause. *"Who will join me and throw a stone?"*

To her horror, Beverly saw thousands of hands waved in response. She looked for Matthew and saw to her relief that his hand was not raised, even though every other hand around him was flailing wildly in the air.

The leader scanned the distant parts of the theater, then brought his eyes to rest on the rows directly in front of him. Beverly saw him narrow his eyes as he saw the only person who did not raise his hand.

Beverly went numb. "Oh, my God, no."

A grin spread slowly across the leader's face. He waved to the crowd for silence. Only the band could be heard, playing the solitary note over and over. The leader spoke.

"All of you are with me. You *know* we must destroy the old to prepare for the new. But how do we teach others?" He pointed at Matthew. "We learn by doing! We learn by acting!" He looked directly at Matthew. "We have someone who needs to learn! BRING HIM TO ME! WE WILL HELP HIM LEARN!"

The mob of people around Matthew grabbed him and started to march him out to the aisle toward the stage. Matthew didn't offer any resistance. Beverly fought her way past the people around her and started to run down the aisle nearest her toward the stage. Matthew was pushed up to the stage and shoved toward the leader, where the three men who had set up the cage had reappeared. The three men surrounded Matthew and held him. The mob then waited at the edge of the stage for further instructions. The leader addressed them.

"You may return." He turned to smile at the crowd. "Their services are no longer needed." The crowd roared its approval. Beverly had made her way down to the edge of the stage, and two security guards posted there grabbed her and held her.

"You've got to stop it!"

"It's all part of the act, lady. Just relax."

"But he doesn't want to be up there!"

One guard grinned at her. "Then he shouldn't have come, lady. What are you, his mother?"

On the stage, the three men brought Matthew over to the leader. The leader grinned at him.

"Tell us your name."

Matthew was silent. The leader addressed the crowd.

"He won't tell us his name."

"Matthew." It was barely a whisper. Beverly could see his face, and he looked genuinely saddened.

"Matthew?" The leader was delighted. "It is ordained! Your namesake was one of the chief liars! You can erase the damage he has done! It is fitting! It is destiny!" He placed the stone in Matthew's right hand, which hung limply at his side. "You have been chosen to complete the circle! *YOU CAN DESTROY THE OLD TO PREPARE FOR THE NEW!*"

The crowd's roar was unbelievable.

Matthew shook his head.

The crowd began to hurl insults at Matthew. The noise was so loud that Beverly could not hear the leader, who was only fifteen feet from her. She saw him remonstrate with Matthew, who continued to shake his head no. The crowd grew uglier.

The leader had improvised when he asked for someone to join him, and he had counted on the force of his mass appeal to sway anyone he selected. Now he didn't know what to do, and he racked his brain as to why Matthew refused. Suddenly he had an inspiration. He again addressed the crowd.

"Our friend here seems to be stuck in his old ways of thinking. And what have we learned tonight? We must . . ."

"DESTROY THE OLD TO PREPARE FOR THE NEW!"

The leader turned to the three men holding Matthew. "I think Matthew here wants the spotlight to himself. Isn't that right, Matthew?"

Matthew remained mute.

"In order to destroy those old thoughts and prepare for the new, we're going to make you the center attraction!" He turned and pointed at the bearded, armored one, then turned to the crowd.

"I think *his* services are no longer needed." The crowd roared as they realized what was coming. The three men started to push Matthew toward the bearded one, who began to take off his armor. The men started to put the armor on Matthew, who didn't resist.

Beverly struggled to free herself, screaming, "Let me go!" The two guards looked at her unemotionally.

"He'll be hurt! You've got to let me go!"

"Look at that armor, lady. He *can't* get hurt."

"I don't care. You've got to get him off that stage!"

"It's a free country, lady. If he wants to be the garbageman, the president or Jesus Christ, it's up to him."

By now Matthew was fully dressed in the armor and had stepped behind the two remaining glass walls. The stage under him began to rotate again. Beverly watched in terror as the band resumed playing, and the leader cocked his arm and threw a stone at what was left of the spinning glass cage. One of the two remaining walls shattered, and the crowd grew louder and uglier. The leader threw once more, and the one glass wall that was left shattered amidst a thunderstorm of sound. He turned to face the crowd and pointed at Matthew, who was now standing alone as the floor under him slowed to a stop. The leader then pointed to one of the buckets of stones on the floor next to him, and held his palms up to the crowd, asking if he should continue. The crowd roared its approval.

Beverly felt tears of rage and helplessness slowly trickling down her face. *I am responsible for this,* she cried to herself. *I arranged for him to sit up front.*

She wanted to turn away but something inside her held her fast and forced her to witness what was about to happen.

The floor under Matthew started to rotate, and Matthew stood holding the cross close to him. The leader bowed to the audience, and took something out of his pocket. It was a large black handkerchief, and he proceeded to blindfold himself. He then reached into a bucket and pulled out a stone. What Matthew did in response to the blindfold was petrifying.

He removed his helmet. The look on his face was of someone removed from the world, already dead.

The roar grew even louder and uglier. There were some screams of panic, but the leader could not discern them amidst the huge volume of sound. He threw the stone.

Beverly watched the unerring accuracy of the throw as the stone hurtled toward Matthew.

She screamed, "Matthew, look out!"

He heard her. She knew he heard her because he turned his head toward her just as the stone was about to strike him, and the stone grazed his head. He fell backward and toppled to the stage. The crowd noise plummeted to a babble of confusion.

The security guards, shocked, had released their hold on Beverly. She took the stairs two at a time as she leaped to the stage, shoved the leader aside and ran to kneel at Matthew's side. She bent over the unconscious youth and cradled his head, dimly aware of others running to surround them. Suddenly the memory of wishing Becky dead flashed through her mind. And her brain hammered over and over again, *I've killed his wife and now I've killed his son. . . .*

9

J oel Alexander was wrenched out of his slumber by the ring of the telephone. He groaned as he squinted at the clock. "1:30 A.M.? What the hell . . . ?" He nudged Michelle, hoping she would answer the call, but she was lost to the world. The phone rang again. Irritated and annoyed at the intrusion, he fumbled for it in the dark and picked it up.

"Hello?"

"Mr. Alexander? Thank God you're there!"

He couldn't recognize the tremulous voice. "Who is this?"

"It's Beverly, Mr. Alexander. I need help!"

"Beverly? What's wrong? Where are you?"

"Mount Zion Hospital, the emergency room. I've been trying to reach Grant, but the hotel in Israel said he never checked in! I can't find him! I can't find him!" She started sobbing.

Joel sat upright in bed and felt Michelle sit up behind him. She whispered, "What's going on, Joel?" He shook his head and returned to the phone.

"Beverly, try to calm down. . . . I'll do whatever I can. Why are you at Mount Zion? Are you all right?"

Her voice steadied. "Mr. Alexander, it's Matthew. He . . . he was . . . injured at the concert tonight. The doctors need permission to operate."

"Why don't they ask Matthew? He's of age."

"They can't. He's unconscious. He was hit in the head by a stone, and the swelling means that they have to relieve the pressure on his brain."

"What?!"

"What do I tell them? Please help me!"

"Do they think he needs immediate surgery?"

"They said that there is no time to lose."

Joel didn't hesitate. "Tell them not to wait . . . to do whatever they think is necessary. I'll be there in ten minutes. You just hang on . . . hang on until I get there, okay?"

". . . Okay . . . okay . . ."

* * *

"Here we are, Mr. Tyler, Mount Zion Hospital."

Grant looked at his watch. 2:00 P.M. He hadn't flown on a commercial airline in years, but he had not even considered flying back to the States on his own jet; his two pilots had just flown for eleven hours and the immediate turn-around would have been hazardous for them. Instead he had called the commercial airlines and flown back first-class on the next available flight.

He gave the cab driver his fare plus a large tip, climbed out of the taxi, and started toward the main doors. They slid open, and he strode through them directly to the front desk. The stout woman on duty raised her head and her eyebrows shot up as she recognized him. Flustered, she managed, "You're . . . are you Grant Tyler?"

"Yes, I am."

The nurse tried to regain her composure. "What may I do for you, Mr. Tyler?" Only the involuntary flutter of her eyelashes and the girlish quality of her voice betrayed her.

Grant wasted no time. "Didn't Mike Hanvill die in this hospital?"

The fluttering eyelashes stopped, the eyes narrowed and the voice became baritone. "Mount Zion Hospital is a fine institution, Mr. Tyler. We did the best we could for Mr. Hanvill."

"I didn't—"

She started waving her right forefinger in his face. "Don't you get tired of tearing the medical profession apart? No matter what anyone says, we are trying to save people here. And all we get from you newspeople is grief."

Grant grabbed her wrist firmly but as gently as he could. "Wait, slow down, slow down. I didn't come here to blame anyone or write a story. I just want some information." He released her wrist.

"Ohhh . . ."

"Do you know where I can find the nurse who was on duty with him when he died?"

"I know he was in the intensive care unit. . . . That's on the third floor. Why don't you let me ring them and ask if someone can speak to you?" She stroked her right wrist with her left hand, and Grant saw a secret pleasure written on her face as she contemplated telling her friends who had held her hand at work today.

"Thanks." He turned away and stared out the front doors at the street while she made the call.

"Mr. Tyler?" Grant wheeled around to face her. "The nurses who were on duty with him are in Mr. Rosenal's office right now. He's the hospital administrator."

"Can you call his office and ask Mr. Rosenal if I can see them when they're through? Tell him I said it's urgent."

"I'll try. Oh, Mr. Tyler?"

"Yes?"

She flashed him a coaxing smile. "I'm sorry I misunderstood."

He understood, and although he was preoccupied, he smiled back. "No problem."

*   *   *

Grant's name did the trick; Mr. Rosenal complied. Half an hour later, three nurses sat in a small conference room with Grant. One appeared to be in her sixties, one in her fifties, and a slender brunette in her late twenties. Grant figured the chief was the middle of the three, and he was right. He sized her up as a no-nonsense type, and he was right again. Good, he thought, I don't have to waste time evading the issue. All three had recognized him, but the fiftyish one's reaction had been to size *him* up, which is why he figured she was the boss.

"Hi, I'm Grant Tyler."

"I know who you are, Mr. Tyler. Is there something you want?"

Grant thought, *Why is this woman acting so uptight?* "I came here to speak to the nurse who attended Mike Hanvill two days ago, right before he died."

She was tough . . . and brief. "What for?"

"I have to know what happened at the end."

"You running short of stories, Mr. Tyler?"

Grant tried to soft-pedal his approach. "I just saw his brother in Israel . . . Rabbi Hanviowitz? He encouraged me to learn the details surrounding Mike's death."

The nurse eyed him distrustfully. "Mike?"

"He was a friend of mine."

"We've heard from many supposed friends in the last thirty-six hours, Mr. Tyler."

"Is there a reason you're so antagonistic, ma'am?"

"I'm not fond of vultures, Mr. Tyler . . . whether it's for a story or for money. Which one are you after?"

He exploded. "Just what the hell is going on here? Look, lady, I don't need his money. I don't need anything but some answers to some questions, so stop giving me the run-around."

She kept her voice maddeningly calm. "Is this the way you treat women, Mr. Tyler? Does your wife have to put up with this, too?"

Grant's rage boiled just below the surface, but he restrained the urge to lash out. "My wife is dead, lady. She died three days ago, and I'm trying to find out *where she went,* okay?" He started to methodically take off his sports jacket. "Does that sound nuts to you? Good. Because if I am nuts, and you don't answer a couple of questions right now, there's no telling *what* I might do to you."

"If you think for one minute—"

She was interrupted by the older, sixtyish nurse, who stepped forward and tapped her on the shoulder. "I don't think he means any harm, Margaret. Why don't you give him a chance to ask his questions and *then* decide whether to answer them." Margaret, miffed that her colleague had given ground, started to retort angrily until she saw Grant's face. For a moment, his face had lost its hardened visage, and he sent the older nurse a look of utter gratitude. Margaret momentarily forgot why she was denying him what he wanted.

Grant's face hardened again. "Are you going to let me speak to that nurse or do I have to speak to your superiors? I'll find her sooner or later, even if I have to turn this place upside down."

A young voice lilted, "You need not search that far, Mr. Tyler." Grant glanced in surprise at the young nurse, who came forward and placed her hand in Margaret's. "It's all right, Mom. Maybe people will believe what really happened if Mr. Tyler tells them the story."

Margaret withdrew her hand from her daughter's so she could place both of her hands on her daughter's cheeks. "You don't have to answer him, Beth."

"I *want* to tell him, Mom." Beth examined Grant's face and seemed to find what she was looking for. "I think Mr. Tyler might be able to help us rather than hurt us." She turned to Grant. "Will you help us?"

"Miss, if anyone is ready to hear your story, I am, if you're ready."

She was ready.

*   *   *

"I just started working here three weeks ago. My mother has worked here for twenty-three years, and we've always been very close, so when an opportunity arose to leave St. Mark's Hospital and work here, I grabbed it. Two weeks ago, Mr. Hanvill checked into the hospital. Did you know he had been ill with lung cancer for months? Anyway, he insisted on any kind of life support that was necessary. He wanted to stay alive even if he were a vegetable, he said. He showed me the numbers they tattooed on his arm at Auschwitz and told me that he didn't believe in God or an afterlife, and that he was going to fight for every last breath. His liver finally failed, along with his kidneys, and he was put on life support."

Grant nodded. The story fit perfectly with the Mike Hanvill he knew.

"Then, two days ago, I walked into his room—and he was dead. I took his pulse . . . he was actually starting to turn cold. I started to call the desk . . ." Her face went white at the remembrance.

"Yes?"

"He . . . he . . ."

Margaret, sitting next to her daughter, spoke. "He reached out and held her arm."

If they were expecting shock and disbelief, they were in for a surprise. Grant never blinked. He just waited intently for the story to continue. Beth, fears mollified, proceeded with her story.

"I almost fainted, and I probably would have, but he said 'Don't faint, young lady. You'll hurt yourself.' I twisted out of his grip and I looked down, and he was smiling! He never smiled!"

"That's for sure."

"Then he said, 'Young lady, I want you to do me a couple of big favors.' I stammered, 'Sure, Mr. Hanvill.' He said, 'I always wanted to be cremated when I died. When I checked into this place I told them that. But I want you to get me the forms for a proper burial. You can call the local Jewish mortuary. They'll help you.' I nodded. But then he said something else that I can never forget."

Grant leaned forward in his chair.

"*He said he wanted to be taken off the life-support system.* I said that I couldn't do that. Then he asked me for a piece of paper and a pen. I took one from the dresser drawer and gave it to him, and he drew a word on it. The letters were foreign to me . . . they looked ancient. I asked what I should do with it, and he said I should send it to his next of kin because he wouldn't be around much longer. Then he told me to go find the burial information right away. I needed some air, I was still in shock, so I left the room to return to the nurses' station. I intended to tell my mother what had happened, but she was talking to someone, so I used the phone and called the mortuary. They said someone would come over to talk to Mr. Hanvill the next day. I went back to his room to tell him, and . . ." She broke off and began to weep. "I was only gone ten minutes!" Tyler wanted to comfort her, but she waved him off. "I went back to his room and he had disconnected the life-support system himself! Would *anyone* believe me if I told them all this?"

"I would."

She stared at Grant and suddenly she flung herself into his arms, rocking him back in his chair dangerously. He stroked her hair and looked over her shoulder at Margaret, who was crying.

Minutes later, when Beth had regained her calm, Grant asked her the question that he had restrained himself from asking. "Beth, can you show me that piece of paper?"

Grant studied the word. There appeared to be six letters written in a very ancient script. "Did Mike say anything about this word that would give you a clue to what it meant?"

"No, and it took us a full day to locate his next of kin so that I could send it to them. We reached his brother in Israel about fourteen hours ago." She looked at Grant in surprise. "Oh, that's right. You were with him when he got the news, weren't you?" Grant nodded. "The mortuary insisted on burying him as soon as possible, so he was buried yesterday. That's probably why his brother didn't fly here, he would have missed the funeral anyway."

"Did you send Rabbi Hanviowitz a copy of the word Mike wrote?"

"Yes, later, but you were probably already on your way here."

What am I supposed to do now? Grant thought. *I've got some ancient word that nobody understands, and I'm supposed to find Becky with this?* He saw Beth and Margaret looking to him for guidance, for some corroboration that what had happened really happened, that the whole incident was real and that they weren't crazy. *What do I tell them?* he wondered.

Beth was serene now. "You probably think I'm crazy. I mean, why would someone commit suicide after they were given a second chance to live? Some story, huh?"

Grant didn't reply. He was confused and drained. The combination of such a flimsy path to follow and the two long plane trips slammed into him mercilessly.

Margaret said deprecatingly, "We'll have a reputation greater than Lourdes, if this ever surfaces. First Perry Lindsay, and then Mike Hanvill the next day."

Grant said, "Perry Lindsay?"

"Yes, didn't you hear how he had a heart attack and sprang right back to life?" She added ironically, "And he wrote down some word, too. Only he didn't tell anyone what it was." She added wryly, "Even though Beth and I have been pestering the emergency room nurses to tell. They all said that he kept it a secret, but that he was out of the hospital like a greyhound as soon as possible."

Grant felt the adrenaline course through him again. "Where's the nearest pay phone?"

Beth pointed down the hall. "Right over there."

Margaret looked severely at Grant. "You're going to rush this story right out there, aren't you?"

Grant said, "No, I'm not. Not only that, but I want you three to keep the lid on it for now while I find out what's going on here. I promise to tell you what I find out if you can keep this story quiet. Deal?"

The three women, relieved and reassured, smiled.

Grant ran down the hall to the phone.

*　　*　　*

"Perry Lindsay's office."

"Hi, this is Grant Tyler for Perry."

"Why, Mr. Tyler, we thought you were in Israel. Mr. Lindsay left an urgent message for you just yesterday. I'll get him for you immediately." Grant felt the same electricity that he had sensed with Rabbi Hanviowitz, and his blood coursed hot and vital.

"Grant?"

"Perry, how are you?"

"A better question is how are *you*? . . . I'm sorry about Becky. I didn't know she had been ill."

"Six months. Strangely enough, though, that's why I'm calling you."

"Do you need some help?"

"Yes, but it's not what you think." Grant told Lindsay everything about Becky's death, the wall she asked him to find, the echo of her story by Willie Daniels, the trip to Israel to see the wall, the encounter with Rabbi Hanviowitz, and, finally, the death of Mike Hanvill and the word he had written.

Lindsay listened intently until Grant mentioned the word Hanvill had written. Then he burst out, "He wrote down *what?*"

"A word in some ancient script."

Lindsay said excitedly, "How many letters did it have?"

"Why? Do you know something about this?"

"That's why I called you!" Lindsay related his shared experience with the other executives, the word they had seen, and their urgent desire to have

Tyler use his resources to decipher what it meant. "Is it possible it's the same word?"

"The word Mike wrote has six letters."

"Oh . . ." Lindsay felt disappointed.

"How many did yours have?"

"Four."

Grant wouldn't give up. "It's still possible that they were in the same language, isn't it?" he asked determinedly. "Perhaps the two words are some sort of a message. This *can't* be a coincidence."

Lindsay's confidence was stoked again. "Sure didn't feel like one yesterday."

"Can you send a copy of the word to my office? I'll head there right now and put my whole staff to work on it right away."

Perry hesitated, then risked revealing his innermost thoughts. "I never gave him much thought before, but do you think God is at work here, Grant?" He waited tensely for the reply.

Grant thought of Becky. He said jubilantly, "Someone sure is! There's an answer to everything if you look hard enough. Send the word over to the office, I'm on my way." They exchanged good-byes, and Grant walked briskly toward the elevator. He pushed the button and waited, humming to himself. The door opened and Grant moved aside as two nurses wheeled out a gurney with a young man whose head was bandaged. Grant barely noticed him, but something clicked in his head. He ignored it as he turned back to enter the elevator and found himself looking directly at an exhausted Joel Alexander and a distraught Beverly Engler.

* * *

Cardinal Benda Cortes's knees were hurting. He had been kneeling in front of the altar for nine hours, praying for guidance. The first three hours he had knelt looking up at the crucifix above him. Then his neck became tired, and he relented to the desire to lower his head. The last six hours he had stared at the floor, searching himself for an answer to his existence.

What was he? Was his mother right when she insisted he was a Catholic by baptism? Or was the grim alternative the truth, that he was a descendant of Jews and possibly a Jew himself?

He knew the Church's position on the subject. Once baptized, a child became a Catholic. That seemed to obliterate any argument. And yet . . .

How could he know if he was indeed a Jew? Who made that decision, the individual or society? Even after the Marrano Jews converted to Catholicism, the Church had been suspicious of them. And in Nazi Germany, the Nazis had gone to insane lengths to ferret out Jewish blood in everyone's ancestry. Would the Nazis have considered him a Jew? He knew that the answer was yes. And even if society did *not* make the decision for him, did *he* consider himself a Catholic?

He had been aware since early childhood of the three sacraments of Christian initiation: baptism, the holy Eucharist and confirmation. He also knew that the latter two were considered the deepening of the initiation, while baptism connoted becoming a Catholic at the moment of baptism. What were the requirements of the Jew? If he was Jewish by blood was he always a Jew?

Cardinal Benda was not a coward, but he was frightened now. At first, he had assumed that his fear stemmed from his ignorance of his identity: Was he a Catholic or a Jew? The very thought that his entire life might have been a sham was shattering to him, not only because of his own self-deception, but also for the others whom he had fought to bring into the Church. He held himself accountable for all his own sins, and he shuddered at the magnitude of this one.

He probed deeper within himself and found a layer of feeling that he had not touched before. He was stunned to discover rage at his mother for leaving him alone in the world. The rage was so intense that it terrified him. This fear was unlike the fear that revolved around his confused identity. That fear he forgave himself for, but the fear of his own rage he found detestable, for it implied that he couldn't control his own emotions.

Why am I so angry at her? he wondered. *I'm not alone in the world. I have friends inside and outside the Church, and she is responsible for that. I've had a very successful career turning people toward Catholicism, and she wanted me to do that. I have . . .*

No children.

Death pervaded the cardinal's thoughts. *I am going to die,* he thought. *Just as my mother did, just as my father did, just as everyone does.* This was what his real fear was, and although he had seen many people die, the thought of his own death had stayed safely hidden in the deep recesses of his mind. Now that his mother was gone, the long line of generations before him would end with him. Suddenly, he had a yearning to know more about his ancestors. If he had no one alive to whom he was connected, at least he could be part of the line that extended back in time. But what if he found he was a Jew? He thought of what Jesus said to the Jews.

"You snakes, you generation of vipers, how can you escape the damnation of Hell!"

After he died, would he go to hell?

Book Two

Good evening, I'm George Nelson. Tonight the Tyler News Network has an exclusive follow-up to this morning's press conference announcing the successful realization of cold fusion in Jerusalem, a breakthrough that could change the world as we know it. Just as the secret of atomic energy ushered us into a new era, the apparent discovery of creating cold fusion may catapult us into an era of unlimited energy and consequent prosperity. We begin with live coverage from our correspondent in Jerusalem, Jerry Grubb."

"Good evening, George. Standing here next to me is the senior member of the team responsible for this momentous discovery, Dr. Steven Aarons. You said at the press conference that you have been working on this project for eight years. Was this the outcome of one path for eight years or did you try many different paths during that time?"

"We tried many different paths during that time, Jerry. What distinguished this path from other paths we have tried was the simultaneity of our inspiration. We all were struck by the same idea at three in the morning while we were sleeping. We called each other immediately on the phone to discuss what we had seen."

"What do you mean, what you had seen?"

"All of us had the same experience. We were sleeping, and suddenly a mathematical formula appeared in our dreams out of nowhere; nothing before or after the formula appeared, just a series of numbers that were unfamiliar to us. It felt to us that we were being directed by some unseen force. After all, for two of us to have had the same dream concurrently would have been fantastic, but three?" He laughed ruefully. "As uncomfortable as I am saying it, that borders on the mystical. And there was something else. . . ." His voice trailed off.

"You mean something else that was mystical about this? What was that, Dr. Aarons?"

"It is involved and rather esoteric. . . ."

"Yes?"

Aarons grimaced slightly. "It involves the use of *gematryia*."

"What is that?"

"*Gematryia* is the method of attributing meaning to a Hebrew word by using its numerical equivalent. For example, in Hebrew each letter has a numeric value. The first letter of the alphabet is equal to one, and each successive letter is one more than the previous one, until the tenth letter, when each successive letter is ten more than the previous one. That lasts until the nineteenth letter, which is equivalent to one hundred, and the last three letters are successively one hundred more than their predecessor. For example, if the principle were applied in English, the word *bag* would equal ten: *b* would count for two, *a* for one and *g* for seven, for a total of ten."

"What was the significance of the numbers in the formula?"

"Both of my compatriots happen to be devoutly religious Jews and familiar with *gematryia*. They calculated the sum, and it turned out to be 1,723. They tried various words and phrases to see if they added up to the same sum and realized that there was a two-word phrase of great significance that added up to the same total."

"What phrase was that, Dr. Aarons?"

"*Acharit Hayamim,* which is found in the forty-ninth chapter of Genesis, the second chapter of Isaiah, and the fourth chapter of Micah."

"What does it mean?"

"It means 'the end of days,' the beginning of the messianic era."

"And you attach great meaning to this, Dr. Aarons? You have intimated that you are *not* religious."

"I said that I wasn't—at least up until now. The reality of this discovery means that energy will be plentiful and constant for as long as man walks the earth. I'm inclined to agree with my colleagues that this discovery reveals the hand of God."

Jerry Grubb paused to allow the full impact of the last statement to be felt.

"Thank you, Dr. Aarons. George?"

"Thank you, Jerry. We will return to you later in this broadcast. We have here in our studio Professor Duncan O'Rourke, one of the world's leading experts on nuclear science, who has been communicating with his peers in Israel. We are grateful to you for joining us, professor."

"Of course, of course."

"Can you explain to us, Professor O'Rourke, what this discovery may mean for all of us?"

"Why, certainly, Mr. Nelson." His patronizing voice had an air of insufferable condescension. "This could mark the end of childhood for the human race. . . ."

*   *   *

"Ahh, bullshit . . ." Pablo de Cardoso grabbed the remote control and turned off the television. The journalist was fed up. The newspaper had printed his story of the bombings at the church and the Ganedos home, but instead of playing up the angle of Jews being murdered for building a Catholic church, the paper chose to feature the narrow escape of Cardinal Benda Cortes from the bombings. The controversy that Pablo had hoped to spawn from a true believer committing murder to purify the holy Church had been relegated to page twenty-five, and the cardinal's narrow escape was page one.

That guy has all the luck, he seethed. *No matter what happens, he winds up looking like a saint. What I'd give—*

The telephone rang. Pablo was in no hurry to answer it, and he took his time sauntering across the room. He lifted the receiver and grumbled, "Hello?"

"Is this Pablo de Cardoso, the journalist?"

"Yeah."

"Are you the one who wrote the article about the bombings of the church and that family's home?"

"You think there are *two* Pablo de Cardosos writing for the same newspaper?"

"Just wait a minute, Mr. de Cardoso. My boss wants to talk to you."

Pablo was not a patient man, especially now. He decided he'd count to ten and if he was still forced to wait, he'd hang up. He was at eight when a voice came on the line.

"Pablo de Cardoso?"

"Yeah."

"This is Cesar Carlos."

Pablo's hand almost dropped the phone. He stammered, "*The* Cesar Carlos?"

"You think there are *two* Cesar Carloses who'd want to talk to you?"

Pablo realized that the drug kingpin must have been listening from the start. "I'm very sorry, Mr. Carlos . . . I was surprised by your call."

"I understand that you covered the bombings this past week."

"That's correct."

"I read your article. It was well written and quite informative. As a matter of fact, I have become familiar with much of your writing."

Pablo was paralyzed. He didn't think a man like Cesar Carlos would call unless he wanted *something*. Pablo knew better than to think he was the recipient of a courtesy call.

"I'm . . . I'm honored that you've read my work, Mr. Carlos."

"I've noticed a certain bias in your work, Mr. de Cardoso. You seem to harbor a profound dislike for the Catholic Church."

Well, there's common ground between us after all, thought Pablo. Carlos doesn't seem like the type of man who is in good standing with the Church either. "They're not my idea of a good time," he confessed.

"They're not mine either, Mr. de Cardoso, although I have given plenty of money to build two churches for them."

"You . . . give the Church money?"

"For the same reason that I give money to the local governments, which I despise, to fund various housing projects for the poor. Just because I detest the institution is no reason to deny people in need. People need homes to live in, and they need churches to forgive them for the sin of being employed by me. You know, I employ more people in my business than any employer in South America."

"I didn't know that."

"Many people regard me as their hero for supplying them with a means of employment. They would bitterly resent the loss of their jobs . . . which brings me to the reason I am calling you."

Pablo waited nervously.

"You have spent much time covering the career of Cardinal Benda Cortes, is that right?"

"That is correct."

"He is constantly vilifying me and my associates in our business. He is unceasingly attacking the gainful means of employment for thousands of people who would otherwise be starving. And yet he is received with great enthusiasm by the general public."

"The fear of the Church, I would surmise."

"I venture to think that there is more to it than that. There are very few people who have a spotless reputation. Usually the public manages to cut them down to size quickly enough, but rarely, an individual surfaces whose reputation remains pure despite the attempts of the public, and then the masses embrace him and follow him like sheep until they realize they've been led astray by their supposed saint."

"That does sound like an accurate picture of the public's perspective of Cardinal Benda Cortes."

"It did to me, too, until the recent event of the bombings. I was wondering, if the cardinal is so popular, why someone would bomb the church where he was speaking? Then I read your brilliant article on the subject and understood that he was not the target, but that the church and the family who built it were the targets."

"That is what I discovered, yes."

"Would you say that this cardinal invariably condemns what he perceives as injustice?"

Pablo agreed grudgingly. "Yes, injustice from his point of view."

"Then, in the days since the attack, why hasn't he publicly condemned the bombings? After all, even though he escaped, a church was destroyed."

Pablo was intrigued. He hadn't considered that angle.

Carlos continued, "Isn't it most *unlike* him to be silent about a matter such as this? Is it possible that he is guarding something from the public about the matter, such as some personal involvement with the bomber or with the victims?"

"It is unlikely. He is from Rio and they dwelled in a village one hundred miles from there. But you are correct to say that it is out of character for him to be reticent about such a matter."

"Is there someone in his inner circle to whom you have access? Someone who saw him or spoke to him after the incident occurred?"

Pablo paused. Should he tell Carlos that he had spoken to the cardinal, Father Juan and Father Antonio the morning after the bombings? He had only a millisecond before Carlos became suspicious. He decided against it. "No, I don't have access, but the nature of my expertise is to gain access where none is available."

Carlos chuckled. "Good. I think that there is something this cardinal is concealing. If you can discover what it is and prove it, I will more than adequately compensate you."

Pablo hesitated. "Forgive me for being so bold, but the money is secondary to the prestige a story of this magnitude would bring to me. My problem is that the newspaper seems reluctant to print a story demeaning this man."

"Did I mention that I have gotten to know the publishers of all the major newspapers on this continent? I'm sorry, I *should* have mentioned it. We have an understanding of what is useful for their health to print and what is not. I'm sure that if you find me the appropriate information I can see that it is widely published. Does that satisfy your needs?"

"How do I reach you when I have succeeded?"

Carlos chuckled again. "You won't have to look far. I'll be there right behind you." Pablo heard a click on the other end of the line and was left to consider what to do next.

He tried to remember everything about his conversation with the cardinal the morning after the bombings. He remembered that the cardinal had been patient to the point of exasperation, questioning Pablo in a direct, calm manner.

Pablo had a gift for reconstructing conversations long after they occurred, which had aided him tremendously in his career. *Let's see,* thought Pablo, *he kept asking me questions until I asked . . . what was it? Oh, yeah, I asked him how much he knew about Ganedos's wife, and Father Antonio, the local priest, went back and forth with me about the mother's maiden name . . . and then I mentioned that the wife used to light candles in a locked closet . . . wait a minute . . . wait a minute . . . somewhere right about there the cardinal became preoccupied . . . it's something about the mother . . . it's something about the mother!*

Think, Pablo . . . think. The mother was the Jewess, right? What does that have to do with the cardinal? He knew he was on to *something,* but it wasn't enough. Pablo knew that he needed more information. *I think I'll just follow him around for a while,* he thought grimly. *He's bound to have a chink in his armor somewhere.*

*   *   *

Cardinal Benda Cortes, back in his office in Rio, pressed the buzzer on his desk. Father Mario's deep voice answered the intercom.

"Yes, Your Eminence?"

"Do you remember three years ago when Islamic terrorists blew up that synagogue in Rio?"

"Yes, Your Eminence."

"There were a number of rabbis who spoke at the press conference that followed the bombing. There was one in particular to whom the others deferred, I remember. He was the rabbi of the synagogue that was bombed, probably in his early seventies, with a white beard and thick glasses, and dressed in a black suit. They referred to him as a tremendous scholar. Is it possible for you to find out who he was and how I can reach him?"

Father Mario's voice became even deeper than normal. "I will try, your Eminence." He cleared his throat. "I am sorry about your mother, your Eminence. When I lost my mother I found comfort in the fact that she believed and had faith. As our Lord said, 'Whosoever liveth and believeth in me shall never die.'"

He said crisply, "Thank you, Father Mario. I hope to find comfort myself, but in the meantime I want you to find the name of this rabbi, all right?"

Father Mario, disturbed by the brusque tenor of the cardinal's reply, murmured, "Yes, Your Eminence."

The cardinal gazed at the crucifix on the wall. His mother had certainly had faith in Jesus, and the cardinal had often quoted Father Mario's excerpt from John, chapter eleven. He had not considered the *exclusive* nature of the statement for many years. In his twenties, he had been so utterly convinced of the rightness of his path and the institution to which he had sworn his life that he had dismissed any argument about the exclusive nature of Jesus' statements as disloyal. Now, though, he was partly seeing matters from the perspective of an outsider. If only those who believed in Jesus' divinity and message would never die, what happened to the rest of humanity? Did their souls stop existing when they died, as opposed to the believers whose souls lived forever? Would his soul stop existing the moment he died if he didn't accept Jesus? He had never been one to jump on the bandwagon simply because it was convenient. He wanted the truth because only the truth enabled him to look unflinchingly in the mirror.

He tried to remember the rabbi from the press conference three years earlier. There had been six or seven rabbis and leading members of the local Jewish community, and they all had been somber. Only the fact that the rabbi of the synagogue had gone home early that day had prevented his murder. The cardinal remembered feeling a kinship with the rabbi, for the first attempt by the drug cartel on the cardinal's life had been two weeks before the bombing of the synagogue. He had observed that the rabbi seemed to have an unusual calm about him when he spoke, until the cardinal noticed his eyes. They had the fire of a prophet flashing from them, and although the voice was calm, the eyes were ablaze with a vision of something magnificent.

Father Mario knocked at his door. "Your Eminence?"

"Come in, Father Mario."

The priest entered and walked over to his desk. "I called the newspaper, and they found the rabbi's name you are looking for. I have his name he lives right here in Rio."

"Who is he?"

Father Mario looked at the piece of paper in his hand. "His name is Rabbi Daniel Hanviowitz. I have his phone number. Would you like me to try to reach him for you?"

"No, thank you. Just give me the phone number and I'll call him myself."

His secretary cleared his throat. "The man at the newspaper said that there are other rabbis who are better known."

"He's the one I want."

"He also said that he wasn't sure if this rabbi was even alive anymore. He also asked why we were looking for a *rabbi,* of all things. I told him that your mother had just died and you narrowly missed being killed last week and this seemed like a good time for you to keep busy by updating our files of local clergymen."

"You didn't owe him an answer."

"I know, but . . . Your Eminence, why *are* you trying to find this rabbi?"

"Just a change from the routine, I guess."

"Oh." He brightened. "That makes sense. I needed a change of routine when my—"

"Can you give me his phone number, please?"

"Oh . . . certainly Your Eminence." He gave the piece of paper to the cardinal. "Is there anything else?"

"Yes, as a matter of fact. Why don't you go to lunch?"

"But it's only 10:30."

"Then why don't you take some time and go look for that new computer you've been telling me about."

"But . . ." The priest looked at him suspiciously. "Don't you need me here?"

"Always. But to see you with that new computer would brighten my spirits considerably. And I could use a little brightness right now."

Father Mario grumbled, "Of course I'll go, Your Eminence. What time would you like me to return?"

"Take a couple of hours and enjoy yourself. But don't come back without that new computer."

"I hope you'll be impressed, Your Eminence."

"I know I will be."

Father Mario grudgingly turned around and headed out of the room. The cardinal waited until the priest closed the door behind him and then he walked to the window and watched Father Mario get in his car and leave. Swiftly pivoting, he returned to his desk and the telephone. He looked at the phone number in his hand, took a deep breath and dialed. The phone rang three times and then a well-modulated female voice answered.

"Hello?"

"Hello, this is Cardinal Isaac Benda Cortes calling for Rabbi Daniel Hanviowitz. Is he in?"

"Yes, he's learning right now, can you hold for a moment?"

"Certainly." Cardinal Benda Cortes found his hands were sweating, and he quickly wiped them on his sleeves. *I haven't felt this nervous since . . . I don't know when,* he thought. *Maybe ever. . . .*

"Hello, this is Rabbi Hanviowitz." The voice was obviously that of an older man but the energy emanating from it was palpable through the phone. He sounded forceful and positive. The cardinal immediately felt more at ease.

"This is Cardinal Isaac Benda Cortes . . . from the—"

"Ah, yes, I know who you are. You have a fine reputation, sir. What can I do for you?"

The cardinal froze. He had subconsciously envisioned a short conversation exchanging pleasantries before the reason for his call was introduced, but the moment was thrust upon him now. How should he start? How *could* he start?

The rabbi saved him. "Your first name is Isaac, you said? That is a beautiful name for our people, too."

Our people, the cardinal thought. *My people?* The cardinal followed the path that was being laid. "My mother had great difficulty in conceiving a child. When I was finally conceived in her middle age, my father insisted that I be named Isaac, since he and my mother had entertained as much hope for a child as Abraham and Sarah did. My mother was later concerned that I would suffer the same fate as my namesake and be offered as a sacrifice, and even though my father reassured her that ultimately Isaac was spared, she insisted that my life be consecrated to God."

"And so your life has been devoted to the Church."

"Yes . . . that's right."

"That's an admirable goal. Everyone should devote their life to God. Your mother must have been a remarkable woman."

"Yes, she was. She just died last week."

"I'm very sorry to hear that." There was a great silence. Then the rabbi spoke.

"Does your call to me have something to do with your mother's death?"

"Yes."

The rabbi's voice became gentle. "You know, for many people it is only when a parent dies that they confront the most central questions of their existence. While our parents are alive, we are protected from the reality of our own finite existence. We tend to see the world from behind a veil, as it were. Then one or both parents die and the veil is torn away, and we are face to face with our own mortality. It isn't a nice feeling."

"No. I've found it to be quite terrifying."

"Still, you have an advantage over many people . . . they go through a crisis of identity. At least your identity is clear."

There was the same great silence.

"Isn't it?"

Silence.

"Is that why you are calling me? Why not speak to your fellow clergymen in the Church?"

Silence.

"What did you say your middle name was?"

"Benda."

"Benda. . . . Was that your mother's maiden name?"

"My mother's and her mother's and her mother's and all my maternal ancestors, for at least five hundred years."

"Where did your mother's people come from?"

"Spain."

There was sharp intake of breath. *"Ribbono Shel Olam. . . ."*

"What does that mean?"

"It means that I understand why you have called me . . . and why we must talk. Not on the phone. In person. I will change my schedule so that we can meet. How soon will you have time?"

"I can meet you tonight."

"Can you come to the synagogue at ten o'clock?"

"Won't that be late for you?"

"At my age sleep is time stolen from a dwindling bank account. We will talk tonight?"

"If God wills."

"He does."

11

"C an I get you some coffee, Grant?" Joel Alexander asked as he sat in the waiting room across from his friend, who sat staring fixedly at the wall.

"No, thanks."

Beverly sat next to Joel, her hands in her lap nervously twisting a hand-kerchief. She hadn't said a word since she and Joel had run right into Grant while following an unconscious Matthew and the accompanying nurses out of the elevator. Grant had whirled around and run after them and stopped the nurses in their tracks. When he demanded to know what had happened, they suggested he wait for a doctor. Grant had turned back to Joel and Beverly, who had caught up to him, and waited for an explanation. Joel told Grant what he knew, then looked at Beverly for corroboration.

Beverly was afraid to say a word because she held herself responsible for everything that had happened to Matthew. She knew that he could never have gotten tickets in the front of the theater without her intervention, and if he had been seated farther back, he would never have been singled out by the band leader. She knew she was guilty. And if Grant ever suspected that once upon a time she had prayed for Becky's demise, too, he would justifiably hate her. *Isn't that what I deserve anyway?* she asked herself. *Take away what I love the most; that would be the punishment to fit my crimes.* But she couldn't summon the fortitude to admit everything to Grant. The thought of being without his presence in her life was too devastating for her to consider. She was saved by the appearance of the doctor, who had been paged by the nurse to explain the severity of Matthew's injury to Grant. Grant had listened in growing horror, then walked to a nearby chair and sank into it.

Now Beverly sat next to Joel, mute, while he attempted to elicit *some* response from his shell-shocked, silent friend.

"You haven't told me why you returned so quickly from Israel, Grant. How did you have time to see the Nuclear Science Institute?"

Grant answered without moving his eyes away from the wall. "I didn't see it."

"You didn't see it? Where did you go?"

"I went to the Kotel."

"The what?"

Grant's eyes closed. "The wall, Joel. The Western Wall of the temple in Jerusalem. That is what it's called in Hebrew."

"You went to the Wall first instead of the institute? Couldn't that wait until afterward? This story may determine the future of the world."

Grant took his eyes off the wall and stared at Joel. He said harshly, "Don't talk to me about the future when *my* future is lying on his back unconscious with a hole bored into his head, okay?"

Joel backed off. "Right, right. I'm sorry, Grant."

Grant's mind worked ponderously. He had thoughts intertwining themselves around each other, making it difficult to examine each one apart from the others. *Be careful what you wish for,* he remembered. He had wished that Matthew would cut his hair and get rid of that earring, and he had gotten his wish. Except that Matthew's head had not been shaved by the marines, but by the nurses in preparation for boring a hole into his skull to relieve pressure on his brain. And the earring had been removed and put in a tiny envelope should Matthew awaken and ask for it. The doctors had told him that Matthew might be in a coma for an indefinite amount of time, and Grant tormented himself with the thought that he would give anything to hear his son awaken and ask to put his earring on.

He had been so sure that the path he had been following would lead him to Becky. He had been positive that he was being directed by Someone . . . Someone.

What for? All that chasing around after some chimera that was based on circumstantial events. He tried to follow the series of events through from the beginning and found that he simply didn't care. What had he been trying to achieve, anyway? No matter what he would have found, did any of it matter if his only thread to the future was being stretched to the breaking point? Without his son he might as well be dead anyway. At least wherever Becky was he would be there, too.

To hell with it, he thought. *Let the world go to hell if only I can have my son back! I'm not leaving this hospital until he is himself again.*

"I'm not leaving," he mumbled.

Joel leaned forward to hear him. "What did you say, Grant?"

"I'm not leaving."

"What do you mean you're not leaving? You mean you're staying here tonight?"

"I mean that I'm not leaving until Matthew wakes up."

Joel looked at Grant in consternation. "Grant, you can't do that. The doctor said it may be days, even weeks, before he awakens. And there's no guarantee of that, either."

"I left him before to travel across the world for some mystical garbage. I'm not leaving him again."

Joel reached over to Grant's arm, but Grant shoved Joel away and said hoarsely, "I'm not leaving. If I have to buy the whole damn hospital, I'm not leaving!"

"Okay, okay . . . I hope to God—"

"Don't put hope and God in the same breath around me, Joel. If there is a God, he's one nasty son of a bitch!"

Beverly was shaken by the vehemence of Grant's anger. He stood up and paced back and forth in front of her, then stopped and looked down at her. She shrank back in her chair as he glanced at her. "You've been very quiet, Beverly," he said softly. "Is there something you haven't told me? Something I should know?" Beverly couldn't speak. Her throat constricted so badly that she could barely swallow. "Did you follow him the way I asked you?" She managed to nod. Grant covered his eyes. "If only he had been sitting farther back in the crowd, maybe none of this would have happened."

Joel, noticing the look of despair on Beverly's face, said, "Forget it, Grant."

Grant's eyes narrowed. "I don't think so. I want to know how this could have been prevented."

"There's nothing anyone could have done, Grant. Sometimes things just happen."

Grant eyed Joel with suspicion. "That doesn't sound like you, Joel. We always agreed that events were ours to control. What went wrong here? There has to be something!"

Joel said evenly, "Drop it, Grant. That's enough. You've flown over eleven thousand miles in thirty hours, you're exhausted and jumpy."

"I'm not exhausted and I'm not jumpy. I leave the country and all hell breaks loose. I—"

"I'm sorry, Mr. Tyler, it's all my fault."

Grant turned his head to see Beverly's face, a face with every ounce of hope gone, a bleak expression that was lifeless and haggard. "I'll submit my resignation in the morning." She rose stiffly and headed painfully toward the elevator without looking back. Joel stood up and grabbed Grant by the shoulders.

"Grant, don't let her go! You need her!" Grant looked at Joel indifferently and returned to his chair. Joel watched Beverly reach the elevator and push the button. "Grant, if you let that girl go, I may just follow her out that door." Grant didn't respond.

"You *can't* stay here, Grant. They'll have to throw you out sooner or later." He flinched as Grant looked up intensely at Joel with a silent expression of pure resolve and will. Joel knew that look, and he knew not to get in its way. Instead, he followed Beverly to the elevator just in time to enter with her as the doors opened. As the doors closed, Joel stared back at Grant, but Beverly never lifted her head.

Grant sat in the chair, looking straight ahead at nothing.

*　　*　　*

Perry Lindsay leaned back in his chair, excited and optimistic. He had every confidence in Grant Tyler. He knew Grant to be indefatigable in his pursuit of whatever he wanted, especially if it was news. Now that he had sent a copy of the ancient word he had seen over to him, he felt a tremendous sense of relief. *He'll find out what those ancient words are,* he thought exultantly. *Wait until I tell the others about Mike Hanvill having a similar experience before he died!* He remembered the meeting with the other four executives; they were completely exuberant when they left Perry's office. All except Robert Hutchinson, who still looked troubled. Why was that?

Something nagged at Perry, trying to penetrate his thoughts. There had been a moment during the discussion of their near-death experiences when Hutchinson had become agitated. He said that he had seen what they had seen, but that he had felt something afterward. Perry tried to remember what he had felt after his vision, but nothing surfaced. *What the heck, I'll call him to give him the good news and see if he'll tell me what bothered him so much,* he mused. He picked up the phone and dialed Hutchinson's office.

"Mr. Hutchinson's office, Mary speaking."

"Hello, Mary. It's Perry Lindsay."

"Oh, hello, Mr. Lindsay. I'm glad to hear your voice. Maybe Mr. Hutchinson will talk to *you.*"

Puzzled, Perry asked, "Why? Has he been incommunicado lately?"

"Ever since he came back from his meeting with you he's either been at home or locked in his office. He's spoken to no one. I've worked for him for twenty-five years and he won't even talk to me. I've tried to catch him on the way in and out of his office, but he's passed me as though I'm not even here."

"Perhaps he won't talk to me, either."

"Oh, please, Mr. Lindsay, please stay on the line. Maybe he'll decide to speak to you."

"Okay." Perry's eyebrows furrowed as he attempted to figure out what was disturbing Hutchinson. It *had* to be what he had been so hesitant to discuss in the meeting, he was sure of that.

"He's not answering when I buzz him, Mr. Lindsay."

Perry was irritated. Just when he had good news . . .

"Mary, tell Robert that I have some great news." Perry decided to take a chance and guess what was troubling Hutchinson. "Tell him that he's not as alone as he thinks he is."

"I'll try, Mr. Lindsay." She put Perry on hold again for about ten seconds. Then he heard a faint sound.

"Perry?" The voice was Robert Hutchinson's, but he sounded distant and remote.

"Robert? Is it you? Are you all right?"

"No."

"What's wrong?"

"Oh, nothing. Just getting ready to go."

Perry was chilled. Go where? From the despondency of Robert's voice, Perry had only one guess; Robert sounded resigned, a man about to end his life. *He can't do this!* he said to himself. *He's one of us! We'll find the answer. I've got to stop him.*

He said excitedly, "Robert, I have some great news. Great news!" No response was forthcoming. "I talked to Grant Tyler and not only is he going to help us, but he discovered that Mike Hanvill saw a word in ancient script, too, just before he died!" He pressed onward hurriedly. "I sent over a copy of our word to his office, and he is going to see if they match. We think it may be some sort of divine message! We may be on the trail of something stupendous! Robert? Robert? Did you hear me?"

"I heard you."

"Isn't this exciting? I mean, to think that we might be receiving some message from on high? Don't you believe me?"

"I believe you all right. I've known this since the beginning."

"What do you mean?"

"Remember when I alluded to having felt something after my vision of the word?"

"Sure. You were extremely upset about it."

"I didn't want to confess what I felt in front of everyone for fear they'd all laugh at me, but what I felt was . . . the presence of God."

"How do you know that's what it was?"

"I just knew, okay? And I knew that all of this was part of a divine plan somehow."

"Weren't you thrilled about it? I am."

"I never believed God was there, Perry. And I've done some things in my life that I'm not exactly thrilled about. Don't you see what I'm getting at?"

"Not really."

"I'm going to die someday, Perry. And when I do, he'll be waiting for me. And he'll have a list of everything I've done, and every sin I've committed, and there won't be any escape."

"Then why does it sound to me like you are in a hurry to go there now?"

"Every single moment that I continue living I'm only making that list longer and longer. I think I'd prefer to keep my sins to a minimum."

Perry said desperately, "Where did you get the idea that you are going to be punished? When you felt God's presence?"

"No, that was the most tranquil I've ever felt. It was only afterward, when I came out of that place, that I realized the implications of what God's reality would mean. I came back to consciousness—or a lesser state of consciousness, as it were—and felt bereft without his presence. And I knew that I was being punished. I knew that the reason that I no longer felt his presence was because I had sinned too greatly in my life. And I want his presence again, even if I have to suffer in order to be close to him."

"But what is the hurry? Perhaps by taking your own life you are committing the greatest sin of all!"

"That's a chance I'm willing to take. I've done so much damage in my drive to get to the top, and I could have done so much good."

"You still can, Robert! You can still do plenty of good!"

"I don't think so, Perry. My habits have grown rigid. I think the damage I'd do is far greater than the benefits I'd create. Do me one favor, though?"

"*No, no, no.* You've got to stay here with me and help me see this through!"

"Oh, I'll be watching. That much I know. Good-bye, Perry."

"NO!"

The sound of the gunshot tore through the phone and ripped apart Perry's heart.

*　　*　　*

"Willie . . . Willie, wake up." Robin Daniels gently pushed her husband's shoulder. Willie hadn't played in any of the Mules' games since his collapse and subsequent recovery on the court, and Robin was grateful for the necessity in late stages of pregnancy to get up and use the bathroom during the night, for it gave her the opportunity to check Willie's breathing and make sure that he was all right. This time she had awakened with a different priority in mind.

"Willie, wake up . . . my water just broke." She pushed him a little harder this time.

"Wha . . . wha . . . what time is it? What's going on?"

"My water just broke, Willie. Can we go to the hospital? The contractions are coming pretty close already."

"Really? Are you all right, Honey?"

Robin smiled bravely. "I just need some help getting my suitcase."

"It's all packed and ready to go." Willie sat up and swung his legs down to the floor, rubbing his forehead with his hands. "Boy, what a dream I was having." He stood up and looked down at his wife. "You stay there, I'll get everything. Don't move, okay?"

"Okay."

*   *   *

Ten minutes later, Willie and Robin were in the car, heading for Mount Zion Hospital. Willie drove with his left hand, because he and Robin were holding hands. Robin looked over at her husband's shining face and clear eyes and fell in love with him all over again. *I adore him,* she thought. *I'd follow him anywhere . . . anywhere. He's such an idealistic, gentle man. And he loves me,* she thought with a thrill. *With his personality and his wealth he could choose any woman he wanted, and he chooses me!* She was well aware that countless athletes were unfaithful to their wives because they were away from home for extended periods of time. Other wives told her as much. She knew Willie, though, and the thought of this man doing something illicit was so incomprehensible that she almost laughed at the thought. *Why me?* she thought.

"Why me, Willie?" she asked aloud.

Willie was lost in his thoughts and was startled by the sudden question. "What, Robin?"

Robin blushed. She had been thinking, and the thought had come to her lips and been uttered without the conscious will to do so. "I was just wondering, why me? I mean, why did you pick me and not some other woman?"

"Because you were the most beautiful girl I ever saw."

"I bet you can't even remember what I was wearing when we met."

"Sure I can." He wrinkled his nose. "You were wearing shining eyes, a dazzling smile . . ."

She smiled in spite of herself. "Oh, Willie . . ."

He continued, "And, of course, the best figure I ever saw."

She looked amusedly at her huge belly. "Say good-bye to that."

Willie disengaged his hand from hers to run his fingers through her hair. "Robin, if there is a more beautiful woman on the planet right now, then she's got to be pregnant, too. I wouldn't trade the way you look, about to bear our child, for any woman who ever lived. Only you and I in the whole history of the human race could share this moment and this child. You must know that without you my life is meaningless."

"I know," she whispered.

"What brought that up, anyway?"

"I was looking at you. Just looking—and feeling lucky."

"After the other night on the court I think we're *both* feeling lucky."

Robin was curious. She hadn't talked to Willie about the other night and his apparent resurrection from the dead. It wasn't because she thought Willie would be reticent; it was because she had been so terrified at almost losing him that she couldn't broach the subject even to herself. But now she was feeling more secure, sitting with him and listening to him say how much he loved her. She shyly asked, "How did it feel the other night, Willie? I mean, when you were supposedly dead? Were you? I know that Mr. Tyler talked to you in the locker room, and everyone else was ordered to stay out. Was there some reason for that?"

"Whoa . . . that's a lot of questions to answer at once."

"Did you see anything special?"

"Not to me, but something told me to find Mr. Tyler and tell him. He sure reacted like something was special."

"He seemed preoccupied that night."

"His wife was dying, Robin. I think she actually died that same night."

"Oh, that's terrible . . . he seems like a nice man. He has been very good to you."

"Yes, he has."

She persisted. "What did you see, Willie?"

"I saw an old man at an old wall talking to Mr. Tyler. That's about it, I guess."

"Oh." She was disappointed.

"The funny thing is, when you woke me up just now I was dreaming what happened next."

"Wow, that's weird. What happened? Oooh . . ."

"What?"

"That contraction really hurt. . . ."

"We're almost there, Robin, hang on." Willie turned into the hospital driveway. "Are you okay?"

Her breath came out in a gasp. "Just when you were getting to the good part . . ." She managed a weak smile.

"We'll save it for later." Willie brought the car to a stop at the hospital doors. As he escorted Robin out of the car, he noticed Joel Alexander and Beverly Engler exiting the hospital. Willie knew Joel from meetings with Grant Tyler, but he didn't know Beverly, and he saw her crying as Joel walked her to the parking lot. As he escorted Robin into the hospital, he glanced back to see Joel and Beverly get into a car and leave.

*   *   *

Two hours later, Willie Daniels was the father of a baby boy. He held his son in his arms and blessed the God who made him. After he followed the nurses to the nursery and walked back to kiss Robin before she dozed off, he was still so excited that he couldn't sit still. He had numerous phone calls to make, and he knew that he should make them, but he needed to walk, to keep moving. He decided to walk through the hospital until he calmed down. He walked through the radiology section, and nuclear medicine, and reminded himself that he was one lucky guy. As he turned a corner, he glanced into a private room and saw to his astonishment that Grant Tyler was sitting in a chair, staring straight ahead at a bed whose occupant Willie couldn't see. Tyler looked drained and exhausted. Willie flashed back two hours to remember Joel Alexander and the crying woman with him. He knew that there had to be a connection.

Boy, Mr. Tyler looks awful. Maybe if I tell him about my son he'll cheer up. He walked over and knocked softly on the door.

"Mr. Tyler?"

Grant slowly turned his head to look at Willie standing in the doorway.

"Hi, Mr. Tyler. I haven't seen you since the other night at the game." Grant looked at Willie disinterestedly. Willie continued, "Did the information that I gave you help?"

"No."

"Oh, I'm sorry." Willie brightened again. "I just had—I mean my wife just had a baby boy."

"That's nice." Grant's voice was flat, toneless.

"Didn't you say once that you had a son, Mr. Tyler? You must have felt sky-high the day he was born."

"I don't remember anymore."

Willie started to feel annoyed. This was the biggest day of his life and Grant was wholly indifferent. He cautioned himself not to jump to conclusions and realized suddenly that the man had just lost his wife. Not only that, but he hadn't thought of asking Grant why he was there.

"I'm sorry, Mr. Tyler . . . I mean about your wife. I just heard about it yesterday. Is that why you're here?" *That was dumb, Willie,* he chastised himself. *She's dead. She wouldn't be here.*

"In a manner of speaking, yes."

Willie suddenly remembered the dream he was having when Robin woke him up. "Did you ever find that wall, Mr. Tyler?"

Grant threw him a piercing look. "Yes, I found it, for what it was worth, which wasn't very much."

"The reason I asked, Mr. Tyler, is that I had a dream this morning which was a continuation of the vision I had when I collapsed on the court." Willie waited for the kind of reaction that Grant had at the game, but no response came. Grant just looked impassively at him. Willie tried to regain the energy and joy that had inflamed him only moments ago, but he found to his frustration that he was stuck in an emotional limbo from trying to communicate with Grant.

"I guess I'll see you around, Mr. Tyler." He walked back toward the maternity ward.

He forgot to ask Grant what he was doing at the hospital.

*   *   *

Perry Lindsay had been sitting in his chair at his office for three hours without moving. His mind was awhirl with a jumble of thoughts. He was quite sure that Robert Hutchinson was dead, and he wanted to call the other three executives and warn them about any suicidal thoughts they might be having, but then he realized that they might not have had the same awareness of God that Hutchinson had felt or the same guilt over sins they might have committed. Yet he wanted to tell them about the fact that Mike Hanvill might have seen another part of the puzzle before he died, and Grant Tyler and his organization were trying to decipher the meaning of the two ancient words. He knew that he should call the other three men, but he was afraid that once they heard about Hutchinson, they might lose heart and give up the search. He felt his sense of urgency wildly escalating, and so he decided to call Grant's office, tell him about Hutchinson and urge him to hurry before another tragedy occurred. He dialed Grant's office, nervously drumming his fingers on his desk.

"Mr. Tyler's office, Pam speaking."

"Hello, this is Perry Lindsay calling for Grant. Where's Beverly?"

"I'm afraid she is at the hospital right now, Mr. Lindsay."

"The hospital? Why is *she* at the hospital? Checking out Mike Hanvill's story with Grant?"

"I don't know anything about Mr. Hanvill, sir. I've just been filling in for Miss Engler."

Perry, trying to stifle his frustration, queried, "Has Grant called in to the office yet? When I spoke to him this afternoon he was at Mount Zion Hospital checking out the death of Mike Hanvill."

"He called me to say he'd be over as soon as possible to examine the document you sent over today, Mr. Lindsay. That was over three hours ago. I expected him back by now."

"Maybe I'll call the hospital and see if he's still there." He tried not to hang up immediately. "Thanks for your help."

"You're welcome, Mr. Lindsay."

Lindsay dialed the hospital.

"Mount Zion."

"Hello, this is Perry Lindsay . . . I was just released from the hospital recently."

"Why, of course, Mr. Lindsay. We all remember you."

"I'm looking for a colleague of mine, Grant Tyler. Would you happen to know if he's anywhere in the hospital?"

"I think he was in his son's room the last I heard."

"His son? What's wrong with his son?"

"He had brain surgery and he's in coma, sir. They just moved him to a private room because he is in stable condition."

"Oh, my God. . . . Can you ring Mr. Tyler in that room, please?"

"He hasn't been answering the telephone, Mr. Lindsay."

"Can you ring the nurses' station, please?"

"Why, surely, Mr. Lindsay." Perry fought off his growing sense of dread.

"Nurses' station, fifth floor. Is this Mr. Lindsay?"

"Yes, hello. I'm looking for Grant Tyler. Can you inform him I'm calling?"

"He's been sitting in his son's room for hours, sir, and he hasn't moved. Every time we've approached him he's ignored us."

"I'm coming right over."

Half an hour later Perry stood in front of Grant, utterly frustrated, as Willie Daniels had been. Grant had shown no interest in Perry's story about Hutchinson, and no interest in pursuing the meaning of the two ancient words either. Perry had tried to impress upon Grant the urgency of the entire situation, but Grant had paid no heed, remaining as comatose in his way as Matthew was in his. Perry left the hospital feeling confused and anguished.

*   *   *

Grant was alone now. No one ventured near him—even the nurses—and his awareness of others had receded from existence. His thoughts centered on the two people he had loved the most: Becky and Matthew, then after a while just Becky. He was not aware that tears streamed down his face. Slowly but surely, his mind compressed all his memories of Becky to the most powerful moments he had spent with her. Finally, his mind was reduced to a single thought.

A wall.

12

ardinal Benda Cortes left his office at nine o'clock to drive to Rabbi Hanviowitz's synagogue. Though he was customarily punctual, this was much more time than he needed. He knew that it was only a fifteen-minute drive, but he had never wanted to get to a meeting so badly in his life. The very *idea* of being late to this meeting was abhorrent to him.

Before he left for the day, Father Mario had reminded him that he had a speech scheduled for tomorrow. He was supposed to speak at the great Metropolitan Cathedral and address the issue of sexual promiscuity in Brazil. The cardinal had addressed the issue before, and his passionate plea for restricting sexual relations to marriage was usually met with indifference or, in some rare cases, outright hostility. Rio de Janeiro had a reputation for licentiousness and libertine behavior, and many people preferred to let the Church preach as it saw fit as long as the citizens could behave as they pleased. This hadn't deterred Cardinal Benda Cortes from speaking repeatedly on the subject, or dampened his enthusiasm for tackling what he regarded as a fundamental problem for Brazilian society. But when Father Mario reminded him of the event, he felt a tiredness wash over him from the essential repetitiveness of it all.

The tiredness vanished, however, when he thought about his upcoming appointment with the rabbi. It wasn't excitement that he felt, but an anticipation of something exceptional . . . something revelatory. Either he would find that he was really a Catholic and his life would not have been for naught, or that he was a Jew, and who knew what would ensue from that? Whether a Catholic or a Jew, his God was still the one God, but whatever path opened before him, he was aware that his life would not be the same after what transpired tonight.

He rounded the corner from the main boulevard to a much smaller street whose buildings showed signs of decay. Flipping on the light inside the car to check the address he had written and realizing he was quite close, he turned the light off and slowed the car to look for the first parking space he could find. He found one directly in front of the synagogue, which was a drab, narrow two-story building. He had taken a long coat and a hat for anonymity, and he wrapped the coat around him and lowered the brim of his hat as he left the car and headed quickly for the front door. Without hesitating, he pushed the doorbell.

The door swung open to reveal a slim woman that he guessed to be in her mid-thirties. She had the darkest eyes he had ever seen, surrounded by hair that was coal black. She wore a simple blue high-necked dress that fell to her ankles, and black low-heeled shoes. Her long flowing hair and steadfast eyes reminded him of the pictures he had seen drawn of ancient biblical figures. She looked at him searchingly for a moment to ascertain if he looked dangerous, then called back over her shoulder.

"Abba, there's a guest here." Her voice had a familiar musical tone, and the cardinal realized that she had answered the telephone when he had called the rabbi earlier that day. She turned back to him and shyly moved to one side to let him enter the long hallway. He heard footsteps coming toward him, and he looked far down the hallway to see an old man with a white beard walking briskly toward him. Cardinal Benda Cortes knew that this must be Rabbi Hanviowitz. Who else would be at the synagogue at this time of night? But the presence of the young woman disturbed him, for what he had to discuss with the rabbi was a private matter.

The rabbi approached the cardinal and held out his hand. "Cardinal Benda Cortes?" The cardinal nodded as they shook hands. The rabbi noticed immediately that the cardinal seemed ill at ease, and he turned to the young woman. "Why don't you wait in the office, Rivkah. The cardinal and I will talk in my study."

Rivkah bowed her head in deference to the rabbi. "Is there anything I can get for you, Abba?"

"No, thank you. Are you sure that you would rather not go home? We may be speaking for some time."

"No, Abba, I'll be here if you need me." She nodded to the cardinal and walked back down the hall to a door on the right side. The rabbi indicated that the cardinal should follow him, and they headed down the hall toward a door on the left side of the hall. The cardinal was curious about the woman and what kind of devotion to the rabbi would keep her at the synagogue far beyond normal working hours.

"Was Rivkah the woman who answered the phone today when I called you? Her voice sounded familiar."

The rabbi looked speculatively at the cardinal as he was about to open the door to the study. "Yes, she was the woman on the telephone."

"She must have enormous affection and respect for you to stay here so late with you. My secretary has worked with me for many years, but still . . ."

The rabbi smiled. "You are assuming that you called the synagogue this afternoon. Actually, you called my home. Rivkah is my daughter."

The cardinal suddenly felt quite dense. Rivkah had called her father "Abba," the Hebrew word for father—a fact he should have known from his knowledge of Aramaic (which was so similar to Hebrew). Then he laughed ironically at himself. He had genuine cause to be preoccupied, hadn't he?

The rabbi entered the study and turned on the light, gesturing for Cardinal Benda Cortes to be seated in the large chair in front of the rabbi's desk. The cardinal looked at the walls of the room, which were covered from floor to ceiling with shelves brimming with books. There was hardly an inch of any of the walls to be seen except for the ledge around the two windows; every spare inch of the walls was hidden by texts of one kind or another. The cardinal took the liberty of walking around the room and discovering what books the rabbi had surrounding him. Virtually all of them had Hebrew titles. There were huge volumes that made up distinct sets of books, and some books that were obviously not part of a larger set. He looked back to see the rabbi studying him with interest.

The cardinal approached a set of enormously tall volumes. "What are these?"

"Those volumes are the Shulchan Aruch. The laws that were derived from the Talmud and codified in these volumes constitute a practical handbook on how to live one's life as an observant Jew."

"That's a large handbook."

"Life requires no less."

The cardinal walked over to a set of twenty volumes on the next shelf and pointed to the titles. "The Talmud?"

The rabbi was impressed. "That's correct. How did you know? By the number of volumes?"

Cardinal Benda Cortes embarrassedly admitted, "No, I read the titles. I've studied Aramaic, so Hebrew is somewhat familiar to me."

"Why did you study Aramaic?"

"It was the language Jesus spoke."

"Of course. Knowing Aramaic would make the study of the Talmud much easier for someone. You see, there is a chain of transmission that started when God gave the Torah to Moses at Mount Sinai. What the rest of the world knows as the Bible, or the Five Books of Moses, is what we call the written Torah. But God also gave to Moses the *explanation* for the written Torah, which was passed down orally through the generations until it was finally written down. We call it the Mishnah. Then later there was commentary and explanation on the Mishnah, which is the Gemara. The Mishnah and the Gemara together comprise the Talmud. Although the Mishnah was written in Hebrew, the Gemara, which is the bulk of the Talmud, was written in Aramaic, because it was the language spoken at that time."

The cardinal closed his eyes. "*Mishnah* means 'teaching' and *Gemara* means 'learning,' if the Aramaic and Hebrew are similar. Is that right?"

The rabbi gave the cardinal a penetrating glance. "You have a remarkable memory. How long ago did you study Aramaic?"

"Twenty-five years ago."

"How many languages do you know?"

"Eleven, but I have had more time than most people to study."

"That is still a prodigious accomplishment. And with your knowledge of the biblical literature you have much to remember. Are you blessed with a photographic memory?"

The cardinal said with fervor, "Yes, although that is not my doing, but a beneficent God's."

The rabbi was impressed with the cardinal's humility; he liked this man. "We have similar stories among our own people of those blessed by God with extraordinary intellectual ability. When they have used their gifts to become our greatest scholars, our *talmidey chachamim*, they become *capable* of becoming our heroes. If, in addition, they exemplify everything that they have learned, that capability becomes a *reality*. To learn for its own sake is not what we expect. To learn in order to make every action holy, to sanctify the name of God in every action, that is how we are taught to live." Rabbi Hanviowitz gestured toward the Talmud and the Shulchan Aruch. "And to make *every* action holy in one's life requires a guide of mammoth proportions, wouldn't you think?"

"That's a difficult goal to achieve for most people, I would think."

"That should not exempt someone from the challenge. You see, because to be good requires not just the *absence* of evil, but rather the *active practice* of proper behavior, a guide is needed. Without a guide to proper behavior, how is one to know which choice to make?" Rabbi Hanviowitz gazed at the cardinal. "And some choices can be agonizing to make."

He saw the cardinal's mouth tighten. Rabbi Hanviowitz said quietly, "Perhaps we should sit down." The cardinal nodded. The rabbi seated himself behind his desk and the cardinal sat down in the large chair across from him. Rabbi Hanviowitz leaned back for a moment, then leaned forward and put both of his arms on the desk, waiting.

Cardinal Benda Cortes tried to slow down the thoughts racing through his head. It was no use; his mind was in a tumult. "I need to ask some questions, Rabbi, but I don't know where to start."

The rabbi interlocked his hands and, putting his elbows on the desk, placed them under his chin. "Our conversation this afternoon is still ringing in my head. Why don't we begin with me asking *you* some questions? Would that make it easier for you?" The cardinal nodded gratefully. Rabbi Hanviowitz closed his eyes. "You said that your first name is Isaac, and you explained why. Then we discussed the death of your mother, and the emotional repercussions. As I remember, the conversation foundered when the issue of the crisis of identity was addressed. You were unresponsive when I asked you whether your identity was clear, and also when I discussed speaking to your fellow clergymen about it. Then you told me that the name Benda was your mother's maiden name and had been the maiden name of your maternal ancestors for five hundred years, and that they had come from Spain." The rabbi opened his eyes and peered at the cardinal. "Is that accurate?"

"It seems that I'm not the only one in this room with an exceptional memory."

Rabbi Hanviowitz smiled. Then he became serious. "What bothers you about any of what we discussed? That your mother's mothers kept their maiden name, that you are confused as to your identity, or that your mother lit candles in a hidden place on Friday nights?"

The cardinal felt goose bumps on his arms and a chill run up his spine. "What did you say? How did you know that? *I never mentioned that!*"

The rabbi closed his eyes again. "It all fits. But why didn't you mention it when we talked today?" Suddenly his eyes flew open with sudden recognition. "You knew what it all meant, didn't you. You knew about the Anusim."

"Anusim?"

"What the Marranos called themselves. The name Marrano was used by the Gentiles."

"Yes, I knew what the candles meant. But the significance of the retention of the name Benda was an enigma to me."

"You don't know why all the women kept their name?"

"No."

"It will all fit together for you in a moment. In our Halacha—"

"Halacha? Walking?"

"Very good. *Halacha* is the term we use for the code of law and guidance that governs our lives. One way of translating it would be 'The Way,' meaning, of course, the way to behave. The Talmud and Shulchan Aruch are part of the Halacha. But getting back to the issue at hand, our Halacha states that any child born to a Jewish woman is Jewish. We are commanded to marry other Jews, of course, but in the event of a mixed marriage it is the identity of the mother that is critical. As a matter of fact, this law was codified in the Shulchan Aruch, although its derivation is from the written Torah."

"Where in the Bible does it refer to this problem?"

"In Deuteronomy 7:3 and 7:4. 'You shall not intermarry with them; you shall not give your daughter to his son, and you shall not take his daughter for your son, *for he will cause your child to turn away from Me* and they will worship the gods of others. . . .' In the Talmud, this is explained this way: that when God refers to the child turning away from him because of the father—'he will cause *your* son to turn away . . .'—the fact that the Torah says *your* son indicates that the child is Jewish because of the mother.

"There is another explanation for the law that is more esoteric. Because women resemble God in his most salient characteristic, the act of creation, they are more intimate with his presence. Therefore, spirituality in the home emanates from the woman. Unlike other religions, for us the home is equal in importance to the synagogue. Thus, many of our most sacred rituals are centered in the home. No matter how religious the father is, if the mother does not project the importance of the religion, the children will not be convinced. Therefore, for a child to be Jewish, the mother must be Jewish. Does this clarify why all the women preceding you kept their maiden name?"

"To preserve their identities as Jews."

"Exactly. Throughout the persecutions, no matter whom they married, when all else was forgotten except for lighting candles on Friday night to usher in the Sabbath, your ancestors insisted on retaining their identity. They must have been remarkable women. In fact, the precedent for retaining our names was largely responsible for the most powerful moment in our people's history."

"The Exodus?"

"Correct. The reasons we were redeemed from slavery were three: The women remained modest in their dress in the midst of the decadent attire of the Egyptian women, the Jews still spoke Hebrew, and the people retained their Hebrew names. On the heels of these events followed our redemption."

"Then according to Jewish law, the Halacha, if indeed all my mother's mothers were Jewish, I am a Jew?"

"Correct."

"There are no other requirements?"

"None."

The cardinal looked embarrassed. "What about circumcision? Isn't that part of the Jewish covenant?"

"Are you circumcised?"

"No . . ."

The rabbi thought only for a moment. "You are still a Jew, by Jewish law, but a huge mitzvah has been left undone."

"Mitzvah means a good deed?"

"The actual translation is 'commandment.' We are commanded to circumcise our sons when they are eight days old."

"Genesis 17:12."

A smile spread across the rabbi's face. "You have the Bible memorized, too?" He grinned, "In how many languages?"

The cardinal looked back at him glumly. "Every one but the original, I'm afraid."

"That can be an obstacle to understanding what God intended. Still, even though you are uncircumcised, if you are a Jew you are required to perform all the mitzvoth commanded by God."

"On the other hand, since I was baptized, part of me still feels I am a Catholic. What do I do? I don't know who I am supposed to be!"

Rabbi Hanviowitz took a deep breath. "I haven't told you why the name Benda struck me with such force, have I?"

"No, that is one issue we've forgotten."

"Very often two names can be contracted as one. My last name is a combination of the Hebrew words *ha,* meaning 'the,' and *navi,* meaning 'prophet.' The *owitz* is an ending glued onto it from my family's living in Lithuania for centuries. My brother, Rabbi Eliyahu Hanviowitz, and I are descendants of the prophet Isaiah."

"And how do you think my name is derived?"

"Every Jewish man is known by his first name and the name of his father. The name *ben* means 'son,' so for example, my Hebrew name is Daniel Ben Yakov: Daniel, son of Yakov. Your last name, Benda, is most likely comprised of *ben,* meaning 'son,' and *da,* which could be an abbreviation of David, so your last name, the name that was so closely guarded by your forebears for centuries, could mean 'the son of David.'"

The cardinal held his breath. "You don't mean *the* David. *King David?*"

"Why else this incredible effort to maintain the name?" The rabbi stood up and looked down at the trembling cardinal. "How far back can you verify your family's history? Can you trace it back three thousand years?"

The cardinal was still dazed by what he had heard. His adrenaline was soaring; his heart pumped feverishly. "I don't know. I don't know. . . ."

"It is not unusual for many religious Jews to have proof of their lineage dating back that far. We even have people who specialize in such a search. Would you like someone's name to help you?" The cardinal nodded. The rabbi reached into his desk, pulled out a battered notebook and flipped through it.

"Here." He wrote down a name on a piece of paper and handed it to the cardinal.

"If I am . . . if I am a descendant of King David . . . how do I make a choice?"

"Remember what I told you about free will? The choice at any given moment is yours. But I would think that you would want to know as much as possible about Judaism before you make the choice."

"That's true. . . ."

The rabbi walked around the desk and put his hand on the cardinal's arm. "Why don't we leave it at this: You find out what you can, and if you decide that you want to learn, call me day or night and we'll start immediately."

"Don't you have enough to do?"

"There is nothing more important to me than to learn Torah." The rabbi raised his eyebrows. "Besides, if you are a descendant of King David—"

"Yes?"

"It's just a passing thought. It can wait."

The cardinal stood up. "Lately, I've felt that nothing can wait."

Rabbi Hanviowitz said, "You have time. That feeling of urgency stems from death striking so close to you." He smiled. "I think that all this is happening to you for a reason, and God is not through with you just yet."

They walked together to the door. As the rabbi opened the door, Cardinal Benda Cortes turned back to look around the warmth of the study once more, and he shivered, feeling spiritually alone. "To return three thousand years," he murmured.

The rabbi quoted, "'And not with you alone do I make this covenant and this oath, but with him who is standing here with us today before God, our God, *and with him who is not here with us today.*'"

The cardinal reached in his pocket for the name the rabbi had given him and nodded grimly. *King David,* he thought. *Is this a dream?*

Mr. President? Mr. President?" Gary Stephens, the national security advisor to the president of the United States, had knocked on the door to the Oval Office but there had been no response from inside. The president's secretary, Angela, had informed her boss that Stephens was there, but when Gary entered the office, he saw the president sitting with his back to the door, looking out the window. Stephens remained in the doorway.

"Mr. President, you wanted me to come right over."

President Robert Evans answered without turning around. "I just received a call from Moscow."

Gary closed the door and swiftly crossed to the chair opposite the president's desk and sat down. "Regarding what, sir?"

President Evans turned the chair around to face Stephens. He said slowly, "You know about the news from Jerusalem."

"Yes, it's been all over the media."

"Only the fact that cold fusion has been achieved. *How* it has been achieved is still a secret."

"I'm sure the Israelis will tell us promptly."

"That's the point. They don't know."

"What do you mean? *They* discovered it."

"*They* are a team of scientists, not the government. And they're *not* talking."

"Why not?"

"Apparently they have a religious authority advising them to keep a lid on it for now."

"A religious authority? Scientists? This is a day that I thought I'd never live to see."

"It's not a joke, Gary. They're dead serious. All three scientists are convinced that they were directed by the hand of God, and so they have a rabbi that they turned to for guidance."

"Which rabbi is this?"

The president looked at a piece of paper on his desk. "A Rabbi Eliyahu Hanviowitz. Two of the scientists had been his students at one time. Evidently he told them that the world was not quite ready for the consequences of their discovery."

Stephens shook his head in disbelief. "These guys are going to pass up the Nobel Prize because of one old rabbi? Do they know how much money they could make? Or the prestige?"

"They know, and when they were asked about that, they said that all the money and honor in the world would not tempt them from contravening the rabbi."

"Well, what about the rabbi? Hasn't anyone talked to him?"

"Yes, and he has been calmly repeating that the world is not quite ready."

Stephens exploded in outrage. "Who the hell does he think he is? These guys have an obligation to the *world!*"

The president said implacably, "That's not the way they see it. Thus, the call from Moscow."

"What do they want?"

"The same thing we do, presumably, but there was another message that they were asked to convey to us. Iran and Iraq, which are always at each other's throats, have decided that this Israeli discovery is a monumental threat to both of them." The president waved off Stephens's attempt to speak. "I know, I know, the Israelis have had nuclear weapons for years and never used them, but the Arab countries are threatened by the discovery of cold fusion."

Stephens nodded. "Of course. With cold fusion, our need for their oil vanishes."

"Not only our need for their oil, but the *world's* need for their oil. They sent word through Moscow that we must pressure the Israelis to release the information on how to achieve cold fusion."

"Or else . . ."

"Or else they will attack Israel along with the rest of the Arab world."

"Did they say how long they were willing to wait for us to succeed?"

"Moscow was rather reticent about that. They seemed to enjoy our predicament."

Stephens rose to his feet. "Where should I start, Mr. President?"

"Start with the Israeli government. Let them know the gravity of letting the scientists remain mute. You can tell them about the Arab response."

"I'm sure they knew before we did, sir."

The president nodded somberly and buried himself in the papers on his desk as Stephens left and soundlessly closed the door behind him.

* * *

Joel Alexander sat at the dinner table and looked disinterestedly at the steaming food that Michelle had lavishly piled on his plate. She cautiously sat down next to him.

"Not hungry? You're not in the mood to eat?"

"No, I'm just thinking, that's all."

"About Grant?"

"Yes. I called the hospital. They said that except for going to the bathroom, he hasn't moved from the chair in two days. No one has even seen him sleep."

"Isn't there anything you can do?"

"I can't think of anything. I did check his desk at the office, though, and I saw something unusual on it."

"What was that?"

"It was a fax from Perry Lindsay, the head of USMC. There was a word in some ancient script written on it with no explanation."

"Did you recognize the script?"

"Are you talking to me? The guy who flunked History 101?"

Michelle laughed in spite of herself. "Did you ask Beverly about it? Wasn't she back at work today?"

"Beverly quit two days ago."

Michelle, shocked, said accusingly, "You didn't tell me."

"She cleared out her desk yesterday. I haven't heard from her. The new girl said that Beverly asked to take one final walk through Grant's office, and that was it." Joel pushed the plate away from him and got up to start pacing the floor restlessly.

"Do you want to watch a really long movie? Maybe that will relax you."

"What's on?"

"The Ten Commandments."

Joel laughed mirthlessly. "Sure. I like fairy tales."

Two hours later, Joel got the surprise of his life.

*   *   *

At the same moment, Beverly was sitting cross-legged on a bed in a cheap hotel two hundred miles away. She had been in a state of semi-shock since her last encounter with Grant at the hospital, and after cleaning out her desk and touring Grant's office for the last time, she had headed down the highway toward parts unknown. Four hours later, she had noticed a sign that read Lonelyhearts Hotel. Something about the name struck her funny bone, and after pulling into the parking lot, she started laughing. She laughed until she started to cry—then she couldn't stop crying. Her tears ran unabated down her face and onto her blouse until the collar was soaked. Finally, she ran out of tears, and summoning the energy to register at the desk and head through the dark of night to find her room, she collapsed onto the bed. Since that moment, she had remained in the room for forty-eight hours watching movies on television. She didn't eat and slept only fitfully.

Now she was watching *The Ten Commandments.* As exhausted as she was, the story still fascinated her. The scene where Moses ascended Mount Sinai came on the screen, and God was about to write the Ten Commandments on the two tablets of stone. The flash came and the words started to be etched into the stone. As the words were written, Beverly's eyes, as tired as they were, widened until she found herself leaping from the bed and pressing her face into the screen. She *knew* it meant something. The words were written in the same script that she had seen on the fax on Grant's desk when she toured his office. *It can't be an accident,* she thought wildly to herself. *It can't!*

She ran to the telephone and dialed directory assistance for the number to Mount Zion Hospital, then called and asked for the nurses' station nearest to Matthew's room.

"Hello, I'm Beverly Engler, Mr. Tyler's assistant. I'm trying to reach Grant. . . . Yes, I know he's been silent. . . . No, that's all right. . . . I guess I'll have to come there."

She called Joel Alexander at home, and nervously paced back and forth. "Joel? Beverly. You won't believe this but I just saw something. . . . You saw it, too? Did you see the note on Grant's desk? It can't be a coincidence. Don't you think it's important that Grant—" She listened for a moment, then sat down stiffly. "Oh, it was just a gag you were pulling for when he returned? Ohhh . . . me? . . . I'm fine . . . yes, I'll stay in touch." She hung up the telephone and sat disconsolately on the bed.

*   *   *

Joel Alexander hung up the telephone and looked at himself in the mirror. He had gasped when he had seen the ancient script in the movie and recognized it as the same script as Perry Lindsay's fax. Luckily for him, Michelle was on the telephone in the other room, and he had regained his composure before she returned.

He had no intention of informing Grant of what he had seen, nor did he feel guilty for lying to Beverly about the origin of the fax. There had been enough mystical crap lately, and all it did was make his best friend one unhappy man. Joel believed that Grant would come out of his predicament when he was ready, and the less mystical and more mundane his life was, the sooner he would be himself again. He knew he was right. He looked at himself in the mirror and reminded himself: *Only believe what you can see.*

*   *   *

Grant sat immobile in the chair at the hospital, concentrating on one thought: a wall. He had been trying for two days to move the wall he was seeing in his mind's eye so he could peer behind it, but it remained immovable. At the beginning, the image he had seen was the Kotel, the Western Wall of the Temple in Jerusalem. Later, that image had been replaced by visions of all different kinds of walls: brick walls, stone walls, apartment walls from his college days, the walls of his present home, but sooner or later his mind always returned to the Kotel. Grant had always been a literal-minded man, and even now, after all the mystical events surrounding Becky's death, his visions of walls were literal, not metaphoric or figurative.

He had become so absorbed in the experience that he began to lose consciousness of himself as a separate entity; he was no longer a viewer of the walls, looking for what was behind them. He started to lose his identity, to merge with the very concept of *wall*. He could feel himself slipping away.

Now something arose inside him, panicked at the thought of losing his consciousness as a separate identity. *Remember who you are,* something cried to him. *Remember who you are!*

And who am I? he asked himself. *Grant Tyler. Who is that?*

The answer came in a flood. The husband of Becky Tyler, the father of Matthew Tyler, the son of James and Dorothy Tyler, the head of the Tyler empire, the best friend of Joel Alexander, the boy who had to win every race he was in or die trying, the teenager who was the most popular boy in the class, third in the graduating class of his high school, the young man who was fair but ruthless in business, the man who only really loved one person—his wife, the father who was too busy in business to be devoted to his son, the boss who expected his employees to renounce compassion wherever it became an obstacle to their work, the man who donated huge sums of money to charity because his wife wanted it and his wife was the one person that he never refused, the man who lived at 100 Whitfield Road in a mansion, drove a luxury car, played golf once a week only to give the pretense of making contact with other human beings.

Hundreds of memories inundated his tired mind. Everything Grant had ever thought about or experienced rushed through him. What had begun as a simple question, *Who am I,* was now a raging river of memories and experiences that threatened to engulf him, drag him into its depths and drown him. The voice that had arisen in panic to ask the question was growing feebler as the river thundered its ecstatic triumph at revealing itself completely now that the dam had burst.

His dying sense of self, on the verge of extinction, managed one last cry. "I don't want this. . . ."

The river abruptly vanished. Silence. More silence. Then, quietly, a question started to poke around his mind.

*What if I give it all up? What if I am none of those things? They are all attached to me. Wait . . . No . . . **I am attached to them.***

He realized that all his life his *self* had taken everything it had ever experienced and attached itself to it. Every memory, every thought, every moment comprised who he *thought* he was. *I am not any of those things. They are all external to who I am.*

Then who are you? Who is asking you this question?

*Maybe it's my mind. That's it, it's my mind asking me that question. My **mind** is who I am! The rest of all this is just confusion!*

My mind. That's who I am.

Terror.

What if my mind can be split?

Mama!

Grant suddenly thought of Dorothy Tyler, his mother. She had been schizophrenic, a woman who battled internal demons daily while she labored to function as a wife and mother. James Tyler had wanted more children, but realized after Grant was born that one child was all that his wife could possibly handle. His own method of dealing with the predicament was to devote himself to his work in order to ensure that his son never had to worry about money. James fully expected, as many men do, that he would die before his wife, and because he expected that Grant would have to take care of his mother in her declining years, he didn't want his son, the great love of his life, to have the financial as well as the emotional burden. The great surprise of James Tyler's life had been to outlive his wife, for Dorothy Tyler had committed suicide two weeks after Grant and Becky announced their engagement, distraught that the only child she had was leaving her for good. Grant had spent his childhood trying to find any pursuit that would enable him to leave the house and avoid his mother's illness. Everyone else thought that he stayed after school studying or excelling in sports or running the newspaper because he was driven. They never knew what really drove him.

Grant knew what a mind split asunder was. *If that's what I am—my **mind**—can I be shattered, too?*

Utter terror.

Then, his vision in his mind's eye was all. Just as a person daydreaming can look at something but inside his head see a vision of something else, Grant's eyes were open, but what he saw inside his mind was a vision that filled his consciousness.

Light. The purest white light he had ever seen. Nothing he had ever seen compared to this; it was so pure that nothing else could even exist in his consciousness. He was aware that it was smooth, like a slate, but not hard like a slate would be. Yet it was not ethereal, either.

A tremendous sense of its indivisibility, its indestructibility, permeated him. There was also a sense of its absolute endlessness in space *and* time, its eternal nature.

And at that moment, whenever it was, Grant did not feel that he was close to God, but even more, that he was a part of God.

He longed to stay there forever. The tranquillity of this moment dwarfed all he had ever experienced.

He was given a glimpse of the Eternal.

God was real.

*   *   *

Later that day—and Grant had no idea how much later it was—he realized that what he had glimpsed was his own soul. He thought that this must be what people who had near-death experiences saw when they referred to the white light. They were separating not only from their own bodies but also from their *selves,* too, and were finally left seeing what was in reality who they were: their souls. And he also realized that every person's soul was made of that same light, that same soul, and that every soul was eternal.

It's all going to be all right, he thought exultantly. *I will be with her again!*

My soul will meet hers when I leave this body.

He realized that there was no hurry to die because he knew Becky's soul was eternal and would be waiting for him whenever he arrived. He followed this thought. *If God knows that I will return to him, why am I here?* he puzzled to himself. *What is my purpose while I am here?* His thoughts returned to the concept of the wall. What was Becky talking about?

It came to him with a clarity he had never felt before. Becky had not been talking about a wall literally; Becky had been talking about a wall *spiritually*. The wall was *his* wall; a wall that *he* had erected.

The wall between him and God.

Grant knew now that the belief in God would have come to him long ago had he not erected a wall barring the way. After all, he did not live in a culture where the concept of God was absent. God had offered numerous chances for Grant to believe in him. And Becky had never completely given up in her attempts to encourage Grant in that direction.

She must have known, he thought. *She must have known that once that wall was gone and I realized that God was there, I'd know I'd see her again.* Everything that Becky had said to him before she died became monumentally significant now.

"A wall." Now he knew what she had meant.

"A man with a beard and black hat and black suit." Grant felt sure that this had to be Rabbi Hanviowitz at the Kotel, especially when he remembered what Willie Daniels had told him at the game. And Becky's description had perfectly fit the Kotel.

"Connect the dots. . . ." Here Grant was stumped. What was she referring to? He dismissed the nurse's contention that Becky had been delirious at the time. It had to mean *something*.

Wait . . . he backtracked. Hadn't Willie just been talking to him about something to do with this? He strained hard to remember. Yes . . . Yes! Willie had dreamed more about the wall!

For the first time in two days, Grant came back to the world. All the mystical events of the last few days were part of a plan; he knew that now. He stood erect and looked down at his son, then swore a fierce oath to himself.

Whatever God has planned for me, my son, wherever he directs me, whatever his plans for you, from this moment I will be his servant.

He left the hospital to begin his journey.

14

Cardinal Benda Cortes hardly slept all night, eagerly awaiting the morning so that he could call the number Rabbi Daniel Hanviowitz had given him. At nine o'clock precisely, he dialed the number, hoping that the man he sought was punctual in his habits. His hopes were realized on the third ring.

A voice growled, "Alfonso Rissolo speaking."

"Are you the man who does genealogical tracing?"

"Who wants to know?"

"This is Cardinal Isaac Benda Cortes. Rabbi Hanviowitz gave me your number last night."

"Yeah, he called me at home this morning, but I was up to my neck with work so he couldn't tell me why you were calling. What do you want?"

The cardinal tried to remain pleasant despite Rissolo's surly attitude. "I want to trace my maternal ancestry."

"And you're coming to *me?* Why doesn't your Church do that for you?"

"Is there a reason you're so hostile?"

"In my line of work, strangers are usually untrustworthy."

"Don't you have to *rely* on strangers to search through other countries to do your work?"

Rissolo said bitingly, "There are strangers and there are *strangers*. When I go to a place where I am talking to Jews, they are strangers that I trust. Otherwise . . ."

"You mean you don't trust Gentiles."

"*Now* we can communicate."

"But why?"

"Listen, Mr. Cardinal, I've had more Gentiles try to bar my way from researching the past than you'll ever know. For some reason they resent the legitimizing of my people's history, and not only have they made my life miserable on occasion, they've even tried to arrange a fatal accident for me three different times. That's what I mean when I say stranger. So why don't you look among your *own* kind."

"That may be what I'm doing."

The cardinal heard Rissolo suck in his breath. "What did you say?"

"You heard me. I may have Jewish ancestry. I may, in fact, be a Jew."

"Right. And *I'm* the pope." The cardinal heard some muttering and then the line went dead. He dialed Rissolo again.

"Is this who I think it is? The meshugge cardinal who thinks he's a Jew?"

"I want to speak to the pope. There may be a mistake on my birth certificate, and I'm going straight to the top for an answer."

Rissolo laughed. "Okay, that's funny. Now, who is this really?"

"Cardinal Isaac Benda Cortes . . . with the emphasis on Benda, which was a name that my mother's mother and all the mothers before her insisted on keeping as part of their name. Does that offer you any incentive to help me in my search?"

Rissolo said uncertainly, "Is this really the cardinal for Rio de Janeiro? People here say you could be the next pope."

"That is precisely why I need to press forward in this matter with the greatest urgency. I have limited time to discuss this matter because I am making a speech at eleven o'clock at Maracana Stadium. Will you help me or not?"

"You realize what this could mean if your suspicions are correct."

"I must know who I am."

"I'll need more information from you. If I meet you at the cathedral, will you have time after the speech?"

"I'll *make* time."

* * *

The cardinal sat in the front row of chairs on the makeshift stage in the middle of Maracana Stadium, waiting for the end of his lengthy introduction from the mayor of Rio de Janeiro, who was standing at the podium. Cardinal Benda Cortes's body may have been there, but his thoughts were elsewhere. He was thinking about meeting Rissolo after his speech and pursuing the story of his own ancestry. He snapped back to attention in time to hear the mayor end with a flourish.

"*Our own* Cardinal Benda Cortes, the fearless champion of justice, the man who has once again escaped the clutches of evil, the man who has garnered support from all corners of the globe, the man who may very well be . . . the . . . next . . ."

Before the mayor could utter the final word, the crowd in Maracana Stadium rose to its feet and gave him a thunderous standing ovation. Maracana Stadium was the world's largest stadium, seating 180,000 people, and the cardinal never suspected that his speech would fill the stadium, let alone elicit such an overwhelming response.

What he was unaware of was the *motivation* for their support. It was not that they were interested in his speech, but that they were protective of him to a greater degree than ever before. In the past, when the drug cartel had attempted to kill him, there had been large outpourings of support from the populace, which was mostly Catholic. What had swollen the numbers of supporters to the enormous crowd packing the stadium was the recent revelation that the pope had cancer and his successor could very well be their own Cardinal Benda Cortes. Brazilians, like other South American citizens, had a fierce national pride, and the thought that a Brazilian could be the head of the Catholic world was a heady feeling, and therefore they were there to show their love and support for him.

The mayor beckoned to him, and the cardinal rose to his feet and hesitantly walked forward to the podium. He was ashamed to acknowledge the adulation he was receiving, for he felt that he was possibly masquerading as something he was not.

He tried to speak and could not. He wanted to confess to them that he had no business being there, but he could not. He shook his head trying to clear it, and the crowd, interpreting this gesture to mean that he was too humble to accept their love and gratitude, roared even louder.

Suddenly, out of the corner of his eye, he saw Father Mario come running up to the mayor, who had seated himself back in the front row. He whispered something to the mayor and handed him a note. The mayor of Rio de Janeiro nodded, rose, and crossed the stage to the cardinal. The crowd, seeing him, fell silent. The mayor whispered something to the cardinal, who was at first surprised, then pointed to the crowd and shook his head. The mayor seemed insistent, though, and the cardinal reluctantly gave in and backed away from the microphone. The mayor stepped forward to the microphone and spoke to the crowd.

"Ladies and gentlemen, I have good news and bad news. The bad news is that Cardinal Benda Cortes must postpone his address to you today." The crowd started babbling. The mayor waited until the noise abated, then continued with a smile. "The good news is that he must leave because His Holiness the pope has sent for him to come to Rome immediately!"

The crowd's roar was so huge that the stage started to tremble. The crowd knew that their cardinal might be going to Rome to be confirmed by the pontiff as his choice to be the next pope. The chant started almost immediately.

"Benda Cortes! Benda Cortes! Benda Cortes!"

Pablo de Cardoso stood alone in a tunnel leading onto the field, disinterestedly viewing the scene, disgusted with the way the event had turned out. There was nothing to interest him here, and his effort to follow the cardinal everywhere in order to ferret out damaging information seemed abortive now. If the cardinal was going to Rome, Pablo had no way to follow him: How could he explain to his employers that he needed to fly to Rome?

Pablo watched miserably as the cardinal uncomfortably acknowledged the ovation. Pablo started to turn away, but just as he did, a man brushed by him to stand at the entrance to the field and wave in the direction of the stage. Pablo couldn't understand why. Then he saw the cardinal glance in his direction, nod his head slightly and descend from the stage alone to start walking directly toward him and the man who had waved. By the time the cardinal had reached the other man, Pablo had hidden himself around the corner of the wall, where he could not see the two men, but he could eavesdrop.

"You are Rissolo?"

"Yes."

The cardinal looked back toward the field to see a mob of people heading his way. "I fear we may have only a few moments alone. I must leave immediately."

"What I need, more than anything, is the name of the town in Spain from where your family emigrated."

"They came from Toledo."

"Then that is where I'll look. How do I contact you?"

"I'll be in Rome for at least the next few days. After that I'll probably be back in Rio. But what about your expenses?"

"We'll worry about that later. Say hello to the pope for me." Rissolo passed by Pablo on his way to the parking lot. Pablo ignored the people hurrying by him to catch one last glimpse of the cardinal and followed Rissolo at a distance until the man reached his car. He memorized the license plate number and humming softly to himself, walked quickly back to his own car. Once inside his car, he picked up a small phone book, found the number he was looking for and dialed it.

"Hello?"

"This is de Cardoso. I need a favor."

"Yes, what is it?"

"I need to identify the owner of the car license plate 2-4-8-3-6-5. And I need the information quickly—within twenty-four hours if possible."

"Should I reach you by pager?"

"Perfect. And please keep it low profile."

"Done."

* * *

Cardinal Benda Cortes rode in the back seat of the taxi to the airport. He had stopped home only to grab a change of clothing and call a taxi. Before he left, he had made a hurried phone call to Rabbi Hanviowitz to tell him of his conversation with Alfonso Rissolo and the subsequent brief continuation of the matter as he left the stadium.

Rabbi Hanviowitz said, "So do you know why you have been called to Rome?"

"No. My secretary took the phone call in my absence, and all he was told was that the pontiff wished to speak to me in person as soon as possible."

"And Rissolo, you were able to give him the information he needed?"

"Apparently all he needed was the name of the town in Spain from where my mother's family came. I would imagine we'll be crossing the Atlantic at roughly the same time."

"And how do you feel about going to Rome?"

"Expectant, confused and guilty."

"I understand. I hope that this trip will help to clarify matters for you. Be well."

"And you also."

*   *   *

Cardinal Benda Cortes waited in the hall for permission to enter the pope's office. The trip to Rome had been uneventful, and it gave him the opportunity to catch up on his sleep and think without interruption. In the past, he had thrilled with anticipation at traveling to the Vatican; the beauty and majesty of the structures had given him great pleasure. He had always been impressed that the Church had shown the foresight to create such beauty in order to attract the world to its center of worship. This trip was different; he no longer had the security of feeling like a full-fledged member of the flock. Not knowing exactly who he was triggered feelings of loneliness and pain, not the usual security and comfort. He spent most of his time trying to understand why the pope had summoned him to Rome without an explanation.

The pope's secretary beckoned him toward the office. He entered the room and saw His Holiness John XXIV seated at his desk facing him. Much to the cardinal's surprise, Cardinal Scoglio was standing to one side of the pontiff, looking grim and dour as usual. Even for an eighty-five-year-old man, the pope looked tired. His once-hearty smile was now a weary grimace of welcome. Was there something else he saw in the pontiff's face?

John XXIV welcomed him with a nod and a slight smile. Cardinal Benda

Cortes neared the desk and started to kneel, but to his surprise, the pope shook his head and directed him to be seated in one of the two chairs opposite the desk, signaling at the same time for Cardinal Scoglio to take the other chair. The cardinal sat in his chair next to an obviously uncomfortable Cardinal Scoglio. The pope wasted no time with formalities.

"The reason I called you here, Isaac, was the same reason I wished Paolo to be here. I don't think that it is any secret that you are the two leading candidates to succeed me."

Scoglio protested, "Why are you speaking this way, Holy Father? You have many years left to you."

The pontiff regarded Scoglio dubiously. "Let's not cheat ourselves of an opportunity to face the truth, Paolo. There are so many opportunities to look at truth squarely, and how many of us can boast that we have been unflinching when we look in the mirror?"

Scoglio looked abashed for a moment, but Benda Cortes saw beyond the overt meaning of the pope's response and intuited that the pontiff was referring to something else. He waited for John XXIV to continue and realized that the pope was looking at him fixedly, waiting for his thoughts.

"I hope that Cardinal Scoglio is correct, Holy Father, although it is certainly in God's hands."

"That is true, and that is why I have summoned you both here. One of you will, in all probability, succeed me, and thus be the safeguard for my name and reputation. If you should continue in the path I have trod, my life will have had significant purpose. If, on the other hand, you should veer from my path or travel in the opposite direction, my life's work will have been in vain."

Scoglio said confidently, "You should have no fear, Your Holiness. The Church has no need of change. It need only be true to itself."

The pope responded, "And what is the focus of that truth?"

"Our Lord Jesus Christ, of course."

"Meaning what?"

Cardinal Scoglio was flabbergasted. "To act in principle with the example of our Lord Jesus Christ, Your Holiness . . . to . . . to . . ."

Benda Cortes saved him. "Holy Father, why are you asking us this question?"

John XXIV had eyes that had been described as "tender as a doe's." But when Benda Cortes looked at them, all he saw was naked fear. Fear of dying.

The pope said quietly, "I am going to die. Whether it is now or in six months, I will soon be in another place where God himself will judge me. And I am afraid of meeting him."

Scoglio burst out, "But why?"

The pope turned his chair around so that his back was to the cardinals. "Please forgive me—I need to tell you a story.

"As you know, I grew up in Rome. When I was a child, there was a girl who lived within a few blocks of me. Every few days I saw her walk past our home with her mother and her many sisters and brothers. She was my height, and I assumed she was my age. She was prettier than a painting by Raphael, more delicate than a painting by da Vinci. Black hair, olive skin and a gay smile that radiated the security of a well-loved child. I would wait at our window every day wishing that she would pass my way, hoping that she would turn and see my face at the window.

"Then one day, I found the courage to stand outside on the road behind a tree and wait for her. I had saved for weeks my meager allowance for my household chores and bought some flowers for her, which I held tightly in my hand. I must have waited for hours. Finally, when I was all but ready to give up and go inside, I saw her coming down the road toward me. Not only that, but she was accompanied only by her mother. I wanted desperately to make her smile at me! As they approached, I darted out from behind the tree and stepped directly in their path, holding in my outstretched hand the flowers I wanted to give to her. I didn't know exactly what to expect, perhaps a shy smile or a hesitant curtsy, but the response I *did* get startled me.

"She froze. The look in her eyes was the look I never fully understood until now. It was fear: fear of the stranger, fear of confrontation with something stronger than she and unmerciful in its power. I *recognized* the look, but I didn't *understand* it. And then, after her mother had swiftly taken her arm and walked past me, I wondered why I hadn't noticed it before. They were Jews. The brothers had always covered their heads, and the one time I had seen their father he had been a bearded man in a black suit, just like the other rare Jews I had seen. I knew that the reason the little girl had been afraid of me was that I was a non-Jew, and therefore not to be trusted. Her mother must have changed her route, because I never saw her again.

"I was bewildered by the whole experience for a long time. I was only a little boy. How could I be frightening to them? I was an adolescent by the time I figured it out. I represented the Christian world to them. Who knew where I came from, or what my relatives or friends would do to Jews?

"By that time, I had become quite knowledgeable about my Church and was committed to serving it. The story of Jesus was as much a part of my life as my own name, and because Jesus was so dear to me, I viewed the Jews as villains, since according to the Gospels they were responsible for his death. The memory of the encounter with the little girl still rankled, for I was determined to be a holy person without a blemish on my character, and the idea that someone would not greet me, for any reason, enraged me. Still, the memory rarely plagued me . . . until the Second World War.

"I had now risen in the hierarchy of the Church to be part of the Papal Secretariate of State. I had many friends in significant places, and Pope Pius XII had come from the same division, so I felt my ascension in the Church hierarchy was cleared of any obstacles. How I wanted to be the pope, to lead the world to recognition of Christ Our Lord! My ambition was not to be suppressed!

"Then, one day, I was given a note. It came from a friend of mine, a correspondent for a French newspaper, who informed me that he had incontrovertible evidence that the Nazis were murdering Jews throughout Europe by the hundreds of thousands. He and I had met when he was covering the installation of Pius XII in 1939, and we remained long-distance friends. He asked me to use my influence to gain the pope's sympathy in order to stop the massacres. I considered the matter carefully. Then I read a response the pope gave to the Vatican newspaper when he was asked if he would protest the massacre of the Jews. 'Do not forget that millions of Catholics serve in the German armies. Shall I bring them into conflicts of conscience?'

"How could I confront the pope with the evidence of my friend when the pope himself was loath to intercede? Had I displeased him, my aspirations and dreams would have vanished into thin air. Besides, I had grown to manhood believing the Jews were responsible for killing my Lord. Were the Nazis only carrying to the extreme what I had been taught to believe from childhood?

"I never confronted the pope. Meanwhile, millions of Jews were slaughtered in a campaign of evil that was unmatched in history. And even though there were a few priests who protested, I, along with many others, did nothing to avert it."

Scoglio questioned, "But you can't *know* that. You alone couldn't have stopped what happened."

John XXIV turned back to face them, trembling. "There is one thing more. When I decided to refrain from delivering the note to the pope, I was consumed by hatred. Not for the Jews as a whole. No, no. But for one small black-haired, olive-skinned girl who had been afraid of a small Catholic boy. I have been looking for that girl for years. Six months ago, I discovered that her family had been exiled by Mussolini in 1938 because her parents were originally from Vienna, not Italy. The entire family was eventually murdered by the Nazis at Dachau."

Benda Cortes trembled, too. *There but for the grace of God . . .*

The pope regained his voice. "And so I have been wondering: Is this what Jesus intended? Was he determined to see the Jews killed? All these centuries that the Church has regarded the Jews as our enemy, is it true? Were all the men who slaughtered the Jews men like me, carrying a secret rage against a small Jewish girl for her fear and rejection of them and venting the rage against the whole people? Has our Church followed the tenets of its founder? Perhaps he will condemn me to hell for my crime."

Cardinal Benda Cortes was shocked to hear the pontiff, who was known as a staunch traditionalist, speak of reexamining history.

Scoglio said, "But Holy Father, the Jews themselves felt they should be punished. In Matthew 27 they say, 'His blood be on our heads and our children's.'"

Benda Cortes was about to respond, but the pope reacted first. "Paolo, remember that Vatican II absolved the Jews of Christ's death. At the time, I was in disagreement, too. But as I near my day of judgment, I have discovered that I am no longer attached to any dogma, and I must seek the truth. And so I no longer avoid the literature that I have studiously avoided reading because it was outside the purview of my beliefs. I cannot take the beliefs of my mind with me when I die. Only my eternal soul and the truth will survive forever."

Benda Cortes asked, "What have you been reading, Holy Father?"

"A number of books of biblical criticism and history."

Scoglio said angrily, "And this is the path you are taking to find peace with God? To tear at the very foundation of the Church?"

The pope was calm. "I love Jesus as much as any man, Paolo. And a staggering thought has occurred to me. If we as Christians are correct, and Jesus is to return, will he return as a Jew? Everyone, Jew and Gentile, agrees that he *was* a Jew. And if he *returns* as a Jew, and anti-Semitism still exists, could he be murdered again? *We must choose between siding with the Nazis, who were the most evil of anti-Semites, and the Jews, or else we are endangering Jesus again, because if he had been alive in Europe in World War II, the Nazis, knowing he was a Jew, would have murdered him!*

"So much of Christian Europe allowed the Holocaust to happen. All genocides are horrific, but this was unique because the Nazis intended the destruction of not only Europe's Jews, but of every Jew on the planet. Was Christian acquiescence in the Holocaust fostered by the way the Gospels portrayed Jews? If that is true, Jesus would have been horrified that such a lesson was drawn from his life. How do I, as a Christian, separate what Jesus really wanted from what was recorded in the Gospel?"

The pope looked anguished. "I *must* know who Jesus was. Not who others thought he was, but who *he* thought he was. And I am exploring different views of him. One is that he never thought of himself as God. That was an addition to his story that was implemented by Paul and the writers of the Gospel who followed him. Jesus *may* have thought he was the Messiah, but the *Jewish* conception of the Messiah: a human being who would free the Jews from the tyranny of foreign oppression and enable them to be free to maintain their own holy nation and be a light unto the world. When he cried out to God at the end of his life, he was despairing of the mission that he thought had been his, to save his people with God's help."

Scoglio asked icily, "And what evidence do you have for these assumptions?"

"Evidence from a number of sources that I intend to publicly support to the world as soon as I finish my reading. And that is why you two are here. If I should die before my mission is accomplished, I want to know that you will continue the quest to bring truth to the world. That, after all, *is* our mission. Then I can look forward to my day of judgment in peace."

Scoglio stood up stiffly. "I cannot promise to destroy the Church."

"I am not trying to *destroy* the Church, Paolo. I am trying to *save* it by purifying it with the truth."

"I know no other truth. And I would assume that my fellow cardinals would agree." He cast a baleful glance at Benda Cortes, who remained silent. "May I be excused, Holy Father?" The pope sighed and nodded his head. Scoglio turned and left the room, closing the door quietly behind him.

The pope looked at Benda Cortes. "Isaac? You have been uncharacteristically quiet."

Benda Cortes was dumfounded. How should he respond? If he was a Jew, shouldn't that disqualify him from any consideration? "Holy Father . . . I love the truth, too. . . . I want to know the truth, but I don't know if I am worthy of this mission. I . . . lately I have been confused about who I really am."

The pope's eyes crinkled slightly. "That has been the enlightening part of my last journey, Isaac. I also thought I knew who I was and what my destiny was. But death seems to be a catalyst for a search for truth. And in the truth of our past we can see the truth of our future, and then we can find the truth of our present, the truth of our destiny. Whatever else you discover about yourself, one thing I know about you with certainty. You are not content with lies and charades: You are an eternal seeker of truth. I have faith in you." He reached both his hands to Benda Cortes. "Go with God." Then smiling, "And pray that he allows me the time I desire to find an answer."

The interview was over.

15

When Grant left the hospital, it was midnight. He kept reviewing the three things that Becky had said before she died. Two of them he understood: the wall was the wall he had constructed between himself and God, and the man in the black suit was Rabbi Hanviowitz in Israel. The third was still a mystery: "Connect the dots. . . ."

It was too late to call Willie Daniels and ask him about the continuation of his dream; that would have to wait until morning. Grant jammed his hands in his pockets in frustration and found a piece of paper. Pulling it out, he realized that it was the note that Mike Hanvill had written and given to Beth, his nurse. It had the ancient six-letter word on it. Then he remembered that Perry Lindsay had said that he would send Grant's office a copy of the ancient word that he and the executives had seen. He decided to drive to the office to see if Mike Hanvill's word and the word that Perry had sent were written in the same script.

Grant reached the Tyler Building and took the elevator to the fortieth floor, which had only two offices: his and Joel Alexander's. As he exited the elevator, he walked to the double doors on his right, where Joel's side of the floor was. He opened them with his key and peered into the dark, hoping irrationally that Joel was there, then backed out and locked the doors. As he crossed to the doors to his office on the other side, he had the uneasy feeling that he was being watched. That's ridiculous, he said to himself. Then he stopped dead in his tracks.

One of the doors was slightly ajar.

He took off his shoes, then swung the door open slowly, silently. There was no light anywhere. Noiselessly, he crept forward into the gigantic room, where Beverly's desk stood directly ahead of him. Behind that was his office, which spanned the entire floor and was separated from the area in front of it by a floor-to-ceiling glass wall interrupted only by a single door. And *that* door was also open.

Grant squinted from one side to the other, trying to see if someone was moving in his office. Suddenly a pencil beam of light was aimed at his desk. Grant couldn't see who was holding it, but the light moved over his desk until it came to an abrupt stop. Grant crept forward until he was crouching just outside the door to his office. The figure in the office picked up a piece of paper and turned toward the door. Grant watched the door swing outward and the intruder start to exit, then sprang at the figure and threw him heavily to the ground. He grabbed the pencil flashlight that the intruder had dropped and pointed the light at him.

It was Joel Alexander.

Grant was flabbergasted. "Joel, what the hell are you doing?" He saw a piece of paper on the floor next to Joel and picked it up and beamed the light at it. He saw, just as he had thought he would, that there was a word of four letters written on it in the same exact script as Hanvill's word. Grant knew that *this* must be what Perry Lindsay had sent to his office. But why was Joel trying to steal it?

He climbed to his feet, walked over to a light switch and flooded the room with light. Joel climbed to one knee, and then stood up slowly, looking at him with an expression Grant didn't understand.

"What's going on, Joel? Why were you trying to take this from my desk?"

Joel blinked and didn't answer.

"Joel, you know I trust you."

"Don't."

Grant walked back over to Joel. "Why did you want this? Is there something I should know that you're not telling me?"

"I know that you haven't been acting normal lately and you're heading for trouble."

Grant said slowly, "I just lost Becky, and I may lose Matthew. Tell me what normal behavior is."

"It isn't running around the world every time somebody has a dream or says something unintelligible. It isn't looking for an answer where none exists. It isn't assuming that you're being directed by some unseen force to act irrationally."

"What does that have to do with this note?"

Joel's voice became acerbic. "All I know is that you're digging yourself in deeper."

"Deeper into what?"

"Into all this mystical crap. So what if Becky saw some wall and Perry Lindsay saw some word when he blacked out. Are you going to let all that crap run you around? What do you think you're getting, messages from God?"

Grant knew the answer to *that*. "I think it's possible. . . . I have to try to understand how."

Joel paced in a circle around Grant. He yelled, "Are you nuts? Becky dies and you go nuts, is that it? Just because everyone else thinks you're God, now you start *believing* it?"

Grant responded calmly, "I didn't say I thought I was God, Joel. I said he may be using me somehow."

"And how about the rest of us? Are we supposed to wait until you deign to give us a message from on high? And what if there isn't someone up there, Grant? Or what if you are getting a message from some alien being out there somewhere? Or what if you've gone crazy, schizophrenic or something like that?" Joel stopped pacing and looked directly at Grant. "How do you know that *you* are getting some message from God?"

"How do you know I'm *not?* Why are you so hostile? . . . I haven't threatened you." Grant looked at the paper in his hand and glanced at Joel. "Why does this piece of paper scare the hell out of you? What aren't you telling me? Sooner or later I'll find out anyway."

Joel's jaw clenched while he decided what to do. Finally he said tightly, "That word you are holding is written in an ancient Hebrew script that hasn't been used for twenty-five hundred years."

Grant looked surprised. "How do you know that? You told me twenty years ago you didn't even know Hebrew."

"It was a coincidence. I saw the paper on your desk yesterday. Then last night I was watching *The Ten Commandments* on TV, and I saw the same script used when God wrote the words on the tablets. I didn't recognize the script, so after Michelle was asleep I got on the Internet and made some inquiries."

Grant smiled. "You really think it was a coincidence?"

Joel sneered, "Come off it, Grant. You think *I'm* getting a divine message through the *television?* You *have* gone crazy."

"I'm not crazy, Joel. But *you* are if you think you're going to stop me from pursuing this matter. I'm going to get that word and Mike Hanvill's word translated and find out what God's trying to tell me."

"Mike Hanvill?"

Grant had forgotten that Joel didn't know about the other word. He pulled the piece of paper from his pocket and held it out toward Joel. "Before he died, Mike had a vision and wrote this down."

Joel looked hard at Grant. "Don't pursue this, Grant."

Grant finally lost his temper. "What the hell is your problem? I may be getting some direction from God, and you want me to ignore it? *Don't you dare stand in my way!*"

Joel said stubbornly, "There isn't any God. There *can't* be."

Grant walked up to Joel until they were almost nose to nose.

"Not only is there a God, Joel, but I can feel him opening a path for me." He thought of Becky and Matthew and the oath he had taken to himself. "And if you get in my way . . ." His eyes bored into Joel's. "I'd advise against it." He walked into his office and closed the door behind him. Joel watched him for a moment, then left for the elevator.

Grant sat down at his desk and reached for the telephone. He knew that Israel was seven hours ahead, so Rabbi Hanviowitz would be awake. He reached into his wallet where he had written down the rabbi's phone number at the yeshiva and dialed the number.

A young man's voice answered. "Yeshiva Tahorah."

"Hello, I'm looking for Rabbi Hanviowitz."

"Rav Hanviowitz?" Then, in heavily accented English, "Who calls?"

"Grant Tyler."

"A moment." There was a flurry of Hebrew spoken between two young men and then the sound of footsteps before the telephone was taken and the voice of Rabbi Eliyahu Hanviowitz came through.

"Mr. Tyler?"

"Yes."

"How has your return to America been? Eventful?"

"More than that." He told the rabbi everything that had transpired since his return: Matthew's situation, his understanding of what Becky had said to him, Willie Daniels's admission of an extension of his dream, and finally his own visionary experience.

"So you had a glimpse of the divine."

"None of this sounds crazy to you, does it?"

"Would that everyone were so crazy. My younger brother Daniel would be a better source for your experience with the mystical, though. He has spent more time studying our mystic tradition of Kabbalah then I have. He lives in Brazil."

"Actually, Rabbi, it's not because of the experience I had that I'm calling you. A part of it is, but the main reason I called you is because of what your other brother wrote before he died."

"Yes, they sent me the note with the word on it after you had left. The one with six letters in the old script?"

"Yes, that's right. What word is it?"

"*Anusim.*"

"What does it mean?"

"Literally it means 'the forced ones.' It refers to the Jews in Spain who were forced by the Church to convert to Catholicism in the fifteenth century. They were called Marranos by their oppressors, which meant 'swine.' The other explanation for the word Marrano was that it was an abbreviation of the Aramaic phrase that these Jews were compelled to repeat frequently, 'maran atha,' which meant 'our Lord has come,' the admission that the Messiah had already come. Of course we believe that the Messiah has not come, so it was a violation of our identities as Jews to say such a thing. But did you call me just to translate that word?"

"No, not just *that* word."

"There is *another* one?"

Grant told the rabbi about the five executives, their heart attacks and their subsequent visions of the same word.

Rabbi Hanviowitz was genuinely excited now. "Can you fax a copy of that word to me right now?"

"Of course. Do you mind if I wait on the line while you translate it?"

"I'd insist on it." He recited a telephone number. Grant laid the telephone on his desk and walked over to the fax machine and sent the fax through, then returned to his desk and the telephone. "Rabbi?"

"It's coming through now. . . . Please wait just a moment. . . . Here it is."

Grant felt his adrenaline start to pump. He gripped the desk with his free hand and watched the second hand on the clock on the wall. Thirty seconds, one minute, ninety seconds. "Rabbi? . . . Rabbi?"

Rabbi Hanviowitz's voice trembled. "Mr. Tyler . . ."

"Is everything all right? Did you receive the fax?"

"Yes . . . yes, I did."

"What does the other word say? What do the four letters spell?"

"They spell . . . *Moshiach*."

"What does that mean?"

Rabbi Hanviowitz took a deep breath. "It means Messiah, Mr. Tyler."

"Messiah? *The* Messiah?"

"That's correct."

"But what does that have to do with the word *Anusim,* the word for Marrano?"

"I don't know, but I can guess. *Somewhere right now there is a Marrano who could be the Messiah.*"

"How do you know that it means right now? Maybe it means in the future?"

"With everything that you've been doing, you haven't heard what the scientists who discovered cold fusion have said, have you?"

"No, I haven't." Rabbi Hanviowitz told Grant about what the scientists had dreamed, their computation of their formula in *gematryia* and their conclusion that it was the onset of the messianic age.

"But I thought the Messiah was supposed to be a divinity."

"No, that is the Christian conception of the Messiah. The original Jewish Messiah was . . . this may take some time."

Grant said humorously, "What *else* should I be doing?"

"All right. Are you ready?"

"Fire away."

"The Jewish concept of the Messiah is that he is the leader of the Jewish people. He is an exceptionally wise and spiritual man, not a divinity, whose primary role will be to bring redemption to the Jews so they can teach the world about God. He will preside over an era of peace, prosperity and moral purity for the entire world. He will gather all the Jews to Israel so that the eyes of the world will focus on Israel, since if the people of Israel obey God's laws, they can serve as an example to the rest of the world."

"But why am *I* involved in all of this? I'm not Jewish, and I've never been a believer in God until now. If it had been Becky it would have made sense; *she* was a spiritual person. I keep thinking that the message came through her because of that."

"That's certainly possible."

"She did say one thing that still puzzles me. The last moments before she was gone she kept saying, 'connect the dots.' And she said, 'you have to go now.'" Grant expected a response but there was none. "Rabbi?"

"Connect the dots, she said?"

"That's right."

The rabbi mused. "It all fits . . . why this has all happened to you. The fact that you command a network that reaches virtually everywhere is the key. You see, as Jews we don't have a need to forcibly convert the world or own large areas of land. All that God intended was for us to live in the land of Israel, follow his laws, and thus serve as a light unto the nations. And if all the Jews could be convinced that their Messiah was here and they returned to Israel and were a kingdom of righteousness, the world would sit up and take notice. And we would no longer be persecuted, the world would follow the seven laws of Noah that we previously discussed, and life would be something that the world cherished, instead of an existence that was viewed pessimistically as a necessary burden before the soul reached a better place."

"But if there is someone out there who fits this description, a Marrano who could be the Messiah, what does he need me for?"

"To understand that, you have to realize that there have been other opportunities for the messianic age. Moses could have been the Messiah had no one told Pharoah about Moses killing the Egyptian taskmaster, and had that not led to Moses' subsequent flight. Moses, as the prince, would have eventually inherited the Egyptian empire upon Pharoah's death, and the physical might of the Egyptian empire could have protected the Jews after their return to Israel so that they would never be exiled. When the Persian emperor Cyrus permitted the Jews to return to Israel under his protection and many did not, another opportunity was lost. Many Jews are still living in the exile forced upon us by the Romans, and for many of them, it would only be the rest of the world's acknowledgment that someone was indeed the Messiah that would convince them to come home and fulfill their destiny."

"So you think that my job is to find this man and convince the world of his importance?"

"I think that the dots that your wife referred to are the Jews scattered all over the world, who need to come home so that we can do the job we were meant to do. You have always had the means, but now you have the *will.*"

"But how will I find him?"

"I don't know. Some things are revealed to us in strange ways. Who would have imagined that my brother, who publicly denied being Jewish and stopped believing in God in 1944, would get a message from someone he didn't think existed?"

"At least until the end, anyway."

"What was that?"

"Oh, I didn't tell you. Right before he committed suicide, he told the nurse that he wanted a proper Jewish burial instead of being cremated."

"He said he wanted a Jewish burial? He identified himself as a Jew?"

"That's right."

"*Baruch Hashem,* blessed be the name of God. Then my brother and I need to sit shiva for him, to properly mourn him. I must call my brother in Brazil immediately."

"What does that mean? Can I still reach you?"

"In seven days."

"But what about helping me to find the Marrano Messiah?"

"Our laws regarding working or doing business during shiva are more than three thousand years old, and the only time I would consider breaking them would be to save a life."

"But I don't know where to start."

"There is still one piece of information you haven't gathered. Your friend

Willie Daniels, didn't he say that his dream had continued? You might start there."

"He won't be awake for another seven or eight hours, though."

"And when was the last time *you* slept, three days ago? For the job you are going to do you will need all your strength. Why don't you sleep now?"

"I'm too wound up."

"There's no law against taking a sleeping pill."

"What about you? Aren't you excited?"

"I know the tragic history of our people too well to get excited yet. On the other hand, you make sure to call me in seven days."

16

ardinal Benda Cortes? Your Eminence, sir?"

Cardinal Benda Cortes rolled over in his bed and painfully opened his eyes in the early light of dawn. For a moment he forgot he was still in Rome staying at the Vatican; he was as unaware of his whereabouts as if he were waking up from a general anaesthetic. He heard the knock on his door again, more insistent this time.

"Your Eminence?"

He sat up in bed. "Yes?"

"I have an urgent message for you, sir. May I slide it under the door?"

"Certainly." An envelope was slid under the door and the cardinal yawned, turned on the light next to his bed and picked up the small envelope. It had been securely taped all around, and *Urgent* was written on the back and front. He grappled with the tape for a moment before he was able to open the envelope and read the letter inside.

Dear Cardinal Benda Cortes:

I have been in Toledo for the past two days, and through visiting the cemeteries I have traced your family back to the fourteenth century. The trail before that goes through the church Mudejar Santa Maria la

*Blanca, which was a synagogue in the thirteenth and fourteenth cen-
turies. When I inquired by telephone as to any records they might have,
they were reticent about showing them to me; in fact, they were
adamant in their refusal. If you want to inquire further, I think you had
better come and ask yourself; I doubt they would refuse you. I am
enclosing the telephone number of my hotel. Please call as soon as
possible and inform me of your intent.*

Rissolo

The cardinal had made reservations to return to Brazil in the afternoon.
Ten minutes and two phone calls after reading Rissolo's letter, he changed
his destination to Madrid. Four hours later he was in Madrid, and ninety
minutes later he and Rissolo were in a car headed for the Mudejar Santa
Maria la Blanca.

Rissolo was driving with a scowl on his face. The cardinal reasoned that
Rissolo's anger was due to the church's refusal to open their records. He
attempted to make polite conversation.

"I've never been here before. Have you?"

Rissolo shrugged. "No, but I've been doing some reading. I read that
Toledo was the chief battleground in the religious war between the native
Spanish, who were Catholic, and the Visigoths, who invaded and conquered
Spain and were Arianists. But I don't know who the Arianists were."

"The Arianists were followers of Arius, who died two hundred years
before the battle between the Spaniards and the Visigoths. He espoused a
different Christianity, a monotheism, the idea that Jesus Christ was not
a part of God made manifest but a being that was *created* by God. This was
a major philosophical battle within the Church."

"He ultimately lost, didn't he? Doesn't the Church hold that the Trinity is
all of the same substance, that Jesus and God are one and the same?"

"It does *now* . . . but then, it was quite a battle. At the same time as Arius
lived, Constantine, the Roman Emperor, was concerned about the disinte-
gration of the Roman empire. He came to the conclusion that if he adopted
Christianity as the state religion he could unify the empire. In 324, he
declared Christianity the official religion of the empire. The growing popularity of Arianism and its divisive effect on the Church concerned him and
so he convened the Council in Nicea in 325 to resolve the issue. It was at

this council that the coequal nature of the Trinity was decided, thus clearly defeating the Arianists. From that moment, Jesus' death was viewed not as a man's but as God's, thus ensuring that whoever killed him was the murderer of God. Since the Gospels identified the Jews instead of the Romans as the killers of Jesus, the Jews became the killers of God."

"But the battle for Christianity in Toledo came two hundred years later."

"The Visigoths weren't loyal to Rome or its religion. They remained Arianists, and it was only when their own King Recarred converted to Catholicism and convened the Third Council of Toledo that Catholicism won and was made the official religion of the state. His successors were brutal to the Spanish Jews, and it was only the successful invasion of the Moors that allowed the Jews to live in peace. That lasted until the thirteenth century, when the Catholics were restored and they again persecuted the Jews."

Rissolo said bitterly, "So Toledo was the site where Catholicism took power again over the Arianists, just as they had over the original Arius in 325. And both times the Jews suffered."

"Correct."

"And we're returning here to find out if you, a candidate to lead the Roman Catholic Church, might be a Jew? Incredible."

"Just think how *I* feel."

Rissolo swung the car into the parking lot of the Mudejar Santa Maria la Blanca. The cardinal's stomach tightened with tension. Rissolo parked the car and waited. The cardinal looked at him and asked, "You're not going in with me?"

"I can't. I spoke with them by phone. I am forbidden by Jewish law to enter a church because of the law against idol worship."

"The cross and the crucifix are viewed as idols?"

"Any physical representation of God is considered as idolatrous."

Cardinal Benda Cortes thought for a moment. "What about a mosque, where nothing is represented?"

"There we may enter."

"Hmmm." The cardinal opened the door, climbed out of the car and started to walk to the door of the church. Rissolo leaned out of his window and called, "Good luck!"

The cardinal reached the door of the church and knocked. The door opened and a rotund, jovial-looking priest appeared. He stared at the cardinal's robe and then stammered nervously, "Good . . . good afternoon."

"Good afternoon. I am Cardinal Benda Cortes of Rio de Janeiro, Brazil. And you are?"

"Father Hernando, Your Eminence. Brazil? Have you come all this way to see our church?"

"By way of Rome . . . I just came from the Vatican. You see, my ancestors came from Toledo."

"Really? And then migrated to Brazil? How long ago?"

"Oh, about four or five hundred years ago."

"You must be a student of history."

The cardinal nodded. "Yes, it is an obsession of mine. Could you tell me about the church's history?"

"Would you like to take a tour of the church while I do so?"

"That sounds perfect."

They started to walk around the church. Father Hernando said, "Before this was a church it was a barracks. That was at the end of the eighteenth century. In the sixteenth century, it was an asylum for women."

"That is quite a contrast."

"Yes, well, it has gone through different incarnations over the centuries."

The cardinal said thoughtfully, "I read somewhere that in the thirteenth or fourteenth century this was a synagogue for Jews. Is that true?"

Father Hernando hesitated. "It is true. But that was a long time ago."

Cardinal Benda Cortes had noticed the change in the rotund priest's mood. "Do you think that there are any historical records of those Jews who lived here?" He saw the cleric look at him worriedly. "I mean, it would be interesting to see just for the sake of history."

"That's funny, someone called yesterday about the church's records." All of a sudden the priest grew frightened. "Is there some trouble that we have with Rome because we had Jews here once? Were you sent here by the Holy Father?"

The cardinal attempted to calm the fearful man. "No, no. I am just here for the sake of historical interest."

Father Hernando breathed easier. "I am relieved. . . . I love this church. Would you like to see our records now?"

"Very much."

"Then follow me."

*   *   *

Two hours later, Cardinal Benda Cortes disappointedly closed the last volume that Father Hernando had put before him. There had been no mention of any family's name that resembled Benda, nor were there any names that sounded remotely Jewish. He looked up to see the priest regarding him anxiously and realized that the priest was still afraid of the Jewish antecedents of the church. All of a sudden, he wondered if Father Hernando had shown him everything.

"Are these all the records you have?"

"Yes, this is all we have."

"Are you sure? I don't see any names of Jews here."

"It is possible they were erased later or lost somewhere."

The cardinal stood up and looked at the priest. "Not a trace of their existence?"

Father Hernando said, "Not unless you count the jewels and furniture they sold to the church when they left Spain in 1497. They had plenty of money under Moorish rule."

"Are any of those jewels or furniture still left in the church?"

"The jewels are in a case in the front hall. The only furniture we have left is an old chair next to the jewel case that looks like it came from the Spanish Renaissance."

"May I see them?"

The priest led him toward the front hall, and when they turned the corner, the Cardinal saw to his amazement that inside a roped-off area was a Spanish Renaissance chair—an exact duplicate of the one in his mother's home. He felt his eyes mist over. . . . Then he turned and saw Father Hernando watching him narrowly. He said wistfully, "In my childhood home, my mother had a similar chair. Could I take the liberty of sitting on it?"

The priest hesitated, "I don't think anyone has sat in that chair for decades. . . . The bishop wouldn't like it. I'm not sure that it would be safe."

"Please, just for a moment. I lost my mother a week ago."

"All right, but please sit gently, Your Eminence."

The cardinal sat down gingerly. As he sat there, memories of his mother flooded into his mind. Tears falling down his cheek, he bent over to put his face in his hands. As his weight shifted there was a sudden snap from below him and the chair crashed beneath him, plunging him to the floor. The priest panicked. "Oh, Mother of God!" He looked in consternation at the floor where the cardinal was sprawled, a three legged-chair and the single leg that had broken off beside him. Anguished, he started to run in panic back to his office, calling over his shoulder, "Please don't touch anything! I'll go call someone!"

The cardinal sat up and looked at the chair and the leg that had broken off. Then he did a double take. Protruding from the broken leg was an old rolled-up piece of parchment. He heard the priest rummaging through the drawers in his office and decided he could take a chance. Removing the parchment from the broken leg, he unrolled it carefully to see a list of Hebrew words written on it. Then he looked at the Spanish signature at the bottom.

It was Devorah Benda.

He heard the priest returning and quickly tucked the parchment into his robe just before Father Hernando reappeared. The cardinal asked solicitously, "Can I help you? I am terribly sorry about this accident."

"No, no. Have you seen everything you need to see here, Your Eminence?"

"Yes, I think I am finished. Are you certain that I cannot help you?"

The priest, who was bent over the chair examining the break, looked up. "If I cannot fix this, will you stand by me with the bishop and tell him that it broke when you asked to sit in it?"

"Should you need me, I will tell him exactly what happened. Tell him that I can be reached in Rio. Thank you once again."

"Fine, fine, you're welcome." Father Hernando bent down to the chair and didn't see the cardinal exit.

*　　*　　*

Rissolo saw the cardinal heading quickly toward him, gesturing to start the car. As he did, the cardinal reached him, opened the door and sat down next to him. The cardinal had a distant look on his face.

"Find anything?"

The cardinal wordlessly pulled the parchment out of his robe and handed it to Rissolo, who took a quick glance and turned to the cardinal. "Did you read any of this?"

"Enough to see my family's name on the bottom."

"Let's get back to my hotel and look it over, shall we?"

*   *   *

"See this? See how each name has 'ben' in the middle? That means 'son of.'"

"I know."

"So we start at the bottom and read up. Here at the bottom, Devorah Benda, daughter of Yitzhak. Then above her is Yitzhak ben Yaakov, then Yaakov ben Yehoshua, then Yehoshua ben Shimshon, all the way up here to . . ." Rissolo's finger traveled up near the top of the parchment. "Chizkiyahu HaMelech? King Hezekiah?" Leaving his finger pressed to the parchment, he stared at Cardinal Benda Cortes. "Then you are descended from . . ." His finger traveled up past twelve names to stop at the name in small writing at the top. He stood up erect and looked at Cardinal Benda Cortes with wonder.

"David HaMelech. King David." Rissolo's eyes started to fill with tears. *"You are a direct descendant of King David."*

The cardinal said distractedly, "Haven't you ever found descendants of King David before?"

Rissolo didn't answer. He fell down on the floor on his knees and began weeping, his face in his hands. The cardinal was dumbfounded to see Rissolo so emotional. "What is it? Are you all right?"

Rissolo said through his hands, muffled, "You don't know?"

"Know what?"

"Who you are?"

Cardinal Benda Cortes felt a chill go down his spine. "What do you mean, who I am?"

"Isn't that what you wanted to know? Who you were? Isn't that why we came here?"

The cardinal was upset. "We know that now. I am a descendant of King David, descended from Jews, and by Jewish law I am a Jew." He bent over the fallen man. "I know why *I* am confused. But why are *you* so upset? . . . Is this the first time you've found out one of your non-Jewish clients was a Jew?"

Rissolo slowly raised himself from the waist and looked up at the cardinal. "First of all, you are the first Gentile client I've had. Second, I am not upset, I am grateful to God for enabling me to be alive for this moment. Third . . ."

"Why does *my* ancestry mean so much for you to witness it?"

Rissolo looked squarely at the cardinal and said quietly, "Third. I have been chosen by God to help discover the ancestry of the Messiah."

All that could be heard was a single bird trilling outside.

"The *what?*"

"You heard me."

The cardinal turned white. "What are you talking about? Me? *What are you talking about?!*"

Rissolo smiled faintly. "I don't think that I'm totally qualified to enlighten you. Why don't you ask Rabbi Hanviowitz when we get back to Rio."

"Is this some sort of a joke?"

"It's no joke. You just have to know Jewish history and prophecy."

The cardinal seized Rissolo by the shoulders. "I am just a man! How can you say this to me?"

Rissolo said, "If you can't believe me, call Rabbi Hanviowitz."

"And what if he says the same as you? How can I believe something so crazy?" He withdrew his hands from Rissolo's shoulders and walked past him to the window.

Rissolo looked at the cardinal's back. He said softly, "Because you are a seeker of truth."

The cardinal spun around to face Rissolo. His lips were tightly pressed inward. "Do you know the rabbi's number?"

"Sure." Rissolo dialed the number on the telephone, then held it out to the cardinal. The cardinal waited for a moment, then crossed the room and took it.

"Hello, this is Cardinal Benda Cortes calling for Rabbi Hanviowitz. . . . Is this Rivkah? I'm fine, thank you. . . . Can your father come to the telephone?" His face looked discouraged. "But it's a matter of great importance. . . . I see. . . . How much longer is his shiva? It's over in two days? Can you please tell him that I'll call him then? Thank you." He hung up the telephone and sat heavily on the bed. "He's sitting shiva for his brother. He couldn't talk just now."

"I heard." Rissolo got to his feet. Then he said grimly, "We've waited almost six thousand years, what's a couple of days?"

Cardinal Benda Cortes was harsh. "I am not the Messiah, Rissolo. I'm just a man whose ancestor happened to be King David. . . . No matter *what* Rabbi Hanviowitz says, I know who I am, and I am *not* the Messiah."

"I guess your voyage of discovery isn't over yet."

The cardinal just looked at him, troubled.

* * *

Pablo de Cardoso shifted his weight from one foot to the other impatiently. He was standing in the hall outside Alfonso Rissolo's office, watching another man pick the lock to the door. Directly after eavesdropping on the cardinal and Rissolo at the stadium, Pablo had obtained Rissolo's identity and address from his license plate, driven by the building, then returned home and waited by his telephone, figuring that Cesar Carlos was as good as his word and would call him, since Carlos had said he would be watching Pablo's movements. Sure enough, that night his telephone rang.

"Pablo de Cardoso?"

"Yes."

"Please hold for Cesar Carlos." Pablo waited for only a moment before Carlos came on the line.

"De Cardoso?"

"Yes?"

"You have made inquiries into a man named Rissolo, I hear."

"That is correct."

"May I ask why?"

Pablo told Carlos about the conversation he had overheard between the cardinal and Rissolo at Maracana Stadium, and his subsequent stalking of Rissolo to the parking lot.

"So this Rissolo was told that the cardinal's family was from Toledo in Spain? And there was no indication what the cardinal was looking for?"

"None." Pablo hesitated before offering a suggestion. "I was thinking that I . . . we should find out what this Rissolo does for a living. I did get his address and I drove by the building, which apparently is his office address."

"That is an excellent idea. Do you think the man has already left for Spain?"

"He seemed in a great hurry."

Carlos's voice became commanding. "One of my men will meet you at

Rissolo's office in two hours. He will enable you to enter, and you and he will search the office for any information about this Rissolo, and possibly any information regarding his relationship to the cardinal. You will give him any information you find, and you will remain silent about this matter until you hear from me." The line went dead.

Pablo started to put on his shoes, then remembered that he hadn't given Carlos the address. *How will his man know where to go?* he thought. Then he laughed to himself. *I'm worried about Carlos finding information?*

*　*　*

Carlos's man, Humberto, finished picking the lock and opened the door, then waved his flashlight for Pablo to enter ahead of him. Pablo had remembered to bring a flashlight, too, and the two men entered silently with the two beams of light pointing in different corners of the small office. Pablo went directly to Rissolo's desk and started opening and closing drawers, while the locksmith crossed to a large file cabinet and began to open its drawers.

Pablo grunted as he pulled out some papers and laid them on the desk. "It looks like this guy traces family histories, all right. Look at all these names." The locksmith came over to the desk to look over Pablo's shoulder. "Look at these dates. 1560, 920, 285. Wow, this guy goes all the way back with this stuff."

The locksmith had returned to the file cabinet. He let out a low whistle as he pulled out an old bridal picture of a young couple. "Look at this . . . look at her." Pablo took a look. The woman was stunning, and he found himself fascinated by her, then looked at the man, who was wearing a skullcap. *Oh, they're Jewish,* he thought to himself. Then he looked at the inscription at the bottom and read "Alfonso and Monica Rissolo." *His wedding picture,* he mused. He started to replace the picture when a sudden thought struck him: *Why is the cardinal of Rio de Janeiro asking a Jew to help him trace his family's roots? The Church certainly has records of its own.* He sat down behind the desk to consider the matter, and though any number of hypotheses came to him, one idea planted itself firmly in his mind and would not let go.

"Hey, do you know Carlos's telephone number?"

"Are you crazy?" Humberto stared, "You can't call him now. If you found something, just give it to me and I'll get it to him."

Pablo was stubborn. "I don't have anything to give him but an idea. How do I reach him?"

"If you think I'm gonna let you call him at this hour of the night, you're nuts!"

"Fine. I'll let him wait until morning before I give him the information he's paying you to find as fast as possible."

The locksmith struggled with himself, debating, then moved to the desk and put his body between Pablo and the telephone and dialed a number that Pablo couldn't see. Then he handed the telephone to Pablo.

The clear, alert voice of the drug lord answered. "Carlos."

"This is Pablo de Cardoso. My deepest apologies for the time of this call—"

"Unimportant. What have you found?"

"The man traces family histories."

"We had figured that."

"He is also a Jew."

The voice was impatient. "Yes, so?"

"So why would a cardinal of the Catholic Church hire a Jew to look into his family history?"

A significant pause. Then, "I suppose that you are thinking what I'm thinking."

Pablo was complimented by the drug lord's estimation of his intellect. He ventured, "That the cardinal may be of Jewish blood?"

"Yes. That would certainly place his candidacy for the papacy in jeopardy." Carlos permitted himself a moment to savor the idea. "Imagine the Church's reaction to the possibility of their leader having tainted blood and claiming it as his own."

Pablo was excited. "He is ruined. Ruined!"

"Not so fast. We need undeniable proof. We need to interview this man Rissolo."

"I don't think it likely that he would talk to me."

"It was not you that I had in mind. I have associates who are quite expert at this sort of thing."

"Violence?"

"De Cardoso, don't become squeamish. This is only one man, and a Jew at that. It will all be kept quiet . . . won't it?"

Pablo heard the implicit threat. "Of course."

"Good. And I'll make sure that if this rumor is true, you alone get to write the story. Is that sufficient for you?"

"I am grateful for your confidence in me."

"But of course. We really have the same agenda, my friend. And I am loyal to those who are on my side. Of course, for the others . . ."

The line went dead.

Grant woke up to feel the bright sunlight warm on his face. It streamed through the windows of his office and bathed him in its glow, awakening in him a boundless optimism. He had fallen asleep with his head on his desk, and as he sat up in his chair his first thought was to see how long he had slept. He looked at his watch, pleased to see that it was only 8:30 and the day was still young. His next thought was to call Willie Daniels and find out if Willie's dream could assist Grant in his search for the Messiah. He started to leaf through his personal phone book for Willie's home telephone number.

The telephone rang.

Grant almost jumped out of his chair, then reached over and picked it up. "Hello?"

"Grant? It's Perry Lindsay. I've been trying you at the office for the past three days. Are you all right?"

"I'm fine, Perry. In fact, I'm better than fine."

"I'm glad to hear *that*."

Grant suddenly remembered that Perry had urgently tried to talk to him at the hospital while he had been noncommunicative. "Perry, I'm sorry about what happened at the hospital. I was . . . well . . ."

"You were in shock. Forget it, Grant. I'm just glad that you're back. How is your son?"

"Nothing has changed."

"I'll say a prayer for him."

Grant seized the opportunity. "You can do better than that. I found out what the word you saw and what the word Mike Hanvill saw both mean. We were right—they both are from the same ancient language."

Perry was intensely excited. "You're kidding! What do they mean?"

"The word Mike saw was *Anusim,* which is Hebrew for Marrano. The Marranos were the Jews who converted to Catholicism during the Spanish Inquisition but practiced their Judaism in secret."

"Yes, I've heard something of them. But what was the word that all of *us* saw?"

Grant had a split second of concern about Perry's reaction, but his innate optimism overcame it. "The word you saw was the Hebrew word *Moshiach.*"

"What does it mean?"

"It means Messiah."

"Wait a minute, wait a minute . . . what do you mean Messiah? Messiah as in Jesus? The Second Coming? But why would that be in Hebrew?"

Grant said, "Because it may be the First Coming, actually. What I have learned is that the Jewish conception of the Messiah and the Christian concept are quite different."

"You're telling me that we were sent a message about a Jewish Messiah?"

Grant grinned. "What's so strange about that? Wasn't Jesus Jewish, too?"

Perry was bewildered. "You can't have it both ways, Grant. Either what you're saying is true and some Jew out there is the Messiah, or Jesus was the Messiah."

"Precisely. I believe we are meant to find this Marrano Messiah and help him fulfill his destiny."

"But don't you think that Jesus was the Messiah that the Jews had prophesied?"

Grant thought for a moment. "I think that the Jews had their own ideas about what their prophecies meant, and they didn't believe he was. Besides, there are many different views of Jesus around the world." He leaned forward and put his elbows on the desk. "What do you think about this? Suppose you and I do a little research into who Jesus really was so we can make a better-informed decision?"

Perry started hesitantly but soon warmed to the idea. "Well . . . okay. That sounds reasonable. I'll contact the other executives and see if they want to do some research, too."

Grant didn't want to be detained by the executives for too long in his search for the Messiah. He remembered that Rabbi Hanviowitz was still sitting shiva. "Why don't we meet in my office one week from today? By then we should be better equipped to move forward."

"Done. I always loved reading history."

Perry hung up, and Grant resumed looking for Willie's number. Finding it, he dialed Willie at home and waited for an answer.

Robin's voice answered. "Hello?"

"Mrs. Daniels?"

"Yes?"

"This is Grant Tyler. I hear that you are the mother of the heir to the Daniels dynasty."

Robin laughed, a warm, sweet laugh. "You should see him, Mr. Tyler. He has the same serious face as his daddy. The same concentration, too."

"If he's anything like Willie, he'll be a fine addition for all of us. Is Willie home?"

"I'll get him for you right now." Grant heard Robin put the telephone down and patter off. Then he heard the receiver being lifted.

"Mr. Tyler?"

"Willie, before I say anything I want to apologize for my behavior at the hospital."

"I didn't find out until I asked the front desk that your son had been hurt, Mr. Tyler. Is he better?"

"He's in a holding pattern right now. Willie, didn't you mention that you had a continuation of your vision at the game?"

"Uh, yes, Mr. Tyler, I did. Could you hold on for a moment while I close the door?"

"Absolutely."

There was a slight pause while Willie closed the door. "Mr. Tyler, do you remember that I saw you at a wall with a bearded man in a black suit?"

"I sure do, and that actually happened to me two days later. That's why I want to know what you dreamed the other night."

"I saw you with a man who looked almost exactly like the man in my original vision. They could have been twins, but this one looked younger; his beard was not as white. He was standing with you, just as the first one had, but this time I was there too, standing next to you. The bearded man told us that we had to protect someone, and he pointed to one side."

Grant could barely restrain himself. "Protect someone? Who?"

"I tried to see what the man we were supposed to protect looked like, but all I saw was a shadowy figure."

"Did you see anything about him that was unique at all?"

"Only that he was wearing a long robe, or something like that. Mr. Tyler, could you tell me what is going on? I mean, the first vision I had involved you, but now *I'm* part of it, too."

Grant felt that he owed Willie an explanation. After all, Willie's vision had helped propel Grant along the path he now followed. He told Willie everything, everything that had transpired from Becky's first revelation to the upcoming meeting with the executives.

Willie was astounded. "You really think this could be true?"

"I wouldn't have called you otherwise."

Willie became shy. "Mr. Tyler, would it be okay with you if I came to that meeting next week, too? I know that they are important men, but the team is in town next week and I'd sure like to be a part of this."

Grant didn't hesitate a beat. "You'd fit right in, Willie. Besides, you're the only one of us who seems to be seeing the future right now. And forewarned is forearmed."

"Thanks, Mr. Tyler. I'll see you there."

Grant hung up the telephone and considered what Willie had said. He had no doubt that the man he was supposed to protect was the Messiah. *But why was he wearing a robe?*

*   *   *

Dr. Abraham Yosef and Dr. Shaul Yonatan sat at the table next to Dr. Steven Aarons and an Israeli government functionary in Aarons's Jerusalem office waiting for Gary Stephens, the National Security Advisor of the United States. Aarons was nervous; the other two scientists were not. Aarons had been nervous since he had received the news from the Israeli prime minister's office that Stephens was coming, but when he informed the two other members of his team that the U.S. government was applying pressure to reveal the formula for cold fusion, they had simply shrugged and gone about their work.

For Steven Aarons, the metamorphosis into a religious Jew was still new. He acknowledged that the discovery was part of God's plan, and he deferred to the other men when they acquiesced to Rabbi Hanviowitz, their teacher, and refused to reveal the formula just yet. Still, the prospect that the U.S. government was leaning on the Israelis to order the team to impart the information intimidated him. Although he agreed that the *discovery* was the hand of God, his *own* participation in its suppression seemed out of the realm of God's decision-making process. He didn't want to lose his career over a political issue.

Yosef tapped his pipe against the ashtray on Aarons's desk. "You still have reservations, Steven?"

"I'm not sure that we're doing the right thing, that's all."

"You don't trust Rabbi Hanviowitz's judgment?"

"I do, I do. It's just that here we are, waiting for the U.S. government to lower the boom, and Rabbi Hanviowitz is unavailable."

Yonatan said patiently, "He has to sit shiva, Steven. He'll be done soon."

"Why is he so sure that we have to conceal everything? What's he waiting for?"

Yosef, the oldest member of the team, answered, "Haven't we all agreed that we've heralded the arrival of the messianic age? The rabbi is waiting for the arrival of the Messiah."

Aarons grunted. "I don't think that the U.S. government is willing to wait as long as we Jews have waited for the Messiah to show up."

Yosef was unfazed. "If Rabbi Hanviowitz says wait, we wait. I've never known him to be wrong before."

"He's never seen the messianic age before, either."

There was a knock at the door. Aarons called, "Come in." The door opened and Gary Stephens walked briskly over to him and shook his hand.

"Dr. Aarons, I saw you on the news. Amazing thing you men have done, simply amazing. And these are your cohorts?"

Aarons introduced Stephens to Yosef and Yonatan, and they all took a seat. Stephens looked from man to man and decided the weak link was Aarons. "You are the head of the team, Dr. Aarons?"

"That is technically correct, but we function as equals. In any disagreement, the majority wins." He grimaced at the other two scientists.

Stephens saw the look. He said carefully, "May I assume that you three are of one mind regarding the information you've discovered?"

Yonatan interrupted quickly. "We are of one mind as to its impact on the world."

"That is not what I meant. Are you all agreed that the formula must be withheld from the public?"

Aarons was apologetic. "We have an advisor who cautioned us to keep the formula private for now."

Stephens acted as though he knew nothing about Rabbi Hanviowitz. "Is this some sort of government official to whom you are referring? We can certainly discuss the matter with him."

Yosef shrewdly appraised the American. "I would imagine that you already know whom we refer to, Mr. Stephens. We have not hidden our loyalty to Rabbi Hanviowitz, nor does he hide from the public."

Stephens sprang. "Then why is he absent from this meeting? Surely you alerted him of its importance. Why is he unavailable at a critical moment like this?"

Aarons said defensively, "He has a religious obligation to fulfill. He will be available immediately after that."

Stephens leaned forward in his chair. "Gentlemen, I will be frank. I do know of your religious advisor, and I am concerned that his influence is crossing into territory that is the province of political leadership. We have heard that some of the Arab world is concerned, to put it mildly, with your possession of a brand of energy that could wreck their oil-dependent economies. In turn, much of the world depends on their oil, and they know it. If they should turn the spigots off, the tenuous structure of the world would be in serious jeopardy. Do you understand what forces you three are playing with?"

Yosef took the bowl of his pipe in his hand and pointed the stem upward. "I think the salient question here is, do you know what forces *you* are playing with?"

Abraham adjusted the skullcap on his head. "We have been advised that the time is not ripe to make such an announcement, Mr. Stephens. Our mentor feels that the moment to make such a revelation has not arrived."

"Then why did you make the initial announcement?"

"He felt that it was a preparatory step in the gradual illumination of the world."

Stephens was frustrated with what he felt were nebulous statements. "Just tell me in real and practical terms what your rabbi is waiting for."

Aarons confessed, "He awaits the coming of the Messiah."

"What?"

Aarons saw his two cohorts look at him warningly, but he continued. "I know it sounds crazy, but that's what he says. He says the Messiah is on his way."

Stephens was politic enough not to sneer or scoff. Instead, he asked, "And just how will we know who this Messiah is?"

Yosef looked straight at him. "When the world is at the brink of disaster, his presence will be as clear to the world as if they had taken off their blinders and *seen* for the first time. I believe with perfect faith in his coming." He flashed Aarons a look. "And until that moment, we are silent." He stood up and offered Stephens his hand, and each of the other scientists followed suit. Stephens shook their hands in turn, but he noticed that Aarons avoided his eyes.

As he left he told himself, *That's the one to watch.*

*   *   *

Grant sat in his office and pondered the identity of the shadowy figure in Willie Daniels's dream. He had two goals now: to research the historicity of Jesus and to locate the supposed Marrano Messiah. He checked his watch: 8:55. *Beverly should be here any minute now,* he said to himself. Then he remembered: She had quit three days ago at the hospital.

Grant dialed Beverly's number at home. No answer. Then he dialed Joel's number at home and Michelle answered.

"Hello?"

"Michelle, it's Grant. Is Joel there?"

"I thought he was at work with you. Are you all right, Grant? Joel told me about Matthew. He said you were still in shock."

"I was. I think I'm better now. I can't seem to locate Beverly, though. Do you know where she might be?"

Michelle, worried, said, "I heard she had quit. Is she missing?"

Grant admitted, "I don't know. I just know that she's gone, and I could use her help desperately. If you hear anything from Joel will you let me know?"

"Sure, Grant. I'll keep my ears open." Michelle hung up and Grant paged the desk of his information bureau chief, who answered immediately.

"Barry Levine."

"Barry, this is Grant Tyler. I want ASAP any reference we have made in the last year, as well as any reference you can find anywhere, that has the word Marrano in it. And if anything comes over the wire like that, let me know immediately. Make this the top priority for everyone in your department."

"Yes sir, Mr. Tyler."

Grant wrote a note for Joel informing him that he would be at home if needed, then headed across the hall to Joel's office and left it on Joel's desk. He decided to head for the library, find any books on the subject of the real identity of Jesus, and then head home.

Two hours later, Grant sat at the desk in his study with twelve books about the authenticity of Jesus and started reading. Every two hours, he called the hospital to get an update on Matthew only to hear the recurrent refrain of "No change yet, Mr. Tyler."

*   *   *

Grant read steadily for five days. The only breaks he permitted himself were to eat, sleep, shower, and call his office and the hospital periodically. He learned that Joel had been running the office smoothly and that Matthew was unchanged. As Grant read volume after volume, he was surprised at what he was discovering about Jesus, albeit less shocked after all he had experienced in the previous week.

The sixth day he received a message to call Barry Levine, who had something to tell him about his Marrano search. He dialed, hoping that there was some nugget of information that he could use. He was in luck.

"Mr. Tyler, I'm sorry it took so long to find, but we finally found something."

"Yes, what is it?"

"Remarkably, it happened only a couple of weeks ago. A Catholic church in Brazil was firebombed by someone who claimed that the family that built it were originally Jews, Marranos."

"Why did this take so long to find?"

"The information about the Marranos was in a Brazilian newspaper, but it was buried in the back."

"But a bombing of a church is big news. Especially in Brazil, where there are so many Catholics."

"Well, it did make the front page, but the story was mostly about the fact that a cardinal of the Church, the archbishop of Rio de Janeiro, was giving a speech there at the time, and he was almost killed. That's why they buried the Marrano issue."

"I see."

Levine continued, "I checked into this cardinal. His name is Cardinal Benda Cortes, and he's a pretty feisty guy. Apparently he's famous for standing up to the drug cartel in South America. They've tried to kill him more than once. He has quite a following. So much, in fact, that he is being mentioned as one of the likely people to succeed the pope. I saw a picture of him. He has one *intense* face."

"I'd imagine that you'd look intense, too, if people were trying to kill you."

Levine joked, "Maybe he's got guns of his own hidden under that robe of his."

Grant sat up straight. "What did you say?"

"I said maybe he's got his own guns under that—"

"Robe of his. He was wearing a robe?"

"Sure. Don't all those cardinals wear robes?"

Grant demanded, "What else did you find out about this cardinal?"

"Let me see. I wasn't really thinking about him, Mr. Tyler, just about that Marrano family."

"Barry, I want you and everyone in your department to spend the rest of today finding out everything you can about this man. I mean *everything*. I have a meeting tomorrow in my office, and once you get that information, you interrupt me immediately. Got it? *Immediately.*"

"Yes sir, Mr. Tyler. I'll get everyone on it right away."

"Faster than that, if you can." Grant hung up the phone and wondered to himself, *I'm looking for the Jewish Messiah in the Roman Catholic Church? This is crazy. . . .*

* * *

Beverly Engler was in her car, being screamed at by everyone on the highway. She was in the fast lane, but she was doing the minimum speed allowed and holding up the traffic behind her. As the cars changed lanes to go around her, each driver rolled down his or her window and hurled epithets at her. She was oblivious. She had sat in her hotel room for five days and finally summoned the will to get up, pay the bill and leave on the road to nowhere. Her hands gripped the wheel tightly, and her eyes looked straight ahead. Random thoughts floated through her mind, random memories, random feelings. She gave up any attempt at ordering her thoughts, instead yielding to whatever her mind conjured up.

One sound began to resonate with increasing frequency. It was the sound of twenty thousand people screaming, "WE MUST DESTROY THE OLD TO PREPARE FOR THE NEW!" Disturbed, she tried to force the sound from her mind, but the harder she tried, the more pronounced it became. She then assumed another tack, letting the sound reverberate through her consciousness until it was ready to leave. That didn't work either.

She realized that the statement wouldn't leave because somehow it resonated within her. Armed with that thought, she decided to examine the statement and consider what part of her it reached. She searched herself and found that the moment at the concert had frightened her, but even on its own terms, the statement frightened her in its implications.

"Destroy." The word by itself was unpleasant. She recoiled at the idea of destruction. *Maybe it's because I'm a woman, and women have an urge to create, not destroy,* she thought. But would the very idea of destruction have disturbed her so deeply?

"Destroy the old." Now she felt some progress. She had always treated people older than she with great respect, and she had spent most of her life in love with the library, which was a repository of historical knowledge that implied a reverence for what had gone before.

"Destroy the old to prepare for the new." She had it now. She saw the statement as emblematic of the entire Western culture, with its preference for innovation over excellence, novelty and trendiness over traditional lasting values. *The "new" is all that matters,* she thought. *A society that thirsts for anything new no matter what the cost.*

Her thoughts started to clear now. *We're like children,* she thought. *Like a child who is thrilled with anything new, no matter how transient its value. Like a child who wants immediate gratification. What was the cause of this? When did it start?* To her embarrassment, she answered herself that much of the fault lay with the field of communications, the field she worked in. *We stress the immediacy of everything,* she reflected. *We don't subscribe to the idea that issues and events take time to understand. But,* she argued with herself, *if the public didn't want everything immediately, we couldn't succeed. So why do they want everything so fast?*

A veil was lifted from her vision and she could see clearly. It was death. *The whole society is waiting to die,* she thought. *That's why the insane urgency of everyone's life, with the emphasis on hurrying and saving time, and insisting on immediate gratification. People think they're running out of time. And they think that this is all they'll get—that when they die it's all over.*

She hearkened back to the concert and surmised that some of the kids had turned on the figure of Jesus because they felt betrayed. He had promised to return and fix the world. He hadn't, and now they were angry at him. Their violence was borne out of the bitterness of purposeless lives, lives that somehow knew that the immediate gratification promised them by society was a chimera that was ultimately meaningless. He had promised them a New Testament of love and peace and harmony, and they didn't see any of it. A New Testament . . .

"DESTROY THE OLD TO PREPARE FOR THE NEW!"

Beverly blinked in surprise as a thought came into her head. It was an entirely new thought, and in order for her to assimilate it, she felt she had to stop driving. Snapping herself back to the cars around her, she cut across the lanes of the highway for the shoulder. More drivers blared their horns at her, but Beverly was intent. Reaching the shoulder, she turned the car off and considered what had implanted itself in her mind.

The story of Jesus had been used to destroy the old to prepare for the new, and the new hadn't come. *That* was why the crowd was angry.

She tried to dismiss this thought. But it had a power of its own; suddenly she remembered Grant's trip to Israel. She now had an incredible urge to see him. Gunning the engine, she headed for the nearest exit to turn around. . . .

* * *

Grant convened the meeting with the four executives the next morning at nine o'clock. Perry Lindsay, Dan Bryant, Bill Eldridge and James Wolford all arrived carrying books with them. The executives all knew who Willie Daniels was, and they were surprised when they walked in together and found him seated next to Grant. His presence was understood when Grant explained to them the entire history of his own journey since Becky's death, omitting nothing.

Grant looked around at each man. "We're all on the same footing now. We know that the two words in question refer to a Marrano who may be the Messiah, and the question before us is whether we believe that it is true. The figure of Jesus tends to complicate the issue, but in what I've been reading things are becoming clearer. Anyone here have a problem with a free inquiry into the matter?"

James Wolford spoke first. "It depends on what you mean by 'free inquiry,' Grant. I believe I am the only religious Christian here. For me, Jesus is, was and always will be my personal Savior. No matter what history shows, it's simply a matter of faith. I also believe that we are being led on a certain path right now, and if that path leads to a more loving and tolerant world, Jesus would approve. As long as I'm convinced of that path, I'll go along. Jesus would want me to."

Dan Bryant was matter-of-fact. "I don't think we'd be here unless we were ready to take this question head-on." He looked to the other executives. They nodded.

Grant turned to Willie. "Willie?"

"Mr. Tyler, I'm just here to listen and learn so I can figure out what the heck is going on in my head." The executives nodded knowingly.

"Okay. Here we go. Let's start with the word itself. *Messiah,* or in Hebrew, *Moshiach.* What have all of you discovered about its meaning and origin?"

Wolford was the most clinical of them, and it showed. "I did quite a bit of reading of the Bible and the Prophets, and the first reference is in Leviticus, chapter four, verse three. There the word means anointed, as the term originally meant the high priest or king who was dedicated to achieve God's purpose. After King David was promised by the prophet Samuel that the throne would remain in his family forever, the title meant a righteous king who would liberate the land from the pagans and bring peace and justice to the world. The primary emphasis was on freeing the land from foreign occupation so that the Jews could live in peace and worship God in the proper manner."

Willie asked, "So he wasn't supposed to be God?"

Wolford answered, "Not in Jewish belief. The idea that God would take human form was, and is, anathema to every believing Jew. It would destroy the idea that God is a perfect unity, which is so central to the Jews that the first words a Jew learns as a child and the last words he says before he dies are, 'Hear, O Israel, the Lord our God, the Lord is one.'"

Bryant cut in. "I did some reading, too, and Zechariah said . . . wait a minute. . . ." He opened a book in front of him and put on his reading glasses. "On that day the Lord shall be One, and His name One."

Willie was puzzled. "Then where did the idea of the Messiah being God in human form originate?"

Bill Eldridge was excited now, for this was what had intrigued him. "I read a lot about this. The critical line of demarcation between the Jews and the early Christians was that Jesus died before he had been successful in the Jewish Messianic mission. The Jews were living under Roman occupation at the time, and the Messiah was supposed to free them politically from the Romans so that they could practice the behavior preached by the Torah. Since Jesus failed to free them, the Christians changed the Jewish concept of the Messiah from God's instrument for freeing the Jews *politically* to the Christian concept of freeing them *spiritually*. But if he was supposed to be God's instrument, why would God allow him to be humiliated and murdered? The answer they gave came from an idea common to other religions of the time: like Attis, Osiris or Adonis, he had died and then been resurrected. These religions also believed that their god had been born of a virgin mother, so that idea was ultimately added, too. All these concepts indicated that he was not mortal. From there it was a logical step to deify him."

Lindsay added, "Especially since he would refer to God as 'Father.' For those unfamiliar with Jewish observance, I have a Jewish prayer book here, and they have been addressing God as 'Father' for thirty-five hundred years."

Bryant took the reins. "Okay, so we know that the *Jewish* concept of the

Messiah was not what Jesus turned out to be. The next question we have to answer is: Who was he?"

Grant had been waiting for this question. "He was an Orthodox Jew."

Willie swerved around to stare at Grant. "What?"

Grant said tersely, "You heard me. Jesus was a practicing Jew. He wore tefillin, also called phylacteries in the Gospels, and fringes on his clothes, and he observed the Sabbath."

Willie asked, "What are tefillin?"

"Did you ever see a picture of an Orthodox Jew wearing one small black box attached to his forehead by a band wound around his head and another strapped on his arm while he was praying? Those are tefillin, and inside those boxes are four passages from the Bible that emphasize loving and serving God by observing his commandments."

Willie was confused. "But if he was a practicing Jew, why would the Gospels be so nasty toward the Jews?"

Grant said, "Now we have come around to the central issue. If Jesus was Jewish, why do the Gospels blame the Jews for his crucifixion? And the answer I've found is so obvious that it amazes me that the world didn't cry out long ago. *Jesus was never killed by the Jews, he was killed by the Romans.* What charge was he condemned with? A Roman charge: sedition, leading a Jewish uprising. They even wrote mockingly, 'King of the Jews' above the cross. Crucifixion was a Roman method of execution, never a Jewish one."

Bryant said, "But the Gospels say the Jews tried him for blasphemy."

Grant was in full gear now. "Historically, that makes no sense. It was *never* considered blasphemous to claim you were the Messiah, indeed, the Jews were *waiting* for a man to lead them to freedom. Besides, the accounts of the trial of Jesus are sometimes contradictory and full of historical impossibilities. For example, it is said that he was tried on the eve of Passover. First, there was a law *prohibiting* a trial on a capital charge at night, and second, an even stronger prohibition on a Jewish festival. Not only that, Pontius Pilate is portrayed as the gentle defender of Jesus, when in fact historical record shows that he was relieved by the *Romans,* who were unusually cruel and brutal, for *excessive brutality*."

Wolford blurted, "Why would the writers of the Gospels direct their hatred toward the Jews?"

Grant asked quietly, "Where are you from originally, Jim?"

"You know I'm from Minnesota."

"Where in Minnesota?"

"St. Paul."

Grant leaned back, waiting. Bryant leaned forward in his chair and said slowly, "You're saying that the Gospels got the whole thing from Paul?"

Grant leaned forward again. "Yes, I am. Paul came first. His letters antedate the three Gospels, of which Mark's was the earliest, and the fourth, very different Gospel of John was much later. There is good evidence that he was most likely a Gentile who had converted to Judaism and attached himself to the high priest's office, then broke with them to create a new religion. Paul never met Jesus, so we can't be sure of the accuracy of his testimony. Also, he claimed to be a learned Pharisee, though the Book of Acts states that Paul came from Tarsus, far from Jerusalem, where a learned Pharisee would have been trained. There are basic principles of Pharasaic legal deduction that Paul never exhibits."

Willie asked, "Just who were the Pharisees, anyway?"

"The forerunners of the Orthodox Jews of today. They were scholarly laymen who taught the Torah around Israel. The Sadducees were the Jews who kept the rituals of the Temple and were supposed to be descended from Aaron, the brother of Moses."

Bryant broke in. "So if Paul worked for the high priest's office, as in the Book of Acts, he would more likely be a Sadducee than a Pharisee?"

"Correct. In fact, the high priest had been handpicked by the Romans and the Greeks before them, and the Sadducees were becoming more and more hellenized, to the despair of the Pharisees. There was one towering difference between the two groups."

"What was that?"

"The Pharisees believed in the Oral Law, the Mishnah, passed down orally through the generations as the *explanation* of the written Torah given by God at Mount Sinai. The Sadducees rejected it, insisting on a literal interpretation of the Torah. Because the Pharisees felt that God intended the Torah to be examined by the human mind, they took a more lenient view of the Torah. Therefore disagreements were normal, and a Pharisee persecuting someone for a different *belief* was unheard of."

Wolford saw the parallel. "Back to Jesus again."

"Right. The Pharisees, unlike what Paul says, wouldn't have had a problem with his claiming to be the Messiah. Now, the Sadducees were largely Roman installees and their henchmen, so *they* would have been furious at an attempt to lead an insurrection against Rome."

Eldridge didn't understand. "But if the Sadducees were angry at Jesus for a supposed rebellion, why didn't Paul simply blame them instead of the Pharisees?"

"How would you offer a new religion in a Roman Empire? By indicting the Sadducees, who were allied with Rome, or indicting the Pharisees, who were admittedly hostile to the pagan ways of the Empire? In fact, there is evidence that Jesus, not Paul, may have been the Pharisee."

Wolford looked disturbed. "*That's* turning the story on its head. How do you figure that?"

Grant rubbed his temples; he found his head starting to ache. "The Gospels go to great lengths to indicate that Jesus' healing on the Sabbath was anti-Pharasaic. But if you consult the Pharasaic law books of the period, they make it clear that the saving of a human life takes precedence over *everything else,* which is the practice of Judaism to this day. But the Sadducees, who took a strictly literal view of the Torah, might have been opposed. And Paul's claim to be a Pharisee makes no sense if you consider the unlikelihood of the Sadducee high priest appointing a Pharisee to such a high post."

Perry Lindsay had been silent, listening and watching James Wolford. "James?"

"I'm thinking, Perry. . . . I suppose even if Jesus is my Messiah, he might not be the Jews' Messiah. What the heck, there are millions of Muslims who think of Mohammed as their Prophet, and billions who worship Buddha. There must be more than one path to God. Why shouldn't we let the Jewish people have theirs?"

Lindsay nodded approvingly. "So where does all this leave us? Looking for the Jewish Messiah, a Marrano who might not exist?"

There was a knock at the door and without waiting for an answer, Barry Levine opened it and walked in to the far end of the table opposite Grant. "Mr. Tyler?"

Grant leaned forward. "What have you found?" Then, realizing the others were unfamiliar with Levine, "Gentlemen, this is Barry Levine, head of our information bureau. He's been looking into someone's background for me."

Levine referred to the notes in his hand. "I called Cardinal Benda Cortes's office. He had traveled to the Vatican at the request of the pope."

Wolford looked at Grant, then expostulated, "A cardinal? You're looking for a Marrano, and you think he's a cardinal in the Roman Catholic Church?"

Eldridge joked, "What better place to look?"

Levine, unruffled, continued, "Mr. Tyler, when I called the Vatican, all they knew was that he had left hurriedly five days ago."

"They didn't know how to reach him?"

"They said the only clue was that he had just received a letter marked urgent."

"From Brazil?"

"No. Spain."

All eyes were on Levine.

"Did I screw up something?"

Grant stood up and looked down at Willie and the four executives. "I am going to Brazil. *Now.* I want to see him when he returns. Anyone want to join me?"

One by one, the executives stood and nodded. Willie stood up last. "I'm going too, Mr. Tyler."

Grant understood, but he said, "Not with that game tonight. And what about your wife and your new baby? I don't think so, Willie."

Willie was firm. "I'd like to go, Mr. Tyler. You know I'm supposed to. I'm supposed to help you protect him, remember? Besides, your son is here, too, and *you're* leaving."

Grant had forgotten Matthew. . . . He didn't have an answer. Who would be there for Matthew if he left?

There was a knock at the door. This time the door didn't open. Grant called, "Come in."

Beverly Engler stood in the doorway.

18

Although they sat next to each other, the cardinal and Rissolo had not spoken once during the ten-hour flight from Madrid to Rio de Janeiro. The day before, after Rissolo had stated his belief that Cardinal Benda Cortes was the Messiah, he had asked the cardinal if he should make reservations for them to return to Rio. The cardinal was so anguished that he didn't respond, so Rissolo telephoned the airlines for reservations to fly home the next day. He insisted on paying for a room for the cardinal, the finest in the hotel, so he could get a good night's sleep. When the cardinal protested the extravagance, Rissolo looked at him, eyes shining, and said that every Jew who ever lived would have envied him this opportunity. This remark made the cardinal more tense than ever, and he decided that further conversation with Rissolo would only elicit more talk of his Messianic identity, so he bid Rissolo good night and went to his room to try to sleep.

It was impossible. All night he wondered why Rissolo would conclude that he was the Messiah. He was the descendant of King David, but so were many other Jews. Did Rissolo think that the cardinal was the Messiah because he wanted to feel important by finding him? He dismissed that angle: Rissolo didn't seem like the kind of man who could stomach fakery in any form. He considered many possibilities, but none of them made any sense. Normally, he would have waited patiently until he could see Rabbi Hanviowitz and obtain an answer, but now he was consumed by anxiety and guilt.

His anxiety was due to the uncertainty of just what Rissolo meant by referring to him as the Messiah. Was he supposed to be God? That was impossible. He knew better than anyone else how human he was.

The guilt, though, stemmed from a different source. If Jesus was the Messiah, and it was sacrilegious to say that anyone else could be the Messiah, what if Rissolo were right? He would be displacing Jesus, the object of adoration his entire life. The guilt accompanying this thought was incalculable and overwhelming. The cardinal spent the night tossing and turning in his bed until five in the morning when he finally fell asleep.

*　　*　　*

As they waited for the plane to land, Rissolo finally spoke. "Are you going to see the rabbi?"

The cardinal, startled, took a moment to respond. "I am going to call him first thing tomorrow morning."

"Actually, you can call him tonight. Our day begins at night, you know."

The cardinal was polite but curt. "I hadn't thought of that. Thank you."

Rissolo asked him uncertainly, "Are you angry with me? Have I done something wrong?"

Cardinal Benda Cortes saw the genuine distress on Rissolo's face and forgot his own. He instinctively tried to comfort the suddenly fearful man. His reply was gentle. "No, Rissolo. I am just confused, that's all."

"Wait until you talk with the rabbi. He'll explain everything to you."

The cardinal had an idea. "Would you like to accompany me when I see him?"

The normally gruff man became shy and self-conscious. "I . . . I would be honored . . . but I don't feel I am worthy to participate in the discussion you must have. Just to have been a part of this is enough to justify my existence."

"Are you sure that you won't come? If it weren't for you . . ."

Rissolo reached in his pocket for his wallet and pulled out a picture of himself and his wife, taken many years before. "This was my wife, Monica, before she was diagnosed with multiple sclerosis. The disease gradually left her in a wheelchair, and almost helpless. Despite it, she used to say to me, 'Alfonso, when the Messiah comes it won't matter where you are, just what you've done, so stop worrying about leaving me while you travel to do your work. Just go and do it. Remember, every person that becomes an observant Jew because you helped them discover their Jewish roots brings the Messiah closer. When he arrives, he'll see all the good you've done.'" He put the picture and his wallet back in his pocket. "She died five years ago while I was away in Russia. I told myself that I was only doing the right thing, that my work was in the service of God, and that she had wanted me to pursue it—but when she died while I was away, I was distraught. As much as I wanted to believe I was doing the right thing, a man sometimes needs a tangible sign that what he is doing is right."

"Are you sure that your need for tangible evidence isn't the reason you think I am who you *think* I am?"

Rissolo actually laughed merrily, something the cardinal hadn't imagined was possible. "You know, you're sorely tempting me to attend that meeting just so I can be there when you learn the truth." He saw the serious look on the cardinal's face and sobered. "I'm going to stop at the office on my way home and write all this down for posterity. After you speak with the rabbi, give me a call, okay?"

"Okay."

* * *

Rivkah Hanviowitz opened the door to the synagogue and smiled at the cardinal. "You certainly have a powerful effect on my father, sir, for him to come here directly after shiva was over. When you called this evening, he insisted that he meet you here tonight, even at this hour."

The cardinal smiled back. "He must have a powerful effect on *you* for you to devote yourself to him so completely that you are here, too, Miss Hanviowitz. I think it's wonderful of you to be so devoted."

As the two of them started down the hall to the rabbi's office, Rivkah said, "I am all that he has. My mother died ten years ago. My father would have no one to look after him. And he is so devoted to learning and teaching that I know he would neglect his health."

"And you? Have you plans to have a family of your own?"

"When I meet a man who is worthy of being my father's son-in-law."

They had reached the office and Rivkah started to turn away to the room across the hall. Cardinal Benda Cortes watched her for a moment, then called after her, "And how will you know?"

Rivkah stopped with her hand on the doorknob and looked back at the cardinal. "He will have to be a man whose soul thirsts for Torah and mitzvoth and the rectification of this world." The cardinal watched her enter the room and close the door behind her. Then he knocked on the door to the rabbi's study.

The rabbi called, "Come in."

He entered and saw Rabbi Daniel Hanviowitz seated behind his desk, poring over a volume that looked ancient.

The rabbi looked up and said, "Please sit down. I got your message from Rivkah this evening, and it sounded as though you needed my help. Did you find anything in Spain?"

The cardinal reached inside his cloak and pulled out the document of his family's history. "I found this in Toledo. It's the genealogy of my family." He handed it to the rabbi and sat down across from him.

Rabbi Hanviowitz studied the ancient document for some time. When he looked at the cardinal again, his eyes looked ageless and tranquil. "Did Alfonso say anything to you?"

Cardinal Benda Cortes took a deep breath, then spoke haltingly. "He said that I am the Messiah." He quickly looked away, embarrassed.

The rabbi said quietly, "This must be at odds with everything you ever knew or believed."

"It certainly is." The cardinal got up from his chair and paced around the room. "It's . . . it's crazy. Forgive me for stating the obvious, but I *can't* be the Messiah."

"And why not?"

Startled, the cardinal stammered, "I'm just a man, not a God."

"But that's who our Messiah is supposed to be. A man, not a God. A man who frees the Jewish people from foreign domination and leads them back to Israel so they can practice Torah and mitzvoth, thereby enabling the world to come to the realization of God's presence so the world can live in peace."

"But under what foreign domination do the Jews live now? And how do I fit into this equation? How am I supposed to free them? I'm still in the dark."

Rabbi Hanviowitz handed the cardinal the volume he had been reading. "The piece of the puzzle you're looking for is in this book."

Cardinal Benda Cortes looked up at the rabbi. "The Book of Daniel?"

Rabbi Hanviowitz asked, "How well do you know the Book of Daniel? Have you memorized the Prophets as well as the Five Books of Moses?"

The cardinal nodded.

"Do you remember his explanation of Nebuchadnezzar's dream of the four kingdoms?"

"The image with a head made of gold, chest and arms of silver, lower torso of copper, legs of iron, and feet of iron and earthenware? Daniel said they represented the four kingdoms that would exist before God would establish his kingdom forever."

"Correct. Do you know what those kingdoms were supposed to be?"

"I'm not sure."

"Those were the four kingdoms that would subjugate the Jewish people until we could complete our mission. The first kingdom was the Babylonian Empire, which exiled us and destroyed the First Temple. The second kingdom was the Persian Empire, which succeeded the Babylonians and tried to destroy us in the story of Haman and Esther. The third kingdom was the Greek Empire, and the fourth and last kingdom was the Roman Empire, which tortured our people, destroyed the Second Temple, and exiled the bulk of our people to the distant corners of the Earth, where we awaited the final redemption."

The cardinal protested, "But the Roman Empire crumbled in the late fifth century."

"In name only. The basic structure of the European states is still the same. And, more important . . . some of our sages said that the Roman Empire was later represented by the Roman Catholic Church."

Cardinal Benda Cortes felt his heart thudding within him. "You're saying that the Roman Catholic Church is the last kingdom that is subjugating the Jews?"

"Didn't it ever seem peculiar to you that the Church, which vehemently contended for centuries that the Jews were exiled from Israel until the Second Coming, still denies us Jerusalem, our capital, and demands that it be internationalized? We have allowed open access to all holy places since we captured the city in 1967. Besides, why should a religion whose worship focuses on a figure who lived and died in Israel be centered in Rome? The reason is that it needed to be adopted by the Roman Emperor Constantine in order to make its way in the world."

"But the Church doesn't prevent Jews from being Jews."

"No. But many children who read the Gospels come away with the conviction that the Jews are responsible for their Lord's death. That kind of hatred bred into people has often led to catastrophic consequences for millions of Jews. Someday the Church may decide to look at Jesus differently and examine what he truly said as opposed to what was added to his message. It makes no sense that a man who was said to have preached tolerance and love would hold that those who came to God in other ways would suffer eternal damnation. There must be a way to see him more clearly than that."

The cardinal suddenly remembered the pope's intention to do precisely that, and he became lost in thought. Then he turned back to the rabbi. "But do you think that the Church itself has contributed to anti-Semitism?"

The rabbi looked at the cardinal. "Do you mind a walk across the hall?"

"Not at all."

The rabbi got up from his desk and led the cardinal out of the study and across the hall. Opening the door, he switched the light on and the cardinal saw a small room that had a map of the world covering the three interior walls. All over the map were colored pins sticking in it, with small index cards attached. Some of the index cards were white, and some were blue. The rabbi indicated for the cardinal to go ahead of him and take a look. The cardinal walked over to the long wall directly in front of him, which was dominated by Europe.

Every white card listed a different decree against the Jews by the Church from the years 306 to 1434. They were promulgated by a synod, by one of the Lateran Councils of the pope, or by the Council of Basel, and next to each card was a corresponding decree by the Nazis in the Second World War. There were more than twenty such cards. Examples included the Synod of Clermont's ban on Jews holding public office and the Nazis' similar laws for the civil service, the Third Lateran Council's ban on Jews litigating Christians and the similar ban by the Nazis, the Fourth Lateran Council's making Jews wear a badge and the Nazis' same order, the Synod of Breslau's erection of compulsory Jewish ghettoes and the Nazis' same order in 1939. There were many others.

The blue cards were a list of all the massacres of Jews around the world through history. Not all of them were in reference to the Church. There were massacres in Mexico, when ninety-six Marranos were burned to death in 1649; in the Ukraine, when seventeen hundred Jews were killed in a pogrom in 1919; in England, whence the infamous lie of the blood libel originated in 1144, and later, when a massacre of Jews took place in 1255 and the Jews subsequently were expelled in 1290 by the first European country to expel them. There was a bloody trail left by the Crusaders, who slaughtered more Jews by the thousands on their way to the Holy Land than the infidels they set out to fight. There were the massacres and torture in Italy in 1475 and the forcible baptisms of Italian Jewish children in 1630. There were the massacres led by Chmielnitzki's Cossacks in Poland in 1648, which killed more than one hundred thousand Jewish men, women and children, as well as fifty Jews burned at the stake in France in 1171. The blue cards were everywhere, and the list of massacres around the world and forced conversions to Christianity were unbelievable.

The cardinal went slowly from card to card, reading and memorizing, his insides churning as he read about his ancestors' people—his people—massacred and tortured and exiled from virtually every European country throughout history. And the great bulk of the violence done to Jews had taken place where the Church had held sway. Instead of tears, the cardinal felt rage—a rage at the world for allowing it to happen.

He became aware of something else—something he had deliberately blinded himself to all his life—the inherent anti-Semitism of the New Testament. All his life he had rejoiced that he was in the bosom of Christ, ignoring the Church's insistence that all others were lost.

Now he saw the consequences of the statement from Matthew: "His blood be on us and our children." Millions of men, women and children had been slaughtered in the name of a religion that spoke of love but damned those who differed; spoke of love and allowed a hatred that had led to the slaughter of innocents. He knew that the Christian principles of love had been derived from the Torah. Jesus had said he had not come to abrogate the Torah, and he had often quoted to others the Torah's statements of love from Leviticus. Why had the later Christians promoted the idea that the Jews were ignorant of love and what they themselves had tried to teach the world?

He looked at the myriad of pins representing massacred millions over the centuries. "It's unbelievable," he murmured. He saw the rabbi watching him and suddenly wondered. "Did you lose anyone in the Holocaust?"

Rabbi Hanviowitz was not surprised by the question. "My parents and baby sister Rivkah were murdered in Auschwitz. My sister was our jewel. My daughter is named for her. She had been the gift my mother was given at the age of forty after raising three teenage sons. When the guards found out that my mother was hiding my sister under her cloak, they pulled out my sister, who was eighteen months old, and shot her to death on the ground in front of my mother. Then they clubbed my mother to death. My father, brothers and I were witnesses."

The cardinal was shaken. "How could you remain a believer in God after that?"

"God did not kill my family. The Nazis did. Although my younger brother, who died last week in America, lost all belief in God."

"What about your other brother?"

"My older brother Eliyahu lives in Israel. He is the Gadol Hador, the leading rabbi of this generation."

"So in spite of your history, you remain a religious man."

"Should I let Hitler or the anti-Semites of the world win by erasing my identity?" The rabbi walked up to the cardinal. "And how about you? According to Jewish law, you are a Jew because of your ancestry. Or are you a Catholic because you were baptized? It's your choice, you know. We are all responsible for choosing who we want to be."

The cardinal said, "Yet you are telling me I am not only a Jew, but I also could be the Messiah. Even if it's true that Jesus was not the Jewish conception of the Messiah, what makes you think it could be me?"

"First of all, I have no doubt that we are living in the messianic age. It was prophesied to us two thousand years ago that in the age of the Messiah, we would once again be in control of our ancient homeland. Who could have predicted that the empires of Babylon, Persia, Greece, Rome, and Islam all would come and go and one ancient people—one tiny people—would survive them all and return to Israel despite the centuries of murder and persecution?

"Second, our mission was always to perfect our society in the land of Israel to function as an example for other nations. But until the late twentieth century, mass communication around the world was unheard of, and such a society would have gone unnoticed. But now, *any* society that became a model of justice and compassion would command the world's attention.

"Third, the world has tried to eradicate us time and time again. We have had few defenders, few allies who unequivocally stand by our side so that we can fulfill our destiny. At best, we have had those who temporize so we can exist temporarily in their grace, before their agenda differs and we become outcasts once again. Much of the world doesn't want a living reminder from *anyone* on how to behave, how to serve God in love and peace. In truth, there are countless nonobservant Jews who encourage anti-Semites by *ignoring* their duty, because the world is aware of how we define our role and they leap at the chance to point out how badly a Jew behaves. But there is a strong possibility you could be the next pope. Imagine what it would be like for the titular leader of the world's largest faith to command that its adherents and its derivatives, the entire Christian world, fulfill the wishes of Jesus by becoming not the *persecutors*, but the *protectors* of the Jews so they could return and make Israel into the model society that was foretold."

The adrenaline racing in his blood left Isaac Benda Cortes's hands trembling and his face on fire. He saw the parallels between his own crisis of identity and the crisis of modern Christianity. If *he* struggled with the choice between his historical identity and the identity given him as a child, how much more tortuous was it for Christianity to reconcile the basic anti-Semitism of its beliefs with the Jewishness of Jesus? Was it his destiny to repair the damage of two thousand years of hatred? Even if it was, there was one gigantic dilemma. "But if I am a Jew, I cannot be a part of the Church."

"That is absolutely true."

"Then how can I possibly do both? How can I be a Jew and still lead the Church to its rightful mission?"

"I would suggest that you answer the first question first. To be a Jew, you must study Torah. We have always believed that every question has its answer in the Torah. Not to mention that if you decide that you *are* a Jew, you'll have a better idea of what a Jew *is*. Then, who knows? Perhaps you were destined to be the leader and deliverer of your people."

The sound of his mother's voice echoed in his mind.

"You are going to be the leader of your people."

* * *

The telephone rang in Alfonso Rissolo's office.

The three men surrounding the man who was tied and gagged in the chair looked at each other, then silently motioned to let it continue ringing. They continued to whisper in the ear of the man who was tied up, and every so often they used a small blowtorch on his body, causing him to writhe in agony and strain violently against the rope binding him to the chair.

The men whispered even though it was late at night, for they had been instructed by Cesar Carlos that if anyone saw or heard them at their work they would be dealt with severely. They looked with disgust at the half-dead man in the chair.

It was Rissolo. He had stopped at his office on his way home, jubilant with the turn his life had taken. Whistling, he opened the door, only to be pinioned and chloroformed by two huge men and then bound to his chair. Even though he had been in danger before, when he regained consciousness something told Rissolo that this might be worse, for his office had been ransacked and the men were completely silent. Finally, the small man accompanying the two huge ones leaned over, removed the gag and whispered in his ear, "We want to know where you've been, Rissolo."

"Who wants to know?"

The small man pulled out the blowtorch. "My friend here. But he gets impatient when I seem to lose my own personal charm. Can we talk?"

Rissolo was frightened, and he didn't hide it. His heart was pounding. "Please . . . don't hurt me. I didn't mean to argue with you."

"Good. Now tell me where you've been."

"I just came back from Spain."

"Where in Spain?"

"Toledo."

"And why were you visiting Toledo, Spain?"

"To do research. I . . . I am a historian of sorts."

The small man smiled. "Yes, we know. Find anything interesting?"

Rissolo was shocked to hear himself say, "No."

"Really? You found nothing? . . . Anyone go with you?"

Rissolo wondered, how much do they know already? "No one went with me."

"You were all alone there? Too bad. So, you went alone and found nothing. That's a disappointing trip. Sort of cold and lonely." The small man turned on the blowtorch.

Rissolo's eyes started to water.

"My employer said that I should tell you that we know of your secret meeting with Cardinal Benda Cortes at the stadium. We need one small piece of information, that's all. Just what did you find in Toledo, Spain?"

Rissolo's voice was strangled. His forehead felt cold and clammy. He saw the blowtorch and was ready to tell them anything, anything they wanted to know. "What is it you want? Who wants to know? I'll tell you . . . just don't hurt me."

The small man looked at the others and muttered, "The courageous killers of Christ." Then he looked back contemptuously at the terrified man and made a colossal mistake. He asked, "What did you find in Spain, Jew?"

*   *   *

Cardinal Benda Cortes and Rabbi Hanviowitz sat back in the rabbi's study while the cardinal waited for Rissolo to answer the telephone. He had promised to tell him of his conversation with the rabbi, and he waited patiently through ring after ring. The rabbi watched him, worried that Rissolo hadn't answered. Just when the cardinal was ready to hang up, he heard a banging as though the receiver had fallen to the floor. Then it was quickly hung up. He turned to the rabbi.

"Something's wrong. I heard someone pick up and then immediately hang up."

"Is it possible that he picked up the telephone and then something happened? Perhaps a heart attack or something of that sort?"

The cardinal thought quickly. "How far is it to his office?"

"About a five-minute ride. Rivkah knows the way."

"You go with her. I'll follow you in my car."

*   *   *

Ten minutes later, the cardinal, the rabbi and Rivkah were climbing the stairs to the second floor of Rissolo's building. The rabbi had two keys Rissolo had given him, one for the building and one for the office just in case he ever needed access. As they reached the second floor and started down the hall, a terrible smell wafted toward them.

The cardinal held his nose. "What *is* that?" He saw Rivkah holding her nose and almost laughed. Then he saw Rabbi Hanviowitz's face, which had gone white.

The rabbi stood motionless, remembering. "I know that smell. . . . I *know* that smell!" He started running down the corridor toward the office, frantically fumbling for the key as he ran. The cardinal and Rivkah looked at each other, startled, then ran after him. They caught up with him just as he reached the door to Rissolo's office. The smell now was almost overpowering.

Rabbi Hanviowitz had the key in the lock but he couldn't turn it; the lock had been jammed. He pounded on the opaque glass window in the door, trying vainly to see through it.

Cardinal Benda Cortes looked around in a frenzy and saw a fire extinguisher at the end of the hall inside a glass case. Running to the case and finding it locked, he smashed his fist through the glass and pulled the fire extinguisher out. Ignoring his bloody hand, he ran back to the rabbi and Rivkah and hurled the extinguisher through the window, shattering it.

The stench that poured out of the window sent them all reeling. The cardinal then realized what the smell was and why the rabbi had been the only one who had recognized it. He had been in Auschwitz.

It was the smell of burned flesh.

The cardinal climbed through the window, his back blocking the view from outside. What he saw made him remain where he was so the rabbi and Rivkah could not see it, too.

Alfonso Rissolo lay naked on the floor next to the telephone, bound and gagged, with his skin charred from his neck to his feet. There was a trail of blood from his right ear where it had been partially severed. The cardinal didn't understand the significance of that until he followed the trail of blood and saw what was on Rissolo's desk and the wall behind it. His body started shaking.

On the wall was a huge cross painted in Rissolo's blood. On the desk was a blood-stained coffee cup that had been filled with the blood from the severed ear. And on the wall under the cross in small letters was written: *From Carlos To Cortes.*

The cardinal managed to say over his shoulder, "Rabbi . . . get Rivkah out of here quickly. Take the car and go home . . . hurry!" The rabbi said something behind him, and the cardinal heard the sound of Rivkah's heels as she ran down the hall. The cardinal reached down for the telephone to call the police. As he bent down, he heard a cry from behind him and he whirled around to see the rabbi still at the door, seeing the bloody cross on the wall and the message underneath it.

The cardinal quickly started to dial the telephone, then stopped. He realized something: The police would not cross Cesar Carlos. Although they would come for the body, no justice would be done. He looked down at the dead man and then knelt beside him.

"Forgive me . . . forgive me."

*　　*　　*

Six hours later, after calling the police and waiting for them to claim the body, after the rabbi tried to console him all night, the cardinal sat at his desk in his office in the early morning light. He felt responsible for Rissolo's death, and he now believed that the rabbi was also at risk, though the rabbi had said that he felt he was a part of the cardinal's destiny and no physical threat would stop him from learning Torah with the cardinal.

What could he do? How much could he fight alone? If even someone as removed from Catholicism as Cesar Carlos used the cross, how could he possibly change the institution whose members regarded it as sacred? Beyond that, how could he convince a world that could harbor a Cesar Carlos of the importance of what he had to say?

He felt alone. More alone than frightened of Carlos. His death, however it occurred, didn't frighten him so much as having lived with an opportunity to rectify the world and failing to do so. He was enormously tired, and, though he had told the rabbi that he would meet him that evening, he was ready to give up . . . give up everything and hide from the world.

Outside, he heard car doors slam and men's voices, and he didn't even attempt to go to the window and see who it could be this early in the morning. He waited stoically at his desk for Carlos's men to find him and end his journey.

There was a knock at the door. The cardinal laughed grimly to himself, *They're going to kill me and they knock first?* He bowed his head and called, "Come in."

A determined-looking man with a face chiseled out of granite entered and walked up to him. "You are Cardinal Isaac Benda Cortes?"

The cardinal exhaustedly nodded.

"My name is Grant Tyler."

Book Three

19

The cardinal looked up. "Grant Tyler? Are you the Tyler who heads the news network?"

"The same."

"Can I help you?"

Grant studied the man in front of him, noticing the exhaustion, the weariness. How should he begin? "I hope so. I have come to Brazil just to meet you, Your Eminence, and possibly offer my support."

Cardinal Benda Cortes, startled that Tyler had heard of Rissolo's death so soon, said, "I didn't think news could travel that fast, even in this day and age. How did you find out?"

Grant thought the cardinal was referring to the discovery Grant had made of his messianic identity. "It's a long story, Your Eminence."

Puzzled, the cardinal said, "I don't understand, this just happened last night."

Grant, ever the newsman, asked bluntly, "What are you talking about?"

"What are *you* talking about?"

"*I'm* talking about your mission. What are *you* talking about?"

Grant thought, *This might be a big mistake. . . . I might have the wrong man.*

There was only one way to find out and one question to ask and Grant knew what it was.

"Forgive me, Your Eminence, but I may have made a mistake. I have just one question for you."

The cardinal sat back, waiting. "Yes?"

"Are you the descendant of Marranos?"

Cardinal Benda Cortes sat forward so quickly that his elbow hit the telephone on his desk and knocked it to the floor. He reached over, picked it up and replaced it on his desk and sat straight again. His face felt hot and flushed, and he saw Grant looking at him steadily. "Why do you ask me that?"

"Because if you are, I think I know who you are, and if I'm right, I'm here to offer anything you need in order for you to achieve your goal."

"Who do you think I am if I am indeed the descendant of Marranos?"

Grant was exultant. He *was* right. "The Messiah." He saw the cardinal looking at him skeptically.

"Are you Jewish, Mr. Tyler?"

"No. Which is even more reason that I'm sure I'm right, if your answer to my question is yes. Is it?"

The cardinal felt a faint hope rising in him that Tyler really knew what he was talking about. He was too tired to evade the truth any longer. "Yes, I am the descendant of Marranos."

Grant leaped to his feet and strode around the room excitedly. He turned and looked back at the cardinal. "You know what I'm referring to, don't you, Your Eminence?"

There was a grim smile in return. "I ought to, I've had enough people telling me." The cardinal suddenly took the initiative. "Please sit down, Mr. Tyler. Please sit down."

Grant reseated himself.

"How do you know who I am? How do you know so much?"

"I suppose I should start at the beginning."

"That always helps."

"It started when my wife, Becky, was dying. . . ."

*   *   *

Outside the cardinal's office, in the waiting room, Perry Lindsay, Dan Bryant, Bill Eldridge, James Wolford and Willie Daniels sat silently. They hadn't spoken since Grant had entered the office thirty minutes before, and they tacitly agreed not to knock and interrupt whatever was transpiring inside.

The door swung open and a grim-faced Grant stood before them. They all looked to him, silently asking him the one question for which they had come five thousand miles to find an answer. Grant understood. He nodded and beckoned them to enter the office. None of them could fathom why Grant looked so forbidding if they had indeed been successful in their quest. They found enough chairs around the room to form a half-circle facing the cardinal's desk.

None of them was surprised by his face, for they had seen his picture. What did catch some of them unaware was his wiry build and relatively small stature. For some reason, the fact that this man was possibly the man who would save the world had made them think of him as larger than life, and, therefore, great in physical stature. Willie had been one of the surprised ones, and then he laughed to himself and thought, *Einstein was no giant, either.*

Grant introduced them one by one. Each man nodded to the cardinal when he was introduced. When he finished, Grant spoke quietly.

"Gentlemen, I have informed Cardinal Benda Cortes of everything we have experienced and everything we have researched so he would understand why we came to see him. I had assumed that what we discovered was something that he already knew. I was wrong. The discovery of his own identity as a Jew, a descendant of Marranos, occurred for the cardinal concurrently with our own recent experiences. There have been fatal consequences already. In order for you to understand the gravity of the present situation, the cardinal has decided that you should know everything he has undergone in the past two weeks."

The cardinal started at the beginning, from the firebombing of the church and the Ganedoses' home to his encounter with Dominic that night, to his subsequent meetings with Father Antonio and Pablo de Cardoso, to his remembrance of his mother's lighting of the Sabbath candles and his journey home to discover the hidden closet his mother had used for the ritual, to his mother's death, to his call to Rabbi Hanviowitz and their discussion of his ancestry that night, resulting in his call to Rissolo, to the sudden summons from the Vatican and the pope's stunning revelation that he intended to reexamine the truth of who Jesus truly was, to Rissolo's urgent letter to him in Rome, to the trip to Toledo and the accidental finding of the document tracing his lineage to King David, to Rissolo's awed reaction and conviction that he was the Messiah, and, finally, to his meeting the night before with the rabbi, where everything was explained to him.

He paused, in pain, before concluding with the story of Rissolo's torture and death, and the bloody message from Cesar Carlos on the wall.

No one moved. Grant waited until he was sure the cardinal had finished, then spoke. "As you may have already realized, my Rabbi Hanviowitz and the cardinal's are brothers. The third brother was Mike Hanvill, as you know. I don't believe in coincidences anymore, and the series of events we have all gone through allows very little room for doubt. One giant factor in the equation that we haven't discussed is the discovery of cold fusion, which in its inexhaustability could make it possible for the world to become prosperous beyond any of our dreams. That solves the long-standing problem of poverty across the world. All that would be left would be a system whereby a just society could be created, a moral guide for the world. We can end irrational hatred around the world by starting with the most widespread kind in the world—anti-Semitism. Even the present pope seems to be headed down that path."

Dan Bryant said thoughtfully, "I agree that this is what we are meant to do. But His Eminence has incurred powerful enemies already. There are obstacles."

James Wolford concurred. "I have already faced death, so the physical threat matters less to me than it did previously. What concerns me is this: If Carlos knows about the cardinal's heritage, can he use it somehow to destroy his reputation?"

Bill Eldridge had been thinking about the Vatican. "And what if the pope dies and someone else is chosen as his successor? I don't see many other cardinals who would agree to review the beliefs of the last two thousand years."

Perry Lindsay allowed himself a look at the cardinal's face, where he saw indecision. "Gentlemen, His Eminence hasn't even agreed to lead our mission."

"He's got to!"

Willie Daniels rose to his feet and gripped the desk with his hands, leaning over to face the cardinal. "You've *got* to, sir. I have a son. He's just a few days old, and I don't want him growing up in a world where irrational hatred exists. I don't want him growing up in a world where a man is judged by the color of his skin, like my ancestors, or the faith of his people, like yours. You've got to *try,* sir."

The cardinal was aware that everyone was waiting for his response, but he didn't know what to say.

Grant realized that although ultimately the cardinal was the captain of their destiny, Grant himself was the catalyst, the force that would enable them to achieve their goal. He needed to clear the path, to have everyone unload himself of whatever baggage he carried so they could move inexorably forward. He asked the cardinal, "We know you have doubts, Your Eminence, or else you would not be hesitant. Why don't you state your concerns and see if we can address them."

Cardinal Benda Cortes said slowly, "I think we are missing one vital cog in our machinery, don't you?" The executives were puzzled, but Grant knew at once what the cardinal meant.

"You mean Rabbi Hanviowitz?"

"Precisely."

Perry Lindsay said, "Let's call him and get him over here right away."

Grant held up his hand. "I think we should do him the honor of going to him, don't you think?" The cardinal looked at Grant, measuring him, and, liking what he saw, he reached for the telephone.

*   *   *

Rivkah Hanviowitz opened the front door to the modest home. She looked exhausted and frightened, but she managed a wan smile when she saw the cardinal. Her eyes widened as he entered followed by Grant and the five men behind him, but the cardinal reassured her with a look and a nod. She ushered them into the living room where Rabbi Hanviowitz rose from his chair to greet them. He spoke to the cardinal first.

"Have you had any sleep?"

"A little."

Rabbi Hanviowitz gestured to the worn chairs and sofa around the coffee table. "Please sit down, gentlemen. I apologize for my exhaustion; the cardinal and I were part of a terrible tragedy last night."

Grant said as everyone was seated, "We know, Rabbi Hanviowitz. I should introduce myself and my friends. I am—"

"Grant Tyler. I know who you are, Mr. Tyler. After Cardinal Benda Cortes called me half an hour ago, my brother called from Israel. We hadn't spoken since a week ago when he informed me of our brother's deathbed repentance and we subsequently observed shiva. He told me that you and others were looking for a Marrano who could be the Messiah, so when the cardinal called and said he was bringing foreign visitors who had reached the same conclusion we had, I guessed it might be you. Who are your friends?"

Grant introduced the five men, then came right to the point. "Rabbi, all of us feel that Cardinal Benda Cortes is the man that we have been sent to find. Apparently, he has some doubts himself. He then suggested, and we agreed, that your presence would be crucial for our mission."

"I am honored." He painfully shifted in his chair to face the cardinal. "Can you articulate your concerns, Cardinal?"

The cardinal felt oddly uncomfortable by the way he was addressed. He surprised himself by asking shyly, "May I make a request?"

The men replied, "Sure . . . certainly . . . of course . . ."

"In present company, can I be addressed as Isaac? That is my Jewish name, and I would like to try it and see how it feels." The men seemed pleased with the cardinal's suggestion, since it implied that he was leaning toward accepting their mission.

Isaac said, "Now, for my concerns. Most important, I feel the danger of failure. To ask the world to rid itself of a hatred that it has nurtured for thousands of years is a mammoth job. I certainly cannot do it alone. Even if I can purify the Church of its prejudice and intolerance—and I am still not sure whether I would do so as a Catholic or a Jew—the world beyond the Church has taken anti-Semitism to its heart and nourished it. People who have never even seen Jews hate them. How do I address such irrationality? And if I fail, will the world's hatred and murder of Jews increase instead of abate?"

Rabbi Hanviowitz interrupted. "And you are not acknowledging the most important part of the puzzle."

Grant raised his eyebrows. "What's that?"

"The Jews themselves. Bullies traditionally pick on those who portray themselves as victims, since they instill no fear in their oppressors."

Perry Lindsay said, "Wait a minute, Rabbi. I don't know many tougher people in the world than the average Israeli."

"Forgive me, I didn't make myself clear. They may be *tough,* but the majority of Israelis are not *religious.* Anyone can say 'I am going to stand up and fight.' The question is not one of *physical* courage, but of *spiritual* courage. What matters is not that a Jew won't be bullied physically, but that every Jew rid himself of the self-hatred that comes from being an oppressed nation for the past two thousand years; that every Jew learn what it means to be a Jew, a practicing Jew, an observant Jew, to realize that God did not make him a Jew by accident, but placed his *neshama,* his soul, in a Jewish body to obey the mitzvoth, to act as an example of how to sanctify God's name. *That's* the biggest challenge of all."

Grant thought of Joel Alexander. How would he convince Joel, who went to synagogue grudgingly twice a year on Rosh Hashanah and Yom Kippur, to keep all the commandments? The rabbi was right. The job of convincing recalcitrant Jews *was* probably harder than ridding the anti-Semites of their mindless prejudice.

Willie asked, "How would *you* convince your people, Rabbi?"

The rabbi responded, "I am a practical man. Remove the hatred of the Jews from the world, and I believe that we will all return to our destiny. That was the original plan with Yaakov and Esav."

Isaac was curious. "Jacob and Esau? How does that fit in here?"

Rabbi Hanviowitz said, "Our sages say that Esau was the progenitor of Edom, which later was Rome, and still later manifested itself as the Roman Catholic Church. Esau, the physically strong one, was supposed to be the protector of Jacob, the scholar and teacher of spiritual matters. But Esau ultimately wound up hating Jacob, and his hatred lasts to this very day."

Bill Eldridge interjected, "But I thought Jacob stole Esau's birthright, and that's what caused Esau's hatred."

The rabbi quoted from memory. "*'V'Yaakov nasan l'Esav lechem unzid adashim.'*"

Aramaic was similar enough to Hebrew for Isaac to recognize the verse from the Book of Genesis, chapter 25. "'Then Jacob gave to Esau bread and pottage.'"

Rabbi Hanviowitz smiled sadly. "There, in a nutshell, is one of the most basic reasons for our troubles: people mistranslating our Scripture. 'Jacob gave' in Hebrew is **VaYisen Yaakov**, not *V'Yaakov nasan*. The correct translation is, 'And Jacob *had given* to Esau bread and pottage,' thus explaining that Jacob had fed Esau *before* they discussed the sale of the birthright. Esau sold the birthright *after* he had been fed, so he was under no duress, which makes the end of the tale, that 'Esau despised his birthright,' explicable, and negates the idea that Jacob 'stole' anything. Unfortunately, that is only one of many mistranslations of the Torah that has been used to justify anti-Semitism."

Isaac mused, "I can't believe so many anti-Semites could be so determined for so long."

Grant countered, "It's the other way around, Isaac. How could your people be determined so long?"

Rabbi Hanviowitz's eyes were clear. "Our existence against all odds is a living testimonial to God's existence. The question is, how do we enlighten the world so people will seek to protect us instead of kill us?"

Everyone reflected on the rabbi's last words for a few moments. James Wolford was the first to venture his thoughts, attempting to summarize the obstacles they faced. "We have discussed four different impediments to our common goal: the apparent mortal threat to the cardinal from the drug cartel, their knowledge of his background and its effect on his influence within the Church, the possibility that another, less sympathetic pope will succeed the present pontiff, and the reluctance of secular Jews around the world to return to the tenets of their faith. Can we surmount all these?"

Dan Bryant suggested, "As far as the first problem, what if we had a security team 'round the clock for Isaac?"

Isaac was normally a fatalist about his mortality, but now he felt an obligation to the others to survive. Not only that, but if he was studying with Rabbi Hanviowitz, the rabbi was in jeopardy, too. He said, "I have made plans to learn with the rabbi. He'll need protection, too."

Bill Eldridge was suspicious of hiring anyone local. "I would suggest that if we hire a security team, we hire men from the States whom we can vouch for. Someone local would have family that the cartel can threaten. And I wouldn't trust the local governments for the same reason."

Bryant agreed. "Good point. I can get friends who are ex-marines to help us put together a team. I could have a team here in three days."

Willie asked, "But what do we do until then?"

Grant interceded. "I suggest that we contact the newspapers and the government and advertise the fact that the five of us are here to visit the cardinal. That ought to hold the cartel until the security team is assembled and ready. I think between the five executives here we can find the money to pay for them." He eyed the executives. "Am I correct?"

They all nodded.

Wow, Willie thought. *Talk about putting your money where your mouth is.*

Bryant continued. "Problem two: Can the cartel destroy Isaac's chances by revealing his Jewish ancestry even if he remains a Catholic?"

James Wolford was dubious. "First, you're assuming that they know of Isaac's heritage, which we cannot prove because the only person who could have told them is dead. Second, even if they do know, how would they influence the Church? I would think that the two entities are mortally opposed to each other."

Grant knew better. "I've heard stories that the cartel has given money for churches to be built. If that is true, they may be more friendly than we think. The other option for the cartel is to simply inform the newspapers of what they know and let public reaction do the rest."

Rabbi Hanviowitz turned to Isaac. "I know nothing about the inner workings of the Church. Could this be an insurmountable obstacle?"

Isaac had been staring out the window. "I don't think we have any control over this issue. My own feeling is that the series of events we have all experienced indicates that the issues we *can* control we *should;* let's leave the others in God's hands. I believe we should also leave in God's hands the third problem, the chance that the pope may be succeeded by someone hostile to changing the Church."

To everyone's surprise, it was Willie who challenged Isaac's statement. "Forgive me, Isaac, but I don't agree with you. In my business, I see the power of the press every day. I don't believe that the Church is unaware of public sentiment. And because of that, I believe that a media campaign that illustrated how you have publicly confronted evil could stir the Catholic world to clamor for your nomination to the papacy. Even if you decided you were a Jew and had to decline the position, you might wield enough influence to demand changes. Furthermore, perhaps the same power of the press could address the fourth problem: how to reach the Jews around the world and convince them to become what God intends them to be."

All eyes turned toward Grant, who thought the magnitude of the job was incalculable. Then he was remembering . . .

Connect the dots. This was what Becky was talking about. Can I do it, Becky? Can I really do it?

What else had she said? There was something else. . . .

You need to go now.

He had assumed that she had meant for him to leave the room. But she had died immediately after that. She was the one who was leaving. What had she meant?

You need to go now and connect the dots.

*I understand, Becky. . . . I understand. I will go **now** and connect the dots.*

The group of men saw Grant's expression grow fierce as he looked at Isaac and Rabbi Hanviowitz—an expression that brought them all straight up in their chairs.

Was the job too big for any *man?* they wondered.

Grant gave them his answer: "May my efforts sanctify God's name."

20

Pablo de Cardoso sat at the kitchen table, eating his breakfast and reading the newspaper. The front page was dominated by the continuing world reaction to the discovery of cold fusion. Even though it had been two weeks since the initial announcement, stock markets around the world were still fluctuating wildly because of the projected effect on the world economy. Overtures were coming in fast and furious to the Israeli government from many poor Third World countries that had spurned Israel for years.

Pablo wasn't interested; his mind was somewhere else. He wondered whatever happened with Cesar Carlos's investigation of Alfonso Rissolo. Carlos had guaranteed Pablo the widest possible access and publicity for the story of the cardinal's Jewish ancestry, and Pablo had subsequently declined to cover two local stories for his newspaper, feeling lazily confident that his ship was about to come in. He turned to his favorite section of the paper, the obituaries. He enjoyed reassuring himself that while others had died, he was still alive and enjoying the pleasures of life. He scanned the list to see if he knew any of the deceased. Then he saw the name: Rissolo, Alfonso.

He's dead! he screamed to himself. *The only witness I had!* He started frantically looking through the paper for the story of what happened but found nothing. As he reached for the telephone to call the paper and ask who had filed the obituary, the telephone rang.

"Hello?"

"De Cardoso? This is Carlos."

Even though it was first thing in the morning, Pablo's armpits started to sweat. "Good morning."

"You have seen the obituaries this morning?"

Keep it simple, Pablo. Just tell the truth. "Yes."

"I would imagine that you're wondering if we extracted any useful information from Rissolo before he died."

"Uh . . . yes, I was."

". . . or even if we had something to do with his death?"

Pablo said quickly, "More the former than the latter."

"The answer to the first question is yes, we did get some information from Rissolo, but only after he was quite resistant to our forms of persuasion. My men felt that they didn't get everything out of him, that he held something back. But we got enough: Our interrogative methods are successful, if a bit enthusiastic. Which inevitably leads us to the answer to the second question, which is, of course, yes. As a matter of fact, we gave him chance after chance, but he proved to be unusually intransigent—until just before the end."

Pablo felt his chest tighten, and it became harder to breathe.

"Are you there, de Cardoso?"

"Yes . . . I'm here."

"Don't you want to know whether your suspicions about the cardinal's ancestry were correct?"

"Yes . . . yes, I do."

"Luckily for you, you were accurate in your hypothesis. Rissolo confessed that the cardinal is indeed the product of Jewish ancestry. Just before the end he also mentioned a word that you had used in your article about the church bombing."

"What word was that?"

"Marrano."

"That was in reference to the family that built the church. They were descendants of Marranos, the Jews who converted to the Church during the Spanish Inquisition."

"This Rissolo said the word just before he died. My men said he had another word on his lips, but he would not say it."

Pablo's mind was at war with itself. On the one hand, he was shaken by what he imagined had happened to Rissolo before he died, and by his own involvement and guilt; on the other hand, he was relieved and a little excited about the story he would now be able to tell and the notoriety he could receive. He tried to find a middle ground between the two ideas crowding his mind, but there was none.

If the ends justified the means, how did writing the story and thus denying the cardinal the papacy absolve Pablo of Rissolo's death? He was part of a murder now, and for the first time in his life, Pablo was afraid of the possibility of a heavenly judgment. Was he just an assassin like Dominic, the bomber of the church and the Ganedos family? Or was he worse, because Dominic was only trying to purify the Church, whereas Pablo wanted to be rich and famous, too. *Forgive me, Jesus, forgive me. It was my own ego. What do I do now? Go to confession? I haven't done that since I was a kid! And where should I confess? To the cardinal?* At this thought, his old hatred and jealousy of the cardinal resurfaced. Then a sudden idea captured him.

Wait a minute . . . purify the Church . . . that's it . . . this Jewish cardinal wasn't a Catholic, he was masquerading as one. I've got this all backwards! He's the one who wants to destroy the Church, not me! If I prevent him from becoming the pope I'm the one saving the Church! I only did what I had to do because I was supposed to save the Church, and all my hostility toward it throughout my life was preordained so I could save the Church!

"De Cardoso?"

"Yes, yes. I'm here. What do we do next? Should I write the story immediately?"

"Yes, write it right away, and then send it to me so I can see if it needs changes"—Pablo winced—"before I contact my friends in the newspapers." Carlos gave de Cardoso his fax number. "Write everything you know. Better too much than too little." Carlos paused. "And, Pablo . . ." Pablo was pleased to hear Carlos address him so intimately.

"I'll make sure you are properly compensated."

"Thank you." Carlos hung up, and Pablo thought, *It isn't the money anymore.* He laughed at himself. *I'm going to be the hero of the Roman Catholic Church!*

* * *

Carlos pressed a button on his telephone that dialed a number automatically. Carlos had learned Italian for one purpose, to enable him to speak directly to the man he was calling.

"Hello?"

"This is Cesar Carlos calling for don Sanguino."

"One moment, please." Carlos waited patiently.

"Carlos?"

"Yes, don Sanguino. I have some interesting information for you."

Sanguino was twenty years older than Carlos, but he had great respect for Carlos's achievements, and they had worked together for years. They were often threatened by a common enemy—usually a government that hindered their shipments of drugs—and Sanguino's knowledge of Europe and Carlos's knowledge of the Americas led to a successful cross-pollination of ideas.

"What have you learned?"

"You know of the many times we have talked of this Cardinal Benda Cortes and the threat to our futures that he poses? I think we have found a way to bury him."

Sanguino couldn't resist the opening. He sighed, "One can hope. He seems to have been quite invulnerable from your attempts to bury him up until now, hasn't he?"

Carlos scowled. "I think we have found a fatal flaw in our nemesis, and it requires no active physical assault on the man. It is a piece of information that ruins any hopes he has of ascending to the papacy."

Sanguino sat forward in his chair. "Interesting. Just what have you discovered?"

"The man is the descendant of Marranos."

Sanguino knew his history. "The Jews from Spain? This cardinal is a Jew?"

"That's correct. Can you imagine the Church selecting someone as the pope knowing he was a Jew? It's unthinkable."

"Are you sure that this is true?"

"We obtained the information from the man who apparently confirmed the cardinal's ancestry for him."

"Where is this man now?"

"Unfortunately, he died under questioning."

"That is unfortunate."

"Still, it was reliably obtained. I have a reporter who has all the information and is writing the story as we speak. I called you because you understand the workings of the Church far better than I do. My question to you is, should we publish this story right away or delay a bit?"

Sanguino thought. "I need to discuss this with my contact inside the Vatican. Give me a day or two and then I'll call you back."

"Fine." Carlos grinned. "God does work in mysterious ways, doesn't he?"

Sanguino grunted. "It doesn't hurt to help him along, either. We will speak soon, my friend." Carlos hung up and Sanguino dialed the Vatican.

"Cardinal Scoglio, please."

*   *   *

President Evans sat in the Oval Office in the bright morning light, waiting for Gary Stephens to arrive. He had just received new information from Moscow that was frightening in its implications, and he wanted to consult his national security advisor before he reacted to it. His intercom beeped.

"Gary Stephens is here, Mr. President."

"Send him in, Angela."

Gary Stephens entered the office. "Mr. President?"

"Sit down, Gary." Stephens crossed to the chair opposite the president's desk and sat down, examining the president's face for a clue of what was coming so he would be prepared.

The president wasted no time with pleasantries. "I have just received further word from Moscow that the Arab countries are planning a quiet summit in the next couple of weeks to discuss their perceived threat by the Israeli discovery of cold fusion."

Stevens was unruffled. "That's no surprise; we expected it. They have been agitated from the day of the announcement in Israel."

"True enough, and the news of the summit would have been public soon enough. It was the information supplementing the news of the summit that was troubling. There is growing sentiment among some of the more fundamentalist Arab countries to use their oil as leverage, forcing us to demand that the Israelis release the cold-fusion formula to the public. I don't have to remind you how unhappy the American citizenry was during the 1974 oil embargo, not to mention the economic jolt we suffered."

"You don't think they are serious about this, do you? The lack of cash inflow would certainly destabilize their own regimes."

"In the countries I am referring to, the governments are becoming more afraid of their own fundamentalists than anything else. From what Moscow said, the Arab countries are considering an oil boycott quite seriously." The president looked over his glasses at Stephens. "Have you made any headway with the scientists at all?"

Stephens grimaced. "No. The lead scientist looked willing but the others held him to their position; they said they are waiting for the Messiah to come before they consider the information."

"The Messiah? Are they kidding? Is that a joke?"

"It's no joke, sir. They insist that this Rabbi Hanviowitz told them that the Messiah is on his way and once he arrives, the scientists can release the information."

"And who is going to recognize this Messiah when he comes?"

"Apparently, it will be pretty obvious. They also said that the world will be on the brink of disaster when he comes."

The president was grim. "Lovely. Are we supposed to wait until that moment without acting in our best interests?"

Stephens held his hands out in front of him, palms upraised. "I don't know, sir. It seems that this Rabbi Hanviowitz is the one to ask. I guess he's the final arbiter in this matter."

"Can we reach him on the phone?"

Stephens said cautiously, "We can try."

The president got on the intercom. "Angela, I need you to get someone on the phone for me right away. He's in Israel. His name is Rabbi—" He looked at Stephens.

"Eliyahu Hanviowitz. At the Yeshivah Tahorah in Jerusalem."

The president continued, "Eliyahu Hanviowitz at the Yeshivah Tahorah in Jerusalem. Got that?"

Angela's voice came through the intercom. "Yes, Mr. President. Do you want me to put him through once I reach him?"

"Immediately."

The president swung his chair around to look out the window, leaving Stephens to stare at his back. They were both silent for a minute. Then the president spoke without turning around. "I hope that this rabbi is more flexible than the Muslim fundamentalists seem to be. Otherwise, we are caught in the middle, and someone is going to get hurt."

"What are you going to do, Mr. President?"

"I won't know until I have talked with Rabbi Hanviowitz."

Angela's voice came through the intercom. "Mr. President, I have Rabbi Hanviowitz on the line."

"Put him through on the speakerphone."

President Evans heard a tranquil, calm voice. "President Evans?"

The president was impressed in spite of himself; he was not used to hearing someone so calm when speaking to the most powerful man on Earth.

"Good afternoon, Rabbi Hanviowitz. How are you today?"

"I'm wonderful, thank God. And you?"

The president attempted to sound jovial. "I'm pretty good myself." He was a veteran at testing people's resolve, and he decided to begin the way he usually did, by measuring the perception and awareness of his target. But before he could start, the rabbi struck first.

"You say you're *pretty* good . . . not *very* good. Why do you temper your words like that? Is there something amiss?"

The president frowned. He didn't like being read so easily. He went on the offensive. "As a matter of fact, there is. And it involves you, Rabbi."

The rabbi didn't miss a beat. "I was wondering how long it would be before I heard from you. I would imagine you are perturbed because my students have rebuffed all attempts at eliciting the formula for cold fusion—and because they say I have instructed them to remain silent."

"Well, have you?"

"Absolutely."

The president's voice became more acidic. "I have also heard that you don't plan to reveal the information until the arrival of your Messiah. Is that also true?"

"Absolutely. That is my position."

"Rabbi, I have been made aware that your adversaries in the Arab world are up in arms about your refusal to go public with this information. They have insinuated that they will launch an attack against Israel unless you divulge what you know."

"That's too bad, even if it's understandable."

"Too bad? Is that all you can say? Do you *want* a war?"

"Have *I* threatened one? I said that their response is understandable; they're frightened of being ignored once the world doesn't need their oil."

The president was frustrated. "But you can avoid all the trouble by revealing what you know."

"How do you know? When someone wants to start a war, any excuse will do. They have always acknowledged in their own newspapers that they regard our existence as temporary, and that ultimately they will wipe us out. Would you feel so comfortable with Canada if they constantly swore they were going to wipe you out?"

The president said, "But we will protect you."

"That's a lovely thought, and your past friendship has been invaluable to us, but what if your protection of us threatened your own interests? If all the oil were turned off, could we count on you then?"

There was no response.

The rabbi knew at once. "I was wondering how long it would be before they threatened you with the oil. Everyone is vulnerable; you can't change the world's dependence on oil to fusion overnight."

President Evans said bluntly, "Just what do you expect of us? Is it reasonable to expect us to watch our country be threatened with economic disaster because of your intransigence? Do you believe that you must bring us all to the brink of disaster before you capitulate?"

"I believe that we are living at the beginning of the End of Days, the era of the Messiah. The rebirth of the State of Israel defied all logic, but it was prophesied as the beginning of this age two thousand years ago. I have perfect faith that God will ensure our survival and the world will know peace. I am sorry that you feel that your country is at risk, but mine is, too. Until I see the Messiah come, the world will have to wait a bit longer."

"Is that rational? After two thousand years of waiting you expect him to come any day now?"

"We have expected him any day for two thousand years. That belief is what has sustained us through all the horrors we have endured." The rabbi concluded, "And when he comes, the world will be ready for what we have to offer."

"I must protect the American people."

"Their bodies or their souls? You may have to make a choice." There was a voice in the background saying something to the rabbi, who said apologetically, "Please excuse me. I have to pray the afternoon service with my students right away. I wish you well, sir."

The president said quietly, "Good-bye." He hung up the phone and looked at Stephens, who looked back helplessly. "What's the name of the scientist that you think may play along?"

"Dr. Steven Aarons, Mr. President."

"Work on him as fast as you can. I don't know how much time we have before this whole thing explodes."

* * *

"This is Cardinal Scoglio."

"Good morning, Cardinal Scoglio, this is don Sanguino."

Cardinal Scoglio said in his most pleasant voice, "Don Sanguino, it is good to hear your voice. I am always glad to hear from you."

Sanguino was unimpressed. "Now that we've exchanged our regards let's get down to business, Scoglio. I have some news for you that you will find compelling. After I brief you, I want to discuss exactly when and how this information should be used. Your opinion will decidedly affect the way this information is treated, although the final decision is mine and our friend's in Colombia. Understood?"

Sanguino had spoken to Scoglio brusquely before, but he had never overtly stated that any decision remained his and not the cardinal's, it was simply understood: a tacit accord between the two men. This new verbal warning was unprecedented in their relationship, and it left Scoglio worried and a little frightened of what he was to hear.

"You understand, Scoglio?"

Scoglio regained his bearing. "Yes . . . yes, don Sanguino, I understand."

"Good. The information is this: Cardinal Benda Cortes, your nemesis and mine, has a defect in his background that can be used to destroy his further advancement."

Scoglio had been nervous before; now he was excited. He interrupted, "What has he done?"

"It is not what he has *done*, Scoglio; it is who he *is*."

"I don't understand."

"He is a Jew, Scoglio. He is the descendant of Marranos from Spain. We know that when he left the Vatican recently he traveled to Spain with a Jewish archivist to verify his Jewish ancestry, which they did. For all we know, he and his family may have still practiced being Jews right up to the present time."

Scoglio was delighted. "Is this information reliable? Where did you get it?"

"Our comrade in Colombia conducted an interview with the archivist upon his return to Brazil."

"The archivist told Carlos himself? Why would he do that?"

Sanguino knew that Scoglio was not stupid; he reminded himself that Scoglio was not used to thinking in violent terms. Still, he hated having to explain simple things to him. "First of all, Scoglio, Carlos wasn't there himself. He sent three of his men to interview the archivist. Second, the archivist was unwilling." He waited.

"Oh. . . . Can the archivist testify in person in Rome?"

"The archivist cannot do anything anymore."

"I see." Scoglio didn't want to know any more details, inferring correctly what must have happened. *Not my affair,* he told himself.

Sanguino, aware of Scoglio's reluctance to probe into the details of Rissolo's death, returned to the matter at hand. "We have this information and can use it however we wish. The question is, how do we use it most effectively? My limited knowledge of the workings of the Church leads me to believe that his Jewish background would eliminate his chances of succeeding the pontiff, yet I don't think it would invalidate his remaining a cardinal, would it? The Church has had cardinals with Jewish background before."

"That is true."

"So we have a problem. He is a major thorn in the side of our friend in Colombia, and by extension, to me. And the information we have only threatens his papal aspirations, not his present status. Have you any ideas of how to proceed?"

Scoglio pondered the matter for a moment, keeping the don waiting. At first he looked up at the crucifix on the wall, but to his chagrin he found it distracting his deliberation. After a minute's wait, he thought he could see a clear solution to their dilemma.

"The pontiff's health is deteriorating, don Sanguino. I believe that the Brazilian cardinal and I are the two candidates to succeed him. If I succeed him, I will have the position to deal with the matter myself. That only leaves the possibility that Cardinal Benda Cortes will succeed the pontiff as a cause for concern. Should it appear toward the end that the Holy Father might designate my rival as his successor, or that the College of Cardinals is leaning in that direction, we can release the information at the appropriate moment."

"Why not just release the information now?"

"I haven't told you about the conversation I had with the Holy Father, have I?"

"No, you haven't."

"That conversation was the reason for Cardinal Benda Cortes's trip to the Vatican. He and I were summoned by the Holy Father for a private conference. During that conference, the Holy Father intimated that he was presently examining the very foundations of our faith. He was convinced that Jesus may have been a Jew."

"But Scoglio, everyone knows Jesus was born a Jew."

"Possibly, but the Holy Father said he believed that Jesus might be only a man—a man who intended to free the Jews from the oppression of the Roman Empire. And he asked that, if he died without purifying the Church of its mistaken beliefs, whichever of the two of us succeeded him would finish his work."

Sanguino was incredulous. "A man? The Holy Father said he thought our Lord might be only a *man?* I don't have much use for religion, Scoglio, but that's beyond *me*. What did you say to him?"

"I told him that I could not be a party to such a mission, that he was destroying the Church."

Sanguino was disgusted. "You couldn't keep your mouth shut? What did Benda Cortes do?"

"He remained silent." Scoglio suddenly became adamant. "On this issue I could not remain silent. I will not allow the Church to be destroyed. But considering the present course of the pontiff, can you see why releasing this information now about the Brazilian cardinal might not be to our advantage?"

"Yes, yes. But what about the course the pontiff is taking? If he lives too long, he may succeed and our man in Brazil would be a logical successor. Is there any way to hasten his decline?" His voice became smoother. "This is no longer about your personal aspirations, Scoglio. This is about saving the Church."

Scoglio looked up at the dying Jesus on the cross. He felt a righteous fury surge within him. "Let me look into the matter, don Sanguino."

"You had better."

21

Grant strode out of the elevator toward his office, fighting the nervousness inside him. The press conference was in half an hour and he knew he faced the challenge of his life, for his return home risked his entire life's work—in more ways than one.

The past three days in Brazil had been riveting in their intensity. Grant, the other four executives, Willie Daniels, Rabbi Hanviowitz and, most of all, Isaac Benda Cortes had discussed and deliberated how to implement their plans. They discussed how each corporation could share the cost of helping Grant's network carry their message worldwide. Willie had been reticent, discouraged that he had nothing to offer of importance, until Grant noticed his silence. They had been discussing how to reach the young adults and adolescents, and Dan Bryant had dismissed the problem as relatively unimportant.

He said, "I don't think many of them give a damn about religion one way or another. They're the most selfish, screwed-up generation in decades. Just look at the television and movies they watch, or the concerts they attend. The more savage the entertainment, the more they are attracted to it. They're about as far from religion as it's possible to get."

Isaac disagreed. "On the contrary, I think everything you say indicates that they are on the verge of a religious awakening. On the one hand, they grew up in a world that has flirted with self-annihilation since the dawn of the nuclear age, so they have a constant awareness of death. On the other hand, much of the world is more affluent than at any time in history, so they are bored. That combination forces them to look for answers."

Rabbi Hanviowitz nodded. "They are angered by what they see as hypocrisy. Often they see their elders attending religious services, promising to act righteously, and then returning to the world and relapsing into improper behavior. What we have to offer them is a different religious perspective than they have had before."

Lindsay interjected, "But I thought that you don't expect everyone to become a Jew."

"That's correct. As a result, they won't feel threatened by eternal damnation or something similar to it, but, rather, reassured that they can examine our perspective freely without feeling coerced. We concentrate on this life, the here and now. We don't yearn for the world to come because once there, the opportunity disappears to do mitzvoth, commandments, as an opportunity to sanctify God's name in the world."

"Why would that opportunity attract these young people?"

"Because young people's greatest resentment is not being taken seriously. But if they knew that every act they executed could be as tremendously significant and heroic as anything their parents did, they would be vitally interested. And it could be fun for them too, since they could feel that every situation was a challenge to their intellect."

Bryant grinned and pointed to his thinning hair. "I'm not sure that they'd listen to what I had to say—I'm from the same generation that they view with contempt." He pointed at Wolford, Eldridge, Lindsay and Grant. "You four gentlemen are too old, too. And Isaac and Rabbi Hanviowitz would be disdained as self-serving. They need someone they admire from their own generation to address them."

Slowly, everyone looked at Willie. Grant looked across the table at him. "You're awfully quiet, Willie." All the men looked at him expectantly.

Willie felt overwhelmed. "You think *I'm* the one to convince them that the Messiah has come?"

Perry Lindsay joked, "From what my grandson says, your biggest problem would be convincing them that it isn't you!"

"But how do I do it? I'm just an athlete, not a politician or something like that."

Isaac said, "Grant told me about your experience at the game, where you had your vision. How many people know about that?"

Grant answered him. "It was a nationally televised game, and it got great ratings. I'd estimate that at least ten million people watched the game, not to mention the millions who read about it in the newspapers or saw it on the news."

James Wolford chimed in, "And don't forget television news, Grant. Your own network made it the lead story the next day, you know."

"I was so busy I didn't notice. What if you held a press conference, Willie? You could bring up the incident and explain what happened and what you saw."

Willie thought for a moment. "But that was only a vision that started you on your path, Mr. Tyler. The rest of the story is yours."

Perry Lindsay addressed Grant. "He's right, Grant. Without your testimony and evidence there isn't much of a story to tell, even if you added what Dan, James, Robert and I experienced. Perhaps the best way is to hold a joint press conference with you and Willie telling the world what happened to us and where it's leading."

Rabbi Hanviowitz suggested, "As long as you're at it, Mr. Lindsay, why don't you and the other executives here also make a statement?"

"Our part in this wasn't as central as Grant's."

"But that's not the point. Because you four are considered the most successful men in the business world, your statements would have tremendous impact. As a matter of fact, the biblical prophets were not poor men on a street corner yelling to passersby; many were wealthy men—sometimes the wealthiest of men. People wouldn't have taken them seriously otherwise. When a hugely successful man testifies to the reality of God and his will, people sit up and take notice, for they feel he has much more to lose than a poor man."

Grant let the idea take root in his mind. Up until now he had envisioned his role as the power behind the scenes, not the spokesman who risked alienating the public. He was surprised to find himself afraid of what he could lose. *What **could** I lose?* he asked himself. *The respect of my peers?* He checked himself and found he was indifferent to that. *Money?* He was certain he had enough to cover whatever he lost. *Then what am I afraid of?*

"It isn't either of those, Grant." Isaac's face had a look of joyous bewilderment on it.

Grant said, "What? . . . How did you know what I was thinking?"

Isaac spoke with wonder. "I don't know. I just heard something tell me to say that to you."

Rabbi Hanviowitz spoke sharply. "You heard something?"

"Yes. A voice told me to say that to Grant. It also said that what he's afraid of is what his mother had—that he's afraid that if he makes a fool of himself publicly people will think he's crazy, too."

Grant stared at Isaac in shock. He blurted out, "I never told you about my mother."

Rabbi Hanviowitz looked back and forth at the two men. He asked Grant gently, "Was she emotionally troubled?"

"She was schizophrenic."

The rabbi's voice reached across the table to Grant. "And you've been carrying that fear with you your whole life—that you might be like your mother? And you fear that somehow this entire adventure is connected with that?"

A small voice answered, "Yes."

The rabbi leaned forward in his chair. "Then how do you explain everyone else's participation in this? Most of all, how do you explain what just happened?"

"I don't know."

Rabbi Hanviowitz spoke powerfully. "Isaac, do you have an idea of what happened to you just now?"

Isaac felt his bewilderment rush out of him, leaving behind only an exultation that surged and flooded through him with such force that he felt lightheaded. "It was so clear. As though I were an empty vessel that was suddenly filled with light and a voice." His eyes grew wide. "Am I hearing . . . ?"

Rabbi Hanviowitz said, "I have to make a telephone call right away."

"But you haven't answered my question."

"That's what I'm about to do." The rabbi reached for the telephone, dialed a number, and waited. After what seemed to Isaac like forever, Rabbi

Hanviowitz spoke. "Eliyahu? Remember when you said we should watch and wait? Well . . ."

$*$　$*$　$*$

Grant reached the door to his office and opened it wide. There she was, seated at her desk just as he had asked her to when he called the hospital from the plane. She looked up, and he was glad to see the warm smile she gave him, suddenly noticing that she had let her hair down around her shoulders, which he had never seen before. She had always kept her long hair tied neatly behind her, and the sight of her hair undone startled Grant into seeing Beverly as a different person; she was not only an attractive woman, which he had noticed before, but a beautifully *feminine* woman, which he had always ignored. He thought to himself that he had been so in love with Becky that any other woman paled by comparison, just as the stars and moon are eclipsed by the light of the sun.

He also realized something else: He didn't want her to call him "Mr. Tyler" anymore. He knew that he had allowed and encouraged her to remain formal with him over the years because he could keep her at an emotional distance that way. But now, he felt an urge to share everything he had experienced with her, with no accompanying guilt, since he felt that when his time came to die he and Becky would be together again.

He walked up to her desk and pulled a chair over to sit across from her.

"Before we talk, Beverly, there's something I would ask of you." She waited, holding her breath. "I want you to call me Grant from now on. No more 'Mr. Tyler,' okay?"

"Yes . . . Grant." It wasn't easy for her.

"I want you to know everything that has been happening to me. I also need to thank you for staying with Matthew while I was gone and alerting the press for the news conference." He checked his watch. "We've only got about twenty minutes before we go downstairs, so I'll have to speak quickly, and you'll have to listen. I want you to know *why* I'm doing what I'm about to do. Okay?"

Beverly had waited for years for this kind of intimacy, but now that it was happening all she felt was tremendous guilt that she and not Becky was the one to share it with Grant. She couldn't look Grant in the face, so she bowed her head.

Grant saw the pain on Beverly's face and recognized the cause. He put his hand under her chin and raised her head to look at him. "I loved her, too, Beverly—more than my life."

"I know."

"If you'll hear me out, you'll see that she wouldn't object. It's because of her that this whole story is unfolding. I think she's glad that I'm sharing it— especially with you."

Beverly started to cry.

*   *   *

Twenty minutes later Grant and Beverly walked into the packed conference room of the Tyler Network. Two hundred reporters were there, and Perry Lindsay, Dan Bryant, Robert Hutchinson, James Wolford and Willie Daniels sat on the dais, staring straight ahead silently.

Beverly took a seat at the side of the dais next to Robin Daniels and her infant son as Grant headed toward the microphone. The hum in the room was expectant, since Grant had never called a press conference before.

Some of the more observant reporters immediately noticed that Joel Alexander was absent, which was unusual. The reporters had often thought of Joel as Sancho Panza to Grant's Don Quixote, the jovial sidekick to the man who would change the world. They threw Joel's absence around like baseball infielders after a putout. Some of the reporters dismissed the news as insignificant, but the more discerning among them saw deeper implications and awaited developments.

Grant stood behind the lectern and waited for silence. The room quieted quickly.

"Ladies and gentlemen, first let me introduce my colleagues to you. From your left to your right, they are: Perry Lindsay of United States Motors, Dan Bryant of Euro-Japan Motors, Bill Eldridge of Intercontinental Motors, James Wolford of Global Computer Systems, and the NBA's MVP, Willie Daniels. What we are about to tell you may cause you to doubt at least our sincerity, and at most our sanity. The saving grace for those of us who will tell our story is the recent news of the discovery of cold fusion in Israel. It is not the discovery itself that heartens us in the task before us, but rather the simultaneous statements made by the scientists that the messianic age is upon us."

The reporters, who were used to decrying the intangible and considered such information grist for the tabloids, were taken unaware. Each one looked around at the others to see if they were skeptical, too.

"My wife died two weeks ago. In that time, I have undergone an adventure that would normally be viewed as incredible, but I can assure you that everything I am about to tell you is true, as well as the testimony from my partners behind me. If you will please refrain from questions I will attempt to describe as succinctly as I can the sequence of events that has occurred.

"On March 10, I was with my wife, who was dying of cancer in the hospital. She said she had a dream that she was behind a wall where I couldn't find her. A bearded man with a black suit and hat told her that I was not to give up looking for her, I would find her behind an ancient, tall wall. Normally, I would have dismissed such a dream as nonsense, but she was dying and I was distraught enough to consider anything."

He turned to face Willie. "The next chapter of the story is Willie's."

Willie smiled nervously at Robin and walked over to the microphone. "I guess most of you know how I collapsed at the game that night. The story got around that I had died and then come back to life." He grinned shyly. "I don't know, because all I was aware of was what I was seeing. It was a vision that was so powerful that after it was over I didn't know where I was, only that I had to talk to Mr. Tyler. I got the word to him from the locker room, and he came down from his seat to see me."

One reporter, putting two and two together, couldn't restrain himself. "Isn't that the same kind of a deal that happened to you executives, too?"

Grant, who was still standing next to Willie, leaned in front of him to answer the question. "We'll get to that in a moment. Willie?"

The reporters were focused now; they started to believe that they were witnessing something historic.

"Well, when Mr. Tyler came down to see me, I told him what I had seen. I told him that I had seen *him* at an ancient wall of light-colored rock with a bearded man in a black suit and hat. In my vision Mr. Tyler asked the man if he could put a message *through* the wall instead of *in* it."

Willie took a step to the side as Grant stepped to the microphone again. "I found out that the wall that Willie had described was the Western Wall of the Temple in Jerusalem, where I immediately went after my wife's death. I met the bearded man of my wife's dream there. His name is Rabbi Eliyahu Hanviowitz, and while I talked to him, a messenger came to tell him that his brother was dead."

The reporters didn't understand the significance of this, but for once they waited.

"The rabbi's brother was Mike Hanvill."

A murmur crept through the room.

"The circumstances surrounding Mike's death were unusual, so the rabbi convinced me to fly home and investigate. What I learned was that before he died, Mike Hanvill had seen a word in ancient script and insisted on writing it down."

Grant beckoned Perry Lindsay to the microphone. As Perry passed Willie, who was heading back to his seat, he held his arm for a moment for encouragement. Then he reached the lectern.

"At the time, I didn't know any of what Grant has described." He gestured to the other executives. "Neither did my compatriots. What happened to us only substantiates our joint credibility. There were actually five of us who suffered heart attacks within two weeks of each other. During the time we were unconscious, we all underwent the exact same experience. We all saw the identical word, a word written in an ancient script. We conferred and decided to contact Grant so he could use his vast resources to discover what it meant, since he had the power to do so quietly. He was in Israel at the time, and by the time I contacted him he had learned about Mike Hanvill's vision of *his* word. Grant compared the two words, ours and Mike's, and found that they were written in the same script, an ancient Hebrew script over twenty-five hundred years old."

The murmur was gone; the room was dead silent. Perry glanced at Grant, then took a step to the side enabling Grant to have the microphone. Grant didn't want to be melodramatic, but he found himself waiting to speak. The tension growing in the room was palpable. He looked at the reporters, then turned back toward his colleagues, and finally looked at Beverly, Robin, and the Daniels's infant son.

"Ladies and gentlemen, the words that were sent to these men and Mike Hanvill when they hovered between life and death were *Moshiach*, meaning

Messiah, and one other word. They were an announcement that the Messiah is here at this moment, alive and among us."

One reporter, braver than the others, stood up and asked, "Are you telling us that the Second Coming is here?"

Grant had expected that question. "Ladies and gentlemen, my office will be publishing a daily news pamphlet to be distributed starting tomorrow explaining in detail who the Messiah is and what we should look for. The pamphlet will be sent to every newspaper, television and radio station in the world so there will be no danger of mistranslation. That will be all. Thank you." Grant signaled the others and they started to file out of the room.

Some reporters yelled after them, "What was the other word, Mr. Tyler?"

Grant, the last one to leave, turned back to them. "In due time, gentlemen."

*   *   *

The next morning the front page of every newspaper in the Western Hemisphere was emblazoned with the biggest headline their editors could muster. Some of the newspapers in the Eastern Hemisphere didn't print the news, either because of repressive regimes or because much of the Arab world reacted as if it were another Zionist plot. The assumption that was most common the first day was that Grant was referring to Jesus and the Second Coming. Speculation was rampant that the Catholic Church had put Grant and his colleagues up to it because the Church was losing ground with its flock.

Grant knew better than anyone else that the press was bound to twist what he had said at the press conference, and so the first day's pamphlet was a word-for-word transcription of what had transpired. The television and radio programs had cut and pasted the story, and Grant's pamphlet ensured the accuracy he wanted. Before he and his colleagues had left Brazil, they had discussed with Isaac whether to reveal his identity immediately or wait for a more propitious moment. Isaac asked Grant to wait; he was still agonizing over whether he was a Catholic or a Jew. The men agreed to wait and see how the world took the news.

The first day, there was general curiosity from most people. Even if Grant and his colleagues were well respected for what they had achieved, the idea that the Messiah was really ready to assume control seemed far-fetched to societies that knew their governments had the power to blow whole countries to bits. Those who hated successful men asserted that Grant was out of control, that he had no worlds left to conquer and had become a megalomaniac, intending to campaign for the job himself. The people most profoundly affected were the religious ones; they believed that there would be a Messiah, and they took the announcement seriously. The religious Christians of all denominations were excited and eagerly awaited the next day's pamphlet. The religious Jews were careful; many historical Jews had been lost following false messiahs. Besides, they also figured that Grant was talking about Jesus, though many secretly hoped that perhaps, just perhaps, Grant was speaking instead about the Messiah that Judaism had introduced to the world.

There was one question that nearly everyone had who heard or read the news: If the Messiah was alive, where was he? This was not so much the question of why he hadn't appeared (the Christians could understand why he was careful about coming forth; he had been crucified the first time), but more directly, where on the planet was he? Was he in America, because the men on the panel were Americans? Was he in Israel, where Jesus was last seen alive? Many Catholics believed he was in Rome because he would want to be at the Vatican. *Where was he?*

Grant didn't answer them the second day. Instead, he decided to start elucidating the meaning and origin of the word "messiah." His pamphlet went into great detail describing its use in the Bible and the Prophets, and he made a point of stressing that the term originally meant the redeemer of the House of Israel from its oppressors. The Christian world was not aware as yet that there was a distinction between Grant's explanation and their conception of Jesus, since they considered themselves the inheritors of the Israelite covenant and their belief in Jesus redeemed them. The third day, Grant planned to address the issue of the Messiah's redemption of Israel as a *political* redemption, a release from the Jews' exile and oppression, but two telephone calls changed his plans.

*   *   *

Beverly caught Grant as he entered the office the second day, holding the newspaper in front of him and grinning at the coverage he was getting.

"There's a phone call for you, Grant."

Grant called cheerfully over his shoulder as he passed her desk on the way to his office, "Only one? I thought I'd be getting a better response than that."

"There are more—it's just that this one can't wait. You'd better take it."

Grant stopped just short of entering his office and turned around. His demeanor changed. "Is it the hospital? I just came from there, and Matthew hasn't changed."

"It's not the hospital, Grant." He visibly relaxed. "It's the president."

"President Evans?"

"He read the pamphlet yesterday and he wants to talk to you immediately."

Grant stiffened, pivoted and quickly walked into his office to pick up the telephone. "Mr. President?"

"Grant? We haven't spoken in months."

"I'm sorry about that, Mr. President. My wife was ill, and everything else had to wait."

"Yes, I heard about that. I'm sorry."

"Thank you."

"Grant, I read your pamphlet yesterday, and I have some serious questions for you."

"I'll help any way I can."

"Good. First of all, how well do you know Rabbi Hanviowitz?"

Grant started to answer, then remembered that the president had read about Rabbi Eliyahu Hanviowitz in Israel, not his brother Daniel in Brazil. "Not too well, Mr. President. Why?"

"Because I'm sitting on a powder keg right now, and he's holding the fuse."

"I don't understand."

"He's advised the scientists who discovered cold fusion to protect their formula and not go public with it, which wreaks havoc with the general state of affairs. And he personally told me that the information will not be released until the Messiah appears. Then I heard that you seem to know who this 'Messiah' is. May I hope that he can make an appearance shortly?"

"Is there any special urgency?"

The president became irascible. "Only if you consider the spigot to the world's oil being turned off. Does that qualify as urgent?"

"The Arab world is threatening that?"

"Only if we cannot convince the Israelis to publicize their information.

And after that, they will most probably attack Israel."

Grant stopped to consider where his loyalties lay. To rebuff the president of the United States was serious, but to destroy what he felt was the destiny that God had intended for him was impossible. He asked, "Did you inform Rabbi Hanviowitz of the imperilment of the State of Israel if he doesn't capitulate?"

"Yes, I did. He stated that God will take care of everything."

Grant smiled inwardly. Rabbi Hanviowitz was certain to say that. "Sounds good to me, Mr. President."

"Look here, Grant, you know what a shock an oil embargo would have on our economy. You've got to tell me where this supposed Messiah is before the world goes crazy."

"Mr. President, when he gives me permission to reveal his whereabouts I will inform you immediately." There was a beep on the line. Grant couldn't believe his ears. Beverly was beeping him with another call while he was speaking to the president? Only one call could be that urgent: a call from the hospital about Matthew. "Mr. President, I'm getting another call. I think it's Mount Zion Hospital—my son is in a coma and I told my secretary to interrupt me if there was any change in his condition."

President Evans had children of his own. "You go ahead and take the call, Grant. But I'd like you to think about what we've talked about. I don't want your son to awaken to a world at war." He hung up.

Grant clicked the receiver and Beverly's voice came on the line.

"Grant?"

"Put the hospital through, Beverly."

"It's not the hospital, Grant."

"It's not?" Grant scowled through the glass wall of his office at her back. "Then why did you interrupt me with the president?"

Beverly stood up from her desk with the telephone, then turned and looked steadily back at Grant through the glass wall. "I thought that this call was more important, considering the path you're taking. It's the Vatican. Pope John XXIV wants to speak to you."

22

Isaac took his eyes off the page for a moment and looked out the window. He was still getting used to the sight of two former U.S. Marines patrolling the front of Rabbi Daniel Hanviowitz's house. Isaac knew that six more marines were stationed around the other sides of the house, and he shifted his gaze to the rabbi across the table from him, absorbed in a talmudic commentary. He thought, *For me to have this security unit around is nothing unusual, I'm used to an entourage . . . but for him, it must be strange to know his house is surrounded by armed men, yet he doesn't even seem to notice.* He glanced toward the kitchen.

Isaac had glanced toward the kitchen more than once during the past three days because he was constantly aware of the presence of Rivkah. She was her father's joy, and each time she softly entered the room to serve them what she had cooked, Isaac found her awakening a devotion inside him that he had only felt for his mother. Her devotion to her father elicited Isaac's growing devotion to her. He found that her very *being* seemed luminous to him; he was aware that something at the root of him yearned to capture her soul, and his heart began to leap at the sight of her. He remembered what she had said to him about the man she would marry, ". . . a man who thirsts for Torah and mitzvoth and the rectification of this world . . ."

He had found two incentives for learning: his quest for his Jewish identity and his desire to impress her. At first he had felt guilty that his attraction to her was as powerful as his desire to serve God, and then he had dismissed the guilt, reasoning that whatever his motivation, learning was a meritorious deed.

Rabbi Hanviowitz had not raised his head, but he knew that Isaac had looked out the window at the armed guard, and he saw Isaac lower his head to study again. He glanced up at the top of Isaac's bowed head and marveled at the man in front of him.

When Grant, Willie and the four executives had left three days ago, the rabbi had given Isaac two thick Hebrew grammar books, expecting him to come back in a week or so. He was already aware of Isaac's prodigious memory, but he was not prepared for Isaac's return the next day with both books entirely memorized. When Isaac asked what they were going to study first, Rabbi Hanviowitz suggested that Isaac memorize the Torah, the Five Books of Moses, in the original Hebrew, since everything stemmed from that. When Isaac returned the next day, the rabbi was perfectly prepared to hear that Isaac had memorized some of the Torah. Instead, Isaac stated that he had not only memorized the Five Books of Moses, but that he was halfway though the Prophets and by the next day would have completed the Prophets and the Writings. When he saw the incredulous look on Rabbi Hanviowitz's face, he said sheepishly that it wasn't as amazing as it sounded; he was reading fourteen hours a day. Rabbi Hanviowitz nodded seriously, suppressing a grin at Isaac's attempt to make the unbelievable achievement sound ordinary.

He called his older brother in Israel after Isaac left the second day and told him of Isaac's phenomenal progress. Eliyahu wasn't surprised.

"After all, Daniel, if God *has* chosen him he was bound to be extraordinary."

Daniel loved his older brother, but he respected him even more. In the rare instances where he felt unqualified to decide a matter of Halacha, he had confidence in Eliyahu's judgment. He was not alone, of course, for rabbis all over the world called Eliyahu for answers, but Daniel was the leading authority in South America and so no one would have suspected that he also had a rabbi to consult.

He broached the worry that had gnawed at him since he had started learning with Isaac.

"Eliyahu, what if we're wrong? What if he isn't the *Moshiach* and I'm teaching Torah to the wrong man? Everything has pointed to him, but it's still a terrible chance we're taking."

Eliyahu had considered the matter carefully. "All the evidence points to him, the other day he heard the divine voice, and you are still unsure? Are we talking about him, or are we really talking about your own place in all this, Daniel?"

"I just worry that we're enticing the world to destroy us."

"Whenever *Moshiach* comes, all prophecies say that the world will be against us. That's a certainty. The most powerful reason for our convictions is the man himself. From what you've told me, he has had an amazing impact on people in his career."

Daniel thought of Isaac's career. "He has enormous courage and personal magnetism."

"Does Rivkah think so, too?"

Daniel was chagrined; he hadn't even been aware of that. *He got me again,* he thought. "You know, I've been waiting all my life to see through you the way you see through me."

"It's one of the privileges of being the oldest." Eliyahu chuckled. "It was the business about personal magnetism that gave you away."

"I've been waiting for her to find the right man for fifteen years, and she falls in love with a Roman Catholic cardinal who's really a Jew and might be *Moshiach?* There go my father-in-law rights of criticism."

"Think of it this way, Daniel. If we're right and he really is *Moshiach,* at his rate of learning, in a year or two he can take all your telephone calls and you can learn uninterrupted."

"Hmmm . . ."

*　*　*

The next day, Rabbi Hanviowitz pulled down two volumes from his shelf. They were matching copies of the first volume of the Mishnah Torah, the code of law and ethics written by Moses Maimonides in the twelfth century. It was the gigantic work that codified all of Halacha and was the bridge between the oral Torah from Mount Sinai (the Talmud) and the Shulchan

Aruch, the sixteenth-century work whose decisions remained binding five hundred years later. Maimonides, also commonly known as the Rambam, started from first principles and in masterful detail and logic covered every angle of Judaism.

The page they were studying now was the beginning, where the Rambam explained the concept of the reality of God, and God as a perfect unity.

Rabbi Hanviowitz said, "If God is a perfect unity, then God's will and his essence must be the same, correct?"

Isaac looked up. "That's logical."

The rabbi continued, "Now, because the mitzvoth, the commandments, were God's will, then by performing them a person becomes attached to God's will, his essence."

Isaac countered, "But Catholics can attach themselves to God simply by declaring their belief in him."

"For Catholics, that is appropriate. But Jews feel that it doesn't result in anything concrete and fixed. Bear with me now, and I'll explain more clearly where I am leading. What is the difference between the physical world and the spiritual world?"

"The physical world takes up space."

"Exactly. So if God is a *spiritual* essence, how do we, as *physical* creations, approach him on a spiritual plane? The answer is that if we perform the mitzvoth, which were willed by God, then our souls, which are joined to our physical bodies, can *bind* themselves to God through performing his will."

Isaac asked, "I have a question. In Leviticus it says, 'You shall love your fellow as yourself.' How do you show your love when so much of Judaism separates you from your fellow man?"

"For example?"

"Keeping the dietary laws and the laws you have about keeping the Sabbath, for a start."

The rabbi leaned back in his chair. "Because our mission is to teach the world about God, we must have a different relationship with the rest of the world than they do with each other. The most successful teachers are always those who love their students but also maintain a certain distance from them. The laws of keeping kosher and keeping the Sabbath are ways God gave us to remind us to remain distinct, even while loving the students."

Isaac glanced through the window. "It must be hard to convince yourself to love a world full of people that have always tried to destroy you."

Rabbi Hanviowitz followed Isaac's glance. "Absolutely. That's why we have lost many Jews through the centuries; they gave up, feeling it was too difficult or dangerous." He looked inquiringly at Isaac. "Imagine if the world not only protected them but *encouraged* them to do their job."

*   *   *

Later, Isaac asked, "What are the central mitzvoth of the practicing Jew besides studying Torah, praying three times a day, keeping the Sabbath and maintaining a kosher home?"

The rabbi answered, "The use of the *mikvah*. Of all these mitzvoth, the most important is keeping the Sabbath. In Exodus, it is required because of God's rest on the seventh day, and in Deuteronomy it is required because God took the Jews out of Egypt."

"Why are there two reasons?"

"They're both needed to show that although God is actively involved in the universe, as he was in the Exodus, he *stopped* being actively involved on the seventh day of creation. He stopped interfering with creation."

"But why?"

"Because when he stopped his involvement with creation on the seventh day, the world stopped changing: It was serene. And when we keep the Sabbath properly, we acquire the same sense of serenity, because we stop interfering with the world. That is why on the Sabbath we eschew anything which involves changing the nature of something. We don't turn electricity on and off, we don't ride in cars, we don't cook."

"There are myriad rules for the Sabbath, aren't there?"

"I would venture to say that there is more commentary on how to keep the Sabbath than any other mitzvah we have. But that's a small price to pay for freeing yourself from the tyranny of earning a living and the hectic pace of dealing with the world. For one day a week, all is peace."

"How about the others: keeping kosher and the *mikvah?*"

"Interestingly enough, they are related."

"How can that be? Isn't the *mikvah* a ritual bath for purification purposes? What does that have to do with keeping milk products separate from meat products?"

Rabbi Hanviowitz was eager to supply the answer to this. "It stems from sensitizing one's soul to the distinction between life and death. The *mikvah's* function is to elevate something's spiritual level. When a woman menstruates, her soul mourns the death of a *prospective* life, and to simultaneously engage in a life-giving act blurs life and death, not to mention being grossly insensitive to the woman's soul. Therefore, the *mikvah* is used to raise the woman's soul back to a state without mourning. It also blurs life and death to mix milk or dairy products with meat, since eating meat means that an animal was killed, and milk is the life-giving sustenance of a mother for its young. By constantly sensitizing ourselves to the difference between life and death, we appreciate life and the tremendous opportunity to serve God."

Isaac said softly, "'For the commandment that I command you today—it is not hidden from you and it is not distant . . . I have placed life and death before you, blessing and curse; *and you shall choose life.*'"

The rabbi looked at Isaac, and their eyes locked.

*   *   *

Grant had never visited the Vatican. He had always viewed it as a shrine to an established religion, and he had never had any use for religion. Although he was a different man now, he was still unmoved by the incredible beauty of its art and architecture. What did strike him came from his newsman's instinct: the Vatican's ability to command the world's attention. He carried that knowledge with him when he was ushered into the room to meet Pope John XXIV. The pope was seated at his desk and looked weaker than Grant had imagined he would, but he slowly rose to greet Grant. Grant noticed that the pontiff's stomach had swollen noticeably and realized that the cancer must have spread to the liver; the pope was precipitously close to death. A matter of weeks, possibly days.

"Please sit down, Mr. Tyler."

Grant was unfamiliar with protocol for the occasion, not being Catholic, so he bowed and then seated himself across the desk from the pope, who winced as he sat down stiffly.

"I'm sorry to ask you to fly all the way to Rome, Mr. Tyler, but this subject is so explosive I considered it dangerous to continue our discussion over the telephone."

"There's no need for an apology, Your Holiness. I was in complete agreement with you."

Pope John XXIV said, "I have been informed of the discovery you claimed to have made. I have read the facts as outlined in the media, and they are fascinating. May I probe into the matter more deeply with you?"

Grant shifted in his chair slightly. "As far as I am willing to go, certainly."

"You have intimated that you have met the Messiah. Is that correct?"

"Yes, Your Holiness."

"And that this Messiah will redeem the House of Israel from its oppressors?"

"That is also correct."

The pope ran his forefinger alongside his nose. "Apparently, the Christian world believes that the 'House of Israel' refers to them, and that the Messiah you are referring to is the Second Coming of Christ." He looked at Grant curiously. "Are they correct?"

Grant didn't answer; he was thinking how much to divulge, how much to risk.

The elderly pontiff saw the indecision on Grant's face, then closed his eyes and tightened his lips as a spasm of pain shot through him. He opened his eyes, and Grant suddenly saw death in his face.

"Mr. Tyler, you should know where I stand. I am currently reviewing all historical evidence related to Jesus. I believe there is a possibility that the Messiah as originally defined by the Jews was not the historical Jesus."

Although Grant had been advised of the pope's activities by Isaac and knew that the pope was dying, he was still stunned to hear the head of the Catholic world make such an admission.

"So, Mr. Tyler, I am not certain that you are referring to the Christian world as the House of Israel, or the Messiah as Jesus Christ. I truly want to know, whom are you referring to? What is his real mission? And who are the oppressors of the House of Israel?"

Grant thought again of the power of the Vatican to impress its views on the world, and he decided to risk everything.

"His mission is to liberate the Jewish people from their oppressors, Your Holiness."

"And who is their oppressor, the Arab world?"

Grant shook his head. "The anti-Semitism within Christianity."

To his surprise, the pope did not erupt in anger, or cry out in denial. His face shining, the pope said, "I am on the right path after all." Seeing the startled look on Grant's face, he smiled. "Since I found out I was dying, I have looked for a way to purify the Church of its anti-Semitism. It is my dying wish to acknowledge our culpability in the forming of anti-Semitism, an anti-Semitism which Jesus would have found abhorrent and bewildering. If we acknowledged our guilt, then we could purify ourselves."

Grant seized the opportunity. "You could go even farther than that, Your Holiness."

"What do you mean?"

"According to what I have learned about Judaism, the Roman Empire, whose last vestige is the Catholic Church adopted by the Empire, was descended from Esau, Jacob's brother. And the original intent was for Esau, the strong, physical one, to protect his scholarly brother so his brother could teach the world. Why not reverse history and use the power of the Church to *protect* the Jews instead of *persecute* them?"

Pope John XXIV closed his eyes again. "To complete the circle . . ."

"What do you mean?"

"To return to what may have been the original intent of Jesus, to accomplish what he thought he would do."

"Exactly."

The aged eyes opened and stared at Grant. "But even if the Church were to do so, there is something we *cannot* do. *We* cannot lead the House of Israel. Only a Jewish Messiah can do that." The pope peered at Grant. "You still haven't told me who this Messiah is."

Grant wanted to tell the dying man, but something told him to wait. "Please forgive me, Your Holiness, but I can't reveal his identity just yet." His jaw set, he continued, "But I would stake my life that he is indeed the Messiah."

The pontiff was visibly disappointed not to know the Messiah's identity, but he left the issue alone. Grant, seeing the disheartened man, returned to the pope's own plans.

"How will you make such a monumental change in the Church, Your Holiness? You're fighting two thousand years of history."

The pope bit his lip from another spasm. "The question is whether to offer our acknowledgment of varying views of Jesus first, or to try to convince the world of the reality of your Messiah so they can see there are other possibilities for other people."

"What if you publicly acknowledged that we had spoken and you agreed that I had indeed found the Jewish Messiah?"

"I think that we need to convince the world of our sincerity first. There are a number of people who don't trust the Church and wouldn't listen to us. They suspect us of intrigue. Of course, some of that is our own fault when every time we elect a new pope there is utter secrecy."

Grant suddenly saw events clearly. The dying pope, the need for openness . . . "What if the election of the pope were open to the world? What if you offered to *televise* it so everyone could see nothing suspicious was going on? If you offered *that,* then those who distrusted you might be more willing to listen to you."

Even in his weakened state, the idea excited Pope John XXIV. He forced himself to sit erect in his chair. "I think that might work. I would announce that we are reexamining our mission and as a result we would televise the next papal election to the world. Simultaneously I announce that I have consulted with you and that I believe you are correct; the Jewish Messiah has come." He gasped as a severe spasm rocked his frame.

"Your Holiness, should I call for help?"

The pope clenched his teeth from the pain. "This will be over . . . soon enough. What we need to do is act quickly."

* * *

Gary Stephens once again sat opposite Dr. Steven Aarons in his office in Jerusalem, only this time Aarons's colleagues were absent. Stephens was determined to wrest the formula from the scientist this time, and he had insisted that they meet privately. Aarons had balked initially, but when Stephens put President Evans on the line, Aarons partially yielded. He agreed that the other scientists could be absent under one condition: His mentor, Rabbi Eliyahu Hanviowitz, had to be present. The president and Stephens were secretly delighted; they knew that the rabbi was really the man in charge.

Stephens heard the door open behind him and saw Aarons stand up quickly and walk to the door to greet the rabbi. Rabbi Hanviowitz shook Aarons's hand and then turned to greet Stephens, who rose and measured his opponent. He was surprised to find that the rabbi's eyes were not the eyes of a fanatic; in fact, they didn't even look serious. They looked clear and positive, even cheerful.

"Rabbi Hanviowitz? I'm pleased to meet you."

The rabbi offered, "Thank you, Mr. Stephens. Your president is a very determined man."

"That's how he got where he is, Rabbi."

Rabbi Hanviowitz said as they all took their seats, "I meant that he may have sent you here needlessly; we had already discussed our refusal to reveal the formula for cold fusion."

Stephens had a card to play and he played it now. "We understand your position, Rabbi. You have said that the formula will be revealed with the coming of the Messiah. Fair enough. But the situation has changed. Grant Tyler said in his press conference that you and he know each other. He also said that he and his colleagues know who this Messiah is. I assume that you must know too, is that correct?"

"That is correct."

Stephens gestured with his palms upraised to Aarons. "Don't you think it is only fair that Dr. Aarons, a Jew who can change the world and must wait until this supposed Messiah reveals himself, should know as much as the colleagues of Grant Tyler, who aren't even Jewish? After all, this *is* a Jewish Messiah we're talking about." He watched Aarons turn expectantly to the rabbi.

Rabbi Hanviowitz didn't hesitate. "We may be talking about a Jewish Messiah, Mr. Stephens, but we're talking about a universal God. My God, your God, everyone's God. The colleagues of Mr. Tyler are just as entitled to partake of his knowledge as anyone else. Therefore the answer to your question is no, Dr. Aarons does not have any special right to privileged information because he's a Jew," he glanced at Aarons before he turned back to Stephens, "any more than you have because you work for the president of the United States."

Out of the corner of his eye, Stephens saw Aarons's disappointment, and he tried to pursue the matter further. "How about it, Dr. Aarons? Do you agree with the rabbi that the Americans have the right to know who the Messiah is while you sit here waiting?"

The rabbi sat back in his chair, calm but alert, studying his pupil. Aarons felt the rabbi watching him and tried not to look in his direction. He started to look down at his fingernails when there was an urgent knock on the door.

Aarons called, "Come in." His secretary opened the door and stepped inside. "Mr. Stephens, there is an urgent call for you from Washington. Do you want to take it in here?"

"Yes, please." Aarons pointed to the telephone and Stephens picked it up.

"Stephens here." Rabbi Hanviowitz saw Stephens's face grow taut. "Yes, sir . . . yes, Mr. President . . . no, sir, not yet . . . yes, I will, sir." He hung up the telephone and glared at Aarons.

Aarons seemed to shrink back from Stephens. "Is there trouble? . . . What happened?"

Stephens said bitterly, "It's an embargo. The Arab world has turned the oil spigots off completely." He approached Aarons, stopping only inches away, and stared into his face. "Are you going to reveal what you know or does the United States prepare to abandon Israel to its enemies?"

Aarons was frozen. Then, at the same time, he and Stephens both looked at the rabbi, head lowered, murmuring a prayer. When he raised his head his eyes were brilliant.

"'You will advance against my people Israel like a cloud covering the earth. It will be at the End of Days that I will bring you upon My land, in order that the nations may know Me'."

23

The limousine stopped at the curb in front of Grant, and Beverly got out, eyes shining. Grant didn't hesitate. He reached out and embraced her, simultaneously throwing his carry-on bag into the back seat. They climbed in and immediately started conferring as the driver pulled away from the curb and headed toward Grant's office.

"How did the meeting go with the pope?"

"Everything's coming together, Beverly. He's ready to make historic changes, provided his health holds out. I think that the cancer has reached his liver, and he may have only weeks to live. He has come to the same conclusion we have regarding who Jesus really was, and he wants to erase all the anti-Semitic references in the Gospels."

"How did he feel about Isaac Benda Cortes?"

"He doesn't know about that yet."

"But I thought that was the reason he wanted to meet with you, to discuss your discovery of the Messiah."

"That's right, and I told him that I would stake my life that my suppositions were correct, but I didn't tell him *who* the Messiah was."

"But you just said that he's dying, Grant. Couldn't you tell him?"

"I wanted to, but something told me not to just yet. I have to reveal the information step by step. We have told the world that the Messiah exists and what the word 'Messiah' means. The next step is to tell them in general terms *where* he is so everyone focuses in that direction."

Beverly said reluctantly, "That's assuming anyone still cares. The oil embargo's effect hasn't totally hit home yet, but it will. And unlike 1973, the Arab states have extended the embargo to all the countries in the world, not just the United States and the Netherlands."

Grant stated, "But won't that make it more difficult for the embargo to be successful? At least the last time they tried to play divide and conquer, isolating us on one side and putting Europe and Japan on the other. This time the whole world can protest against the embargo together."

"You're forgetting something, Grant. The Arab world's ostensible reason for the embargo in 1973 was because they demanded Israel retreat to the pre-1967 borders. The world had been amazed by the Six Day War in 1967, and the thought of abandoning the tiny heroic state of Israel wasn't popular. But now, Israel is powerful; they have the formula for cold fusion, something the whole world wants. And Israel seems to be reluctant to hand it over."

Grant's eyes narrowed. "So the world would cave in to Arab pressure and abandon Israel?"

"That's the current sentiment. The president said yesterday that he was frustrated with Israeli intransigence on this issue. The embargo may wipe your discovery right off the front pages. What are we going to do?"

Grant didn't know whether he was making the right decision, but he figured it was all in God's hands anyway. "I'm going straight ahead. No matter who people think the Messiah is, they all agree he's supposed to bring peace. The embargo may increase everyone's interest in the Messiah if they see it as the beginning of another world war. Let's start by telling the world where he is."

Beverly reached for a pen.

*   *   *

An entire continent went crazy. The only way that it could be described was to say that South America was giddy, exulting in a sense of importance on the world stage that it had rarely if ever experienced before. From

Colombia and Venezuela in the north to Cape Horn in the south, the continent burst forth with pride and joy, especially since the testimony to the Messiah's presence there came from North America, long viewed by the rest of the world as the *only* important America. The reversal of the traditional roles of power was a heady one; North America's seeming helplessness in the face of the oil embargo and South America's powerful identity as the home of the Second Coming.

For the Second Coming was exactly what South America thought Grant was referring to when his campaign resumed. The information he released actually blew the oil embargo off the front pages; he stated that he had conferred privately with Pope John XXIV who had confirmed that Grant had indeed found the Messiah. The Vatican simultaneously released a statement that corroborated this fact.

It was natural that the South Americans would assume that the Messiah Grant referred to was Jesus; the Vatican had confirmed Grant's discovery, and South America was mostly Catholic. The question on every South American's mind was, Where was Jesus hiding? Which country had the honor of his presence?

$*$ $*$ $*$

Cesar Carlos was not thinking what other South Americans were thinking. Because he had never believed Jesus to be God or the Messiah, he had no preconceived ideas of who the Messiah might be. Not only that, but the idea of a Messiah had no meaning for him. He wouldn't have cared about the whole issue except for one thing; he could foresee it affecting his business. He was concerned that many heretofore indifferent citizens might suddenly become ferocious with moral righteousness. And when that happened, who knew how his business might suffer?

And there was something else nagging at him. After the murder of Alfonso Rissolo, he *had* planned to continue his intimidation of the cardinal, and he had been surprised when the newspapers blared that Grant Tyler, the executives and Cardinal Benda Cortes were holding meetings. He had then heard that the cardinal, under armed guard, was meeting with Rabbi Hanviowitz. Now Grant Tyler was meeting with the pope, and they were declaring that the Messiah was in South America. But Carlos knew that the Messiah was supposed to be Jesus. What the hell was going on?

*   *   *

Cardinal Scoglio slammed the newspaper on his desk in a fury. He didn't know what the pope was trying to pull, but he suspected that Cardinal Benda Cortes was behind it. *Cortes*, he thought savagely, *Cortes is trying to wreck the Church, and I have to stop him.* He jumped to his feet and headed toward the pope's chambers.

*   *   *

Grant and Beverly were seated at the desk in his office when they heard a knock at the window. They looked up to see Joel Alexander standing there. He was holding the next day's bulletin in his hand, and he looked frustrated and furious. Grant hadn't spoken to Joel in person since the night he had caught Joel in his office, but he had a good idea why Joel was angry now. He waved Joel in.

Joel entered but didn't bother to take a seat. He stood opposite the other two, gripping the bulletin, and tried to speak in a controlled, measured tone. He didn't succeed.

"Are you really going to print this tomorrow?"

Grant said quietly, "You bet I am. Do you have a problem with that?"

Joel's face started to redden. "Listen, Grant. Up until now your information about the Messiah has been harmless. When you said you discovered him and defined the origin of the term 'Messiah,' people were fascinated. When you said he was in South America, that made the adventure even more intriguing. But if you print this," he waved the bulletin, "people will go nuts and lives will be endangered. Are you totally unaware of what will happen?"

"And what do you think will happen?"

"To start, people equate Israel with Jews."

"As they should."

Joel, ruffled, said, "And right now the world is not too fond of Israel. If you print that this Messiah of yours is not Jesus, but a Jew, you're endangering all of us."

"Us?"

"You know what I mean. Every Jew will be in danger from the backlash. The whole Christian West will go crazy." He stared intently at Grant. "Does the Vatican know that you're referring to a *Jewish* Messiah?"

"Pope John does, yes."

"How does he reconcile that with Catholic belief?"

"He intends for the Church to reexamine their beliefs. Don't you think that he has some influence with the Christian world?"

"Not as much as you think. You're still playing with fire if you propose a Jewish Messiah."

Grant studied his oldest friend. "Is that all that upset you about what I wrote?"

Joel's face reddened further. "What do you mean by that?"

Grant looked squarely into Joel's eyes. "You know what I'm referring to. The section that addresses the Jews directly. The idea that all Jews must follow the commandments in order for the Messiah to be successful. That didn't bother you?"

Joel snapped, "I think you've gone over the top. Where in hell did you get the idea that you're free to lecture Jews on their responsibility? You aren't one of us. You're endangering all of us for your private little whim?"

Beverly retorted, "Grant's trying to say that your people have a mission to enlighten the world. Is that responsibility too much for you to handle?"

Joel exploded, "I didn't ask to be born a Jew. It just happened. Why should I single myself out from the rest of the world and ask for trouble? For *what?*"

Grant waited for the outburst to finish, then replied quietly, "For a chance to turn Israel into a true light unto the nations. For a chance to teach the world how to behave properly and to do it in a nonthreatening manner."

"Let me tell you something, Grant. The world doesn't *want* to be taught. And I'm not sure that my—or any other Jew's—practicing 613 arcane commandments is the way to teach them."

Grant actually felt sorry for Joel. "If *you* don't believe that the millions of Jews who died in the last three thousand years to sanctify God's name died to guard something vital for the world, then how do I convince you?"

"And how do you think dying sanctifies God's name?"

"Dying itself doesn't. But to die for the idea that there is a guiding force in the world, to protect the idea that the world progressed toward a messianic age with peace among all nations, that kind of death is a constant testimonial to God's existence."

"I'm not interested in that kind of death, thank you. I just want to live in

peace with my family. And if you insist on continuing the path you've taken
. . . I'll fight you in the media."

Grant stood up to face his antagonist. "You do what you have to do,
because I'm going to do what I have to do. *Now get out of my office.*"

"Wait!" Beverly grabbed Joel by the arm. "Mr. Alexander, please stop and
think what you're doing. Please . . ."

Joel shook himself loose. "He's not giving me any choice, Beverly. If I
don't stop this now, there's no telling how bad it might get." He opened the
door and walked back toward his office.

*　*　*

President Evans sat eating his breakfast, about to read the front page of
the newspaper, when the telephone rang.

"Mr. President?" It was Gary Stephens.

"Yes, Gary?"

"You'd better turn on the television, sir. Joel Alexander's about to make a
major announcement to the press." The president knew how close Joel and
Grant were, and he quickly turned on the television, hoping that Alexander
had news that would help solve the current crisis. Joel Alexander stood
behind a lectern in front of the press to read a prepared statement:

*Ladies and gentlemen, I have a brief statement. I have reluctantly
decided to come forward in order to disassociate myself from the statements made in the press today by my friend Grant Tyler and his associates. I have known Grant Tyler for almost thirty years, and the
campaign he has waged in the press the last week has convinced me
that he is suffering from an emotional breakdown—a breakdown that
was caused by the recent death of his wife and the accident that left his
son in a coma. He has said that he is convinced the Messiah is alive
and well in South America, and today he has made further statements
that persuade me that severe emotional stress has affected his powers
of reasoning.*

*I would urge the public to disregard the nature of his latest state-
ments and worry more about the current oil embargo and how to solve
the Israeli government's obstinacy in refusing to share the cold-fusion
formula. I hereby resign from the Tyler Network and offer my services*

to pressure the government of Israel to release the formula and end the crisis. I also call upon the public to please view all of Mr. Tyler's and his associates' statements as inflammatory, misguided, and not to be taken seriously. Thank you very much.

He left the podium amid calls and questions from the press.

President Evans turned the television off and started to read the front page and the latest statement from Grant.

Grant claimed that the Messiah he had been speaking of was not Jesus. He then clarified that the House of Israel (which the Messiah was to save) meant exactly that; the House of Israel—the Jewish people—had a mission to live in the land of Israel, protected by the world while keeping the commandments, thus acting as an example. He mentioned that the Gentile world was only enjoined to keep the seven laws of Noah, and explained what they were. He listed the numerous massacres of Jews throughout the ages, their survival against all odds, and their fierce will to safeguard the Torah and its teachings.

He ended with a plea for understanding; he said he knew that many in the Christian world would be violently opposed to a Messiah other than Jesus, and many in the Arab world would be just as violently opposed to the idea of Israel as a Jewish theocracy.

President Evans threw the paper on the table. "Oh, my God . . ."

*   *   *

Willie Daniels walked onto the gym floor toward his teammates, who were in a circle talking animatedly. When they saw him approach, the circle opened and he saw a look of contempt on their faces. Donald Walker, the Mules' other starting guard, stepped in front of the others and addressed Willie sardonically.

"We're glad you returned before the playoffs, Willie. We're only three games out now."

"We were two games in front before," growled someone behind him.

Walker continued, "We want to know about your world travels while we were playing basketball. Meet any interesting people?"

Willie stood ramrod straight, silent.

Travis Davis, the Mules' center, pushed his way forward through the circle. "You have a chance to go to church while you were gone, Willie?" Some teammates snickered behind him.

Walker fixed Willie with a frozen grin. "You preparing for your next career, Willie? Are you gonna go into scouting for talent?"

"He's gonna scout the bushes . . ."

"Yeah . . . burning bushes . . . like Moses . . ."

There was general laughter.

Willie stood erect, tall, quiet. He spoke slowly. "You guys angry at me?"

Walker's grin thawed into a scowl. "Maybe we are, maybe we are. None of us got a vacation to go looking for some hero."

Willie took a step toward them. "I'm sorry about that. Then again, none of you dropped dead on the floor, either."

Davis moved his giant frame in front of Walker and looked down at Willie. "I woulda been sorry about that before, Willie, but I'm not sorry now. I never heard anything about this kinda thing in church." There was a murmur of agreement.

Willie took another step forward until he was standing in front of Davis. "Travis, you can't even remember the plays when I call them. How are you going to remember what some preacher said years ago?"

Donald Walker stepped between the angry giant and Willie. "He's not the only one who remembers the Gospel that way, Willie."

Willie said mildly, "Maybe I read a different version." All the players tensed up. Willie grabbed a nearby basketball and started to dribble for the hoop at one end of the court.

"You gonna turn Jew, Willie?"

Willie turned around, ball in hand, "No, just the most tolerant, loving Christian I can be."

*   *   *

Rivkah Hanviowitz, carrying a coffee urn, entered the study and saw Isaac asleep in his chair and the rabbi sitting at his desk, examining a page of the Talmud. Her father looked up as he heard her enter and tried to clear his desk of the volumes strewn all over it. Rivkah put down the urn and helped him move the heavy volumes to one side. Then she took his coffee cup and began to pour.

"Is he all right, Abba?"

The rabbi glanced at Isaac and smiled gently. "For a man who spends seventeen hours a day learning, he's in remarkable shape. I don't know where he finds the strength."

"I know it's not proper for him to live here while I'm here, Abba. Maybe I should stay somewhere else for a while. Then *he* could stay here and sleep here, and he wouldn't have to go back and forth every day." She looked down at the sleeping man. "He must be so tired."

"Your home is here, Rivkah. He must do what he must do. He has chosen to learn as quickly as humanly possible, and that always entails a sacrifice, no matter what you're learning."

"How is he doing, Abba?"

The rabbi sipped some coffee. "We have been traveling from the Rambam backward to the Gemara and forward to the Shulchan Aruch at such a rate of speed that I feel young again. I never have to repeat myself, and his understanding is astonishing. I have never seen anyone like him."

Rivkah asked shyly, "Do you talk about anything else?"

"There simply isn't time . . . although twice when I brought the coffee he asked where you were. I told him that you were sleeping, and he said he liked your brewed coffee better than my instant version."

She smiled down at Isaac. "He is a kind man, Abba. . . . I like him very much." Suddenly there was anguish on her face. "I am afraid for him."

The rabbi reached for her hand. "What frightens you, my darling?"

"When the news broke that the Messiah was from South America, the people here were ecstatic. But today the news said that the Messiah was Jewish, and when I called the synagogue, they said that they had received threatening telephone calls."

"And you are worried for him?"

Rivkah's anguish broke through. "When it becomes known that he could be the Messiah, people will hurt him, Abba! People will hurt him!" The rabbi shushed her, but it was too late.

Isaac yawned and painfully opened his eyes to see Rivkah and her father. "I'm . . . I'm sorry I fell asleep, Rabbi. I must have been . . . how long have you been waiting for me?"

The rabbi glanced at Rivkah and back at Isaac, then said thoughtfully, "About thirty-three years, I think."

Rivkah blushed and said, "Excuse me, Abba." She hurriedly left the study.

Isaac was still brushing the cobwebs from his mind. "Where did we leave off, Rabbi?"

The rabbi moved his coffee to one side in order to reset the volumes on his desk. "We were discussing property rights and the laws about returning a lost object. Now if there an identifying mark on the object, it must be returned. If there is none, the finder must try to ascertain whether the owner would reasonably expect the object to be returned . . ."

*   *   *

Cardinal Scoglio knocked on the door to the pope's study. He heard a faint voice.

"Come in, Paolo."

Scoglio entered and saw the pope hunched over at his desk, writing laboriously. When he saw Scoglio he put his pen down and attempted to rise, but his strength failed him and he slumped back into his chair. Scoglio moved to kneel and kiss the pope's ring, never looking the pope in the face.

"Please be seated, Paolo." The pope's eyes glinted despite his fatigue, and he watched Scoglio carefully as the cardinal reached the chair opposite him. "You wanted to see me?"

Scoglio coiled his emotions tightly around himself. He said evenly, "I didn't know that the Holy See was consulting with non-Catholics about Church doctrine. I had believed that such matters were the province of the Church hierarchy, not the laity, and certainly not those outside the Church."

Pope John XXIV's voice was barely more than a whisper. "You are referring to Mr. Tyler, I presume?"

"That's exactly whom I'm referring to, and I would like to know who put him up to it."

"No one that I know of, Paolo. His mission arose out of his own experience."

Scoglio's voice became grinding. "Did you know that when he referred to the Messiah he was referring to a Jew? *A Jew?*"

The pope's eyes crinkled slightly. "What's wrong with that, Paolo. What does it matter as long as the world is made right? Jesus himself was a Jew."

The emotions started to uncoil into a venomous rattle. *"We're not talking about Jesus here, Holy Father.* We're talking about a Jew in South America who has convinced all these executives that he's going to save the world." He pointed at the pontiff. "And in the meantime he is going to destroy the

Church. With your help! Are you going to let Benda Cortes do this?"

The tired eyes flew open. "Benda Cortes?"

"Don't tell me that you are ignorant of his background, Holy Father."

"I . . . I don't know what you're talking about."

Scoglio didn't know whether to believe the pope or not. He said suspiciously, "Didn't you know that Isaac Benda Cortes is a Jew? That his ancestors were Marranos?"

"He wouldn't be the first cardinal to have ancestors who were Jewish, Paolo."

Scoglio felt stifled. "I happen to know for a fact that he has researched his background and his ancestors were all Jewish, right up to his mother. He thinks he's a Jew! And not only that, but he's plotting to take over the Church after you are gone! *He's* the one whom Tyler is referring to! *He's* the one who thinks he's the Messiah!"

"Isaac thinks he's the Messiah?" The pope used his remaining strength to swivel his chair around so his back was to Scoglio. He whispered, "Isaac Benda Cortes . . ."

Impatiently, Scoglio said coldly, "What do you intend to do, Holy Father?"

The chair swiveled back. "I must address the situation . . . while I have time left to me. Can you arrange worldwide access?"

"I can announce that you will make an emergency address tomorrow, Holy Father."

"Yes . . . yes . . . please do that. . . . I must prepare what I will say."

"Will you need help, Holy Father?"

"God is getting closer and closer, Paolo. . . . He will be my help." He waved weakly to dismiss the cardinal, who rose quickly to his feet, kissed the papal ring and exited confidently.

Pope John XXIV bowed his head and began to pray.

24

Isaac was jolted awake by the shrill ring of the telephone. He wasn't sleeping much, only five to six hours a night, and so this intrusion was more than annoying; it caused him to fold his pillow around his ears in the hope that the noise would go away.

It didn't. The telephone kept ringing until finally he wearily rolled over and yanked the receiver to his ear.

"Hello?"

". . . Isaac?"

Isaac strained to hear the ghostly, elderly voice. It sounded like a long-distance call, but even beyond that, the voice was remarkably faint. Who would call at this time of night? And who would not address him as Cardinal Benda Cortes but Isaac?

"Isaac . . . my son?"

He felt goose bumps on his arms. His first reaction was, it's my father. Then he shook his head awake, remembering that his father was long dead. The brief rush of longing for a father pained his heart.

He forced himself to respond. "Yes . . . this is Isaac. Who is this?"

"Isaac . . . I must know . . . are you indeed a Jew?"

The chill around his heart petrified his lips. He couldn't shake the thought that he was speaking to the ghost of his father. Was his father accusing him of betraying his Catholic ancestry?

He asked again, frightened, "Who is this?"

"I must know . . . I must know. . . ."

Why wouldn't the voice tell him who he was? And who would have his home telephone number? Make it go away! Tell the truth!

"Yes, yes, Father, I am a Jew! I am a Jew!"

"Ahhh . . . Isaac . . ." The line went dead. Isaac looked stupidly at the useless telephone in his hand and felt the chill around his heart turn to numbness. He reached up to his face and touched hot tears.

*　　*　　*

Five hours later, at eight in the morning, the telephone rang again, waking him out of a restless sleep. Checking the clock by his bed, he silently berated himself for oversleeping . . . then he remembered the call of five hours earlier and chills ran through him. At first he wasn't going to answer, but the sunlight streaming through the window reassured him enough to lift the receiver.

"Hello?"

"Your Eminence, it is Father Mario. I apologize for calling you so early, but there was a call this morning from Rome."

"Who was it?"

"The papal secretary said that the Holy Father was making a major announcement on television, and he asked that you watch tonight at eight o'clock our time."

"Was that all?"

"He also said that the Holy Father's illness has worsened considerably. This morning he was delirious for a brief period, and the secretary warned that the end may be near. The Holy Father insists on giving this speech tonight." His tone grew accusing. "I've been holding all calls for days now, Your Eminence. How much longer are you to be gone from your office?"

Isaac thought of the admission he had made to the ghostly voice. Had he made up his mind that he was a Jew? Was he sure?

"It won't be much longer, Father Mario," he said uncertainly. Suddenly, he had a vision of his mother.

I will be the leader of which people, Mama?

*   *   *

"Good evening, this is George Nelson. Tonight we have an abbreviated news report because Pope John XXIV is scheduled to speak fifteen minutes from now. The Tyler News Network will carry the pontiff's remarks live immediately following this broadcast.

"Around the world tonight the ugliness of anti-Semitism has raised its ancient head. Apparently there are two driving forces, the Arab oil embargo and the news of a Jewish Messiah. From Buenos Aires to Toronto, from London to Moscow, from Sydney to Johannesburg, there have been incidents of synagogue burnings, anti-Israel demonstrations, and abuse of Jewish citizens. Here in the United States, the Dow dropped more than three hundred points, and there have been sporadic outbreaks of anti-Semitism in urban areas around the country.

"In the midst of the turmoil a unique coalition has arisen. From Wall Street to Hollywood, voices are condemning the state of Israel. The spokesman for CANT, the Coalition Against the New Theocracy, is Mr. Joel Alexander. He spoke today in Los Angeles."

The television screen showed Joel standing at a podium, flanked by members of the coalition. He addressed a large contingent of reporters, punctuated by occasional flashes from their cameras.

"Ladies and gentlemen. The state of Israel has always prided itself on its tolerance of opposing viewpoints. As a bastion of democracy in the Middle East, it has been invaluable as a reflection of what the region could achieve. Today, regrettably, the state of Israel is being held hostage by a religious minority, a minority that has convinced itself that the messianic era is upon us. This minority has intimidated the scientists who discovered cold fusion into hoarding their secret, a secret that they will divulge with the coming of their Messiah, who can only be acknowledged by the religious authorities.

"We who live in an age that believes in the essential goodness of man declare that there is no need for such a Messiah or for secrecy among nations. The formula for cold fusion must be revealed, and the concept of a Messiah debunked. We declare our support for the Arab nations' demand that the Israeli government release the information, and we reject the notion that any Messiah has arisen.

"This is not a Jew versus non-Jew issue. Along with me, many members of our coalition are Jews, and we reject the notion that we have any agenda or set of rules to follow that differs from the rest of the world. We don't want to live in fear of being different. We are Jews because we were born as Jews, and we alone will decide what constitutes our Jewishness. We categorically deny that any set of rules compiled in a bygone age has any hold over us; we are free to follow our own paths.

"The time for an idea of a Jewish theocracy in Israel has passed. Israel must become like other nations, a democratic state that shares its communal responsibility with the nations of the world. We demand that Israel release the formula, and we also demand that Mr. Grant Tyler and his colleagues desist from their advocacy of a Jewish Messiah."

The screen returned to George Nelson. "We have in the studio Mr. Grant Tyler, the head of the Tyler News Network." The camera panned to Grant seated next to Nelson.

"Mr. Tyler, we have only a few moments. Just the other day, Mr. Alexander stated that your championing of a Jewish Messiah was triggered by an emotional breakdown. Now he and his coalition demand that you cease your support for such an idea. How would you respond?"

Grant looked directly into the camera. "I find it significant that Mr. Alexander's coalition calls itself CANT. I'm sure they mean to suggest that our cause *can't* be permitted to succeed. There is another meaning to the word *cant,* however. It can also mean the insincere use of pious language. When Mr. Alexander utters phrases like 'the essential goodness of man' and 'communal responsibility with the nations of the world,' he tries to pose as a moral spokesman instead of being what he really is—the high priest of a xenophobic cult."

"Xenophobic?"

Grant smiled grimly. "I'm sorry, George. Xenophobic means to be unduly fearful of foreigners or foreign concepts."

"But Mr. Alexander himself is Jewish, Mr. Tyler. The Israeli people and the Messianic concept he condemned are Jewish."

"What is foreign and fearful to Mr. Alexander and his ilk is the idea of personal responsibility, which is the linchpin of the messianic age if you are a Jew. Suddenly they can't blend in with society the way they want to; their destiny is to teach, and they must follow more stringent rules in order to purify themselves for the task."

Nelson interrupted, "But as we just reported, there is tremendous resistance to this idea from all over the world. The anti-Semitic acts that have been reported give further ammunition to Mr. Alexander when he implies that your cause is a suicidal one for Jews."

Grant said calmly, "This was all prophesied by the Jewish prophets long ago. They said the Messiah would arrive when the Jewish nation was imperiled. And . . . ," he glanced at Nelson, " . . . although I know him, I cannot announce his arrival until he deems it fitting."

*　　*　　*

Isaac sat next to Rabbi Hanviowitz in his living room, watching the small television he had asked a member of the armed guard surrounding the house to obtain, since the rabbi had no television. They had started watching the Tyler News Network at 7:58, expecting the pope to speak at the top of the hour. When the news came on instead, Isaac would have preferred to study, but George Nelson's first words not only froze Isaac and the rabbi to their seats but also brought Rivkah in from the kitchen. As Nelson described the worldwide anti-Semitic reaction, Rivkah put her hand over her mouth and backed away from the screen. Isaac's eyes started to narrow. Only the rabbi remained unaffected, intently following the report.

When Grant finished, " . . . until he deems it fitting," the rabbi glanced at his pupil. Isaac sat still, mulling it over, as Nelson continued.

"We now go to Rome, where Pope John XXIV is about to speak."

The television screen shifted to the fragile, dying figure of the pope seated behind his desk. The camera closed in to let his face fill the screen.

"Good evening . . . ladies and gentlemen."

Isaac sat straight up at the sound of the ghostly voice speaking in English.

"In the name of God . . . I take the liberty of addressing all of you as . . . my brothers. . . . Brothers who saw their ancestral home become . . . a broken home with all of us as runaways . . . ," the pope coughed weakly into a handkerchief, " . . . dispersed to every corner of the earth . . . waiting for the moment we can return to be one family again. . . ." His hands fumbled with the handkerchief.

In another room at the Vatican, Cardinal Scoglio was watching the speech on television. That morning he had asked the pope if he could accompany him when he spoke, but the pope had refused, saying that he preferred to be alone. Scoglio momentarily doubted that the pope was going to reveal Isaac's background as a Jew and condemn the whole messianic charade; but then the pope continued that the reason he wanted to be alone was that Jesus had been alone when he faced his greatest trial. The pope's mention of Jesus as his role model had reassured Scoglio.

Now he watched the pope closely, waiting for the moment when Benda Cortes would be destroyed, the Church saved and his own aspirations fulfilled.

The pontiff continued haltingly, "I recently met a most . . . remarkable man, Mr. Grant Tyler. . . . He said he had found the Messiah . . . the man who will bring universal peace and," he coughed again, "brotherhood. . . ." A spasm shook the pope and he trembled. "I know this man. . . ."

Five thousand miles away from each other in Rome and Rio de Janeiro, two cardinals sat paralyzed with shock.

"I realize some suspect us of intrigue. . . . That is false . . . we hide nothing . . . we seek the truth. . . . When I die . . . I wish the papal election to be televised . . . to allow the world to see that . . ." Another spasm shook him and this time his head drooped downward. With a massive show of will, the pope feebly raised his head.

"As to my successor . . . I wish to urge the . . . I wish to . . . urge . . . I . . . I . . . I . . . saac . . ." His face fell forward onto the desk.

The pope's physician, who had been watching out of camera range, rushed to the fallen pontiff, waving at the cameras to cut away from the scene. There must have been prior warning given to the cameramen, for the screen immediately cut back to a shaken George Nelson looking offscreen at the monitors. He had been warned that they might have to cut back to him, but he had not really believed that the pope might die during the speech.

"Ladies and gentlemen, out of respect for the Holy See, we will not intrude on Pope John XXIV in his distress." He suddenly looked offscreen at something. "What?" The screen showed Nelson waiting, waiting . . . He faced the camera again. "Just a moment, ladies and gentlemen. . . ." Nelson looked offscreen again, his eyebrows raised. Then suddenly his eyebrows fell and his face went slack. He slowly turned back to face the camera.

"Ladies and gentlemen, the Supreme Pontiff of the Roman Catholic Church, His Holiness Pope John XXIV, is dead. . . ."

*   *   *

Scoglio sat frozen to his chair, his mind chaotic. *What am I going to do?* he thought wildly. *What am I going to do?*

He felt sure that everyone had heard the pope say "Isaac," Benda Cortes's name, as his successor just before he collapsed. The whole world had heard it! There was no way that he could stop the juggernaut now. Now that the pope was dead, the attention and sympathy given the dying man's last words would catapult Benda Cortes to the papacy, and he would systematically destroy the Church!

His mind raced through everything the Church had meant to him during his lifetime. During his youth, the warmth of being part of a group; in his early adulthood, the people he had advised; the years of middle age, when he had seized the chance to be ambitious; and the last stage, where he could use what he had achieved to serve God as his viceroy.

Although he sat immobile, the hatred that was kindling inside him roared to a firestorm, launching him out of his chair to pace furiously around the room, looking fiercely at the crucifix on the wall.

The telephone rang. Scoglio walked over and almost swept it off his desk in his fury. He snapped, "Cardinal Scoglio here."

"Sit down, Scoglio. We need to talk."

Scoglio's fury was punctured and released; he recognized his benefactor. He sat down, chastened, like a schoolboy. "Don Sanguino?"

"You will listen?"

"Yes, don Sanguino."

"I will assume that you were also watching. From the sound of your voice when you answered my call, I assume you are concerned."

Scoglio knew better than to reply petulantly that *of course* he was upset. He said humbly, "But you heard what he said. He said that he knew who this Messiah was. And he named his successor. He said 'Isaac.' That's Benda Cortes's first name."

"That's not what I heard."

Scoglio's eyebrows rose. "Forgive me, don Sanguino, what did you say?"

"I heard him say 'I—sick,' not Isaac. *He was saying that he was sick.*"

"You don't really believe that, do you, don Sanguino?"

"Try to convince me otherwise. . . . We have to work quickly to make this clear to the press."

"But everyone knows—"

"What? That Benda Cortes is this Messiah they keep talking about? They know nothing. How many of them know that Benda Cortes's name is Isaac? Probably none. That means that they won't put his name together with the Messiah the pope spoke of. All we have to do is convince them that the pope was slightly delirious when he spoke of the Messiah, and he even acknowledged that fact when he said 'I sick' at the end."

The cardinal objected, "But even if we deflect the pope's acknowledgment of the Messiah and the choice of his successor, can we also negate his idea of televising the next papal election? Benda Cortes has a magnetic appeal that could sway the college to vote for him, and it seems he has powerful allies. I'm not even sure that revealing he's a Jew would work; he could deny it, and it would only be our word against his."

"I'm afraid that we must go through with the open election, Scoglio. Once the world heard the pontiff equate honesty and openness with open elections, it's too late to go back without jeopardizing your influence."

Scoglio muttered, "Then what do we do? We cannot stop Benda Cortes's plan for control."

There was a pause while Sanguino considered the possibilities. Then he directed, "I want you to handle the press immediately. Inform them about the delirium that affected the pope, and make sure you convince them that his last words were an admission of his condition."

"But what about Benda Cortes?"

"Your job is to handle the press, Scoglio. I have to call Colombia."

*　*　*

Cesar Carlos didn't have any trouble adding two and two. When he had heard two days before that Grant Tyler had announced that the Messiah in South America was a Jew, Carlos had known where to look: Isaac Benda Cortes. The fact that the pope had confirmed Tyler's discovery confused him, though, because he knew nothing of the pope's desire to reform the Church and couldn't understand why the pope would support a Jew as the Messiah.

He sat in his office at home, looking out the window at the night sky covered with stars. He suddenly realized that even though a Messiah could be a threat to his business and his wealth, he wanted to confront such a man face to face and measure himself against him. He knew that he would emerge triumphant—he had risen to power by virtue of his cunning and fearlessness—and whoever this Messiah was, he hadn't been forged from the same steel. The thought of such a meeting was intoxicating.

"Cesar, I am sorry to interrupt you but there is news."

Carlos turned to see his advisor Rodrigo standing in the doorway. The older man waited for Carlos to beckon him forward.

"Come in, Rodrigo." Rodrigo crossed the room to sit across from Carlos, who reluctantly left his dream of confrontation.

Rodrigo noticed Carlos's distraction. "Cesar, the pope is dead."

The eyes flashed into focus. "When?"

"Within the last hour. Apparently, he was giving a speech, and he collapsed. I only learned of this because there is a call for you from Sicily."

"Sanguino."

"Yes. He wishes to speak with you right away."

"Put him through, Rodrigo. And make sure that no one comes near the room."

"Yes, Cesar." Rodrigo closed the door quietly behind him. Carlos leaned back in his chair and waited for the call to come through. Ten seconds later the telephone beeped and he answered.

"Sanguino? You are keeping late hours for a man your age."

Sanguino had no time for banter. "Carlos, did you see the speech?"

Carlos grew serious. "No, I didn't."

"Let me enlighten you as to what has happened." Carlos listened carefully, unemotionally at first, but slowly he sat forward until both elbows were on the desk and he gripped his chin with his free hand. His face shone with excitement.

"It is as good as done."

*   *   *

Isaac stood at the door to the rabbi's house.

"I must go. Even if it is just to pay my respects to him, I must go."

Rabbi Hanviowitz understood. "What will you do if they want to elect you?"

Isaac shivered. "I will tell them the truth, if they can hear it."

"There are those who wish to harm you."

"I know it."

Rivkah stood quietly behind her father. She said in a steady voice, "Must you go?"

Isaac wanted to tell her exactly what she had awakened in him, what she meant to him, but he was afraid of her reaction. Instead, he responded, "How can I ask them to make such a fearful change if I am afraid myself?" He looked at the rabbi and admitted, "I am frightened, too."

Rivkah said quietly, "I will wait for you."

Isaac swiftly turned his head, startled. He saw Rivkah with her hands clenched by her sides, waiting apprehensively for his reaction. He stared at her, realizing that she loved him and was terrified of giving her love to a man who might not have the slightest interest, having lived his entire life as a man of the Church—a celibate.

A picture of his mother flashed through his mind, and to his astonishment, he heard himself burst out, "I want to come back to *you*."

Rivkah's hands unclenched and she folded them and put them to her lips, her eyes radiant with love and fear. The rabbi put his hand on Isaac's shoulder and said gently in Hebrew the blessing God gave Aaron to bless the children of Israel: "May God bless you and protect you . . . may God illuminate his countenance for you and be gracious to you . . . may God turn his countenance to you and establish peace for you."

Isaac turned toward the armed guard outside and left, without looking back.

*   *   *

Grant awakened at home to the aroma of eggs and coffee, wafting upstairs from the kitchen. He was confused because nobody else was at home, and no alarm had gone off.

The night before in the studio with George Nelson he had witnessed the pope's collapse and the resultant chaos in the studio. After thirty minutes of issuing orders to those in the studio and those in Rome, he extricated himself and quickly called Rabbi Hanviowitz in Brazil to consult with Isaac. By the time the rabbi answered, Isaac had left for the airport. Grant, frustrated, worried for Isaac, told the rabbi that he would see Isaac in Rome, since the election of the new pope was going to be televised. Then he went straight home to bed to get some sleep.

Throwing on his robe, he silently headed downstairs. Near the bottom of the staircase, he peeked around the corner to see Beverly cooking at the stove. Then he remembered that he had given her a key to the house when he had gone down to Brazil, just in case she had needed something for Matthew if he regained consciousness. She heard him pad down the stairs and turned around with the frying pan in her hand, smiling at him. Grant forgot about the pope or anything else and smiled back instinctively, then stopped in his tracks, suddenly remembering another woman standing with the same frying pan.

Beverly stopped, too, seeing Grant halt abruptly, and she held her breath, waiting tensely to see what he would do. After a long moment, his eyes focused on her again, and he forgave her for rekindling his memory of Becky. He smiled again and walked over to the kitchen table. Beverly exhaled deeply, slid the eggs on the two plates she had placed on the table, and sat down with him.

Grant sipped his coffee. "Mmmm . . . that's great. This is just about the—" A thought struck him, and he started laughing at himself.

Beverly asked tentatively, "Did I do something wrong?"

Grant saw her hesitation and said quickly, "No, no, Beverly. It's just that I was marveling at how good the coffee was and how you would know what I like, and then I realized something . . . of course it's great, Grant, you dope, she's been making it for you for years." He reached out and squeezed her hand and they both started to laugh until they were roaring.

Beverly shyly said, "Can I tell you how proud of you I was last night when you spoke on the news?"

Grant said, "You can say whatever you wish. You haven't let me down yet."

"I *was* proud of you. You've got a lot of people gunning for you right now."

"Let them shoot at me as long as they leave Isaac alone."

Beverly's protectiveness asserted itself. "I understand, Grant, but I want you in one piece, too."

Grant sipped some more coffee. "One way or another, everything will come to a head soon. Isaac's on his way to Rome now. And I'm going there to cover the election."

"Do you really think the Church will televise it?"

"Since the pope brought it forth last night and then died, the impetus from his announcement will grow until it is driven through. I've got to go to Isaac. Can you turn on the radio? I want to get the traffic report to estimate the drive to the airport."

Beverly walked over to the counter and flipped on the radio.

This is KTNN, the Tyler News Network, with an update on a breaking story out of Brazil. . . . The daring kidnapping of the cardinal from Rio de Janeiro on his way to the airport to fly to Rome has the world aghast. Cardinal Isaac Benda Cortes was taken after an ambush in the midst of gunfire that left five members of his entourage dead, and one severely wounded. A group of approximately twenty men has disappeared with the cardinal, and there have been no claims of responsibility from any terrorist group . . . further updates as they occur . . .

Beverly turned to look at Grant, but he was already gone, racing up the stairs.

I saac was silent. Nor had his captors spoken to him since they had blindfolded him and shoved him into a car following the attack.

The ambush had been so unexpected that Isaac's six bodyguards never had a chance to use their weapons. Of the six, three rode on motorcycles in front of his car and two others rode behind it. The sixth drove the car while Isaac sat in the back seat, finishing the last volume of the Mishnah Torah. He was most struck by Maimonides's assertion that Jews could *consider* someone to be the Messiah if he was learned in the law and compelled all Jews to be observant, but they could be *certain* he was the Messiah if he also gathered the dispersed of Israel and eventually rebuilt the temple in its proper place. He finished the concluding paragraphs of the monumental work and reflected for a moment on another assertion of Maimonides: that the deeds of Jesus and Mohammed were to improve the world to prepare for the messianic age.

He was pondering all this when the car slowed down, and he peered forward through the windshield. Two cars had smashed into each other just ahead, blocking the road, and two men were arguing furiously next to them. The three motorcyclists in front of Isaac's car slowed to a stop and dismounted to encourage the drivers to move their cars to the side of the road.

Isaac's driver stopped and Isaac had returned to his contemplation when he heard a sound of thunder outside. For a millisecond he thought to himself, *It can't be thunder, the sky is blue,* and then he knew and he threw himself down on the back seat.

Even through the window of the car he could hear the screams from his guards outside, and he wondered how they could sound so clear until he realized that the front windows of his car had shattered when the gunmen targeted the driver. It seemed only a moment later that the door next to Isaac's head was thrown open. He raised his head instinctively, but someone slammed it back onto the seat face down and fumbled to blindfold him. Quickly, he was dragged out of the car and pushed into another car. As he fell into the other car, he heard someone cursing, and he strained to hear the reason. Apparently, one of Isaac's bodyguards to the rear of the car had never come to a full stop, sized up the number of assailants and gunned the motorcycle past the ambush, leaving them to fire after him. Though he had been shot in the shoulder and back, he had managed to ride out of sight to find help.

The getaway car sped along without a sound from its occupants; the only sound Isaac heard was the hum of the engine. He knew that there were at least two men in the car with him: the driver and the man next to him in the back seat sticking a gun into his ribs. He was frightened, but he was still rational enough to realize that if the men responsible for the ambush had wanted to kill him he would have been dead already. Forcing himself to breathe slowly, he tried to figure out where his kidnappers intended to take him, and who was responsible.

Soon, to his surprise, he heard the roar of airplanes taking off. He couldn't believe that they would go to the airport with him in tow. No one was that brazen.

But when the car came rolling to a halt, the back door thrown open and his body pulled from the car, he knew he was at the airport; he heard different airplanes taking off and landing. He had only three walking steps to recognize that fact, however, because with his fourth step he started ascending a ramp into an airplane and barely had time to be forced into his seat before the whine of the engine started and they were catapulted into the air.

How his captors could have avoided the usual security and gone straight to their airplane amazed him. Who would have that kind of clout? Only one man he could think of . . .

*   *   *

At the Vatican, Cardinal Scoglio walked nervously toward the room where the press waited for him. He had hardly slept after the call from Sanguino, and the next morning, without consulting any of his fellow cardinals, he had arranged a press conference for that evening. He intended to swiftly confront the issue of the pope's credibility and convince the world that the pope had been delirious when he spoke of the Messiah and named Isaac as his successor. After the press conference was scheduled, he secluded himself and let it be known he was not to be interrupted so he could work on his speech.

He wouldn't have been nervous about addressing the press except for one thing; as he left his quarters at the Vatican to head for the conference, one of the young priests in the building had begged his forgiveness for intruding and asked him with tears in his eyes if he had heard the news: Cardinal Benda Cortes had been kidnapped.

Scoglio was slightly shocked, not because of the kidnapping (Sanguino had *said* he would handle Benda Cortes), but because the young priest was obviously distraught. It was an unwelcome reminder that Benda Cortes was a well-loved man. He suddenly wondered, *How will that affect the press?* And there were other questions, too. He doubled back to his quarters and called Sicily.

*   *   *

Scoglio shuffled the papers of his speech and cleared his throat.

"Ladies and gentlemen, I apologize for being a little late. . . . The tragic death of the Holy Father in the middle of his address last night left many questions unanswered. As you know, I was close to the Holy Father for many years, and I watched him gallantly fight against the disease that threatened his life. He was a noble man, and consequently it was all the more painful to witness his delirium in his last days. It is not unusual in some cancers for the poison to ultimately affect the cognitive process, and what made the Holy Father's fight even more poignant was his awareness of his losing struggle.

"Even in his extremity, when he was moments from death, he wished to disavow the delirious thoughts he had previously articulated, so much so that his last words were the English words 'I sick,' acknowledging the loss of his mental faculties. He fought through his delirium to recant what he had said previously about the coming of the Messiah. At the moment he was to leave us, he wanted to make sure that there would be continuity, a proper succession that would continue the glorious history of our faith, not heretical ideas that would jeopardize it."

He paused briefly to examine the faces around him. Were they persuaded?

One reporter had the audacity to seize the moment. He asked, "Your Eminence, are you saying everything the pope said was false, a product of dementia? He mentioned that he had met Grant Tyler of the Tyler News Network and confirmed the Messiah's existence. Do you think that he imagined such a meeting?"

"I think we should ask Mr. Tyler if he took advantage of the Holy Father's condition and misled him into false beliefs."

Another reporter jumped in. "Your Eminence, are you implying that the pope's desire for the succession to be televised and open to the world was also an error?" The journalists waited intently for the answer.

Scoglio thought, *Don't make any enemies with these people.* He responded smoothly, "In an age where the public is skeptical of established institutions, I think it is in the Church's interest to allow the world to see how we elect our leadership."

The reporter realized that Scoglio was subtly evading him; he had given the journalists what they wanted, access to the election, but he was dodging the question of how the pope had been wrong on the Messiah issue but right on the open election issue.

A voice called from the back, "What about the kidnapping, Your Eminence?"

Scoglio knew he would get that question sooner or later. He replied thoughtfully, "You mean of Cardinal Benda Cortes?"

"Yes. Will that impede the selection of a new pontiff? He is, after all, your most likely rival for the papacy."

The cardinal's demeanor became icy. "I do not view anyone as a rival. The papacy is not a contest to be won; it is an honor and duty to be conferred on the one best suited to serve the interests of Christ here on earth."

The same reporter murmured to a colleague, "Although his absence wouldn't hurt Scoglio's candidacy either." All within earshot nodded knowingly. Emboldened, the reporter continued, "How soon will the Church have a statement regarding the kidnapping, Your Eminence?"

"Ladies and gentlemen, you may rest assured that every member of the Church condemns the kidnapping of the unfortunate cardinal. We urgently await word from him or those who committed such a heinous crime. But until we have information regarding his whereabouts, all we can do is pray for his safety and continue with our primary mission: convening the conclave to elect Pope John XXIV's successor. I thank you for your indulgence and urge you to inform your constituents that they should disregard the pope's statements in his extremity. The Church does not recognize the statements as binding or accurate." He started to leave the room.

"Just where do you think Cardinal Benda Cortes is, Your Eminence?"

Scoglio, irritated at the insistence of the reporters regarding Benda Cortes, restrained his impulse to lash out at them. "We all pray that he is in God's hands."

*   *   *

After Grant had heard the news of Isaac's disappearance, he had dressed hurriedly and yelled downstairs to Beverly to get in the car. Five minutes later she sat beside him as he drove, listening intently to the news on the radio.

In Paris early this morning an Orthodox synagogue was fire-bombed. Fifty-four year old Rabbi Shimon Halevy was killed along with twelve other men praying with him. This occurred eight hours after a similar incident occurred in London, where another Orthodox synagogue was bombed. As in Europe, the flurry of anti-Semitic violence continues to grow around the world. There are numerous reports of rioting in Jewish areas of South America, and in Australia the prime minister has stated that he cannot protect the Jewish population from random violence.

Here in the United States there were three more firebombings of synagogues last night, two in New York and one in Atlanta, and in Chicago a kosher market was vandalized and burned to the ground. This morning President Evans implored the American public to avoid such outrageous acts while simultaneously condemning the Israeli government for its stubbornness.

President Evans's voice was heard:

Fellow Americans, our history as a tolerant people is being tar-nished by internecine acts of hatred and violence against some of our citizens. These despicable acts are to be condemned; we are not a nation of barbarians. I plead with all of you to respect the rights of others and focus your attention on the genuine cause of your hostility: the reluctance of the state of Israel to share their momentous discov-ery of cold fusion with the world. We must unify the global forces of reason to insist that Israel acknowledge the duty to its fellow nations. I have asked for a special session of the United Nations to condemn Israel's intransigence and make the world's position clear on this point. I ask all of you to refrain from attacks on our Jewish citizens and institutions; such behavior is not in our interest.

Grant was incredulous. The president had offered a carrot but no stick to the dark forces of hate surfacing in the country. He had simply given them an alternate target for their sickness—the State of Israel—and stated that *evil behavior was not in our interest.*

Beverly felt sick to her stomach. "What do we do now?"

Grant swung the car into his parking space. "First we have to figure out how to save Isaac."

"*If* we can find out where he is."

∗   ∗   ∗

When they opened the door to Grant's office five minutes later, the tele-phone on Beverly's desk was already ringing. She ran over and answered it.

"Hello?"

"There's a call for Mr. Tyler from Brazil, Miss Engler." As Grant reached Beverly she whispered to him, "It's from Brazil." Grant's eyes narrowed, and he mouthed to Beverly, "See who it is," as he headed for his desk.

"Who's calling, operator?"

"A Rivkah Hanviowitz." Beverly knew who Rivkah was since Grant had told her about his trip to Brazil, but she was surprised that Rivkah, not Rabbi Hanviowitz, would be calling.

"This is Beverly Engler, Mr. Tyler's assistant. Can I help you?"

Rivkah's voice was quiet because she was shy about her English, but

Beverly could still sense the undercurrent of desperation. "I am Rivkah Hanviowitz, daughter of Rabbi Daniel Hanviowitz in Rio de Janeiro."

"I know who you are, Miss Hanviowitz."

"I need to speak with Mr. Tyler. Can you reach him?" Before Beverly could respond, Rivkah added, "I will give anything if he can help me. It's . . . it's about Isaac Benda Cortes."

"Isaac?"

"I am sorry . . . you think of him as Cardinal Benda Cortes."

Beverly twisted to see Grant looking questioningly at her through his office window. "Do you have some information related to the kidnapping, Miss Hanviowitz? Otherwise let me take your number, and Mr. Tyler will call you back as soon as he can."

Rivkah's voice trembled. "I *must* speak with him. I *must* speak with him."

Beverly saw another call coming through. Distracted, she waved to Grant that she was putting Rivkah's call through to him. "Please hold for Mr. Tyler, Miss Hanviowitz." She put the call through to Grant and then clicked back to the operator.

"Another call from Brazil for Mr. Tyler, Miss Engler . . . a Mr. Cesar Carlos."

Cesar Carlos? Beverly had spent the last seven years of her life working for the head of the world's biggest news organization; she knew who Carlos was. She also was quick enough to guess the reason he was calling all the way from Brazil: Isaac.

"This is Beverly Engler, Mr. Tyler's assistant. Can I help you?"

His voice sounded exactly as she thought it would, despite his heavily accented English: suave and controlled. "Miss Engler, may you let me speak to Mr. Tyler?"

Her voice apprehensive, she asked, "May I ask what this is regarding?"

"Tell him I have a very . . . important guest. He is a friend of Tyler's. An *eminent* friend."

Eminent? *Eminence.* She was right. It *was* about Isaac. She waved frantically to Grant, who was standing at his desk talking animatedly with Rivkah. He held up his hand to forestall her.

Forcing herself to speak evenly, she said, "Please hold, Mr. Carlos." She put the phone down and almost ran into Grant's office. She hissed, "Grant,

I've got *Cesar Carlos* on the line. You've got to take this call! He's holding the cardinal!"

Grant's eyes snapped to her. "Rivkah, stay there." He put her on hold. "Beverly, you take Rivkah at your desk while I take Carlos." Beverly ran for her desk as Grant changed lines.

"Grant Tyler speaking."

Carlos didn't pretend to be convivial. "Mr. Tyler, a friend of yours is staying with me. You refer to him as a hero of the Jews. This confuses me because all the years he was fighting me he looked like a Catholic priest. Do you know who I mean?"

Grant said shortly, "I understand you. What do you want with him? If you harm him—"

"Oh, do not threaten me, Mr. Tyler. We have killed cardinals and bishops before without fear of punishment."

"What is it that you want?"

"Just a small change. We want you to say you made a mistake . . . that you were wrong, there is no Jewish . . . what is the word? . . . Messiah."

Grant wanted to probe deeper. "Why is that your concern? Besides, he was going to Rome to elect a new pope. Why did you stop him?"

"I don't understand this kind of 'Messiah.' Maybe he goes to Rome to change things. I don't like changes, Mr. Tyler."

"Why not just kill him then?"

"I will . . . I will. But first he and I will talk."

"If you're going to kill him, why are you calling me?"

Carlos started to grow violent at Tyler's confrontational attitude. "Because you may have another man who can be this hero, too. *I want you to say you made a mistake.*"

"And if I don't?"

Carlos paused for effect. "Then he is not the only one who will die." He waited for Grant to respond, but Grant was silent. "I will give the Jew three days." He said cheerfully, "One more thing, Mr. Tyler. If you try anything, I will kill him immediately and you next." He hung up.

Grant slowly put the telephone down and desperately tried to think. Beverly had been watching him while he spoke with Carlos, and she saw his face turn ashen at the end. When he hung up she called, "Grant? Do you have anything you want to say to Rivkah?"

Grant picked up the telephone and pushed the button for Rivkah's line. "Rivkah, I didn't speak with him . . . yes, Carlos has him . . . I don't know what I am going to do . . . I'm sorry. . . ."

Beverly came back to his desk. "How bad is it?"

"It's bad, all right. He has Isaac and he says he is going to kill him."

"Kill a cardinal of the Church? He can't do that."

His eyes distant, Grant said, "This man can kill anyone he wants."

Beverly stared at him. "What do you mean, *anyone?*" When Grant didn't answer she grabbed his arms and turned him to face her. "I asked you what you meant, *anyone.* Did he threaten to kill you, too?"

"If I don't retract everything I've said about the Messiah, yes."

She hurled the words at him. "Then retract them! Retract them! The world can't be made perfect anyway! What difference does it make if the world changes and you're not here? *Think,* Grant! How can I—how can I—*Damn it, I've finally reached you, and you want to leave me!*"

Grant reached out to hold the weeping woman close. Her head buried in his chest, he let her sob. When he finally spoke, it was with great tenderness. "I want you to promise me something."

She looked up at him through the tears, hoping . . . hoping . . .

He stroked her hair and looked away. "If something should happen to me, will you take care of my boy?"

*   *   *

Carlos hung up the telephone and turned to the man sitting across the desk from him. He studied the man's face, looking for a hint of some emotion. The man had listened to the entire conversation without reacting, even when his own death was discussed, and Carlos was forced to admit that his captive possessed unusual self-control.

In fact, Isaac was experiencing a psychological severance from anything he had known, a total lack of control over his destiny. After being flown to Carlos's private airfield in Colombia, he had been driven to Carlos's villa and placed under a comfortable house arrest. He had a bedroom with its own bathroom and food was brought to him immediately. When he was finished eating, the two armed guards outside the bedroom had escorted him to Carlos's study, where another armed guard trained a rifle on his heart as Isaac was led to the chair opposite Carlos's empty desk. Five minutes later

Carlos appeared and waved the armed guard out of the room. Without speaking, he sat at his desk and made the call to Grant.

Now Isaac saw his captor appraising him and he wondered what would happen next. He hadn't spoken a word since his abduction, and he intended to flow with the tide of events; if control over his destiny was being taken from him, he thought, he might as well give it up.

Carlos had intended to wait until Isaac spoke, but he sullenly realized that Isaac was willing to wait for him to make the next move. He was damned if he would give the cardinal the satisfaction of seeing his irritation. He said casually, "After all this time, Your Eminence, we can confront each other without the use of any intermediaries—like the press."

The memory of Alfonso Rissolo's death suddenly seared through Isaac's consciousness, impelling him to speak. "Or your employees in Rio de Janeiro."

Carlos was pleased. There was a chink in the cardinal's armor after all. "That was a necessary step, Your Eminence. I make it my business to gather useful information. How else would I know that you have been masquerading as a Catholic all your life?"

As long as I'm going to die anyway, Isaac thought . . . "And who told you about Rissolo?"

The drug lord smiled. "Ah, yes . . ." He called to the door, "Bring our other guest in, Roberto." Isaac twisted around in his chair to see the door open and Roberto, the armed guard that Carlos had dismissed from the room, enter followed by a familiar face: Pablo de Cardoso. Pablo didn't flinch from the look of amazement on Isaac's face. Instead, he gave Isaac a look of triumph which the cardinal found unfathomable. *Why would the journalist feel such pride?*

Isaac soon found out. Roberto carried a chair to the side of Carlos behind the desk and then exited. Carlos indicated for Pablo to sit down.

"Pablo, our guest just asked me how I knew to gather information from Alfonso Rissolo." He smiled benignly at the journalist. "Would you care to enlighten him?"

Pablo coolly looked at Isaac. "I overheard your conversation with him at the stadium and put two and two together. The rest was just a matter of following him when you returned from Spain."

Isaac forgot the peril he was in and asked savagely, "And do you know what happened to him, Mr. de Cardoso?"

Pablo looked boldly at him. "There are times when extreme measures are justified, if truth is to prevail."

"And which truth are you defending?"

"The truth that you are a Jew, and not a Catholic at all! If you are pope, you will destroy the Church!"

Isaac was amazed. "*You* are defending the Church from *me?*"

Carlos was enjoying the reversal of roles immensely. He said blandly, "Sometimes a man finds his destiny in the strangest ways. Isn't that what happened to you, Your *Eminence?*"

"Something like that, yes."

"And from what I have learned from your friend Grant Tyler's outbursts in the media, you are supposed to be this 'Messiah' person? You are supposed to lead the Jews to . . . 'freedom,' is that right?"

Isaac was silent.

Carlos leaned back in his chair. "I always wanted to see a real live miracle. The Church always talked about the miracles of Jesus. Is that what you do?" Pablo snickered. "But I forgot something . . . Jesus has nothing to do with this, because you're a Jew." He smiled beatifically. "Why don't you start freeing the Jews by freeing just one—you. Now *that* would be a miracle."

Pablo added, "And Carlos, what I've been hearing in the news is that the Jews around the world are being attacked because of this Messiah business. Many people are *very* upset about it."

Carlos said, "Now see what you've done, Your Eminence? More Jews are suffering just because of you. Is that what you want?"

Isaac remained silent despite the taunting, wondering where Carlos was leading.

Carlos came to the point. "Have you thought about denying this whole 'Messiah' business, Your Eminence? You might save a lot of Jews that way."

With a faith that he himself found astonishing, Isaac affirmed, "I have faith that God will not abandon his people."

Pablo was scornful. "So where was he in World War II? And if the Jews are his people, why don't you rule the world, instead of being so pitifully small?"

Isaac said quietly, "God has his plan. I am reconciled to waiting for him patiently, whether I have three days—" he looked at Carlos pointedly—"or three years, or three decades."

Carlos's telephone beeped. "Carlos here." He listened for a moment, stroked his chin and answered, "Enough." He hung up and gazed at Isaac with anticipation. "You insist on continuing this game you are playing even at the risk of your people? You were speaking of patience with God, I believe. Apparently some are more patient than others. The Arabs have just declared war on Israel."

26

Isaac sat down on the bed heavily. Everything seemed to be happening just the way that Rabbi Hanviowitz had said it would at the advent of the messianic age, with the Jews around the world being threatened with violence and possible extinction. Now that the Arab world had declared war on Israel, and the rest of the world looked as if it might jump on the bandwagon, too, the extinction of the Jewish people was a grave possibility.

Although he had answered Carlos that God would protect his people, the news that the Arab world had declared war had left him with a creeping doubt. How far was too far? Had he endangered his own people by viewing himself as the Messiah? If he renounced the idea, would he save Jews instead of endangering them? Was this his own ego and vanity or was he genuinely the instrument of God's plan?

He wasn't certain of anything now. He tried to examine himself, to recognize what parts of himself were fundamental to his identity. His lifelong passion for justice? When he tried to summon it, all he could find was emptiness. He realized that his passion had been bulwarked by his faith in God; his courage and dedication predicated on the belief that God stood behind him, watching over him. But was he?

Isaac didn't doubt God's existence; he was powerfully aware that every blade of grass testified to it. Among the thousands of texts he had read in his life were numerous science books, and he had found it poignant that they acknowledged that the chances of the world arising by accident were microscopic if not impossible, and yet insisted that there was no creator simply because he could not be quantified and measured by their own techniques.

The question that now haunted him was not whether God existed, but whether he had acted in concord with God's design. *Am I really a megalomaniac?* he asked himself. *Has this adventure been simply my reaction to the discovery that I am a Jew and therefore unfit to be a cardinal who can exert power? Am I looking for another avenue to exert my will over others?*

I don't know . . . I don't know. . . .

He temporarily freed his mind from the tyranny of self-doubt and asked himself: *Where does this indecision originate? Am I waiting for a sign from God that I'm on the right path?*

What am I trying to do, anyway, take on the whole world?

All his life Isaac had found the answers he needed in the Bible. But the example of leadership put forth in Christian Scripture was the example of Jesus, who ended by being crucified and later deified. *That's not who I am,* he thought. *I'm not going to save the world by dying, and I'm certainly not God.*

Was there another example of someone willing to confront the entire world for the sake of God? Here he had imagined himself as the man to awaken the world's eternally dormant knowledge of God. If he was the *end* of the line, where had it *begun?*

And then he thought of one man, one solitary man who had shattered the world's illusions of no gods, or many gods, or gods limited by their connection with the physical. A man who saw that limiting God in any way was inherently antithetical. A man who risked his life to insist that God was eternal and indivisible, and intimately involved with his creation. A man who was constantly hearkened back to by Judaism, Christianity and Islam as their patriarch.

As he looked back to his partner in the huge historical arc of enlightening the world about God, Isaac realized he had been asking himself the wrong question. He didn't need a sign from God; *God needed a sign from him: the same sign that eternally bound Abraham.*

And he knew that his indecision stemmed from leaving one thing undone.

*   *   *

Monsignor Giovanni Bentivoglio had been weeping on and off since Pope John XXIV collapsed during his speech. As the man responsible for looking after His Holiness's household affairs, it fell to him to supervise the gathering of the pope's possessions for safekeeping. He had loved his pontiff deeply, and watching the pontiff struggle valiantly against the fiery disease consuming him had been the most painful time of Giovanni's life. When he heard Cardinal Scoglio disparage the pope's last days as marked by delirium, he was infuriated.

As the chamberlain of the pope's household, he was not unaware of the books that the pope had been reading regarding the historicity of Jesus. He had seen the titles and wondered why the pope would be reading such material. But the pope's gentle demeanor had convinced him that any suspicions were groundless and any speculation pointless. A sensitive man like His Holiness, Bentivoglio rationalized, was certain to be beyond any radical notions.

Although he had aides to help him collect the pope's belongings, there was one job that Bentivogloio insisted on doing himself: removing the papers from the desk in the pope's study. He excused the others from the study and opened the top drawer of the desk with a key. He was surprised to find only one item in the drawer: a manila envelope. On the envelope was written, "In the event of my death deliver immediately to Mr. Grant Tyler." As he pulled it out of the drawer, a small piece of paper fluttered down from the drawer to the floor. Bentivoglio bent over to pick it up and saw Grant's name followed by a phone number. Bentivoglio looked at the telephone and hesitated but a moment; even after the pontiff's death, he was His Holiness's faithful servant.

*   *   *

It was only a moment after Grant had asked Beverly to look after Matthew when the telephone rang. Beverly had a brief impulse to hold Grant a moment longer, but she forced herself to let go of him and unsteadily walked to her desk.

"This is Beverly Engler, Mr. Tyler's assistant. Can I help you?"

"I am Monsignor Bentivoglio . . . the chief of Pope John's household. I have found an envelope His Holiness left for Mr. Tyler but I have no address for Mr. Tyler, just a telephone number. Can you tell me your address?"

Beverly said quickly to Grant, "It's a Monsignor Bentivoglio, chief of Pope John's household. He says the pope left an envelope for you."

Grant jumped at the telephone. He snapped, "This is Grant Tyler. Did you say the pope left something for me?"

"That's correct, Mr. Tyler. It's a sealed envelope that he wanted delivered immediately in the event of his death."

"Open it."

"I don't know if I have the right to do that, Mr. Tyler. It's addressed to you."

"I give you my permission. Open it." Grant waited, eyes boring into Beverly, who was watching him intently.

"It's a document, Mr. Tyler . . . it's about twenty pages long . . . the front page is titled The Holy See's Choice of a Successor and . . ." There was a giant pause; then the Monsignor continued unsteadily, " . . . the Evolution of the Church."

Grant reacted swiftly. "Do you have a fax machine nearby?"

"Yes, there is one down the hall."

"Do you know how to use it? Can you send me a copy right now?"

Bentivoglio's voice was shaky. "Maybe I should ask my superiors first. I don't know if this should leave the Vatican. . . . The Holy Father may have made a mistake. . . ."

Grant took a chance that Bentivoglio's loyalty to the deceased pope was even greater than his loyalty to the Church as an institution.

"Monsignor Bentivoglio, you knew the Holy Father as well as anyone. He is no longer here to supervise his affairs, but he did address the envelope to me, did he not?"

"Yes, he did . . ." Bentivoglio's voice grew anguished. "And he always was clear in his thinking, *always*."

Grant was unaware of Scoglio's press conference and so he didn't understand the undercurrent of fury in Bentivoglio's voice. He only knew that for the moment, Bentivoglio had sided with him. He seized the opportunity. "Then don't you think that we should carry out what may have been his last request?"

Bentivoglio's smoldering anger at Scoglio surfaced. He said defiantly, "I will send it to you right away, Mr. Tyler."

"Good. As soon as you have sent me the copy, I want you to reseal the envelope and put it in a safe place." Grant dictated his fax number to the Monsignor, then wondered if Bentivoglio might have a change of heart after he sent the document. "I should be in Rome tomorrow morning."

"I will fax it to you immediately."

Grant hung up the telephone and grabbed Beverly's hand as he hurried them both back into his office to wait by the fax machine. They stood in front of it, staring at it, hardly moving. When it reeled out the first page, Grant grabbed it and started reading rapidly. Beverly watched his eyes running back and forth across the page, and she barely had time to pull out the next page before he grabbed it from her while handing her what he had just read. Twenty minutes later, Grant looked sideways at her as she finished reading the last page.

She said, "I'll get the plane ready."

*   *   *

Carlos sat at his desk, pleased with himself. He had watched Cardinal Benda Cortes closely when he suggested that the cardinal was endangering his own people by continuing on his present course. And when the news was delivered that Israel was under attack, he could feel the noose tighten around the cardinal's neck. The whole scenario was unfolding better than he could have hoped.

Carlos prided himself on his own personal courage even more than his cleverness. He was not afraid of dying; in his youth he had figured that he would have some sort of tragic, heroic death. He thought that his attitude hadn't changed, but in truth, he had gotten comfortable with his situation and didn't feel that he was endangered anymore. The thrill he had once gotten from evading death as he ascended the rungs of power had evaporated once he reached the top. Evading death was delegated to his subordinates.

He realized he was bored with the lack of personal combat. He was middle-aged, and too old for physical combat now, but there remained the option of mental confrontation. It didn't bother him that he himself was not at risk, that this was a one-sided confrontation; he had become an observer of others' lives and risks anyway. The real battle was between the cardinal and death, with Carlos as the catalyst.

The guard Roberto knocked on the open door and entered to stand at attention.

"Yes, Roberto?"

"I put the articles from today's newspaper in his room as you asked, sir. Ten minutes later he called for a guard, and when I answered, he asked me to bring him something from the kitchen."

Carlos asked impatiently, "Yes, what was it he wanted?"

"A knife, sir."

"A knife?"

"The sharpest one we had, sir."

A knife? Carlos wondered what the cardinal intended to do. There was no way for him to use it for attack purposes; his door was locked and three armed guards stood outside. To commit suicide? Carlos had already said he would kill him, so the cardinal's death was not the issue. In fact, if it could be proven that he *did* commit suicide, that would truly kill the Messiah idea. The cardinal's supporters couldn't view him as a man of great personal courage if he committed suicide.

He was disappointed that the cardinal had capitulated so quickly, but he decided that even if he refused the cardinal's request, the cardinal would have to be killed anyway. Much better for the cardinal to commit suicide.

Carlos sighed. "Roberto?"

"Yes, sir?"

"Get him the knife."

*   *   *

The articles that Carlos had carefully provided for Isaac lay on the bed. One referred to the Arab world's coordination of their military forces, and two more delineated the world's refusal to take sides, with the exception of Russia, which offered the Arab world the use of Russian arms if needed. Their offer was politely held in abeyance by the Arab nations, which stated that they were quite self-sufficient, thank you. A third article described the plight of Jews worldwide. More than fifty Jews had been killed in various bombings, and there was a two-fold response: Some were leaving their homes and flying to Israel, and others were remaining where they were, fearing they would be in worse straits under attack in Israel.

As Carlos had hoped, Isaac was tormented by the articles. And though he had already decided what he had to do, he could only hope and pray that he was right.

He heard the door open and watched as Roberto silently entered and put a tray with a gleaming silver knife on the table next to the door. The guard then exited and locked the door from the outside.

Isaac walked over slowly and picked up the knife; his lips grew tight for a moment. Then he walked to the bathroom, picked up the soap from the counter, turned the hot water faucet on and began to scrub the knife harder than he had scrubbed anything in his life.

Ten minutes later, Isaac sat on the bed, dressed only in his robe, summoning every bit of courage he had. His clothes lay on the floor near him, and he mentally reviewed the steps and accompanying blessings that had been outlined in the Mishnah Torah. He knew that he was about to undergo intense pain but he also knew that whether he died two days or twenty years from now he was finally sure of who he was.

Knowing he had to recite the blessing while clothed and then uncover himself for what he must do, he quietly acknowledged the commandment he was to perform: *"Baruch Atah Adonai, Elohaynu Melech Haolam, Asher Kidshanu B'Mitzvotav V'Tzivanu Al Hamilah."*

Reaching down with his left hand to hold himself steady, he unwaveringly brought his right hand and the knife to within range of the foreskin. As he cut the flesh the pain forced him to grit his teeth in agony, but in spite of the pain, he felt something even more powerful: a triumphant ecstasy at joining the people whose improbable existence was a testimonial to the living God.

* * *

George Nelson had never flown on Grant's private jet before, let alone with a whole camera crew. Grant was taking no chances with an Italian crew; he wanted the crew that Nelson normally used so the anchorman would be totally comfortable. As they headed for Rome, Grant told Nelson about the fax with the pope's choice of a successor and his plans for a reformation of the Church.

Nelson stated, "No wonder that Cardinal Scoglio said what he did. He held a press conference yesterday saying that the pope was delirious when he died. He said that just before the pope collapsed his last words were an admission of delirium."

"Where did he say that?"

"You haven't read the papers this morning?"

"Not yet." Grant reached over his seat to grab the newspaper folded next to his briefcase. He saw the article headed "Cardinal Argues Pope Was Delirious" and started racing through it, suddenly understanding what had infuriated Monsignor Bentivoglio. When he finished he turned to Nelson.

"Wasn't this Cardinal Scoglio considered one of the heirs apparent to the pope?"

"That's right. He and Benda Cortes were the two choices heading the short list."

Grant mused, "I'll have to call Rome to set up the videotape of the pope's speech for you to use. Get them to preset it for the pope's last words. He wasn't saying 'I sick,' he was saying 'Isaac,' acknowledging his successor. And I want to disclose only a part of the pope's plans for reformation, not everything."

Nelson was confused. "You're the boss, Grant. But I still don't understand why we are going all the way to Rome. Why don't we just announce it from here in the States?"

"Because when you disclose that information to the millions of people watching, I want you to have the original document in your hand."

"So what's the rush? Why didn't we wait for them to send it to you? It would only take a couple of days."

"I don't have a couple of days, George. And the reason for that is the other piece of news I want you to couple with this one."

$$* \quad * \quad *$$

Good evening. I'm George Nelson speaking to you live from Rome. Tonight the Tyler News Network has obtained startling evidence from the world seat of Roman Catholicism. A document written by the late Pope John XXIV has been found that identifies his personal choice of his successor as well as plans he had made for an epochal metamorphosis of the Church itself.

The pontiff was ready to call for a reexamination of the Gospels themselves, indicating that they were not an accurate picture of the historical Jesus and were an attempt to vilify the Jews in order to gain influence with the Roman Empire. Along with the unprecedented direction of the late pontiff's arguments, he also identified his choice of his own successor, an extraordinary action. He called on the Roman Catholic Church to elect Cardinal Isaac Benda Cortes of Rio de Janeiro as the next Supreme Pontiff of the Roman Catholic Church, citing his courageous stands against the drug cartel as just one example of the fearlessness required to lead the Church through this monumental change. The last words of the pontiff were his identification of his successor.

The screen cut to a videotape of the pope's last words.

"As to my successor . . . I wish to urge the . . . I wish to . . . urge . . . I . . . I . . . I . . . saac . . ."

Nelson continued, "Apparently Pope John XXIV collapsed before he could finish pronouncing the full name of Isaac Benda Cortes."

Grant stood out of camera range, waiting for the next words out of Nelson's mouth, knowing that they were the gigantic gamble, one roll of the dice, that put his own life and Isaac's in terrible jeopardy.

As we have reported previously, Cardinal Benda Cortes was kidnapped on his way to Rome. The Tyler News Network has learned that he is being held captive by the head of the South American drug cartel, Cesar Carlos, and that Carlos has threatened to kill his longtime adversary within the next forty-eight hours. Carlos has stated that the people of South America have witnessed murders of cardinals before, and he has no qualms about killing another.

The question left dangling is, if the Church respects the desires of the late Pope John XXIV and elects the cardinal from Rio de Janeiro, who would be the first pope from the Western Hemisphere ever elected, could they act swiftly enough to present the drug chieftain with the staggering prospect of killing the leader of the Catholic world?

*   *   *

World reaction was instantaneous.

While on the way to Rome, Grant had contacted Beverly and instructed her to alert every major network in the world to cut to the Tyler News Network for George Nelson's broadcast; a historic and dramatic announcement was going to take place. When various networks balked, saying that the Arab-Israeli conflict was erupting, Beverly asserted that the Roman Catholic Church was at risk and a major upheaval was imminent. As a result, virtually every network worldwide broke into their regularly scheduled programming and joined Nelson's broadcast.

Within an hour, every government in the Western Hemisphere condemned Cesar Carlos, and every South American government called on the Church to immediately elect Isaac as the next pope and call Carlos's bluff. The South American governments were forced to choose between alienating Carlos and alienating the rest of the Christian world, and in an age of economic interdependence the choice was difficult but inevitable. The rest of the Christian West had planned only to condemn Carlos without endorsing Isaac, but hour by hour, as they heard about South America's demand for Isaac's election, they found themselves confronted by a dilemma. If they didn't endorse Isaac, and he was murdered because he was a cardinal and not the pope, they would be accused of provincialism, or worse, tacit complicity in his murder. One by one, the countries of Europe called on the Church to elect Isaac the pontiff without delay.

*   *   *

Scoglio looked around the Sistine Chapel in consternation. It had been thirty-six hours since the pope had died, and nearly all the cardinals from around the world were already present. This was most unusual since the Church's constitution stipulated that a pope be mourned for nine days and there was a minimum of fifteen days between the old pope's death and the opening of a conclave to elect a new pope. This scheme allowed the cardinals ample time to make their way to Rome.

But it was only a day-and-a-half after the pope's death and nearly all the members of the college were present. Since the cardinals had not secluded themselves in the conclave yet, they were aware of what was transpiring in the outside world. Most specific to their concerns was the perilous situation of Isaac and the Christian world's near unanimous demand that he be elected and saved from Carlos.

After a pope's death, it was customary for the College of Cardinals to meet daily and decide how both the election of the new pope and the burial of the late pontiff should be handled. At this moment no one was speaking of the burial, everyone was speaking of the election and Isaac. Virtually every cardinal's office had been contacted by his secular government and urged to vote for Isaac.

Scoglio heard the talk of doing the unthinkable: burying the old pope immediately and electing a pope the next day. He couldn't believe the situation was out of hand to this degree. He hadn't reckoned on Pope John XXIV's enormous popularity with the College; cardinals were human, too, and the drama of Isaac's position and the pope's dying words were an emotional thunderclap to them. They were also aware that at this moment, even a Middle East war was taking a back seat to their predicament.

But most of all, the possibilities of focusing the world's attention on the Roman Catholic Church's perennial fight against evil were crystallized and personalized in the forms of Isaac and Carlos. What a chance to make the leader of the Roman Catholic Church a hero for all mankind!

Scoglio's mind was feverishly confused. If ever there was a moment for revealing that Benda Cortes was a Jew, it had to be *now*. But if he did, how could he prove his assertion? Without any documentation, he had no proof. The only way to demonstrate that Benda Cortes was truly a Jew was for Benda Cortes to be confronted and admit it himself. But would he? Scoglio didn't think that Benda Cortes would lie; but who knew how a man would react if offered the most powerful position in the religious world?

He didn't believe that Grant Tyler would admit anything either. The opportunity to reveal Isaac's true heritage had been his, and he had concealed it. How could Scoglio stop the juggernaut that was inexorably building?

Then he had an idea. *The new pope had to accept the position verbally before he could be enthroned. Even if the college elected him and Carlos freed him, he would still have to be informed of his selection and accept the post.*

He thought rapidly, *The same passion that has been ignited to elect him can turn to a passionate denunciation of him if he comes to Rome and I confront him and demand that he reveal himself a Jew. Then the college will turn to* me.

Scoglio signaled the secretary of state that he wished to address the assembly:

My Lord Cardinals, we have heard the discussions of what we would heretofore have considered unthinkable: to bury the Supreme Pontiff immediately and elect our Reverend Brother from Brazil, Isaac Benda Cortes, our new pontiff. In other circumstances, we would view this as a distortion of what our Church demands from us, but there seems to be no doubt that we are witnessing the workings of the Holy Spirit. The entire Catholic world seems to be in unison that we must act—and act quickly—to elect our endangered brother. We have weighed the precipitateness of such an action against the certainty that such an action, even if intemperate, would be viewed as the Church at its most heroic.

We may have erred in suggesting that the late Holy Father was not fully cognizant and coherent before he died. His intention may well have been to nominate Cardinal Benda Cortes for the papacy. His desire to open the election process to the world could be achieved by giving the public access to Cardinal Benda Cortes when we bring him to Rome to accept our nomination.

To those who would seek to nominate me for the position of pontiff, I can safely say that my own aspirations pale in comparison to the chance to yield to the world's apparent fervor for the election of this man. Therefore I say to you that we should pursue the course being laid for us, and elect our Reverend Brother Isaac Benda Cortes without delay and force the man Cesar Carlos to free him so that he can come to Rome and accept his nomination.

There was silence. The cardinals had considered Scoglio the only legitimate rival to Benda Cortes for the nomination, and now Scoglio was withdrawing himself from nomination and nominating Benda Cortes. Slowly, one by one, the cardinals stood in front of their thrones and slowly repeated, "I shall elect Benda Cortes."

Scoglio spoke with apparent humility. "If my Reverend Brothers would permit me, I will inform the media immediately." There was no dissent.

* * *

Isaac lay on his bed, in terrible pain and exhaustion. The circumcision had been excruciating and terrifying because of the amount of blood he had lost. He had used the knife to slit a towel from the bathroom for a makeshift bandage, but he was more aware of the pain now than when he had cut himself, for the spiritual exaltation had ebbed and been supplanted by the prosaic realization that far worse pain might be forthcoming.

The door to the room suddenly opened and Isaac forgot the pain and instinctively sat up to see Cesar Carlos walk in.

Carlos said softly, "You're alive."

Isaac couldn't tell if Carlos was furious or relieved. Then he realized that Carlos had thought the knife was for a suicide attempt.

Carlos looked at Isaac's robe and saw the blood. He said indifferently, "I must release you." He suddenly seemed amused. "Your Church has elected you pope and they need you in Rome to accept your election. How does a Jew do that?" He chuckled. "No one would believe me if *I* told them the truth, but what will *you* do?"

Isaac was still too stunned to answer. Carlos said, "One way or the other something in you has to die, Your Eminence. Either you stay a Jew and give up the Church, or become the pope and lie to yourself. Either way you're half a man."

Isaac thought, *He doesn't realize why I'm bloody. Nothing has to die in me; I'm whole.* He tried to think of his next step, but events were moving too fast for him.

"One more thing, Your Eminence. You'd better hope the world has a long memory, because the day you're no longer the popular favorite, you're open season." Carlos went to the closet, pulled out some clothes and threw them on the bed.

"Get dressed. I don't have all day."

*   *   *

Pablo de Cardoso sat in Carlos's office where Carlos had left him. He had screamed over and over at Carlos that he had blown his chance; he should have killed Isaac right away. He yelled that Carlos should ignore the rest of the world and kill Isaac anyway. Carlos had taken all he could until finally he said coldly that he was cutting his losses, and Pablo should do the same. When Pablo angrily cursed Carlos for leaving him out in the cold with nothing, Carlos asked icily if Pablo considered his *life* enough of a parting gift. Pablo had been silent, but Carlos saw his eyes and locked him in the office until the cardinal had left, just in case Pablo tried to do something crazy.

Pablo trembled with rage. Everything had gone wrong: no Pablo as savior of the Church, no heady career as a muckraking journalist, not even an article for which he had been an accomplice to murdering Rissolo. As he sat locked in the office, stripped of what remained of his self-respect, denied an opportunity to make a name for himself, he decided on another path to immortality. Pulling out his wallet, he reached inside it to find a scrap of paper with a telephone number on it. He picked up the telephone and dialed, not caring if he was being listened to or not.

"Father Antonio? This is Pablo de Cardoso. . . . Yes, that's right, the journalist. How quickly can you reach your brother Dominic?"

27

President Evans sat in front of the television, scowling. He didn't like taking a passive position, and yet that is exactly what he had done since the oil embargo started. He had only half-heartedly condemned the acts of violence against American Jews. He had remained uninvolved in the sudden Middle East conflict, ignoring the traditional role the United States played as defender of Israel.

Now he watched footage of Lod Airport in Tel Aviv, where thousands of Jewish immigrants from all over the world were landing by the hour. As they landed, every immigrant was given a gas mask to protect him or her from threatened missiles from Iraq and Iran. The president winced as he watched a mother put gas masks on her two small frightened children.

He had argued to himself that supporting Israel was a luxury that he couldn't afford; not with the world condemning the Israelis for hoarding cold fusion and the American public ganging up on Jews in their midst. His first responsibility was . . . was . . . "to faithfully execute the office of the President of the United States and to the best of my ability preserve, protect, and defend the Constitution of the United States." Not to preserve, protect and defend the *people* of the United States, but the *Constitution*.

Where would the Constitution draw the line between protecting one group of citizens, the Jews, from real danger, and protecting the American public from incipient danger, the threat of living without oil? He didn't like using the endangered Jews as pawns to force Israel to share the formula, but if that was what it took, he was ready to take the hard line. *All because some rabbi is waiting for the Messiah,* he grumbled to himself.

At least I was forceful on the Cesar Carlos issue, he thought. He had joined the chorus of leaders who had condemned Carlos for holding Cardinal Benda Cortes and demanded his release. He thrust aside the nagging reminder that the condemnation of Carlos had been a no-brainer without any risk. At the time he had not given the situation with Carlos much thought: the Middle East was his primary concern.

But now, he suddenly wondered why Grant Tyler hadn't come to *him* for help with the kidnapped cardinal. He knew that the report by George Nelson must have involved Grant because it had been broadcast on every channel.

Ten minutes later, after a phone call to Grant's office, the president was speaking long-distance to the Tyler News Network's studio in Rome.

"Grant?"

"Hello, Mr. President."

"Why didn't you come to me with this problem of the cardinal? I could have lent you a hand rescuing him."

Grant didn't have time for dissembling. "Your participation in the rescue wasn't as problematic as your participation afterward, Mr. President."

"What do you mean?"

"I mean that you would have detained the cardinal from going to Rome."

The president said heatedly, "What are you talking about? You're putting me in the same league as that Colombian hoodlum?"

"When you figured out just who the cardinal was, you'd hold him in Washington."

"And why would I do that?"

"Because he's the man you've been looking for, Mr. President."

It took a moment for the president to realize what Grant was saying. Then his vision cleared. "*The* man? *He's* the Messiah you've been referring to?"

"Yes, he is, and I didn't want you interfering with his trip to Rome. He has a job to do."

"Like hell he has! He needs to tell the Israeli scientists to release the information so that everything can get back to normal." The president suddenly remembered something. "Wait a minute . . . you said that this Messiah was supposed to be a Jew." He waited for a response and heard nothing. "Grant? . . . Grant? . . ." He slammed the telephone down. "Damn, damn, damn . . ."

He tried to think. *Events are out of control. . . . How fast can I get to Rome? I've got to speak to this Cortes. . . .* He quickly checked his watch and beeped his secretary.

"Angela, get Air Force One ready ASAP. I've got to go to Rome."

*   *   *

Beverly sat at her desk surrounded by Perry Lindsay, James Wolford, Bill Eldridge and Dan Bryant. The executives had been on tenterhooks since Isaac's kidnapping, calling Grant's office repeatedly for updates. Grant had told them of Carlos's threat, advising them to sit tight until he figured out what to do. They had *watched* George Nelson's broadcast of Isaac's election and the resultant world reaction. They had *watched* as Nelson later reported that Carlos had released Isaac.

Now they were tired of being observers, and they had consulted each other and traveled to Grant's office to find out what was going on.

Perry spoke first. "Can't you call Grant and ask him what's happening?"

Beverly threw up her hands. "I'm sorry, Mr. Lindsay, but he is unreachable. I've been trying him for the last two hours."

Wolford cut in. "We saw that the cardinal was released. Have you heard from him?"

"Not a word. All the information I've got is thirdhand. Apparently, the cardinal was dropped off by Carlos's men at a taxi stand in Bogotá near the airport, and he called Rabbi Daniel Hanviowitz in Brazil and said he was on his way to Rome. The rabbi called his brother in Israel and Rabbi Eliyahu Hanviowitz called our office looking for Grant. I gave him Grant's number in Rome and that's all I know."

Eldridge looked at Lindsay and raised his eyebrows. "What do you think Isaac will do?"

Lindsay said uncertainly, "Your guess is as good as mine, Bill."

Bryant decided the issue. "We've been talking about how we're frustrated because we're only observing, haven't we? I say we go to Rome and see this through to the end. Anyone want to join me?"

*   *   *

At their latest press conference in Los Angeles, the members of CANT were growing more desperate. Many of them were Jews who had been receiving threatening calls, and they felt their position increasingly precarious. They had divorced themselves from the religious wing of Judaism by denouncing the concept of the Messiah, hoping to ingratiate themselves with secular society, but now that same secular society was targeting them anyway. Joel Alexander stood before the microphone denouncing the state of Israel once more to a largely bored group of reporters when he saw a familiar face enter the room from the rear and heads turn one by one to see the visitor.

Willie Daniels, impeccably dressed in a suit and tie, walked proudly down the aisle toward the podium. The Mules were on a road trip, and they were staying at the same hotel that held the press conference. Half an hour before, Willie had been talking to his wife Robin, and she had informed him that some members of their church had openly shunned her because of Willie's participation in the Messiah controversy. Even those mothers who normally would have *oohed* and *aahed* over the Danielses' new baby boy were treating Robin as a pariah. While Willie was talking to her the television was tuned to the news, and, as he spoke, he watched the same footage from Israel that the president had seen: the mother putting gas masks on her children. Because he was feeling vulnerable with his wife and child home alone without him, the scene from Israel upset him profoundly.

Ten minutes later and in a sweatsuit, Willie exited the elevator on the main floor, intending to go for a walk to shake off his distress. He was passing through the hotel lobby when he noticed on the board listing the day's activities a press conference being held by CANT half an hour later. His eyes narrowed, then he pivoted decisively and headed back toward his room to change clothes.

Now Joel saw Willie coming toward him and tried to look over his head to the crowd, which was buzzing with the anticipation of a conflict. Willie seemed oblivious and didn't stop his approach. He walked right up to the lectern and stood next to Joel, who looked up at Willie, flustered.

"Excuse me, Willie."

Willie picked Joel up and placed him to one side, then stood before the lectern himself. "No, I'm afraid you'll have to excuse *me*, Mr. Alexander."

The press roared. They were sick of CANT's self-pity and whining by now. Willie addressed the crowd.

"I have a few words to say. As you may know, I was one of six men who met with the man we think is the Messiah. Mr. Alexander and his group here have said that they have a problem with the whole messianic concept, claiming that 'the State of Israel is being held hostage by a religious minority, a minority that has convinced itself that the messianic era is upon us.' They say that 'the concept of a Messiah must be debunked,' and that they 'reject the notion that they have any agenda or set of rules to follow that differs from the rest of the world.'

"I beg to differ. I have experienced hostility from members of my own race over this issue, and I can see a clear parallel between Jews who agree with Mr. Alexander, and black Americans who hurl the epithet 'whitey' at those of their own race who have become successful. Both groups deny the legitimacy of their own race to succeed."

He turned to Joel. "Forgive me for sounding presumptuous, Mr. Alexander, but the Jewish mandate has always been to act as living testimonials to the existence of God. When a Jew acts in a dishonorable manner, when he takes no responsibility for each act that degrades society, he desecrates the name of God. You have more precise laws about how to behave than any people on the face of the earth. Your people taught a pagan world that routinely sacrificed children that life had an inherent sanctity and dignity—how can you desert your heritage?"

Turning to face the press again, Willie said quietly, "A wise man once said that there is no dignity without responsibility. Mr. Alexander and the members of CANT who cravenly deny the coming of the Messiah are wrong. Wrong about the Messiah, wrong about the state of Israel and wrong to assume that they won't have to answer to God after they die."

Although they only stood four feet apart, Joel shouted at Willie, "So who is he, Willie? Who is this Messiah?"

No one uttered a sound. Willie waited a long moment before he replied. "No gifts, Mr. Alexander. In order to know how God works you have to make the first move."

And Willie left.

*   *   *

When Cardinal Scoglio called the Tyler Network's studio in Rome to alert them of Isaac's election, the news was immediately forwarded to Grant at his hotel. He rushed back to the studio to watch George Nelson announcing Isaac's election. He had remained there, tense and worried, until Rabbi Eliyahu Hanviowitz called from a sealed room in Jerusalem informing him that Isaac had been freed and was on a flight to Rome. When Grant asked the rabbi how Isaac was, Rabbi Hanviowitz replied that his brother Daniel thought Isaac sounded remarkably tranquil, and that he would be arriving in Rome sometime that evening.

"Did Isaac say what he was going to do?"

"Apparently not. He asked Daniel to contact you with some urgent requests: to set up live coverage of the Kotel and to inform the Vatican that he wants the ceremony tomorrow morning to be open to the public outside in the piazza, not inside the Sistine Chapel. He asked that there be as many giant television screens around the piazza as you can afford, and, not knowing that you were there, for you to meet him in Rome at the airport tonight. Daniel called me figuring that I would find you, and I got your number from Miss Engler in your office. Can you arrange these things?"

After the call from Jerusalem, Grant had worked in a frenzy. He had George Nelson announce Isaac's release, called the Jerusalem office of the Tyler News Network and arranged live coverage of the Kotel, and called Cardinal Scoglio at the Vatican to forward Isaac's request for the use of the piazza instead of the Sistine. Their conversation was terse and to the point: Grant was ready for a pitched battle over the use of the piazza, but Scoglio was remarkably amenable and eager to respect Isaac's wishes. He assured Grant that he would get quick acceptance from the cardinals, and he was right; after the momentous decision they had made to elect Isaac, the college was not about to argue with their future pontiff. Their acceptance was astonishingly swift; the Vatican called back within the hour.

Grant was riding the crest of the wave now, and although he was unsure what Isaac would do, his confidence in their mission together was growing rapidly. That afternoon President Evans called, only to wind up furious that Grant had hung up on the most powerful person in the world. What he didn't know was that Grant was in a hurry to get to the airport to meet the most *important* person in the world.

*   *   *

The most important person in the world was experiencing visions that would have terrified anyone who didn't have complete trust in God. They had started while he was driven from Carlos's villa to the airport in Bogotá. He had been blindfolded before Carlos would allow him to go; Carlos was reasonably paranoid about revealing the exact location of his residence in the Colombian mountains.

On the way to the airport, Isaac had let his thoughts wander where they would, and he first wondered how the College of Cardinals had agreed so quickly to elect him. What kind of pressure had been brought to bear on them? Who could have concentrated the world's attention on his plight with a war simultaneously starting in the Middle East?

Only one person that Isaac knew: Grant Tyler. His eyes shut because of the blindfold, he pictured Grant's face.

Suddenly another face came into his vision: a young man's face that looked quite similar to Grant's. The young man was lying on a bed with his eyes closed, but he was slowly awakening, blinking his eyes once, then twice. Isaac blinked his eyes and saw Grant enter his vision peripherally and approach the young man with tears in his eyes. Then, just before the vision ended, Grant reached over to hold the young man. From what Grant had said about his son's accident, Isaac knew that the young man had to be Matthew. *Somehow, he was foreseeing Matthew's awakening from his coma.*

His thoughts drifted for a moment until he wondered what had happened in Israel. He had never been to Israel, but he had seen many pictures. Again, suddenly he had a vision: this time of the Kotel, where he was standing preparing to blow an instrument that could only be a shofar—the ram's horn—the ancient ritual herald of the revelation of the Torah at Mount Sinai that was sounded every Rosh Hashanah to call all men to repent.

He strained to understand exactly what was happening to him and tried to bring himself back to the reality of his situation: He was being called to Rome to accept the papacy. He knew he would have to refuse it and inform the college that he was really a Jew, but he also realized that the opportunity to reform the Catholic Church was at hand; it might be in his power somehow to enable them to fulfill part of their destiny as guardians of the Jewish people.

For some reason, the number 476 kept interfering with his thoughts. He repeatedly tried to dismiss it, but it stubbornly kept intruding. He was quite aware that 476 was the year that the Roman Empire finally ended, and he was aware that the Roman Catholic Church was considered by Judaism as the last vestige of the Roman Empire, but there was something else nagging at his mind, attempting to surface.

For the third time a vision came to him. This time it was the Vatican, and his vision oscillated between the Vatican and the number 476. Irritated, he shook his head, trying to cast off his vision, and the picture of the Vatican trembled.

Then, from somewhere deep in the recesses of his memory, he remembered what had also happened in Rome in the year 476, and although he felt completely a Jew now, his lifelong attachment to the Church and the Vatican as its focal point caused him to cry out at his understanding of what he had seen and remembered.

He understood now. He saw everything clearly as a part of the divine pattern, and he only wondered if what he had seen was a foregone conclusion or whether he could avert the disaster he had foreseen. Searching for an answer, he remembered the response he had learned when memorizing the Jewish prayer books. In response to the passage delineating how God decides on Rosh Hashanah who will live and who will die in the coming year, the prayer stated: "But repentance, prayer and charity remove the evil of the decree!"

Now he was sure. If he could change the Church and rid it of its ancient misconceptions, he could save it from the disaster that awaited it. He knew that as a Jew, he was forbidden from entering any church that had a cross or crucifix. That eliminated the Sistine Chapel as a forum for his confrontation with the college. He wondered if the piazza . . . with television screens all around . . . broadcast to the world . . .

The car stopped abruptly and Isaac was jolted forward despite his seat belt. Without warning, the back door was opened and the blindfold ripped off his face. Isaac winced at the bright sunlight as he was pulled from the car and an envelope was thrust in his hand. The man handing it to him quickly hopped back in the car as it sped off.

Isaac heard the whine of airplanes and realized he was at a taxi stand near the airport in Bogotá. When he inspected the inside of the envelope, he found a wad of bills and two airplane tickets: one for a flight from Bogotá to London and another from London to Rome. He checked his watch; he had two hours before the flight to London departed. There was a telephone booth next to the taxi stand, and before he hailed a taxi, Isaac headed for the telephone to make one call.

"I'd like to reverse the charges on this call, operator. It's to Miss Rivkah Hanviowitz."

*   *   *

Eighteen hours later, Isaac walked off the airplane into Leonardo da Vinci Airport and saw Grant waiting for him with an envelope in his hand.

"We're ready for tomorrow, Isaac. And I have a gift for you that Pope John left with me."

Isaac opened the envelope and quickly perused the title page. "Thank you."

Grant said, "Don't thank me, thank him. He was the one who wrote it."

Isaac raised his eyes from the document and looked directly at Grant. "That's not what I meant. The steward on the flight told me what's been happening in the world. I can recognize your work. Thank you."

Grant was embarrassed. "I wasn't about to abandon you at this late juncture. How many cardinals—" He broke off and stared past Isaac. "I'll be damned."

Isaac swung around to see Perry Lindsay, James Wolford, Bill Eldridge and Dan Bryant walking toward them. As they reached the two men, Lindsay extended his hand to Isaac. "What in hell are you going to do tomorrow?"

Isaac said grimly, "Offer the world a chance to redeem itself. It's all up to them now."

28

The Piazza di San Pietro was jammed. More than two hundred thousand people packed the piazza, and they were fascinated by the ten gigantic television screens arranged around the perimeter to face inward toward the crowd. At Scoglio's request, the Vatican had announced that Isaac's acceptance was to be made in historic fashion: Instead of his accepting inside the Sistine Chapel and then moving outside to the loggia above the piazza to address the world as the new pope, the entire process would take place on the loggia in front of the public.

Isaac had called the Vatican from the airport, and despite their protestations, he informed them that he would be staying at a hotel for the night instead of the papal palazzo. Grant had anticipated this and arranged for the room across the hall from his to be registered under his own name so Isaac would have some anonymity. As it turned out, the executives had already made reservations at the same hotel.

By the time they arrived, it was early evening and the ceremony was scheduled for noon the next day, so everyone decided to go to bed early and try to get some rest. As the executives walked toward their rooms, Isaac turned to Grant.

"Would you have a moment to speak alone? There is something I must tell you."

Grant raised his eyebrows. "Strategy?"

"That, too, but afterward there is a personal matter that involves you."

Grant pointed toward his room. "Let's use my room. Want some coffee?"

"That would be fine."

Ten minutes later, sipping their coffee, Grant and Isaac were discussing the details of what the screens in the piazza should be showing. Grant was puzzled by Isaac's choice.

"But why do you want them showing all these places? They should be featuring you."

"Remember in Rio when I heard that voice telling me to reassure you that you weren't crazy? Well . . ." Isaac told Grant about his visions of the Kotel and the Vatican and what he thought they meant. He explained the significance of the number 476 and disclosed what he was going to do the next day. Grant listened, eyes widening, until Isaac concluded, "Perhaps you should not attend the ceremony. It could be dangerous. And we should warn the others."

Grant was adamant. "If you intend to do what you said, the least I can do is to be there offering moral support. I will warn the others after we're done talking, though. . . . What was the personal matter that you mentioned?"

"I had another vision. It involved your son."

"You saw my son? Matthew?"

Isaac nodded. "I saw him awaken from his coma, and I saw you embrace him."

For some reason that Grant couldn't explain, he suddenly felt uncertain about Isaac's visions. When Isaac had spoken of the Kotel and the Vatican, Grant had blindly accepted what Isaac was saying, but now that it involved the matter closest to his heart, the matter without which the others were meaningless, Grant was tense and fearful.

Isaac studied his friend's face. "You are having doubts, aren't you."

Grant managed to nod.

Isaac sighed. "You're not the only one." He said humbly, "Perhaps these visions are my own concoction. Although I feel sure of them, there's a part of me that is pretty frightened that this is all a delusion."

Grant tried to reassure him. "This can't be a mistake, Isaac. Too many people have been involved." He put his hand on the worried man's shoulder. "You'd better get some rest."

Isaac rose from his seat and headed for his room across the hall. As he opened the door he looked back at Grant somberly, "You know, if someone had told either of us a year ago that all of this would happen we would have thought he was drunk." He closed the door quietly.

Grant called his home office to put Isaac's plan in motion, then buzzed Lindsay's room to deliver Isaac's warning. There was no answer. The same was true when he buzzed the other three executives. He figured he'd call them back in twenty minutes after taking a brief nap.

He hadn't counted on his exhaustion catching up with him.

* * *

Everyone had fallen asleep; everyone but Isaac. He was feeling a terrible isolation from the world of reality. He knew it stemmed from the magnitude of what he wanted to accomplish. He felt a sudden sense of anxiety and looked around the room for something mundane, something ordinary. What he saw instead was the envelope Grant had given him with the pope's document. He didn't want to think about it right now—he was planning to read it in the morning—but something inside him commanded him to read what the pope had written regarding the Holy See's choice of a successor and the evolution of the Church.

He read it slowly, but as the document was just twenty pages long, it only took fifteen minutes. Isaac thought of the old man and the terrible struggle he had waged to reinvent his entire life's philosophy at the same time he was battling the disease consuming him. That kind of fearlessness in changing oneself while time was running out was a signal example of the glory of the human spirit, and Isaac could identify with the effort it must have taken.

To his relief, his anxiety had disappeared. He felt less alone now and calm in the mission he had accepted for himself.

* * *

Grant awakened at five in the morning. He shook himself awake and leaped to his feet, only to realize that he'd fallen asleep fully dressed. *I'll change later,* he thought. *I've got to warn the others about what Isaac has foreseen.* He called Lindsay in his room and woke him up.

A groggy voice answered, "Hello?"

"Perry, it's Grant. Sorry to wake you, but I've got to speak to you and the others *now*."

Five minutes later the four executives were in Grant's room in their bathrobes, rubbing their eyes and drinking the warmed-over coffee that Grant had made the previous night. Grant explained what Isaac had envisioned and the possible catastrophe that could occur.

He said bluntly, "There's a good chance we could all be killed by staying here." The men were silent, thinking. Grant sensed the need for the four men to discuss the dilemma. He stood up, stretched his arms above his head, and suggested, "I'll go make some fresh coffee."

When he returned, Lindsay spoke for all the executives. "You know, Grant, death doesn't have the same power over us since all of us had those near-death experiences. We want to stay and see this thing through whatever happens."

Bryant added, "It's also possible Isaac is mistaken, isn't it?"

Grant said, "Isaac and I talked last night. He isn't certain of the validity of his visions either." He thought of Matthew. "I hope he's right, though. And, if he can succeed in convincing the Church, perhaps he can elicit God's mercy."

The shrill ring of the telephone pierced through their absorption. Grant reached over to pick it up. "Hello? . . . Yes, sir, I'm awake. Yes, sir, I can wait here for you." He hung up.

The executives were puzzled. "Sir?" They looked at Grant quizzically.

"That was President Evans."

Bryant blurted, "He's in Rome?"

Grant replied, "He's downstairs in the lobby and he's on his way up—now. I don't think he knows Isaac is here or he would have mentioned it. . . . I've got to get Isaac out of here." He dialed Isaac's room but there was no answer. "Where is he?" Throwing his door open, he crossed the hall to Isaac's door and saw a note folded with his name on it.

Grant,

I could only sleep for three hours, and I didn't want to wake you. I called the Vatican to pick me up, and they're on their way. I told them to reserve five seats for you and the other men in the section reserved for foreign dignitaries at the front and side of the piazza. Forgive me

for not waiting for you—I wanted to see the city one last time while it
slept. With God's help, I'll see you afterward.

* * *

Grant folded the note and put it in his pocket just as the elevator at the
end of the hall opened and four Secret Service men escorted a very angry
president of the United States toward him. Grant gestured toward his room.
"Please come in, Mr. President."

* * *

In the midst of the piazza were two men who had barely arrived in time.
They were both out of breath from shoving their way through the crowd, and
only the fact that one of them had identification as a member of the press
enabled them to push past the onlookers.

Pablo de Cardoso had met Dominic at the airport in Rome just two hours
earlier, and on their frenzied taxi ride toward the piazza he had informed him
of everything that had occurred and his fears that Cardinal Benda Cortes was
about to destroy the Church. Dominic's reaction had been exactly what
Pablo wanted. His eyes shone with the fanaticism of the zealot, and Pablo
handed him a gun that he had secured in Rome immediately after his arrival.

"He is a Jew, Dominic. And he will Judaize the Church. He will say
Christ is not God."

"He is the Antichrist!"

Pablo tried to ease Dominic down with directions. "You must wait until
you are close enough to be certain. You may have to wait until he finishes
speaking."

Dominic's voice was barely under control. "I will act . . . carefully. But
he will not escape me. He is not Jesus. He cannot walk on water."

Pablo said caustically, "And if he could?"

Dominic looked at Pablo with such intensity that Pablo shivered. His
voice was deadly. "Do not joke about what only Christ could do."

* * *

Grant, the four executives and President Evans sat together in the front
row of chairs set up for foreign dignitaries, waiting for Isaac to appear on
the loggia above them. Security was everywhere. Grant had felt it was

incumbent upon him to give the president the same warning about Rome that he had given the others, but the president had scoffed at the suggestion that Isaac could be having prophetic visions and demanded that Grant bring him to Isaac as soon as the ceremony was over.

The president looked around at the massive blank screens and nudged Grant. "Why the television screens? Is that usually done? It looks like a political convention."

Grant just shrugged. "It's what the cardinal wanted." He looked at his watch. It was 11:45. Suddenly there was a roar from the crowd. The screens had come alive with pictures of the White House, the Statue of Liberty, the Eiffel Tower, Big Ben, the Kremlin, the Great Wall of China, Sugar Loaf Mountain in Rio de Janeiro, and the Kotel and the Dome of the Rock in Israel. The roar destabilized to a confused cacophony.

President Evans said angrily, "What the hell is going on? Why are you showing all those places up there?" He stared at Grant. "What haven't you told me?"

Grant was imperturbable. "It's in God's hands, not yours, Mr. President."

A voice thundered through the speakers placed around the piazza. The crowd fell silent automatically. From the loggia, the voice of Cardinal Paolo Scoglio addressed the multitude.

"Welcome, my brothers and sisters. In the name of Christ, you are welcome to witness this historic moment, a moment that has been inspired by the commitment of millions around the world. The Holy Mother Church has opened its doors to the world and let God's fresh air rush through her. We have heard the world's anguished cry that evil must be confronted, and we have acted." The crowd roared. Scoglio waited for the roar to cease, then continued, "We have heard the world urge us to elect a man of singular courage as our Supreme Pontiff and throw down the gauntlet to evil, and we have acted." The roar was twice as loud as it had been before.

In his peripheral vision, Scoglio saw Isaac standing off to one side, waiting. *Now I throw down the gauntlet to **him**,* he thought with relish.

"We have acted in the love of our Lord Jesus Christ, and our champion has come to bring knowledge of Jesus Christ to the world." Isaac hadn't moved. Scoglio beckoned to Isaac to come forward in order to accept his election. "Come forward, Cardinal Isaac Benda Cortes."

Isaac crossed to Scoglio as the crowd went absolutely berserk. Scoglio waited for the crowd to become quiet. It took more than two minutes. Once they were silent, Scoglio slowly intoned the offer in Latin to accept election as the leader of the Catholic world, the branch of Christianity from which all others were derived.

"Acceptasne electionem de te canonice factam in Summum Pontificem?"

The crowd roared in anticipation; the roar grew and grew until it was deafening. Isaac waited for the noise to reach its peak. Only then did he speak forcefully into the microphone in *Italian.*

"Aspetta."

A quarter of a million people in the piazza went into a shocked silence. The president looked at Grant. "What did he say?"

"He said to wait a moment, Mr. President." The president caught his breath.

All over the world, hundreds of millions of people watching reacted in identical fashion. And two brothers separated by seven thousand miles knew that their efforts to alter the history of the world and save their people rested on the shoulders of one man, and one moment. And one woman waited for the man she loved to offer himself as the human beacon who would light the path for the world to follow.

Isaac had decided to speak in English, since it was rapidly becoming the lingua franca of the world. In order for the Italian crowd to understand him, he had also decided to follow each English sentence with its Italian equivalent. He looked sharply at Scoglio, then turned to the microphone.

"I have been chosen by the Roman Catholic Church to serve as their leader. For this, I am honored. I know that many of you listening were instrumental in influencing events so that I could reach this moment. For this, I am grateful.

"I am aware that I am about to make a claim that will seem sacrilegious to some and outrageous to most: I have been chosen by God to show the world a new path. It is a new path, but in reality it is the acknowledgment of an old path; older than the fifteen hundred years of Islamic faith, older than the two thousand years of the Christian faith, older than the twenty-five hundred years of the Buddhist faith. It is a way that does not demand, as the other Western faiths do, that the entire world succumb to its dictates, but that its emissaries practice its laws to produce a just society and serve as a shining beacon whose light will radiate to the nations.

"I speak of Judaism. Of the world that has gone mad with anti-Semitism I ask, were 6 million not enough? Were one million children butchered not enough? Of the Christian Church that from its inception damned the people from which arose their chosen divinity I ask, is two thousand years of hate insufficient? Of the Islamic faith that claims the same inheritance but refuses to allow the Jewish people the right to live in their ancestral homeland I ask, were you not descended from the same father?"

The crowd was numb with shock. Why was their pontiff speaking of Judaism? And while they were numb, Pablo and Dominic surreptitiously moved closer and closer to the loggia.

"For the members of the Church that elected me at the behest of a great man, I bring word from him. Our late pontiff Pope John XXIV had prepared an encyclical from which I am about to read a portion." Isaac read from the document itself:

> We, the Holy Mother Church, have been guilty of fostering a hatred that has spanned the centuries. The anti-Semitism that abounds in the world we live in has been nurtured by the Gospels we hold dear. As my great predecessor, Pope John XXIII, wrote just before his death in 1963, "Forgive us the curse which we unjustly laid on the name of the Jews."
>
> Can we call ourselves practitioners of love when our Gospels portray an innocent, God-fearing people as villains? Would the Jesus we worship have condemned those who find other ways to God? And, if Jesus is to return, will he return as a Jew? Everyone, Jew and Gentile, agrees that he was a Jew. And if he returns as a Jew, and anti-Semitism still exists, could he be murdered again? How do I, as a Christian, separate what Jesus really wanted from the anti-Semitism recorded in the Gospel?
>
> When early Christianity wanted to spread its message of the one God to the pagan world, it found that the laws of the Torah were too difficult for pagans to accept. As a result, there were statements such as, "Christ is the end of the law," and "Where there is no law there is no transgression." Not only was the Torah vilified, but also those who loved it and practiced its directives. Yet it was not long before Christianity developed laws of its own, some of which were far more

severe than what the Torah had prescribed. What the Church failed to understand was that there are many different ways of serving God. Judaism understood this; instead of saying, "No salvation outside the Church," they said, "The righteous among the Gentiles will have a place in the world to come." If Jesus intended a message of tolerance, it was a Jewish message.

In this age of more and more forms of spirituality which are not rooted in actual historical events, Christianity must make a choice. If it is rooted in history, bound to the real Jesus who existed, it must know who he was. The loving ideals we ascribe to Jesus came from his people—the Jewish people. In Leviticus, long before Jesus lived, it was stated, "You shall love your neighbor as yourself."

Dominic and Pablo had moved within two hundred feet of the loggia.

Isaac paused a moment before continuing. "Those were some of the words of Pope John XXIV. These words are my own. When Jacob and Esau were born, the intent was for Jacob to be the scholar and teacher, and Esau to guard and protect his brother. The Jews are the descendants of Jacob, who became Israel. The descendants of Esau became the Roman Empire. And the last vestige of the Roman Empire is the Roman Catholic Church, which placed itself at the service of Rome in order to spread the message of monotheism. But can any religion claim to spread the awareness of God while fostering hatred of others who also believe in him?"

Isaac thundered, "It is time that the Church held itself responsible for its history. Not just for its inaction during the Holocaust, not just for the persecutions of the Jews since the Gospels were written, but for its own anti-Semitism. For telling the story of Jesus in such a way that the Jews are villains, *when Jesus as a Jew would have been murdered in the Holocaust had he been alive.* For weeping for the Jewess Mary's pain over her lost son while ignoring millions of other Jewesses through the centuries weeping for their murdered children. For taking the Torah that God gave the world and fostering hatred for it instead of acknowledging its ability to teach the world how to coexist. For portraying the Torah as vengeful when the Jewish mandate, unlike the Church's, *was always to live in peace in the land God gave them without a need to convert the rest of the world.*"

His voice grew quieter. "There is a universal syndrome that children going through adolescence question their parents' intelligence and often regard them as too severe. It is only when they have children of their own that they realize the full necessity of the severity their parents employed. Christianity and Islam are the children of Judaism, and they both turned on their parent when the parent refused to stray from the path given to it by God. Only after the two thousand years of Christianity and the fifteen hundred years of Islam can they see that *perfecting a world should not require its submission.* Now, in an age of communication where everyone in the world is aware of everything around him, any righteous society, whether it be Jewish or not, can impart its message *without forcing its will on others.* Judaism *always* knew this. It just needed a Messiah to free it to fulfill its destiny."

Isaac thundered again. *"And I am that man. I am a Jew, and I tell you that God has chosen me to lead my people to freedom. And I do not speak to the pharoah of Egypt—I speak to every living being on this earth: Let my people go! Let them live in peace!"*

The wave of sound that carried through the piazza was earsplitting. The ground literally shook from it. Isaac closed his eyes. *Now,* he thought.

He called out, "I will prove to you that I have been chosen to lead because God has granted me visions of what is to happen. Unless the world renounces anti-Semitism it will be shaken to its very core." He pointed to the screens. *"Look and see the hand of God."*

A quarter of a million faces turned to watch every site on the giant screens start to tremble: from the White House to the Great Wall of China, from the Eiffel Tower to Sugar Loaf Mountain, from the Kremlin to the Kotel. Dominic stood as if paralyzed. The crowd shouted with alarm and shock, and Isaac, shaking from the knowledge that his visions were true, righted himself and seized the moment to deliver the rest of his message.

He cried, "I speak to the Jewish people. Your place is not among other nations. Your place is in the land God gave to you more than three thousand years ago. For the many who have emigrated out of fear, I will be with you. For those who are left in exile I offer you a chance to realize your destiny and come home with me. *But you must promise to return to the mission God gave you."*

He pointed to the crowd. "To the world I have a message. God granted me another vision, a vision that will be fulfilled unless you stop persecuting my people. Just as the end of the Roman Empire in the year 476 was marked by an earthquake, an act of God, the world will experience the same act and be ripped apart unless it acknowledges the right of the Jewish people to fulfill their destiny."

Many in the largely Italian crowd had experienced earthquakes in Italy, but never in the vicinity around Rome. And the thought of God threatening the Vatican was almost absurd, despite what they had just seen on the television screens.

Isaac pleaded with them, knowing that they didn't have much time. "We have only seconds before we are struck. Please . . . *Make this promise,* 'I will help guard the children of Israel.'"

Only a few thousand people in the multitude repeated the phrase. Dominic, who had temporarily regained his emotional equilibrium and regarded the scenes around the world as a trick, looked contemptuously around him at the few who obeyed Isaac.

Isaac pleaded once more, "All of you who are watching all over the world, promise with me, 'I will help guard the children of Israel!'"

Only a few more people joined the initial group.

Isaac froze to his spot, and waited for the trembling to start.

It did.

The movement of the ground was almost as if the Earth were convulsing. Twice the ground was yanked straight up and straight down. The screams from the piazza couldn't have been louder than when Isaac announced he was the Messiah, but they were much higher in pitch, and terrified. Isaac shouted over the din, "'I will help guard the children of Israel!'" The ground was yanked again. A quarter of a million people were on their stomachs and knees on top of each other, and the sound started to grow.

"I will help guard the children of Israel."

Another convulsion.

Much louder. "I will help guard the children of Israel."

Another convulsion.

Unbeknownst to anyone but Isaac, who saw it with his eyes closed, tens of millions of people around the world experiencing the same convulsions of the earth joined the quarter of a million people in the piazza and cried, "I will help guard the children of Israel!"

And one assassin saw his own evil and rose to his feet, standing alone among the hundreds of thousands of fallen-over bodies.

The convulsions ceased.

Isaac cried out, "Will you help me? Will you help restore the children of Israel to their rightful place so that I can lead them to give their light unto the world?"

"Yes!"

Isaac turned toward Scoglio, who was white with shock and guilt, and said, "Cardinal Paolo Scoglio, will the Church rid itself of its anti-Semitism and protect us?"

Scoglio stammered, "Y . . . yes!"

"And we will share our discovery of cold fusion with the world, and we will share the world in mercy and justice! And we will all share in God's blessings!"

Pablo slowly climbed to his feet and saw the tears streaming down Dominic's upturned face. He seized the would-be assassin by the shoulders, yelling, "Why are you crying?"

And the man who had murdered a family for simply being Jews did not speak, but pulled out the gun . . . and used it to pronounce final judgment on himself.

*　*　*

Half an hour after the earthquake, Isaac informed the College of Cardinals that he was taking the first flight to Israel. Two of the cardinals fell to their knees when they saw him until Isaac lifted them to their feet, gently reminding them that although he was the Messiah, he was still only a man and that one should bow only before God. Grant appeared at precisely that moment and Isaac excused himself to talk with him.

"We can fly to Israel on my plane right away, Isaac."

Isaac smiled at Grant. "You're not going with me, Grant."

"What do you mean, I'm not going with you? You're going to sound the call to God for the world, and you don't want me there?"

"You have more important business elsewhere."

Grant said in exasperation, "After all we've been through, what's more important than helping you acknowledge the call to God?"

Isaac said quietly, "Being there when your son awakens tomorrow. He needs you more than I do."

Grant said weakly, "Tomorrow?"

"Yes."

Grant was numb. Through a blur of sudden tears he heard Isaac say, "Love of God means honoring your responsibilities, Grant. Isn't that where you belong?"

*   *   *

Three days later, Isaac, flanked by Rabbi Eliyahu and Rabbi Daniel Hanviowitz, stood at the Kotel amidst tens of thousands of Jews. Grant stood next to Matthew's wheelchair and watched as Isaac spoke to the world the words of his ancestor, from the psalms of David, the sweet singer of Israel:

"Behold, how good and how pleasant is the dwelling of brothers in unity. I will exalt You, my God the King, and I will bless Your name forever and ever."

He blew the shofar and from every corner of the earth, it was heard. And the call was clear: Something special was beginning.

Healing Leaves

Many of us, faced with the ups and downs of everyday life, are searching for the inner strength and confidence to renew our lives in a positive and meaningful way. Reb Noson's letters, based on the understanding and love he learned from the great chassidic master, Rebbe Nachman of Breslov, show how each of us can find that strength.

Code # 7656 Quality Paperback • $7.95

New Age Judaism

Many people will be surprised to find that Judaism is fundamentally aligned with what we think of as the New Age. Many of the things we associated with the New Age are not new but are part of Kabbalah, the Jewish mystical tradition. *New Age Judaism* is not about Judaism modified to meet the needs of the moment, but rather it makes age-old Judaism, traditional and kabbalistic teachings accessible to the modern person in a new way.

Code # 7893 Quality Paperback • $9.95

Praying for Recovery

This book is dedicated to helping all recovering addicts find and deepen a connection to their Higher Power. The author presents his own experience in overcoming his skepticism about a personal God and learning to pray for recovery with an open heart. He has specially translated for this book, Psalms that were instrumental in helping him to make the Twelve Steps a spiritual path for himself.

Code # 7885 Quality Paperback • $7.95

From HCI, *The Life Issues Publisher*
DISCOVER THE MAGIC
OF THE JOURNEY

Catherine Lanigan, best selling author of *Romancing the Stone* and *Jewel of the Nile*, returns with a sweeping tale centered on the courage and irrepressible spirit of its heroine.

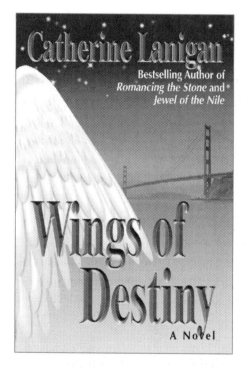

Code #6900 Hardcover • $24.00

This is the story of Jefferson Duke, who sacrifices the most precious of life's gifts—his heart—and of his granddaughter Barbara, who must betray him and, ultimately, learn the truth about herself and her own secret past.

About Simcha Press

Launching its first titles in the spring of 2000, **Simcha Press** has emerged to sustain and nurture the burgeoning interest in Judaism. As an imprint of HCI Books (Health Communications, Inc.), best known for the beloved *Chicken Soup for the Soul* series, **Simcha Press** carries on the tradition of publishing titles that make a positive difference in the lives of its readers.

The imprint is currently accepting submissions through literary agencies and independent authors. Please refer to "submission guidelines" on our website: ***www.simchapress.com***.

Submissions should be mailed to:

Simcha Press
3201 SW 15 Street
Deerfield Beach, FL 33442

In the spirit of *simcha*, the symbol of celebration and joy, Simcha Press offers titles for those on the path of Jewish enrichment. We wish all our readers a loving and wonderful adventure along the way.